WEAPONS FREE

DAVID BRUNS

J.R. OLSON

SEVERN RIVER
PUBLISHING

Severn River Publishing
www.SevernRiverBooks.com

ISBN: 978-1-64875-663-4 (Paperback)

ALSO BY BRUNS AND OLSON

The Command and Control Series

Command and Control

Counter Strike

Order of Battle

Threat Axis

Covert Action

Proxy War

Line of Succession

The Third Option Series

Weapons Free

Alpha Strike

Also by the Authors

Weapons of Mass Deception

Jihadi Apprentice

Rules of Engagement

The Pandora Deception

To Baron Castle Lord Carnarvon Olson
2008-2025

J. R. dedicates this book to his long-time co-pilot, Baron, who passed away on Tuesday, April 8th, 2025. Baron was the first dog in the Olson household. He welcomed every new adopted or fostered dog with eagerness, support, and pack camaraderie, and up to his last week on Earth, he continued to lead the pack. Baron succumbed to kidney failure at the age of 16.5 years, but what an impact he had in those years.

He is deeply missed.

Map of the South China Sea

When faced with a national security threat, the President of the United States may call upon the State Department to resolve the issue through diplomatic means.

When the situation demands a military response, the President calls on the Department of Defense.

In rare instances, when diplomacy and military force are insufficient or inappropriate, the President of the United States calls on the brave men and women of the Central Intelligence Agency.

They are the Third Option.

1

107 miles southeast of Hainan Island, South China Sea

Commander Janet Everett, captain of the USS *Illinois*, leaned toward the monitor as if proximity might help her unlock the meaning of the lines and squiggles that cluttered the screen. The sonar waterfall display graphically depicted the broadband noise in the ocean waters surrounding the *Virginia*-class fast-attack submarine. It updated from top to bottom in a slow drip of new information that appeared as bright lines and dots against a darker background.

The ocean was full of life—noisy life. Most of it was natural: Waves, shrimp, and fish created a cluttered backdrop of snap, crackle, and pop. But the bright line that ran down the right side of the screen was most definitely manmade. It was, in fact, a Chinese People's Liberation Army Navy Type 039C *Yuan*-class diesel-electric submarine. The ship was at periscope depth, and the bright line on Janet's display was caused by running her diesel engines to recharge the ship's batteries.

The smells of cooking in the galley circulated through the control room, triggering a rumble in Janet's stomach. The midday meal would begin in a few minutes. Like all US Navy ships, her submarine ran a rigid schedule where meals were served every six hours, at the change of each watch section.

Behind her, the watchstanders in the control room spoke in soft tones as they went about their duties. Today, the talk was mostly of home. After more than three months at sea, the USS *Illinois* was heading back to Hawaii.

The crew was excited. Janet, not as much. For as long as she could remember, she'd wanted command of her own submarine, and now that she had it, she didn't want to give it up. But that wasn't how the US Navy worked. After three years as commanding officer of the *Illinois*, it was time for Commander Everett to move on. When they returned to Pearl Harbor, she'd receive new orders, and a new captain would take command of her ship.

In these waning days of her time as captain, Janet found herself spending more and more time in the control room. Not for any specific purpose, just to soak up the atmosphere.

Three months at sea had turned a good crew into a finely tuned unit. She loved to watch them in action. She'd done a lot of things in her nearly two decades of service, but this command, this kick-ass crew, was the thing she was most proud of.

It was also the thing she would miss most.

The bright line on the waterfall display ended abruptly. She counted in her head: *one...two...*

"Officer of the Deck," reported Senior Chief O'Malley, "Sierra two-six has secured snorkeling. I'm getting hull-popping noises, sir. He's going deep. Last good bearing three-one-zero, range three-six hundred yards."

"Very well, Sonar." Lieutenant David Taylor stood behind the sonar supervisor's chair, peering over O'Malley's shoulder at the monitor. "Tell me when you see an aspect change. I need an intercept course."

"Aye, sir."

Janet hid a satisfied smile. This was the game they'd been playing for weeks. Once submerged, diesel-electric submarines ran on battery power, which made them extremely quiet and difficult to track, even for the *Illinois*'s state-of-the-art sonar system.

But this particular Chinese boat had a flaw. A pump on the port side of the submarine was sound-shorted to the hull, creating a sonic signature in the water called a tonal. The *Illinois*'s ultra-sensitive towed array streaming behind the ship was able to track that frequency—provided they stayed on the left side of their target. It was a tricky bit of maneuvering to keep the *Illinois* in position, but her crew had proven up to the challenge.

Janet wondered idly if her counterpart on the PLA submarine knew he had a sound short. Her own crew ran routine sound checks on their hull to identify problems. Surely, the Chinese did the same. Nevertheless, since they'd encountered Sierra two-six almost three weeks ago, the use of the pump had only increased.

By cross-checking intel reports and mining the top-secret sound signature library, they'd identified the contact as the CNS *Changcheng* 346, based out of Yulin Naval Base on Hainan.

They'd first encountered the PLA submarine during the two-week Chinese war games exercise in the underwater test range ten miles to the north. The *Illinois* had been ordered to observe the exercises and gather intel on new Chinese weapons and tactics.

The exercises had ended forty-eight hours ago, and all the PLA warships except for the *Changcheng* had departed the area. The fact that it had stayed on station made her curious, but her request to SUBPAC to extend their patrol had been denied. Commander, Submarine Force, US Pacific Fleet had other plans for the *Illinois*. On their last trip to periscope depth, they'd received orders to return home to Pearl Harbor.

"He's turning to the west, OOD," O'Malley reported. "Recommend course of two-four-zero to give us the best angle on the array, sir."

"Very well, Sonar," Taylor replied crisply. "Pilot, come left to new course two-four-zero."

He waited for the repeat back. The submarine heeled gently to port as the big ship started to turn.

"Pilot, all ahead two-thirds. To Maneuvering, make turns for ten knots."

Janet nodded to herself. She'd taught Taylor that move two years ago when he was just a wet-behind-the-ears Lieutenant Junior Grade. Increasing speed moved the sub through the turn faster and helped to stabilize the towed array.

"Captain?"

The woman who interrupted Janet's reverie was a head shorter and sported a mop of blond curls that matched the gold oak leaves of a lieutenant commander on her collar. The block letters on the name badge of her blue coveralls read AVERY.

"What is it, Jen?"

"I have the transit home laid out, ma'am, if you'd like to review it before lunch. It's pretty straightforward."

"Let's do it." Janet got to her feet, following the ship's navigator to the large horizontal display in the center of the control room.

Avery threw a questioning glance at Taylor for permission to use the navigation display table and he nodded his approval. The navigator's nimble fingers accessed a file and the monitor changed to a chart of the entire South China Sea. The *Illinois* showed up as a blue dot southeast of the mass of Hainan Island.

Another few touches and a large square enclosed the blue dot. "This is our current op area, Captain," Avery began. "At midnight, our track home opens up."

The United States and her allies used a system called waterspace management to minimize the risk of an underwater collision. When on patrol, submarines were assigned separate operational areas to ensure that friendly submarines never shared the same water. When a submarine needed to transit submerged to a new location, it was assigned a moving rectangle of ocean. The rectangle was large, usually tens of miles wide and three times as long, and the sub could operate anywhere inside the box. As the transiting sub advanced, the water behind them closed and new water opened up at a set speed of advance.

"We head northeast at an SOA of fifteen knots," Avery continued. "When we hit Taiwan, we hang a right and our SOA increases to twenty knots for five thousand miles. About two weeks from today, we should be home." She smiled brightly at her commanding officer. "My wedding anniversary is on the thirtieth."

"Well, it looks like you'll get to celebrate this one at home." Janet had seen the wedding picture that the navigator kept on the tiny fold-down desk in her shared stateroom.

"First time in five years." She held up crossed fingers, her smile wide.

"Sierra two-six reacquired, OOD," the sonar supervisor reported.

"Very well, Sonar." Taylor smiled, and Janet knew that look. He was going to turn over the watch to his relief with the trail of the PLA sub locked in.

A young man in a T-shirt with the ship's logo appeared next to the display. "The Supply Officer sends his respects, ma'am. Lunch is ready."

Janet nodded. "I'll be right down." She approved the first twenty-four hours of their track home, hiding her regret behind a smile. In twelve hours, they'd be homeward bound.

The officers in the wardroom stood behind their chairs, waiting for her to arrive. "Seats, please," she said as she drew out her own armchair at the head of the table. The soup course arrived promptly and she busied herself with a heavily seasoned clam chowder.

This far into a patrol, Janet would have committed a felony for a leafy green salad and a tall glass of fresh milk. All the perishables were long gone. No vegetables, no eggs, no fresh milk. If the food wasn't frozen, canned, or powdered, it didn't exist.

Lieutenant Commander Tom Savarino, her executive officer, offered her a basket of rolls. Mechanically, she buttered the bread and bit into it. It was warm and chewy. She nodded her approval to the enlisted food attendant, who beamed back at her.

The junior officers spoke in low tones at the other end of the table. She couldn't make out the words, but the undercurrent of excitement told her they were talking about home. Good for them, she thought. They'd earned it.

The main course of steak sandwiches arrived on a platter. Janet took a small one. She wasn't really that hungry, but she also wanted the galley staff to see her enjoying the meal.

Just as she was about to take her first bite, the phone near her right knee buzzed. She reached under the table and pulled out the heavy black handset.

"Captain."

"OOD, ma'am. We have a new sonar contact that I think you need to see."

"What's the range?"

"It's not close, ma'am, but the characteristics are unusual."

"What does Senior Chief O'Malley say?"

"He's never seen anything like it, ma'am."

Janet's eyebrows went up. There wasn't much in the sonar world that O'Malley hadn't seen. "I'll be right there."

She replaced the handset and stood, gesturing for the wardroom to stay seated.

"I'll be back in a few minutes. Mr. Taylor says there's something I need to see in control."

Janet watched the junior officers for a reaction—Taylor was known as a practical joker and this was the last few hours of a deployment—but she sensed nothing was amiss.

In the control room, she found Taylor posted behind the sonar supervisor's chair, a worried expression on his face. If this was a practical joke, this guy deserved an Oscar.

"Report, Mr. Taylor."

The OOD's glance flicked between O'Malley and the captain. "I'm going to let Senior explain it, ma'am."

Janet turned to O'Malley, who slipped a pair of headphones off one of his ears. His face was pressed into a frown of concentration.

"Fifteen minutes ago, we recorded a loud transient to the north, Captain. It was a convergence zone hit, over a hundred miles away." He pointed to the monitor. "Then this happened."

The waterfall display showed a bright stripe indicating a very loud noise in the ocean moving at a high rate of speed.

"This thing is fifty miles away from us and closing, ma'am."

Janet shook her head. "You just told me that you picked it up fifteen minutes ago and it was a hundred miles away."

O'Malley nodded.

"So it's..."

"It has to be a rocket, Captain," the sonar supervisor said. "It's going something like 150 knots *underwater*."

Janet had taken enough hydrodynamics courses to know that was not possible. "Let me listen."

O'Malley passed the headphones to her. She slipped them on as he placed the cursor on the noise source. A rushing, rumbling sound filled her ears. It sounded like a freight train.

Janet pulled off the headphones. "Sound general quarters, Mr. Taylor."

"Aye, ma'am."

The rhythmic pulse of the general quarters alarm rang through the ship, followed by the thunder of running feet. New voices filled the control room as replacement watchstanders entered and took up their posts. The movements were quick and practiced. In less than two minutes, reports came in from all stations that general quarters were set throughout the submarine.

"Attention in control," Janet announced. "We have an incoming unknown submerged contact moving at a very high rate of speed headed in our direction. I intend to remain in this area and learn everything we possibly can about this new contact." She decided to leave out the part that if this thing was really moving at 150 knots, there was no way the *Illinois* could outrun it. "Sierra two-six is a known PLA submarine and is in the area, bearing two-niner-zero, range four thousand yards."

Her eyes sought out the Weapons Officer at the fire control station. "Weps, give me a firing solution on the Sierra two-six and the incoming contact."

"Aye, Captain."

"XO, pull the last twenty-four hours of intel reports. See if we can figure out where this incoming contact came from."

"On it, Captain." Savarino departed for the radio room, where the intel briefings were stored.

Janet's gaze rested on O'Malley. "You're recording, Sonar?"

The Senior Chief nodded. "Every channel, ma'am."

Janet took up her post in front of her own monitor, studying the information as it came in. A picture began to emerge.

The incoming underwater rocket—she decided to call it a rocket—was traveling at a rate of 167 knots, nearly 200 mph. Although everything she knew about current technology told her that moving that fast underwater was impossible, she put that thought aside. The first rule you learned in nuclear power school was to believe your indications. The data was telling her how fast this device was moving, so she would believe what her instrumentation told her until proven otherwise.

At the current heading, the incoming rocket was going to pass on the far side of the PLA submarine and head straight down the center of the underwater test range. In Janet's mind, this meant the PLA submarine was there to witness whatever was happening out there.

The XO appeared at her elbow. The look on his face told her he had news, so she stepped back to allow him access to the monitor.

Savarino called up satellite coverage from twenty-four hours ago. He pointed to the grainy image of a surface ship on a field of open water. "This is the only PLA ship within a hundred miles of the origin of that..." He seemed to search for a word to describe what they were seeing.

"I'm calling it a rocket," Janet said.

"I guess that's as good a term as any. Every other ship, except for Sierra two-six, cleared the area two days ago, after the war games. They're all back in port and accounted for, including the submarines."

Janet nodded at the screen. "What type of ship is it?"

"It's a missile test platform, ma'am. But it was in shipyards for three months last fall, so maybe it got an upgrade?"

"Okay," Janet said. "Let's play this out: At the end of the war games, when the Chinese think the ocean is clear of any enemy submarines, they want to test a new weapon, so they set up a test barge here." She pointed at the screen. "And they shoot it downrange into this underwater test area. Sierra two-six is set up as a monitor."

Savarino nodded. "That sounds right to me."

"But what the hell is this thing?" Janet asked. "Who shoots a rocket underwater?"

"Captain?" Senior Chief O'Malley's voice cut through the buzz of the control room.

"What is it, Senior?"

"It's not a rocket, ma'am," the sonar supervisor said. He handed her a headset.

Janet slipped them over her ears. The rushing noise she'd heard before was gone. The new sound was familiar to her: a high-pitched whine, like an angry bee.

"It's a torpedo," Janet said.

O'Malley nodded. "It's a high-speed, long-range torpedo, ma'am. And we've got it on tape."

The whining sound ended.

Janet kept her face still as she handed the headphones back to O'Malley, aware that every eye in the control room was on her. She fought to suppress the bubble of excitement that rose in her chest.

This was *big*. Her ship had just witnessed the test of a brand-new Chinese weapons system. She made an effort to reel in her imagination that was spinning out the strategic implications of this new weapon. That was for the analysts in DC to work out. Her job was to supply them with the best possible raw intelligence of what they had just seen.

"Navigator?"

"Captain." Jen Avery stepped forward.

"Pull together a first-draft intel package that we can send off within the hour. Details to follow. You know the drill."

"Aye, Captain." When she turned away, Janet caught the look of disappointment in her eyes.

Even if the rest of the crew hadn't figured it out, Avery knew the score. The *Illinois* was not going home anytime soon.

2

White House Situation Room

The emergency meeting of the National Security Council was a packed house—standing room only. Between the principals and their respective staffs, Harrison Kohl estimated there were close to fifty people in the room, including a sizable number of US Navy uniforms. Some of the Cabinet-level officials had even given up their seats at the main table to make room for a line of grim-faced naval officers.

For his part, Harrison was happy to take a seat against the wall behind his boss, CIA Director of Operations Don Riley. Don's head partially obstructed the viewscreen at the front of the room, but Harrison was happy to be as far away from the main table as possible.

Since he'd seen the presentation already, he spent his time gauging how the news was landing with the audience members who were hearing it for the first time.

It was not sitting well. Secretary of State Abel Cartwright, a man who was never at a loss for words, stared silently at the screen throughout the entire twenty-minute presentation. The tight scowl across his square jaw spoke volumes.

That was understandable. In the forty-eight hours since Janet Everett's flash intel brief had landed in Washington, DC, Harrison had learned enough about submarines and torpedoes to last a lifetime.

The briefer was Bob James, a retired Navy O-5 who now worked at CIA as an analyst specializing in PLA Navy submarine technology. In addition to his credentials as a former submarine captain, Bob was an engineer's engineer and looked the part. He had thinning gray hair and square glasses, and he spoke in precise, clipped terms as he described the damage to US national security that would be caused by a fully operational Chinese superfast, ultra-long-range torpedo.

"I've read Commander Everett's strategic assessment of the situation, Madam President," James said, "and I agree with every word of it. With this capability, the Chinese have the opportunity to rewrite the submarine playbook that we've all been following for the last fifty years."

He paused for a sip of water, seemingly unperturbed that he was delivering bad news to the most powerful person in the free world.

"Up until now," he continued, "our main weapon in undersea warfare has been stealth. A submerged platform needs to be quiet so they can get close enough to their target to attack. This weapon turns all of that upside down. It's the opposite of quiet—it sounds like a freight train—but it's faster than anything out there by a factor of four. Imagine a world where a submarine can launch a salvo of superfast torpedoes at a carrier strike group a hundred miles away. We have not seen this kind of fundamental change in naval warfare since aircraft carriers were introduced at the start of World War Two."

James mercifully left out a reference to Pearl Harbor, but judging by their faces, Harrison could see that everyone in the room was filling in the blanks.

"A weapons platform of this nature presents strategic challenges for the United States Navy, ma'am," he continued. "On a global basis, a stand-off torpedo like this is a direct threat to the US Navy's dominance of the sea lines of communication. But I think the real threat is closer to home for the PLA."

President Eleanor Cashman spoke for the first time. "Be specific, please, Mr. James."

James bobbed his head. "Bluntly, ma'am, a weapon like this could shut down the South China Sea."

James let the comment settle in the humid atmosphere of the packed room.

Harrison knew what they were thinking. A third of the world's shipping traffic transited the South China Sea en route to the Suez Canal and markets in Europe and the US. For the last thirty years, China had systematically built up their military presence in the region, claiming ownership of most of the South China Sea and their so-called First Island Chain, which included the island of Taiwan.

For the last quarter century, while the United States military was consumed with Afghanistan, Iraq, and the Global War on Terror, the Chinese were annexing tiny islands and turning them into fortified military bases. The fact that the Philippines and Vietnam already claimed these bits of land mattered not at all to the Chinese.

Diplomatic protests were lodged, adverse rulings were handed down by international courts. The Chinese response was to continue building. They now had a string of military outposts that continued northward to the island of Taiwan—the crown jewel in the First Island Chain strategy.

The US Navy still ran freedom of navigation operations, FONOPS, around the Chinese strongholds, but it was too little, too late. The PLA wasn't going anywhere.

The room was strangely still. No rustling papers or whispering aides attending to their principals. All eyes were fixed on the retired Navy submarine commander.

James offered a tight smile. "This new weapons test has answered some long-standing questions for us, though." He flashed a satellite image of a submarine under construction.

"This is the newest class of Chinese fast-attack submarine, the Type 097, codenamed Barracuda. The boat is under construction in the Bohei shipyards in Huludao, on the Yellow Sea in northern China. Bohei is the lead shipyard for all nuclear-powered submarines in the PLA Navy. Submarines aren't built from the keel up like other ships. They are constructed in sections, sort of like slices of bread, and welded together in the shipyard."

He used a laser pointer to highlight the missing front section of the submarine. "This build has not changed for the last six months. Our assumption was that the Chinese were developing a new bow-mounted sonar system, but now we think otherwise. A new long-range torpedo like the one that Commander Everett discovered would be larger than a normal torpedo, requiring a total redesign of the front end."

"How much larger, Mr. James?" asked the Chief of Naval Operations.

"It would be a beast, sir," James replied. "We're guessing this weapon is twice the diameter and a third again as long as anything we're using today."

"That means new torpedo tubes," the CNO said.

James nodded with emphasis. "New torpedo tubes, new handling system, new weapons loading hatches. A complete redesign of the front end of this submarine."

The President cleared her throat. "If I'm following you, Mr. James, you're telling us that even if the Chinese had this weapon, they don't have a platform to put it on yet."

James changed the display to show a surface ship that looked like a barge to Harrison. "That's correct, ma'am. The weapon was launched from this test platform, the CNS *Shinyan*." He zoomed in on the bow section. "This ship underwent a refit last year and the bow section was replaced. Our belief was that the PLA was testing a new bow-mounted sonar. Again, current events have caused us to reconsider."

Cashman's eyes sought out Carroll Brooks, the Director of the CIA. "And we knew nothing about this?"

"No, ma'am." Carroll's voice was flat. "The analysis at the time fit the assessment of a new sonar system."

"Maybe you need a different narrative, Director," said Todd Spencer, the National Security Advisor.

Harrison frowned. There was no need to pile on like that.

Cashman shot her advisor a cutting look that said she agreed with Harrison's assessment.

James spoke up again. "I realize I've painted a grim picture, Madam President, but I think we have reason to be hopeful."

"Really?" Cashman's skepticism was evident.

"Absolutely, ma'am. What the USS *Illinois* witnessed was a propulsion test, nothing more. For this to be a functional weapon, it needs both a guidance and a search system. There's no way the torpedo can find any target while at top speed. It needs to slow down and run a search pattern. What we saw was only the first step in the weapon's development."

"I think you're going to have to spell it out for me, Mr. James," the President replied.

"What I'm saying, ma'am, is that I believe we have a window of opportunity to stop the Chinese development of this weapon system. They're under tremendous pressure right now. The PLA has a multi-billion-dollar new submarine design that's been sitting idle in the shipyards for months, waiting for a decision about this weapon. That's expensive and embarrassing. It's also taking up space for ongoing submarine production."

"How long do you think this window of opportunity will remain open?"

James shrugged. "If this were a US-based weapons system development, I'd say a year or more. But for China, given that this new platform has been on hold for the last six months? I give it three months. Maybe four."

The estimate landed like a lead balloon in the center of the mahogany table. The President made a show of closing her leather portfolio and folding her hands.

"Thank you, Mr. James. I believe we have the picture." She stood and the occupants in the room rushed to their feet. A din of rolling chairs, shuffling papers, and babbling voices filled the space as aides rushed to brief their principals on what had transpired in the last hour outside the confines of the Situation Room.

As the room emptied, the President stayed at her place. Harrison caught her nod at the Director and Don. *Stay here.*

Don cast a look over his shoulder at Harrison. He was being told to stay as well.

That could only mean one thing: Don had plans for Harrison and his team at the Special Activities Center.

Harrison pressed his back against the wall and let the room empty out until only the President, the National Security Advisor, Carroll Brooks, Don Riley, and Harrison remained. The three CIA officials took seats facing the NSA. The President remained at the head of the table.

"Mr. Riley, it's been a minute. How have you been?" Cashman said in a conversational tone.

More than any other individual at CIA, including the Director, Don Riley had a strong relationship with the President. She trusted him in the same way her predecessor, President Serrano, had trusted him.

Harrison hadn't seen Cashman in person since he'd briefed her about the assassination attempt on the Russian President six months ago. This close to her, he could see the signs of strain beneath her carefully applied makeup. He could not imagine the pressures of the office of the President of the United States, but it seemed he was watching Eleanor Cashman age in real time.

"Now that it's just us," Cashman said, "I'd like to understand how this happened."

Director Brooks answered, "Madam President, about a year ago, the PLA moved all their new naval weapons development to Hainan Island. It's a high-security facility with state-of-the-art countersurveillance capability. That means the only real access is via human channels. In a world of biometrics, there's no hiding who you are. We are recruiting native-born Chinese, but it takes a long time to develop assets. Years, in some cases. We've had much better success with the shipyards, which is why we were aware of the new submarine and the construction delays."

The President nodded, but her lips were pressed into a firm line of red lipstick. Her eyes rested on Don Riley.

"I have a mission for you, Donald."

Don sat up in his chair.

"You heard Mr. James. We have a limited window of opportunity to change the direction of the Chinese weapons development program. We need them to believe that deploying this new torpedo would be a mistake. That the whole program has been a waste of money, time, and resources."

"I understand, ma'am," Don said.

Cashman shifted her gaze from Don to Carroll, then to Harrison. He felt like he was being scanned. No wonder. His last covert action in Russia had not exactly gone smoothly.

"There is no room for failure here. If the Chinese succeed in deploying this weapon, we will have given up de facto control of the South China Sea. I will not allow that to happen."

It wasn't a question, it was a statement. No response expected.

"Whatever you need, whatever assets you have to burn, whatever it takes," Cashman concluded. "I will pay that price, but you have to get the job done. No excuses."

The President stood and they all followed suit.

"You have work to do. I'll leave you to it."

3

CNS *Changcheng* 346, Type 039C *Yuan*-class diesel-electric submarine
94 miles southeast of Hainan Island

It was shortly after 2000 hours when the knock sounded at the door of Captain Kai Jun's stateroom. As commanding officer of the CNS *Changcheng* 346, he was the only person on board the ship with private quarters, but they were modest in comparison to the spacious staterooms on board surface ships in the PLA Navy. He didn't mind. The small space was well-appointed with a folding desk, a single bunk, en suite lavatory, and two chairs. Everything he required to accomplish his mission.

Thirty minutes had passed since their last trip to periscope depth to download radio traffic from the satellite. He'd scanned the message traffic on his stateroom computer, then closed the lid of the laptop and used the remaining time to compose himself.

This would be a difficult meeting, but this confrontation had been building for weeks. It was time he met the challenge head-on.

In the hours before the test of the new Hu Jing torpedo, he'd sent a private message to his chain of command recommending that they post-pone the testing of the new weapon. Kai believed there was an enemy submarine lurking in the vicinity. He requested an additional forty-eight hours to sanitize the underwater test range.

Surely, he reasoned, a test of this significance would warrant extraordinary security measures. The Hu Jing torpedo was the most important underwater weapons development in the last fifty years. In the past, China copied the weapons of Western nations, but not anymore.

The Hu Jing was 100 percent Chinese-developed and like its namesake, the Orca, it would be the most fearsome predator in the ocean.

But his entreaty was ignored by his superiors. He was not granted extra time to search for the elusive enemy submarine. In fact, he'd received no answer at all.

Until tonight.

Contained in the recent radio traffic was a P4, a personal, eyes-only message for the political officer of the *Changcheng* 346.

That could only mean one thing, he reasoned. Instead of responding to the captain of the submarine, Beijing had sent a message to his embarked political commissar.

He drew a deep breath, locking the anger he felt tight in his chest.

You are right, he told himself. Don't let this fool convince you otherwise.

He'd arranged the two chairs in the room—his own armchair and a metal straight-back chair—so they were facing each other. He squared his shoulders and called out.

"Come."

The door eased open and Commander Mao Li entered. Mao was junior to Kai by seven years but infinitely more senior in the pecking order of the Chinese Communist Party.

Kai did not rise to greet the political officer. They were the same rank, after all, so it was not necessary. He surveyed his counterpart with undisguised distaste. Mao had a lean physique, a swimmer's build, and long dark hair that skirted regulations. He was a handsome man with an easy smile, and when he saw the seating arrangement, the corners of his mouth turned up with humor.

"You've been expecting me, Captain," he said in a soft voice.

Kai grunted. So, the man wasn't even going to pretend. Good. At least that would keep this meeting short so he could get back to things that mattered.

He stabbed his hand forward to indicate that Mao should take a seat. The younger man swung into the chair easily, crossing his long legs. The stateroom was small enough that only a few centimeters separated their knees as they faced each other. Mao touched the tablet he was carrying and handed it to Kai.

"Can we talk about this, Captain?"

His voice held not a trace of irritation, and that infuriated Kai. He wanted to have an argument with this idiot, but Mao's entire persona was one of calm patience. In Kai's experience, most political officers wore their jobs like a shield. They were chosen by the Party to be the official arbiters of right and wrong. If they couldn't convince you, they beat you to death with the weight of their office.

Mao was different. From admirals to apprentice seamen, he was able to talk to men of any social station with ease and confidence. People instinctively liked and trusted him. The crew of the *Changcheng* loved him. Kai had often seen him on the mess decks chatting with the sailors, laughing.

Kai took the proffered tablet and scanned the short message. He expected the missive to be critical, but it went beyond that. The words jumped off the screen like sparks: *incompetence...stupidity...embarrassment*. It was a harsh personal attack on Mao's performance as political officer and finished with a veiled threat that if he did not rein in his commanding officer, there would be severe career implications. Kai scrolled up to review the message distribution and his eyebrows ticked up involuntarily. This scorching reprimand had been copied all the way up to the regional staff.

Kai felt his face redden in shared humiliation. By any reasonable measure, Mao should be furious at Kai, but his quiet manner barely showed irritation, much less anger.

"Why did you feel it necessary to send the message without consulting me first, Captain?" Mao asked softly. A question, more conversation than confrontation.

"Our chain of command needs to know the truth," Kai responded.

He registered the harshness in his own tone. He knew he should moderate, but he couldn't bring himself to do it. He was right, dammit. How could this idiot not see that?

"The truth," repeated Mao. Kai listened carefully for any trace of mocking, but he heard none.

"The truth," continued Mao, "is that we have no solid evidence that there is an enemy submarine in these waters."

We, not *you*, realized Kai. His political officer viewed himself as part of the crew, not just an overseer of the submarine.

"I understand you have far more experience in these matters than I, Captain, and I respect that experience deeply. But without evidence, it's just speculation. Recommending to your chain of command that we delay the test of a critical new weapons system without just cause was not wise, sir."

The fury that Kai had been holding back breached the dam.

"You don't know what you're talking about." He was shouting, but he couldn't help it. "You're a political officer. I am a line officer. I *know* there's another submarine out there; I can *feel* it."

Mao's lips grew tight at the corners. The first sign that he was losing his patience.

"The weapons test of the Hu Jing torpedo was a highly classified operation, Captain. If we can *prove* there was an enemy submarine in the vicinity, that is information our leadership needs to know. Otherwise, we should keep our speculations to ourselves."

Again, *we,* not *you*. Kai's fingers gripped the arms of his chair, his knuckles white with tension.

"We've picked up a tonal on the flank array," Kai insisted. "It's intermittent, but I know it's another submarine, Commander." How could he explain to this staff officer that the way sound traveled in the ocean was not predictable? Sonar interpretation was an art, not a science.

Mao's voice was infuriatingly patient. "We've been over this, Captain. We have followed this signature multiple times to no avail."

"There is an enemy submarine out there." Kai swung his arm toward the ocean beyond the bulkhead. "I know it."

Mao steepled his fingers. "The future of the First Island Chain strategy depends on a successful weapons test and we are a key part of that effort. If you want to search for an enemy submarine in these waters, I support you in that endeavor. But until you actually show proof of the enemy's presence, you need to keep your opinions to yourself. Otherwise, you risk making your command look foolish."

Kai flushed a deep red as the barb struck home. Even now, the political officer refused to make his attack personal. Kai wasn't making a fool of *himself*, he was making *his command* look foolish. There were over a hundred men on the *Changcheng*. He was embarrassing all of them with his actions.

Kai felt a fresh rush of anger at this political creature. Everything in Mao's life had been presented to him on a silver platter. Kai had scrapped and scraped for his entire career. First at the Academy, then in submarine school, then as a junior officer. He'd never had the right connections, befriended the right people to clear his path to promotion. He'd worked hard for everything he had today, including this command. He was not foolish. He was right.

Mao spoke again, his tone soft with understanding. "Captain, I support you. I will always support you. If you believe there is an enemy submarine out there, I want to help you find it." He paused. "But you have to trust me."

Kai felt his lips twist into a grimace. He glared at the younger man, trying to read his face.

Trust, he thought. Trusting a political officer was like playing with a cobra. Their trust only went one way. When your head was turned, the venomous fangs struck deep.

He forced his anger down into the center of his chest, locked it away. He bent his lips into a smile.

"Of course, Commander Mao," he said. "I apologize for my actions. Rest assured, it will not happen again."

Mao sat back in his chair and laced his fingers over his lean belly. The wattage of his ever-present smile increased.

"That's all I ask, Captain. I want you to trust me. I am on your side."

Kai abruptly got to his feet.

"If that is all, Commander," he said firmly, "I'm going to make my evening rounds."

Mao stood without effort, extended his hand. "Thank you for your time, Captain."

Mao's hand felt limp in Kai's intense grip. He gritted his teeth as he resisted the urge to crush the long, elegant fingers.

"My door is always open, Commander Mao."

He stayed on his feet even after the door closed behind the political officer. Sending the message had been foolish, even he could see that now, but he was still right. There was an enemy submarine out there.

Kai busied himself bringing order back to his tiny stateroom. He placed the armchair in front of his desk and secured the second chair against the wall as a precaution against unexpected ship movement.

He drew in a deep breath, held it, then expelled it in an explosive blast. Kai stalked out of his stateroom and into the control room.

"Captain in control!" announced the enlisted man on the helm. The watch section came to attention. The watch officer came forward to offer his report, but Kai waved him aside and stepped into the darkness of the sonar room.

Three operators sat at monitors, headphones over their ears. The sonar supervisor was a chief petty officer who had served under Kai for the last two years. He looked away from his monitor to meet the captain's inquiring gaze.

"Anything?" Kai asked.

"No, sir." The chief's eyes were red with fatigue. Since the weapons test, Kai had put the sonar teams on port and starboard watch. Six hours on watch, six hours off. It was a risk—tired sonar operators were less alert—but it was a risk worth taking. He would do what it took to find the enemy submarine that he knew was out there.

The sonar supervisor returned his gaze to his monitor. The captain stood in the darkness, fists clenched. The angry box in his chest threatened to burst open again.

"Keep looking."

4

Special Activities Center, CIA Headquarters, Langley, Virginia

The last three days had given Harrison Kohl a whole new level of respect for his boss, Don Riley. All his career, Harrison had sought positions away from headquarters, telling himself that his skill set was better suited to the rapid-fire, seat-of-the-pants adrenaline rush of the field operative.

That was a lie, he knew now. He wasn't an adrenaline junkie; he was just afraid of managing other people.

He wondered how Don did it. How did he deal with the stress of sending people out into the field knowing they were walking into dangerous situations? The responsibility seemed overwhelming to Harrison, like a giant rock hanging over his head waiting to crush his skull like a robin's egg.

But as head of the Special Activities Center, that was what he did every day: He sent people into harm's way for the good of the country.

The latest assignment to derail the Chinese torpedo development program was no exception.

All of Harrison's years of experience told him that there was real danger in this mission. For starters, they were moving at light speed, trying to cram what should have been months of vetting and prep into a few days inside a meeting room.

He pushed aside the cup of cold coffee, telling himself that the sick feeling in the pit of his stomach was because he was overcaffeinated.

Great, he thought. My number one coping mechanism for dealing with managerial stress is lying to myself.

"Let's go through it again, Mike," he said.

Mike Beason, the targeting officer Harrison had seconded from the CIA's China Center, cleared his throat. Mike's job was to select targets and match CIA case officers to recruit them. The man had a patient smile that matched his placid demeanor. If he was being torn apart inside by the stress of sending officers into the field, he certainly didn't show it.

"Given the parameters of the mission, Harrison," he said, "we have two candidates."

His briefing tablet displayed a silver-haired Chinese man in his mid-sixties. His flat, square face wore a no-nonsense expression.

"Wei Chan, sixty-six years old, is a project manager in the Hainan Weapons Development Center. He'll be at a conference in Australia next month. Party loyalist, family man with two grandchildren, minimal profile on social media. Research shows that he plans to retire next year, which gives us a possible money angle on him."

Harrison nodded, studying the screen. Wei looked like a grandfather, and not the kind who took you out for ice cream, either. The set of his jaw spoke of inner conviction, and his thirty years of service as an engineer, patiently making his way through the ranks, indicated he was a plodder.

"What's Door Number Two?" Harrison asked.

The screen changed again to the image of a younger man. Mid-thirties, dark hair that touched his collar. He wore a faint smile, like a man who had a secret.

"Zhu Shufen, thirty-six, level two engineer in the Advanced Propulsion division in Hainan. Unmarried, no steady relationship that we could find. Both parents dead, no siblings, no grandparents. Modest presence on social media. Likes to gamble a bit. Makes a trip to Macau two or three times a year."

Harrison raised his eyebrows hopefully. "Any signs that he's in debt?"

Beason shook his head. "Finances look good. He either doesn't gamble much on these trips, or he's the luckiest son of a bitch ever. He spent almost the exact same amount on every trip."

That answer felt off to Harrison, but he set the feeling aside. "What's our first contact opportunity?"

Beason met his gaze. "Four days from now in Singapore."

Harrison scrubbed his face with both hands. A month from now was too long, but four days? Could he get a case officer prepped in that amount of time?

"If you want my input, Harrison," Beason prompted, "Zhu Shufen gives you more to work with. Younger, unattached, seems to have a taste for the finer things. The older guy? I think he'd be more risk-averse, and this operation..." His voice trailed off. "I can keep looking, maybe expand our search outside of propulsion?"

Harrison stopped him. "You're right. It has to be Zhu."

"Good choice," said Beason. "Peter Chen's going to be your best bet for Singapore."

And that was how it went, Harrison reflected. One decision automatically led to another. As they moved farther along the decision tree, there were fewer branches and fewer options. His stomach clenched. Fewer options did not mean less risk.

It just meant he had less control.

Peter Chen joined Harrison and Beason after lunch. He sat opposite Harrison, hands folded on the bare table as Beason briefed the case officer on his target.

He seemed not to care that Harrison studied him with the intensity of a professor inspecting a new addition to his butterfly collection.

On paper, Peter Chen was the perfect candidate for the assignment. He was in his mid-thirties with short dark hair and round glasses that slipped down his nose when he nodded at Beason. His cover—an industrial systems engineer at a small Midwestern company that made ergonomic computer equipment—was perfect. Because the company had manufacturing facilities in Singapore, Peter traveled there multiple times each year. He spoke fluent Mandarin, and his engineering background gave him the ability to talk to the target in technical terms.

Still, Harrison worried. His first impression of Chen left him wanting more, but more what? Confidence? Personality?

They would get only one bite of this apple. Chen would need to read his target and react in real time. Could this bespectacled engineer pull that off?

Beason finished the brief. Peter Chen turned his attention to Harrison, pushing his glasses up his nose. His demeanor was calm, face impassive.

"You understand the target profile?" Harrison asked.

Chen nodded. "I'll want to study him in more detail, but I have the high points."

"You think you can cold pitch him?"

Chen took a few seconds to answer. "It's a risky move, but I understand the urgency. I can do it."

"Tell me the setup."

Chen put his hands flat on the table. "I'd have him picked up in Customs. Put him in an interrogation room and let him marinate. Meanwhile, we can go through his luggage and scan his laptop."

"What if he makes a scene in Immigration?" Harrison pressed.

Chen shook his head. "I've worked with Singapore before. They're pros. We can cut him from the herd without a fuss. No problem."

One point for Chen, Harrison thought. He knew Singapore in practice, not just on paper.

"I'd examine the luggage to see if we have any new angles to use on him," Chen continued. "Assuming no new information, I think we go in hot."

"Meaning?"

"He'll be nervous and vulnerable. We're roughly the same age, both engineers. I play myself off as a friendly face. Speak to him in his own language, build some basic trust."

Harrison raised a skeptical eyebrow. This was Case Officer 101. Chen caught the look.

"I lay it out for him," he continued. "He's been flagged as having access to a top-secret weapons propulsion system design. I want to hire him as a consultant. Big money, benefits up front."

"What do you say when he asks who you work for?"

Chen shrugged. "I work for a large international defense contractor with deep pockets. I drop hints that it's based in Europe—France, maybe—but I'm assuming he's not an idiot. He's going to know that's a lie. If he wants the money bad enough, he'll make himself believe the lie so he can sleep at night. Make the conversation about the money, not about his loyalty to his country."

Harrison nodded. It was a good answer, as good as anything he'd be able to come up with on the spot. The engineer could think on his feet. Another point for Mr. Chen.

A cold pitch was the riskiest of recruitment tactics. Under normal circumstances, developing Zhu would take place over months, maybe even years. Through a series of meetings, the case officer would vet the asset, making increasingly larger asks of classified information until they found his comfort level.

The cold pitch bypassed all that prep work, but that came with a massive downside. Once the offer was out there, you lost all control. Your target could lose his shit or—worse yet—tell you what you wanted to hear, then turn himself in to the Ministry of State Security as soon as he landed on the Chinese mainland. If the MSS was smart—and they were very good—they'd turn Zhu into a double agent.

A cold pitch required finesse, salesmanship, an ability to think on your feet, and no small measure of luck. Even then, it had a small probability of success.

Their pitch was a guess at what motivated their target. If they were wrong, they were back at square one.

For all their sakes, Harrison hoped Zhu Shufen was a greedy bastard.

Harrison cut a glance at Mike Beason, who gave a slight nod. Peter Chen was their best option.

"Okay," Harrison said to Chen, "talk to me about how you'd set up covert comms."

5

Changi Airport, Singapore

Zhu Shufen opened his eyes as the wheels of the Singapore Airlines flight touched the tarmac at Changi Airport. He yawned and stretched. Two Bloody Marys and it was lights out for the entire four hours.

He pushed up the window shade and peered into the bright midday sunshine. He was looking forward to a week in this tiny island country. It was a work trip, but his only firm commitment was to sit on a panel on Wednesday afternoon for two hours. In his mind, that meant the rest of the time was his own. He'd show his face each morning—assuming he wasn't too hungover from the prior night—and collect a few business cards to show off to his boss. Then he'd hit the town again.

If you had money and connections, all the doors opened in Singapore. You could buy anything—or anyone—you wanted. The city had all the glitz of Shanghai but with an added flair of Western decadence that made it so much more exciting.

Zhu shivered with anticipation as he zipped open his computer bag and fished in the front pocket for his mobile.

There were two phones in the bag: his work mobile, a sleek iPhone knockoff, and a brand-new flip phone. His fingers lingered over the flip phone, but Zhu stopped himself.

Jiecheng's instructions were very clear: Turn the phone on at eight o'clock in the evening on Sunday, no sooner. You will get a text message with an address. Go there and bring cash.

"Shufen." Jiecheng had gripped his arm. "They only accept cash."

It was a lot of money. Enough money that Zhu had needed to tap into his savings for this trip—and that was just for one night.

"Is it worth it?" he asked Jiecheng.

His friend's eyes rolled back in his head in mock ecstasy. "It will be a night you will never forget! I can promise you that."

Zhu's stomach tightened with anticipation, but he left the burner phone in place and extracted his work phone from the bag. He powered the device on and logged into his unclassified work email. He sighed in frustration. He already had four messages from his boss. Yang Min was working on a Sunday.

All of the emails were what you'd expect from a paper-pushing bureaucrat who had no life. Yang wanted to know if he'd filed his weekly status update before he left on Friday afternoon—Zhu had not—and two separate emails questioning a small charge on his last expense report.

Yang Min was not half the engineer Zhu was. In fact, his boss owed his career to Zhu. He'd taken all of Zhu's best ideas and repackaged them as his own for management. If not for Zhu's brilliance, Yang wouldn't even have his position in the advanced underwater propulsion lab. He'd be pushing paper in some backwater research center in Wuhan instead of being part of the most important subsurface weapons development in the last fifty years.

Zhu deleted all the emails without responding. He was on vacation, he reasoned, and his moron boss should respect his time off.

The plane made a wide sweeping turn as it pulled into the gate, then jerked to a halt. Instantly, everyone around him jumped to their feet, opening the overhead bins.

Zhu looked out his window in disgust. What sheep these people were. They were at the back of the plane. They wouldn't even start moving forward for at least another ten minutes.

Across the aisle, a tall, thin teenage girl dressed in a baggy sweatsuit stretched to reach into the overhead storage bin. Her shirt hiked up, revealing a smooth lower back the color of milky coffee. Zhu couldn't help staring. She seemed to sense his eyes and turned around. He quickly looked out the window.

He waited until the girl and her mother had traveled up the aisle before he got out of his seat and made his way forward. He'd checked a large rolling suitcase in Hainan. It was only half full so he could bring home all sorts of goodies. Souvenirs to remember his week in exotic Singapore.

It was just past noon as he strolled down the concourse to the huge Changi immigration hall. Two dozen desks were manned by customs officers. He queued up in the shortest line.

As the line moved forward, Zhu mentally planned the rest of his day. Taxi to his hotel, then a late lunch, he decided. He'd walk a bit, maybe do some shopping, then take a nap so he'd be fresh for this evening. Just the thought of the night's activities gave him a secret thrill.

He was debating what to have for dinner when he arrived at the Immigration desk. Absently, he handed over his passport to the official. Something light, he decided, but nothing that might give him gas later in the evening.

The customs officer opened the passport to the picture page with a gloved hand. His eyes flicked from the page to Zhu's face. He tapped on his keyboard with an index finger and fed the passport into a scanner.

"What is the purpose of your visit to Singapore, Mr. Zhu?" the customs officer asked in Mandarin.

"Business," he replied.

Zhu's hand slipped into the open pocket of his computer bag and touched the flip phone. After dinner, he'd shower and turn on the phone.

He smiled to himself. Business, with a little pleasure on the side.

The man nodded and stamped the passport. Zhu held out his hand to receive it, but instead of passing it across the desk, the official handed it over his shoulder to a uniformed security officer.

Zhu drew his hand back, unsure what was going on.

When the security officer stepped from behind the desk, Zhu could see he was armed. A second man appeared from behind Zhu and stood on his other side.

"Would you come with us, please, sir?" the first man said.

"What is this about?" Zhu demanded. He did his best to keep any trace of concern out of his voice. "I'm here on a business trip. I've been here before."

The officer was unmoved. "Just come with us, sir. Please."

He put his hand on Zhu's elbow and steered him out of line, toward the wall of the high-ceilinged hall. People were staring at him and Zhu felt his face grow hot.

They turned behind the row of Immigration desks to where a third man waited next to an open door. He had Zhu's checked luggage at his side.

"What's going on?" Zhu demanded. He spoke in a stern voice because he didn't want them to see how freaked out he was. The three men simply formed around him and herded him through the open door. Zhu heard the door close behind them and the solid clunk of a magnetic lock slamming home. His heart rate spiked.

He hadn't done anything wrong, he told himself. This was all some sort of mistake.

They moved down a wide hallway, closed doors on either side. The floors were linoleum, cream-colored with flecks of gray and black to conceal the dirt. The walls were vinyl, punctuated every few meters with white steel doors labeled with bold black numbers.

The quartet stopped next to a door labeled 4. Zhu's eyes widened when he saw the number.

The first guard used a keycard to unlock the door. He pushed it open to reveal a square white room with a table and two chairs. A sturdy metal screen covered the fluorescent lights.

An interrogation room, Zhu realized. He started to speak again, but his mouth was dry.

"Could you wait in here, please, sir?" the security man said.

Zhu found his voice. "Why? What have I done?"

"I'll need your computer bag and your mobile phone, please."

"I don't have to—"

"Please." The guard cut him off. "Computer bag and mobile phone, Mr. Zhu."

He didn't have a choice. He gave up the requested items and stepped into the room. The door boomed as it closed behind him. The magnetic lock chunked into place.

Zhu kept his back to the door. When he crossed the threshold, he'd seen the dome of smoky glass protruding from the ceiling over the door. A camera.

He composed his face, squared his shoulders.

You have nothing to fear. You have done nothing wrong. There is nothing in your luggage that can incriminate you.

Face impassive, he took the chair facing the door, placed his folded hands on the bare table.

He wondered what time it was. He wasn't wearing a watch, and they'd taken his phone. It had been after noon when he'd gotten off the plane and he'd taken his time walking to the immigration hall. In line for ten minutes, he guessed, maybe fifteen.

Then the guards came and took him away. How long had that taken? Although it had seemed like an hour, it was probably less than ten minutes. He did the math. It was about one in the afternoon.

He drew in a deep breath and let it out.

This was a mistake, he told himself. *Any minute now, an Immigration officer will walk through the door full of apologies.*

He waited, counting his breaths, deep and even. When he reached twenty, he started over again.

Zhu Shufen kept his face still, but when he looked down, he could see that the skin around his knuckles was white with tension.

6

Changi Airport, Singapore

The security center for immigration control at Changi Airport was dark and cool enough that Peter Chen was glad he'd worn a suit. The room was spacious, with three officers and a supervisor manning workstations in front of an interactive monitor that covered the entire wall. The officers, all wearing headsets with boom mikes, spoke in low tones as they manipulated the images on the screen.

It was a controlled, professional atmosphere, and Peter was impressed. The cooperation from the Singaporean security services had been excellent. He asked for what he needed and they delivered, no questions asked. It was clear the authorities valued a close working relationship with the United States.

At a standalone monitor along the back wall, he studied the detained Chinese engineer, Zhu Shufen. He'd been in the interrogation room for just under two hours and he was showing signs of strain.

Good, Peter thought. They'd used all the classic pressure techniques—turning up the heat in the room, removing all ways to measure time, and isolating him. For the first seventy-five minutes, Zhu had sat completely still and quiet. The only sign that he was nervous was the way he clenched his hands on the table. At the ninety-minute mark, the Chinese engineer began to stir. He got up, paced.

"The room number was a nice touch," said a voice behind him.

Peter allowed himself a smile as he turned toward Genevieve Matcombe, who was running tech on the operation.

"My grandmother used to tell me that the number four was unlucky," he said. "The word sounds like the word for *death* in Mandarin. I don't know whether that's just an old wives' tale, but I figured it couldn't hurt."

Genevieve leaned over his shoulder to study the monitor. She was a tall, willowy black woman with deep experience in banking and technology. "It certainly got his attention."

Peter nodded. "What did you find out about our guy?"

Genevieve consulted a tablet. "Zhu Shufen has a reservation for the whole week at Raffles downtown. He flew in a day early. The conference doesn't start until tomorrow afternoon. One piece of checked luggage, half full, which I take to mean our man is planning on doing some shopping while he's here. Carrying quite a bit of cash, over five grand, but that fits with the shopping theme, I guess.

"His laptop is a travel model, stripped down. It has his presentation for later this week, and basic office functions like unclassified email. His boss is a bit of a prick. He's already sent him four emails, on a Sunday."

"What about his phone?"

"Which one?"

Peter glanced up. "He has more than one phone?"

"Work phone is a Huawei Mate XT smartphone. We hacked it. It's got email and some games, but nothing out of the ordinary. The other phone is a flip phone, Motorola knockoff. Clearly a burner."

"Any calls?"

Genevieve shook her head. "Never even been used as far as we can see. Fully charged battery, but it's only been turned on once in Hainan last week. No calls made or received. Ever."

Peter frowned. "Odd. Why does an engineer need a burner? You think it's just a backup for his work phone?"

"Your guess is as good as mine." She consulted the tablet again. "We ran an AI scan on his entire unclass email history. No big scores there. We got a few hits that might help us piece some intel together, but it'll need some human intervention."

Peter nodded, his eyes on the screen.

"Does he have any appointments this evening?" he asked.

"He's got a hotel reservation, but nothing else is on his calendar. You going to keep him overnight?"

On the screen, Zhu ceased his pacing and sat back down. As he brought his hands up, Peter saw them tremble. He laced his fingers together and placed them on the table in front of him.

"I don't think that will be necessary. Besides, if we detain him for too long, it might raise suspicions. We don't want that. I'm going in."

"Good luck," Genevieve said.

"Four is my lucky number," Peter returned with a smile. "I don't care what Grandma says."

Genevieve took his vacated seat and leaned back in the chair. "I'll get the popcorn."

Peter visited the restroom, splashed water on his face, and reknotted his tie. He took his time walking to Interrogation Room 4. He paused outside the heavy steel door. He filled his lungs, held the breath for a four count, then let it out slowly. When he pressed the keycard against the pad, the red LED light turned green, and the magnetic lock snapped open.

The sharp smell of armpit sweat pervaded the warm room. Zhu Shufen was nervous. That was good; he was off-balance.

Peter stood in the doorway, letting the cool air from the air-conditioned hallway draft into the room. He released the door and it swung closed. The magnetic lock slammed home with a metallic snap that made Zhu wince.

The engineer's gaze flicked across Peter's face, taking in the suit, the polished shoes, the neutral smile. He swallowed. "Who are you?" he asked in Mandarin.

"My name is Peter Chen," Peter replied in the same language.

"You're not with Immigration. Who do you work for?" The tone was hostile—and fearful.

"We'll get to that."

"I want to see some ID," Zhu continued.

"That's not how this works."

Zhu's eyes narrowed. "You're not with the police."

The response took Peter by surprise and he fumbled his answer. "No, I'm not with the police."

Zhu's face seemed to soften. He sat back in his chair. "Who are you? You're not with Immigration and you're not with the police, so that leaves... what?" The hostility had dropped from Zhu's tone.

Peter pulled out the empty chair. This was moving fast, much faster than he'd expected. "I work for a European company," he said. "I'd like to hire you."

Zhu unlaced his fingers, rubbed his palms along the thighs of his trousers. "Have I heard of this company?"

"They're well known in their industry," Peter replied. "Very wealthy."

Zhu leaned forward. "And what industry are we talking about?"

There was something off about this guy, Peter realized. He'd moved from nervous to engaged, almost relaxed, in the space of just a few minutes.

"We're in the defense industry."

"What do you want with me?" Zhu's black eyes were wary, but Peter clearly had his full attention.

"My company is interested in the latest advancements in undersea propulsion systems."

"And I suppose you would be willing to pay for information about these developments." Zhu leaned back in his chair, folded his arms. His face was flushed from the heat, but there was a trace of a smile on his lips.

"Handsomely."

"How much?"

Peter tried to keep his face neutral. Step by step, he reminded himself. He had a live one. Don't blow it now. "It depends on what you have to offer."

Zhu smiled wolfishly. "What do you want to know?"

Peter withdrew a folded sheet of paper and a pen from inside his jacket. "Explain the basic propulsion concept behind the high-speed torpedo that was tested recently in the Hainan underwater test range."

Zhu immediately went to work, drawing what looked like a series of nozzles around a shrouded propeller. Peter studied the diagram, asking a few follow-up questions. Finally, the Chinese engineer held up his hands.

"No more," he said. "Not until we reach terms."

"You'll be paid well, Mr. Zhu."

"How much?"

Peter named a figure. He saw the greedy flare in Zhu's eyes, then concern. "What do I have to do?"

Peter pointed at the pen in Zhu's hand. "May I?"

The engineer returned the pen. Peter held it up between his thumb and forefinger. It was a thick, heavy cylinder of black plastic, trimmed in brass, the kind of pen where a user twisted the shaft to make the ballpoint appear. Engraved on the side of the pen was the name of the conference Zhu was attending in Singapore. The conference logo was encased in a clear plastic bubble on the end of the pen.

"Hundreds of these pens will be given out at the conference tomorrow, but this one is different." Peter twisted the shaft so the ballpoint retracted, then continued twisting through two slight detents. He pointed the end of the pen at Zhu and depressed the gold pocket clip. "I just took your picture."

Zhu's eyebrows went up. "It's a camera?" he said with a note of wonder.

Handing the pen back, Peter nodded.

Zhu inspected the end, depressed the trigger. "How many pictures can it hold?"

"More than you can possibly take, Shufen." He slipped Zhu's first name into the conversation to see if he got a negative reaction. He did not. "The entire assembly is built into the back end of the pen."

"What about an X-ray?" Zhu asked. He held the pen up to the light, squinting at the pinpoint lens.

"The camera appears on radiography as a pellet about the size of a mung bean. Any cursory X-ray in a security queue will never see it."

"Amazing," Zhu murmured.

Peter took the pen back. "Imagine you're sitting at your computer at work." He mimed slumping in his chair. He held the pen in his fist with the camera pointed out. He rested his fist against his chin, finger over the pocket clip of the pen. "You're thinking as you work. You call up a screen and take a picture, then put the pen aside while you do some work. A little while later, change the screen and do the same thing again."

"And then what?" Zhu asked.

"Next month, you're scheduled to attend a symposium in Korea, correct?"

Zhu hesitated, then nodded.

"You bring the pen with you. At the hotel bar, someone will ask to borrow your pen to sign a check. They will keep the pen."

"And that's it?"

"That's it. We'll analyze the pictures, confirm they're legitimate, and then you get your money."

"Two million dollars?"

"Two million dollars, Shufen."

Zhu's face broke into a wide smile, then a frown creased his brow. "What time is it?" he demanded.

Peter checked his watch. "A little after four."

Zhu set his chin. "I want fifteen thousand dollars. Cash. This afternoon."

"That's not how this works, Shufen."

"You get it for me, or I walk out of here and get back on a plane to China. I'll tell them everything."

What the hell just happened? Peter wondered. Assets making demands was not unusual, but this was all happening on an accelerated timetable.

He folded his arms. "Why?" Peter challenged. "Why do you need money now?"

"That's my business. You want the designs of the Hu Jing? I'll get them, but I have demands—and they will be met. Or else."

Hu Jing. They called the torpedo the Orca, the killer whale, the most fearsome predator in the ocean.

Peter hesitated. In normal circumstances, the right answer was to push back, reestablish control in the relationship. But these were not normal circumstances. He'd just recruited a valuable asset on a cold pitch. This entire operation had been one step above a Hail Mary from the start...and he'd done it. Why fight success?

Peter rubbed his chin like he was making a difficult choice. "I can arrange that," he said finally.

Zhu grinned. "Let's get this wrapped up. I'd like to go to my hotel. It's been a long day."

At just after seven in the evening, Peter watched from his monitor in the security center as Zhu Shufen hurried to a waiting taxi outside Changi Airport. He tossed his bag in the trunk and slid into the backseat.

Genevieve joined him. "That went well."

"It did," Peter agreed. "He barely batted an eye when I asked him to spy on his country."

"We all have our reasons, Peter. Money talks."

"Yeah." Something about the interview still nagged at Peter, but it was hard to argue with success. He'd been sent here to recruit a spy and now they had a man on the inside of the Hainan weapons development facility.

"Did you tell Harrison the good news yet?"

Outside, the sun was setting. The taxi pulled out of the queue and disappeared into the Sunday evening flow of traffic.

"Not yet."

7

USS *Illinois*, 120 miles southeast of Hainan Island, South China Sea

"The ship is rigged for ultra quiet, ma'am," Lieutenant Taylor reported. "Request permission to proceed to the rendezvous point."

Janet crossed her arms more tightly across her chest. In the last half hour, she hadn't moved from her position behind Senior Chief O'Malley's back, studying the sonar displays over his shoulder. According to their sensors, the ocean around them was free of contacts.

Janet gave a curt nod. "Proceed, Mr. Taylor."

"Pilot, all ahead one-third," Taylor ordered. "Left five degrees rudder, steady new course two-seven-zero."

The repeat back was crisp.

"Nice and easy, Pilot."

"Aye, sir."

Janet let out a shallow breath. At this speed, it would take them almost forty-five minutes to reach the rendezvous point where they'd recover their underwater drone.

The Narwhals, so nicknamed for their long snouts that connected them to the submarine for recharging batteries and downloading data, were extensions of the submarine's sensor capabilities. Over the last two weeks,

Janet had been using them to map the seafloor of the PLA Navy's underwater test range off Hainan Island, including the exact placement of the hydrophones. She'd even managed to get a few photos of the seafloor sensors, something she was sure would be of great interest to the analysts back in DC.

She stepped away from the sonar stack to join Lieutenant Commander Avery at the navigation plot in the center of the control room. The soft light from the horizontal display lit Avery's face as she readied the system to accept a data download from the incoming sensors.

The area they'd already surveyed showed detailed seafloor topography. The hydrophones showed up as red dots with accompanying data tags. Janet touched one of the tags and a pop-up box provided the exact lat-long of the device and a picture. The sensor was not something she was familiar with. It looked a little like a mechanical starfish.

"We should be filling in this area right here, Captain," Avery reported. "After today, we'll be about 60 percent complete."

Janet nodded. The process was excruciatingly slow. Since the drones were assigned a few square nautical miles each mission, watching the chart fill in was about as exciting as watching paint dry. Still, if the US Navy ever had cause to penetrate the underwater test range, the data would be invaluable.

Janet certainly hoped it was worth it, because it was giving her an ulcer. Twice a day, she had to move her multi-billion-dollar submarine to the perimeter of the underwater test range to recover one drone and deploy a second. Janet took no chances. She knew there was a PLA Navy submarine out there on patrol. Each time, she rigged the ship for ultra quiet, stopping the normal activity of her submarine. All nonessential watchstanders were confined to their racks, all maintenance ceased, and all watertight doors were latched open. Even the galley was shut down for the three hours it took them to transit in, swap the drones, and clear the area.

Like the rest of the crew, Avery looked tired. The excitement of heading home had evaporated, replaced by the routine monotony of a long-term deployment. The crew had accepted that their mission was extended, and Janet was proud of the way they were performing, but the signs of strain were everywhere. She saw it in the faces of the crew and fraying tempers.

Although their captain might secretly relish the fact that their deployment was extended, she was definitely in the minority.

"Carry on, Nav." Janet leaned in and lowered her voice. "I'm sorry about your anniversary. Thank you for staying so focused. I appreciate your professionalism."

Avery forced a smile. "Thank you, Captain. It's all part of the job."

Janet returned to her post behind Senior Chief O'Malley. She and the sonarman had reached an understanding: She would be a pain in his ass and he would ignore her. It was an imperfect détente, but so far, it was working for them.

"Anything, Senior?" she asked in a low voice.

He shook his head without removing his headphones or taking his eyes off the screen.

"No, ma'am. That signature tonal is nowhere to be found. If he's out there, he's a ghost."

That was not strictly true and they both knew it. The tonal was directional. If the enemy sub was facing away from them, they'd never hear it.

"He's out there," she said.

"Officer of the Deck," the fire control operator said. "I have contact with Narwhal One."

"Very well, Fire Control. Pilot, all stop. Adjust trim for hovering."

Another ten minutes passed before the massive ship slowed to a full stop and was suspended in the ocean.

"Officer of the Deck," called out the Pilot. "Ship is one-five-zero feet and hovering."

"Narwhal One is one hundred yards astern, OOD," Fire Control reported. "Depth match is tracking."

Taylor approached Janet. "Captain, request permission to light up the runway and recover Narwhal One."

"Permission granted."

Along the spine of the *Illinois*, a line of blue-green lasers—dubbed the runway by the crew—energized to guide the drone to its recovery position over VLS tube number twelve.

Janet moved to a spare monitor and called up the Narwhal recovery screen.

The graphic showed a side view of the *Illinois* with green dots indicating the positions of the lasers. The drone approached from the stern, a long device shaped like a hypodermic needle, traveling along the centerline of the submarine. It passed over the sail and stopped over the vertical launch tubes.

Janet hated this part. Opening the VLS tube made noise. There was no way around it. "You have permission to open VLS twelve, OOD."

"Pilot, open VLS twelve."

"Opening VLS twelve." The chief at the controls touched his screen. A second later, there was a soft thump like someone punching a pillow. Everyone in control flinched together. The green circle on the screen extinguished. A few seconds later, a red dot replaced it.

"OOD, VLS twelve indicates open."

Janet shot a glance at O'Malley to see if the noise had stirred any response in the ocean around them. As if he knew she was watching, he slowly shook his head.

"You may commence recovery, Mr. Taylor," Janet said.

"Commence recovery, aye, ma'am."

The fire control technician, a short, skinny kid, repeated back Taylor's order as he worked his screen. On her monitor, Janet watched the long tip of the drone's nose slowly tilt downward until the device was vertical, pointed straight down at the sub.

"Laser lock is intermittent, OOD," Fire Control reported.

The drone used a laser sensor to maintain a straight approach into the vertical tube. The primary had failed last week and now the secondary laser was acting up. It might be something as simple as a dirty lens, but there was no way for them to access the VLS tube when the ship was underway.

"Proceed, Mr. Taylor," Janet prompted.

"Aye, ma'am."

The graphic showed the cigar-shaped drone moving downward.

"Five yards and closing," Fire Control reported.

Taylor murmured an acknowledgment.

"Three yards...OOD, the laser just quit."

Janet cursed to herself. "You have permission to cycle power, Mr. Taylor."

It took ten more precious minutes to cycle power to the laser and reboot the system.

"Laser is back online, sir," Fire Control reported, "but the drone is out of alignment."

Janet's gaze snapped up to the clock in the corner of the display. They'd been hovering in enemy territory for twenty-eight minutes. The idea that her ship had been exposed for that long made her skin itch with anxiety. There was an enemy submarine out there.

Taylor went through the procedure to return the drone to a neutral position and line up for another docking attempt. Janet fretted about the time it took, but she kept her face still, her shoulders relaxed. The only outward sign of the stress she was feeling was the death grip her fingers had on the edge of the console.

"Two yards," the fire control tech reported on their second approach. He paused. "Laser is out again, sir."

"Continue the recovery, Mr. Taylor," Janet ordered.

"Aye, ma'am." Taylor's voice was tight with tension.

Janet felt more than heard the body of the drone impact the rim of the open VLS tube. Then, a scraping sound like a key being dragged across the body of a sports car.

"Captain—" began O'Malley.

"I hear it, Senior," Janet snapped. "OOD, get that drone in the tube now."

"Yes, ma'am."

"Sir!" The fire control technician's thin face was sweaty with anxiety. "It's misaligned! We missed the connection—"

Taylor dropped a hand on the kid's shoulder. "Take a breath, Jackson. We just need to burp the baby. We do this all the time."

"Captain," O'Malley said again.

"Chief, I know we're making noise—"

"He's back," O'Malley blurted. "Sierra two-six. I've got the tonal, bearing zero-one-zero."

"Get that drone back in the tube, Mr. Taylor," Janet snapped. "Now."

She moved to the sonar stack, where O'Malley had the narrowband display called up. The dancing line of frequencies showed a sharp spike. As she watched, the amplitude of the spike shot up.

"Aspect ratio is changing, ma'am. He's close and he's turning toward us. It's possible he heard us."

Janet cursed. "Mr. Taylor?"

"Working on it, Captain."

"Work faster."

"Sierra two-six is increasing speed, Captain. I'm getting a broadband signal. He knows something's out there."

I'm out of time, Janet thought, and I'm vulnerable. This is not going to end well.

"Attention in control, this is the captain. I have the conn."

She swung toward the fire control station. "Petty Officer Jackson, eject the drone."

"Captain?"

Taylor reached over the young man's shoulder and punched a button on the display. "Drone ejected, Captain."

"Pilot, close VLS twelve."

"Closing twelve, ma'am." Her eyes were fastened on the hull display. "Green board, Captain."

"All ahead one-third, Pilot." Janet turned to Taylor. "Where's my layer, Mr. Taylor?"

"Three hundred twenty feet, Captain."

"Pilot, make your depth four hundred feet."

"Four hundred feet, aye, Captain."

The deck angled down.

"Sonar, what's two-six doing?" Janet demanded.

"He's turning towards us, Captain," O'Malley said. "He knows we're out here, ma'am."

"Pilot, all ahead two-thirds. Make your depth five hundred feet."

"Passing two hundred on my way to five hundred, ma'am. Engine room answers all ahead two-thirds."

"Best bearing to Sierra two-six, Senior?"

"Due north, Captain."

"Pilot, steer new course one-eight-zero."

The ship adjusted course gently. The deck leveled out. The Pilot reported steady on course and speed.

Janet gritted her teeth. Getting discovered by the PLA Navy would be a disaster. They were under the thermal layer, and she'd steered the ship to give the lowest possible cross section to any sonar search. She'd done all she could do.

"He's going active!" O'Malley reported.

Janet's eyes snapped to the broadband waterfall display. The screen saturated white.

8

CNS *Changcheng* 346, South China Sea, 115 miles southeast of Hainan Island

Captain Kai Jun worried at the ragged edge of a fingernail. His eyes flicked around the control room, taking in the rigid posture of his watch officer and the equally straight backs of the rest of the watchstanders on duty.

These days, it felt like he rarely left the control room. Indeed, he experienced mild anxiety if he was absent for more than an hour. The feeling was silly, he knew. The submarine wasn't that big. He was never more than a minute or two away from control. But that did nothing to ease the sense that if he left the watch team alone for too long, they would lose the intensity necessary to find their prey.

Kai knew his actions probably made the crew nervous, even less effective, but he couldn't help himself. There was too much at stake.

There was an enemy sub out there. He knew it was true. The fact that no one in his chain of command shared his belief did not matter. This had nothing to do with his sense of pride; it was a matter of duty. Honor to his profession. He was the commanding officer of one of the finest submarines in the People's Liberation Army Navy, and he would fulfill his mission to the best of his ability.

From the mess decks below the control room, strains of island music drifted up the stairwell. Out of the corner of his eye, he saw the fire control tech on watch bop his head in time with the heavy beat.

Kai wanted to snap at the enlisted man but restrained himself. It wasn't his fault. Commander Mao had been after Kai for the past week to allow the crew a night off, and Kai had finally relented.

Tonight, the galley was serving a beach-themed menu. Mao had produced a box of garish Hawaiian shirts for the crew to wear—Kai had no idea where he'd stored them—and following the evening meal, there were games and dancing planned in the crew's mess. When Kai imagined his crew doing the limbo on his mess decks, it made him gag.

But Mao was persistent and even Kai had to admit that the crew needed some diversion at this point in their patrol. He could see they were all tired. Hell, he was exhausted.

Turning his mind back to the enemy submarine, he drew a small notebook from his breast pocket and flipped to a marked page. Over the past two weeks, they'd had intermittent contact with an unfamiliar narrowband frequency. It was tenuous, no more than the occasional spiking signal in the noisy ocean. Each time, the faint signal lasted for fifteen minutes before disappearing. If he hadn't been so present in the sonar room, he was not convinced that the sonar supervisor would have reported the odd signal.

But he had been there. He had identified the signal and left specific instructions that he was to be informed if the frequency reappeared. No matter how weak or tenuous the signal, he was to be called immediately.

And his tenacity paid off. Twice a day, roughly every twelve hours, the sonar team had detected the tonal in their patrol area. They tried to track it, but the elusive signal always slipped away as quickly as it arrived.

Kai checked his watch. Twelve hours had come and gone with no sign of their quarry. In minutes, the galley would open and the crew would be distracted for the next few hours by the political officer's ridiculous festivities.

Kai stowed the notebook in his breast pocket and rubbed his face. He needed a nap, maybe a shower and a shave. Maybe it was time to reset his thinking and admit to himself that he was chasing ghosts in the ocean. Sound did not travel in a straight line underwater, and the South China Sea was one of the busiest shipping lanes in the world. The ocean was filled with random noise. He was seeing patterns where none existed.

The chief engineer appeared in the doorway of the control room and came loosely to attention. "Request permission to enter control."

The watch officer looked at Kai, who nodded.

The chief engineer approached Kai. "May we speak in private, Captain?"

Of all the officers in his crew, Kai identified most with his chief engineer. Kai had done that job and knew it to be demanding and thankless. The engine room of a submarine was a place of complexity, with thousands of moving parts and millions of opportunities for things to go wrong.

In the engine room, something always needed fixing and there was never enough time or manpower to complete the task fully. It was a job of constant interruptions and setbacks, but also ripe with opportunities to rise above the chaos and lead his engineers to success. Like himself, he knew his chief engineer took quiet pride in accomplishing his mission.

Kai led the way to his stateroom and offered the chief engineer a seat. The man sank into the chair with a tired groan. It was possible his chief engineer looked even more tired than Kai felt.

"When was the last time you slept, Jin?" Kai asked him.

The man gave up a weak smile. "When was the last time we were in port, sir?"

They laughed together—it was an old joke between them—and Kai felt a rare moment of kinship with a fellow officer. He and the chief engineer had come from humble roots and worked hard for their commissions, unlike the political officer with his private school education and family connections within the Party.

"What can I do for you?" the captain asked.

"The leak rate on the shaft bearing has increased, Captain," the other man said, his tone all business now. "I'm estimating five liters per minute—enough that I have to run at least one bilge pump almost continuously to keep up."

Kai sighed. The shaft seals always leaked a little bit, that was part of their design, but this leak rate was well above specification. He'd instructed the chief engineer to leave the failing seal out of his daily ship status report to keep the information away from Commander Mao. He worried that the political officer would use the failure as an excuse to get the ship sent back to port. A damaged shaft seal could mean weeks of refit, possibly even a trip to the drydock.

"What if you ran both port and starboard bilge pumps? Would that keep the level under control?"

The engineer nodded. "For now, sir, but the problem is getting worse."

Kai nodded. "I understand your concern, Jin, but I need you to get us through this patrol. Can you do that for me?"

The chief engineer straightened in his chair. "Of course, Captain. But I think I need to start reporting the condition in the daily status report, sir."

The phone on the wall next to the desk buzzed. Kai snatched up the heavy plastic receiver. "Captain."

"Captain, Sonar reports a transient in the starboard baffles, sir."

Kai was in the control room before the watch officer hung up his own handset. He strode into the darkened sonar room.

"Show me," he said to the sonar supervisor.

The man was already pointing to the waterfall display. In the staticky background, Kai spotted a bright dot, then a trailing white line like smeared ink.

"Intermittent mechanical noise, sir. Just a few seconds in length. A bump, then a scraping sound. The contact is in our starboard baffles." He handed the headphones to his captain.

Kai closed his eyes and listened. When he heard the noise, his eyes snapped open. He roared through the open door into the control room. "Watch Officer, bring the ship to general quarters!"

The alarm sounded through the ship like a throbbing heartbeat. The crew came alive with action. Pounding footsteps, lockers being opened, sound-powered telephones appearing from containers, the sharp rap of issued orders.

Captain Kai reentered control. "Come right to new course two-two-zero. Increase speed to ten knots."

The watch officer gave the orders and the *Changcheng* banked into the turn.

Kai posted in front of the sonar waterfall display. In the intervening minutes, the transient noise that had started the entire chain of events had traveled to the bottom of the screen. He watched it disappear. Kai stared at the display as if he might be able to will another signal to appear, but the line of bearing remained empty.

"The ship is rigged for general quarters, Captain," the watch officer reported. "Steady new course two-two-zero."

"Very well," Kai replied. "Sonar, report when the towed array is stable."

"It will take at least two more minutes, sir," came the reply.

Kai cursed to himself. Repositioning the ship was a risk, but the enemy contact was behind them. He needed to close the distance and try to acquire the elusive signature frequency.

"Captain?" the watch officer said in a tentative voice.

Kai looked up to find the political officer standing in the doorway of the control room. For once, Commander Mao did not look composed and at ease. In fact, he looked ridiculous. He wore a brightly colored Hawaiian shirt that was two sizes too large, so it swam on his lean frame like a sack. A gray flash hood pooled around the base of his neck and he had an emergency breathing mask slung over his shoulder. His complexion was dark with anger.

Kai looked away, ignoring him. He crossed the room to Sonar and leaned in.

"Anything?"

The sonar supervisor shook his head. "No, sir, but the array is just stable now. It takes a few minutes to process the incoming data."

Kai nodded and turned to find the watch officer waiting for him. "Captain, the political officer wishes to speak with you."

Kai let his gaze settle on Mao. He nodded once, and the man stormed into control. Mao drew close to him and said in a low voice, "What are you doing, Captain?"

"I am prosecuting an enemy submarine in the territorial waters of the People's Republic of China, Commander Mao." He dropped his eyes to take in the oversized shirt. "What are you doing, sir?"

"Captain." Mao's voice was rigid with anger. "The crew is tired. You agreed to give them a night off. No drills, no evolutions."

"Is that what you think this is, Commander?" Kai's own voice sang with tension. "A drill? Something to mess up your party?"

Mao struggled with his composure. "No, but you promised, Captain."

A white blip appeared on the waterfall display. He put his hand on Mao's chest and pushed him back, leaned closer to the monitor.

"Sonar! Report on that transient."

"Not sure, sir…it could be manmade."

Kai strode into the sonar room, his hand reaching for the headphones. The sound was like a soft pop, or a muffled thump. It could be manmade… or not.

There was one sure way to find out.

"Line up to use active sonar on that bearing," he ordered.

"Captain." The political officer's voice was behind him. "The admiral's standing orders prohibit the use of active sonar near the underwater test range."

Kai spun around. He'd had enough of this meddling. He knew he was shouting, but he was unable to stop himself. The frustrating weeks of endless searching took their toll and he unleashed on the political officer.

"Commander Mao, you will not interfere with the execution of our mission. I order you to leave the control room immediately."

Shocked silence. Kai instantly regretted his words. He'd placed the political officer into a position where he couldn't back down. Mao was right about the admiral's standing orders and they both knew it. To his surprise, the younger man raised his hands, palms out. He stepped back.

"My apologies, Captain. You are correct. You have operational control over the submarine. I was wrong to question your authority."

Kai, who had expected an argument, opened his mouth and closed it again.

"Good," he said finally.

"Sonar is lined up for active transmission, Captain," Sonar reported.

Kai hesitated.

"Captain," the watch officer said. "Sonar is standing by, sir."

Kai cursed his own indecision. "Transmit, Sonar," he ordered.

"Transmitting."

The pulse of energy entered the water in front of the submarine. Kai studied the monitor where the reflected energy showed as bits of brightness like dust motes in sunlight. A metallic target the size and shape of a submarine would show up as a bright blob.

But there was nothing.

"We have a strong layer at one hundred meters, sir. We're reflecting off it. Recommend higher power."

Kai gripped the sides of the monitor with both hands.

"Increase transmission power by fifty percent and retransmit, Sonar," Kai ordered.

Ten seconds later, the next pulse blanked out the screen. Kai stared at the display, willing it to update.

The additional power was enough to punch through the layer, but there was no bright return.

"Weak return at nine thousand meters, Captain. Possible submerged contact."

Or it could be a school of fish, Kai thought.

"Transmit again, Sonar. Maximum power."

"Transmitting."

The display blanked out as the sonar system blasted energy into the ocean. Kai watched the screen update. He didn't need the sonar supervisor to tell him what he could see with his own eyes.

"No return, Captain."

Kai straightened up, his back rigid with disappointment. The political officer had departed the control room.

"Watch Officer, secure from general quarters."

9

Yulin Naval Base, Hainan Island

Although it was just after eight in the morning, the day was already hot and humid. By the time he arrived at the bus stop, Zhu Shufen had sweated through his shirt. He mopped his brow with a handkerchief as he waited in the queue. He hated taking the bus, but all private vehicle traffic on the secure area of the base had been curtailed since they had begun testing the new torpedo.

The bus arrived, an ancient groaning monster that smelled of body odor and diesel. The open windows did nothing to lessen the stench. The man across from him pulled a small jar of menthol from his pocket and dabbed it under his nose. He saw Zhu watching and offered the open jar, but Zhu shook his head. The bus lurched forward.

Normally, a morning like this—arriving to work late, riding a stinking bus to a job that he hated—would have made him angry, but not anymore. Zhu Shufen was a new man, a man on the cusp of greatness. He drew a satisfied breath of the fetid bus air and let it out slowly, imagining his life after he got paid.

Two. Million. Dollars. It was hard to tamp down the shiver of joy he felt every time he thought about all that money.

On his last trip to Singapore, he'd had $15,000 extra in cash. That first night had exceeded his wildest dreams—and he had some pretty extravagant dreams. With $2 million in the bank, he could experience that level of pleasure every night of the week and twice on Sunday for the rest of his life.

One more week. He just had to get through one more week at work. By this time next week, he'd be in Korea for the conference, Peter Chen's contact would take delivery of the pen, and he'd be a very rich man.

Zhu clutched his knapsack against his chest, feeling the pen in his shirt pocket. At first, he'd worried about being discovered, but he followed Chen's instructions to the letter. Put the pen in his shirt pocket, wear it in plain sight. Use it often. Why not? After all, it's just a pen. Use it to write notes, sign documents, let everyone see you using your favorite pen.

He'd been doing that ever since he got back from Singapore and the results were astonishing to Zhu. No one gave him a second glance when he pulled out the pen. It was comically easy to gather the documents that were going to make him two million dollars richer.

The pen was like a superpower now. He'd even used it in a staff meeting to take a picture of a particularly useful slide in his boss's presentation to the admiral of the weapons development section.

One night, after a few shots of baijiu, he thought about taking the pen apart to see if he could figure out how it worked. Despite the overconfidence of the grain alcohol, he stopped himself. He had two million good reasons to resist the temptation.

The bus drew to a shuddering halt outside the Advanced Propulsion Lab, where Zhu worked. He disembarked and climbed the steps into the building two at a time, pulling his security badge from his knapsack as he walked. He was more than twenty minutes late as he scurried past Yang Min's office. His boss did not look up from his desk, and Zhu breathed a sigh of relief.

He laughed to himself as he arrived at his cubicle. In another week, none of this would matter anymore. Zhu would be a free man.

A few minutes later, a fresh cup of tea at his elbow, Zhu used his computer to call up the new design specs for the rocket nozzle that drove the high-speed torpedo. There was a pending design change and he wanted to make sure he captured the details.

Casually, he removed the pen from his shirt pocket and twisted the barrel counterclockwise. He felt the first detent, twisted more, then the second. He settled the pen in his fist and rested his hand against his chin, contemplating the screen. He placed his thumb on the pocket clip.

"Mr. Yang wants to see you," said a flat voice from directly behind his chair.

Zhu startled, upsetting his tea. He spun his chair around to face Ms. Cheng. Yang's secretary was in her mid-fifties with a face like slapped dough and a sour demeanor.

"Why did you sneak up on me?" Zhu demanded. "You could give me a heart attack."

"Mr. Yang wants to see you," she repeated.

"About what?"

She eyed the spilled tea. "I'll tell him you need a moment to get cleaned up."

Zhu mopped up the spilled tea and tried to compose himself. There was no way she saw anything, he told himself. Nevertheless, he found his pulse beating faster as he made his way to his boss's office.

The glass walls of Yang's office jutted out from the corner of the advanced propulsion floor like the prow of a ship looking over a sea of engineering cubicles. From his perch, his boss could see who was at their desk and who was coming and going by the secure entrance. The engineers in the division shared a private joke that Yang kept a piss bucket underneath his desk so he never had to leave his office.

Yang represented everything Zhu hated: a company man who had done his time. He wasn't a good engineer, but he was an excellent bureaucrat and masterful ass-kisser, and that was what was rewarded in this business.

Zhu's lip curled. If this loser knew what he was doing right under his nose, the fat bastard would probably have a stroke right at his desk.

As always, Mr. Yang dressed in a short-sleeve white shirt with a narrow black tie. The white cotton was stretched taut across his considerable belly. His thinning hair was greased back, and he had an oily smile on his face.

"Come in, Shufen," he said, half rising from his desk. "Have a seat."

Zhu knew something was wrong. The use of his first name was out of character for the by-the-book manager and his manner bordered on friendly. He decided to play along.

"I'm sorry I was late this morning, Mr. Yang," Zhu said with as much contrition as he could muster. "The bus—"

"It's not about that, Shufen," Yang interrupted. His insincere smile tightened.

Zhu tried to read Yang's face and came up blank.

"I'm afraid I have to cancel your trip to Korea next week. I know you were counting on it, but it's just not possible. Two of our engineers are on leave for family emergencies and I need you here."

"But that's not fair," Zhu blurted out. It was a stupid thing to say, but it just fell out of his mouth. "You promised me I could go to that conference." He sounded like a child.

Yang's soft tone mimicked a patient parent talking to that child. "As I've already explained, Shufen, there are exigent circumstances."

"Exigent circumstances?" Zhu's voice rose, his face hot with anger. It was all slipping away. Two million dollars.

"I want to appeal to the department head," Zhu demanded.

"It won't do any good, Shufen. I've already discussed it with him. He agrees with me. You are needed here."

"I want to talk to him anyway."

The patient smile evaporated. "You have that right, but I would suggest you think carefully about your situation. You are working on a highly secure project that is vital to the national security of the People's Republic of China and all hands are needed. End of discussion."

Zhu returned to his desk in a daze. In the space of a few moments, his world was shattered. The tantalizing image of the bank balance he'd dreamed about now seemed like a hazy mirage in his mind's eye.

Zhu didn't use the pen for the rest of the day. In fact, he barely worked at all. When he wasn't shooting angry glances at Yang's office, he stared blankly at his computer screen, too upset to work.

He left the office at four, an hour earlier than normal, walking past Yang's office with a stiff back, eyes forward. The smelly bus to the parking lot was only half full at that hour and he sulked in his seat. He drove straight home and took out the bottle of baijiu.

The first shot of baijiu was always harsh. Today, he barely noticed the sting of the alcohol in his throat. Zhu placed the pen on the table next to the shot glass.

This is a disaster. Everything I've worked for is at risk.

By the third drink, Zhu had come up with a plan.

Although Peter Chen had set up a means of covert communications, he'd warned Zhu that he should only use it in extreme emergencies.

Zhu poured another shot. Two million dollars was an extreme emergency to him. Besides, Chen was not going to get his precious pen back unless he came up with a new plan.

Zhu considered destroying the pen, smashing it with a hammer and throwing the pieces out of his car window. Pretending none of this ever happened.

But memories of that night in Singapore intervened. Money satisfied his desires. And two million dollars would satisfy any desire he could think of.

No, he needed to fix this. Take action. Now.

Zhu got out his computer, fortified himself with another shot, and logged onto the website of a popular outdoor clothing supplier. Chen had made him memorize these details, but at the time, Zhu had been anxious to be on his way with the $15,000 in cash, so he'd only been half listening.

Hiking boots, he recalled. He found the brand and ordered two pair in different sizes, then he ordered a rain slicker and a linen shirt, also in two sizes. After he verified that all the items showed up in the cart, he closed the browser.

Zhu polished off another shot as he stared at his email inbox.

Five minutes passed, then ten. Zhu started to fidget, but another drink calmed him down.

A new email appeared in his inbox, subject line: *Did you forget something?*

He opened the email and scrolled to the bottom, to the link that read, *Do you have questions about this order?* He clicked on the link.

His screen went blank. The cursor blinked once, twice, then a line of text appeared.

How can I help you?

Zhu typed the answer to the challenge phrase.

A journey of a thousand miles begins with one step.

The cursor blinked again. Then:

Is there an issue with your order?

Zhu's mouth was dry and another shot did nothing to moisten his tongue. He recalled Chen's instructions.

Keep the message short, he'd said. If you're under duress, use the word *shipping* in your message.

Keep it short, Zhu thought. The baijiu was hitting hard now, a pleasant, floating feeling.

Conference attendance canceled, he typed. *Need instructions.*

He eyed the screen. It was short enough. Zhu logged off, cleared the cache on his browser, and restarted the machine. He sat back in his chair, realizing for the first time that he was covered in sweat and his hands were shaking.

His nerves were shot, his thoughts a toxic mix of anger and frustration. There was nothing he could do. Chen had told him they would need at least twelve hours to respond.

He poured himself another shot. He needed a distraction, something to take his mind off all his worries.

Zhu got unsteadily to his feet and lowered the blinds on all the windows. Then he went to his hall closet and took out his hard-sided suitcase. He unzipped the lining and felt along the wheel well for the square of duct tape. It was right where he'd left it. Using his fingernail, he peeled the tape back and extracted the tiny plastic chip.

He left the suitcase open on the floor and returned to his computer, turning off the lights as he went until the only illumination in the room came from the laptop screen.

The mini-SD memory chip slid neatly into the slot on the side of the machine. Zhu waited for the computer to recognize the external storage device. The prompt appeared, asking if he wanted to open the file.

Hands trembling with anticipation, he clicked on the button.

He leaned back in his chair as the movie began to play.

10

Special Activities Center, CIA Headquarters, Langley, Virginia

Harrison Kohl buried his face in his hands as if he could hide from the bad news that was raining down around him.

Breathe. Focus. Every mission has setbacks. What separates professionals from amateurs is how they handle bad news.

Still, the little voice in his head countered, it was rare that the news got this bad this fast. Maybe you really are screwed, buddy.

His morning had begun with a briefing from Bob James, the retired Navy O-5 who now ran the CIA's submerged threat analysis shop. James was his normal, thorough self, delivering alarming facts in a dispassionate tone.

"In the last forty-eight hours," James reported, "we've seen new activity on the Chinese Barracuda submarine in the shipyards. So far, it's mostly prep work, but that's still significant. Until now, they'd basically ceased all construction work on the platform."

"Which indicates what?" Harrison asked.

"Shipyards are like trains, Harrison. They don't start and stop on a dime. It takes a lot of effort to get them moving and a lot of effort to get them to stop. If they're putting resources into this platform again, it tells me that they've made some decisions."

James paused, ran a hand over his close-cropped gray hair in a nervous gesture. Harrison eyed the man with a sinking feeling. Bob James did not strike him as a guy who got anxious very often. "Don't keep me in suspense, Bob."

James called up an image of a drydocked Chinese military ship on his briefing tablet. The vessel looked like a science experiment gone feral. Mismatched missile launchers dotted the deck of the ship, and three cranes hovered over the vessel.

Harrison studied the high-resolution color imagery. The details were sharp and clear enough that Harrison could see a man smoking a cigarette in the parking lot next to the drydock. A trained imagery analyst would have a field day with this level of detail.

James cleared his throat, prompting Harrison to look up.

"Okay, I'll bite," Harrison said. "I see this is the torpedo testbed platform, but I assume there's more that I'm missing?"

James assumed the tone of a professional briefer.

"After the test of the new torpedo propulsion system, the test platform went right back into drydock." He pointed to the screen. "Before they put that crane in place, we got this shot."

He tapped his tablet and Harrison saw an oblique shot from space. The image wasn't great, it had been enlarged and enhanced, but it was clear enough to see the alteration. Beneath the waterline, a gaping hole the size of a drainpipe protruded from the bow of the ship. Harrison let out a low whistle.

"That opening is about a meter across," James said. "That's what the squints are telling me."

Harrison smiled to himself. James was dating himself. The term *squints* went back to the days when imagery analysts used microscopes to study grainy satellite photographs. These days, the National Geospatial Intelligence Agency employed AI-driven algorithms to process and interpret images almost as fast as they could be downloaded.

The torpedo launch system on the Chinese test platform was a jerry-rigged affair. Harrison could see rusted support struts holding the massive tube to the bow of the ship. James pointed to a huge hatch, hinged on the right, that stood open.

"The ship needs to be dead in the water to launch the torpedo." A note of excitement crept into James's tone. "If they have sea state at all, that barge is not leaving port. The giant chunk of metal they've welded onto the bottom of the ship means that thing has the seaworthiness of a two-by-four."

Harrison frowned at the image. "What else does this tell you?"

"If we assume they're keeping the same hydrodynamics as our Mark 48, then this thing is about as long as a Greyhound bus."

"Which means what?"

"It means everything about the front end of the new Barracuda submarine will be redesigned. Weapons loading and handling, for starters, but almost every ship-wide system you can think of will need a complete update. Sonar, the trim system, high-pressure air, hell, even the berthing area will change. Every design the PLA has built to date has been a knockoff of one of ours. This is new territory for them, and if they get it wrong, they'll spend tens of billions on a white elephant."

Harrison set aside the tablet. "So they're under the gun to make a huge design decision and it all comes down to the new torpedo. How much time do we have?"

James scraped his knuckles across his chin. "All they've got right now is a successful propulsion test. They were able to shoot a torpedo from point A to point B. To make it an actual weapon, this torpedo needs to do a lot more."

Harrison sighed. "Pretend I'm a second grader, Bob. Spell it out for me."

"A modern torpedo, like a Mark 48, is wire-guided. You can update instructions, even steer it after you launch it. There's no way this new torpedo has a wire. The distance it travels, the speed...it's impossible."

James put his mobile phone on the desk. "This is your target." He walked to the other side of the desk and placed a pen on the surface. "This is the torpedo. Imagine you're over a hundred miles away when you shoot the torpedo." He pushed the pen across the desk. "You program the torpedo to drive to a point in the ocean where you think the target will be.

"But your target won't be there. This torpedo is superfast, but noisy as hell. The target will hear the torpedo coming and run away bravely." He slid the mobile phone to the edge of the desk. "The new torpedo needs a guidance system that gets it to the search point. Then it slows down and runs a search pattern. If it doesn't find the target, it repositions and runs another search pattern. It keeps doing that again and again until it either runs out of fuel or finds its target."

James stabbed the pen into the mobile phone and pantomimed an explosion.

"The torpedo search function already exists," James concluded. "The next weapons test needs to demonstrate the guidance system."

"Will that be enough to approve the new weapon?" Harrison asked.

James retook his seat across from Harrison. He shook his head. "My guess is no. They'll want to see a SINKEX that shows the whole package works the way it's supposed to."

"You mean shoot a live torpedo and blow up a target?"

James nodded. "Standard operating procedure. Take a hulk that's going to be scrapped, tow it out to deep water, and sink it. If that test is successful, then the PLA has demonstrated the most advanced subsurface weapon in modern history."

Harrison sat back in his chair, deflated. "You didn't answer my question from before: How much time do we have?"

"Before the guidance test?" James ran his hand over his crew cut again. "Weeks, a month at most. If they've restarted work on this boat in the shipyards, that means they're planning for success. The Chinese move fast, Harrison."

Bob James's seat in Harrison's office hadn't even cooled before the next bombshell burst over his desk.

He read the daily update from the Office of Naval Intelligence. Janet Everett's submarine had lost one of their UUVs. Worse news still, there was a possibility the *Illinois* had been detected by a PLA submarine.

Harrison chewed his lip. The drones were mapping the underwater test range off Hainan Island. Did they need that information to assess the upcoming guidance test of the new torpedo? He needed Bob James back for that answer.

As Harrison reached for his phone, there was a knock at his door.

"Come," he called out.

Peter Chen entered. One look at the case officer's face made Harrison replace the receiver on his desk phone.

"What?" he demanded.

Chen handed a single sheet of paper across the desk. Harrison scanned the page in a glance. Covert communications from their asset in the Advanced Propulsion Lab in Hainan weapons facility.

Conference attendance canceled. Need instructions.

"It just arrived this morning," Chen explained. "I don't have all the details yet, but if his attendance at the conference in Korea is canceled, then we won't get the design plans for the weapon."

Harrison stared at the nearly empty page. "This is it? No other information?"

"I told him to keep it brief. Covcomm was always a distant plan B. He was certain that he'd be at the conference. Said his boss owed him one."

"Well, he followed your instructions," Harrison said wryly. "It is brief. How will he handle the setback?"

Chen's face twisted into a scowl. "I don't think well. He's money-focused and he knows he doesn't get paid unless he delivers the goods." Chen hesitated. "I have rapport with him. I could travel to China and retrieve the pen."

Harrison was already shaking his head. "Not gonna happen, Peter. You've built up a bulletproof commercial cover and you know too much. I won't risk it."

"Harrison," Chen pressed, "he's impulsive. He agreed to the deal in no time at all, without even thinking about it. What if he decides to throw the pen in the ocean and cut his losses. We need to get that intel."

Harrison nodded. After his briefing with Bob James, he needed the intel on that pen now more than ever—and the clock was ticking.

"You're right. Let's set up an in-person handoff."

Harrison scrawled a name on the paper and handed it back to Chen.

"This is our operative in the Guangzhou consulate—that's the closest US installation to Hainan. Get on secure comms this morning and work out the details for a no-contact pickup."

Chen picked up the paper. "Got it."

"Peter," Harrison called after him. "Time is not on our side on this one."

Harrison watched the door close, then he dialed Bob James's number.

11

Hainan Island, China

Never. Again.

Zhu Shufen promised himself as he retched into the toilet. I will never drink baijiu again.

He slumped back against the wall, pressing the cool tile against his cheek, and closed his eyes. His hand searched for the handle to flush the toilet. Even the gentle rush of water sounded like the pounding of surf on the beach.

Zhu forced himself to his feet, placing both hands on the edge of the sink, and inspected his face in the mirror. His skin was gray and sweaty.

"Never again," he said to his reflection.

Twenty minutes in the shower, four aspirin, and two glasses of tea were all it took to return him to the land of the living. Unfortunately, he was now very late for work. Late enough that Yang Min might write him up this time.

But before he left for work, he needed to do one more thing.

He opened his laptop and checked his email. There was a follow-up email from the clothing company.

Subject line: *Did you forget something? More savings await!*

His fingers fumbled through the process of entering the covert communications portal, but finally he got there. The message from Peter Chen was succinct:

Laogedou Sichuan Dish at 7. Contact will carry a copy of Financial Times. Sit beside them and leave the item when you go. You will be paid in full.

He read the lines twice, then a third time. They were sending someone to pick up the pen! And he was getting paid!

The instructions were simple. He knew the restaurant; he'd eaten there many times. Go in, order the spicy crab appetizer, leave the pen, and walk out.

But first, he had to get through the workday. Maybe he'd even add a few pictures to the trove he'd already stored on the pen, just as an added bonus to make sure Peter Chen was delighted with his work.

His headache receded as he drove the fifteen minutes to the employee parking lot and waited for the old diesel bus to arrive. The bus was mostly empty, but the sour smell was still there. He took a seat next to an open window to avoid getting sick again.

He passed the time by imagining the scene in the restaurant. His contact would be a businessman, he decided, dressed in a blue blazer, white shirt, and tie. He'd be sitting at the bar, with an open seat next to him.

The man folded the pink pages of the *Financial Times* into quarters and propped the paper up against a water glass so that Zhu would see it when he came in. The man would be eating the spicy crab—Laogedou was famous for the spicy crab—and he would shrug when Zhu asked if the seat next to him was taken.

Zhu would eat quickly—no, he'd order takeout—and leave the pen on the bar.

The bus groaned to a stop outside the engineering building and Zhu struggled to his feet. He was the only one who got off the bus and he climbed the stairs into the building alone. The foyer was empty. There was no line at security.

Zhu dropped his messenger bag on the conveyor belt that ran into the X-ray machine. He dropped his wallet, mobile phone, wristwatch, and the pen into a separate small container and placed it on the conveyor belt. He flashed his security badge at the guard, who offered a bored nod in return.

On the other side of the magnetometer, Zhu stowed his wallet and phone in his pockets, then buckled the watch onto his wrist. A smug smile tugged at his lips as he slipped the pen into his shirt pocket.

His sense of self-satisfaction was short-lived when he saw the time on his watch. He was almost ninety minutes late now.

Zhu hurried down the hallway. He turned into the Advanced Propulsion section, squaring his shoulders as he marched past Yang Min's office.

Except Yang wasn't there, which was odd. Yang was always at his desk. He was there when Zhu arrived in the morning and there when he left at night. Always.

But not this morning. What a stroke of luck! Zhu thought. He quickened his pace and turned into the third aisle of cubicles.

Yang stood outside Zhu's workstation. His back was to Zhu and he had a mobile phone pressed to his ear, his free hand cupped next to his mouth to shield what he was saying. He stopped and said something to someone inside the cubicle.

"What's going on?" Zhu asked in a loud voice.

Yang turned. He ended the call and put out his hand, palm out.

"Stay where you are, Shufen," he ordered. "Don't come any closer."

Zhu ignored him. He increased his pace, closing the distance between them.

A head popped up over the divider of the cubicle. He shot a glance at Zhu, then at Yang as if to say, *Is this him?* Then he stepped into the aisle.

"Who are you?" Zhu demanded. "What are you doing at my desk?"

The man said nothing. His hard, dark eyes scanned Zhu's face with enough intensity that Zhu dropped his gaze.

That's when he saw the badge. The man was dressed in a dark blue business suit, but he had a gold badge clipped to his belt. When the man turned to Yang, his suit jacket fell open, revealing a handgun in a shoulder holster under his left armpit.

Police, Zhu realized, and a cold finger of fear probed his roiling stomach.

"Is this him?" the policeman asked.

Yang nodded. Zhu looked from the cop to his boss. Yang's normally pasty complexion had a gray tinge, and a line of sweat beaded his upper lip.

"Shufen, we had an IT security audit last night—"

The cop held up a hand to stop Yang. Zhu's stomach convulsed and he let out an involuntary burp.

The policeman reached over and removed the messenger bag from Zhu's shoulder with a touch that was surprisingly gentle. He opened the bag, searched it briefly, and held it out to Zhu. "Wallet, mobile phone, wristwatch, please."

Zhu's hands felt clammy as he complied. The policeman started to close the bag, then almost as an afterthought, plucked the pen from Zhu's pocket and dropped it into the bag.

"Follow me," he ordered, and brushed past Zhu.

Zhu could feel the eyes of his coworkers raking over his skin, wondering what Zhu had done to warrant a visit from the police. Behind him, he could hear the labored breathing of Yang Min.

The cop entered Yang's office like he owned it. He took a seat behind the desk, then scanned the windows that looked out over the sea of cubicles. "Don't you have blinds?" he asked Yang.

Yang shook his head. "I believe in an open-door policy. Transparency."

The policeman barked out a short laugh, then got up. He gestured for Zhu to sit behind the desk, facing the windows.

Zhu complied. He could see eyes peeking over the edges of cubicles, wide with curiosity. Whispered comments, maybe even a few laughs from the jealous ones. His face grew hot with shame.

"What is the meaning of this?" he demanded. He tried to put some bravado in his voice, but the policeman was unmoved.

"I'll give you one chance to come clean, Mr. Zhu." His tone was matter-of-fact. "Just one."

"Come clean about what?" Zhu responded immediately. "I haven't done anything wrong. I'm one of Mr. Yang's best employees. Just last month, he sent me to Singapore to represent the division at an engineering conference."

The policeman nodded thoughtfully. "Singapore...beautiful city. Did you enjoy your stay there, Mr. Zhu?"

"Yes," Zhu snapped back.

"Is there anything you'd like to tell me about that trip? Anything unusual?"

Of their own accord, Zhu's eyes found the messenger bag that held the pen. He should have left the pen at home. His stomach convulsed. He felt acid crawl up his throat and he clamped his mouth shut.

"No," he said through clenched teeth.

The policeman shrugged. He placed an open laptop in front of Zhu.

"Your IT department ran a routine security scan last night. The AI that's used to power these scanners is remarkable. You can ask it to search for anything." He manipulated the cursor over a square icon of a file. "Anything," he repeated.

Zhu crossed his arms.

"You took a work computer with you to Singapore, right, Mr. Zhu?"

Zhu didn't trust his voice, so he nodded.

"Did you know that if you view a video on a computer, a copy of that video is saved in a temporary file?"

Of course, Zhu knew that. Any idiot with half a brain knew that. He nodded with more confidence now.

"Did you know that the most recent software update keeps a permanent copy of any files viewed, even if the temp file is purged?"

Zhu felt the room go still. The wall clock behind him hammered out the seconds. Yang's breathing hitched.

"It's a recent update to government computers, Mr. Zhu. Not many people know about it."

Zhu tried to swallow, but his throat was stuck. He felt a rising panic in his chest.

The policeman touched the screen. The icon opened to a video.

Zhu recognized the room on the screen. The sounds were familiar, too. A child's laughter...The video slewed to a bed...

Zhu put his head between his knees and vomited.

Zhu pressed the side of his face against the cool concrete wall. He wanted to weep and scream, but his tear ducts had no moisture left to give. Anyway, the last thing he wanted to do in this place was draw attention to himself.

He wormed his shoulder deeper into the corner of the cell block as if he could burrow into the concrete and make himself invisible.

He'd lost all sense of time. It had been late morning when they brought him to the jail in handcuffs. The interview had taken most of the afternoon, he supposed. Then processing and finally to this holding cell that smelled of cold piss and hot fear. Or maybe that was just him.

It was probably evening, he guessed. The guards had brought food in a while ago, but Zhu had not left the safety of his corner. He peeked across the room.

The man with the scar was still watching him.

Zhu pressed his face back into the wall. Every bad prison movie he'd ever seen flashed behind his closed eyes. He'd never been so scared in his entire life.

Zhu had told the detective everything. The burner phone, the pre-planned call, the address. He even gave them Jiecheng's name.

Well, not everything, he thought. They didn't know he'd been pulled aside at Immigration in Singapore, didn't know about Peter Chen or the pen. And he was going to keep it that way.

He would go to prison for what was on that video, but if they found out about the pen...

"Zhu Shufen!" a deep voice roared.

I'm dreaming, Zhu thought.

"Zhu Shufen, come forward. If I have to come in after you, you'll regret it." There was a sound of banging on metal bars as if for emphasis.

Zhu struggled to his feet. His legs were asleep from squatting in the corner for hours and his hands shook with fear. He staggered to the door, where a fat guard waited. He pointed to an open space between the bars.

"Hands," he said.

Zhu stared at his hands dumbly.

The guard rolled his eyes. "Put your hands through the hole."

Zhu did as he was ordered. The guard cinched handcuffs around his wrists.

"Step back," he ordered, pulling out a baton from a ring on his belt.

The door swung open. The guard motioned with the club, and Zhu stepped into the hallway. The door slammed closed behind him.

The baton pointed down the hall, so Zhu shuffled forward. The door at the end of the hall opened to another hallway. The club directed him to make a right turn.

Zhu recognized the line of doors. He'd been here for the interrogation in the afternoon. It seemed so long ago.

"Stop at number 4," the guard ordered.

Number 4, the same as in Singapore, Zhu recalled. His bad luck continued.

The door opened and the guard pushed him inside. The door closed behind him. The magnetic lock slammed home. Just like Singapore.

He was alone in the room. Zhu shuffled to an open chair and collapsed. He laid his head on the table and closed his eyes.

He had no idea how long he'd slept. The metallic snap of the lock jerked him awake and he sat upright.

Two men entered. One was the detective from earlier, the second a tall man dressed in a charcoal-gray suit. He had pale skin and fine features and his hair was carefully parted on the right side. He did not have a gun or a badge that Zhu could see. A faint scent of expensive cologne followed the man into the room.

Neither introduced himself. Behind them, Zhu saw the red light on the wall camera in the corner wink out.

The policeman looked at the tall man, who nodded. The cop cleared his throat.

"Mr. Zhu, because of your security clearance we were required to report your crime to the Ministry of State Security. We have turned over all the evidence in this case to the MSS for processing."

Zhu looked from one face to the other, said nothing.

The tall man reached into his suit jacket and drew out a pen. The pen that Zhu had brought back from Singapore. He placed the device carefully on the table between them.

The tall man's voice was soft, feathery. "Tell me where you got this pen."

Zhu felt his bowels turn to water.

12

Sanya, Hainan Island, China

Shannon Petersen cast an eye skyward as she hurried down the city street. She wasn't alone in her actions. All around her, pedestrians eyed the dark thunderclouds that huddled over the tropical city as they scurried to safety. The air seemed charged with electricity.

She reached the entrance of the restaurant out of breath. Thunder growled ominously as she pulled open the glass door.

The interior of the Laogedou Sichuan Dish bustled with the energy of a restaurant readying for a busy dinner hour. The two dozen tables in the space were about half full and already the noise level was high. At the four-top next to the hostess, four businessmen—two Germans, two Chinese, ties off for the evening—polished off a liter bottle of beer and toasted loudly to some business success.

Shannon nodded in satisfaction. This place would work for the handoff.

The hostess arrived back at her station and Shannon pantomimed that she wanted to sit at the bar. The hostess waved her through.

The long bar was mostly empty, so Shannon selected a seat near the wall. She dropped her handbag on the adjacent chair, then pulled out a copy of the *Financial Times* and placed it on the bar top, angled toward her as if she were about to read it. The salmon-colored pages seemed brightly conspicuous against the black stone, but she knew she was overthinking it. Besides, the distinctive color was the point.

She pulled off her blazer and hung it carefully on the back of her chair. As a petite woman, barely five feet tall, Shannon loved the fit and selection of the clothes available to her in China. Back in the US, she was often relegated to shopping in the pre-teen section to find clothes that fit her well, but in China, her body type was the norm. Shopping here was a joy that she often indulged in.

She ordered tea from the bartender. Casually, she scanned the room in the mirror behind the bar. She did not see her target. Tapping the face of her mobile phone, she saw the time was 1842.

The bartender was back with her tea.

"Thank you," she said.

"Menu?" he replied in accented English, proffering a laminated page.

Shannon studied it for a moment. "What is your best dish?" she asked in English.

He pointed to a picture. "Spicy crab. Very famous." His voice reflected the pride he took in his work.

"I'll have that."

The bartender nodded and left.

Shannon sipped her tea, annoyed by the situation. She spoke Mandarin fluently, skillfully enough that most Chinese were surprised at her proficiency. And that was the problem. If the bartender was questioned later, the last thing she wanted was for him to remember the short, white woman with curly hair who spoke fluent Mandarin.

Better he should think of her as just another ignorant foreigner. As much as it galled her, that's what was called for.

The minutes dragged by. The spicy crab appetizer arrived in record time and she dug in, surprised at how hungry she was. Her day had started before dawn with a trip to the Guangzhou Airport and a seven a.m. flight to Hainan Island. She'd conducted three site visits during the day, all to Chinese factories looking to entice American businesses into manufacturing contracts. As an economic development liaison, Shannon's day job consisted of visits to Chinese factories all over the People's Republic. It also provided excellent cover for her occasional assignments with the CIA as a field operative.

Those assignments were usually benign courier activities. An active pickup operation like the one planned for tonight was rare and it made her nervous. Still, she knew the Special Activities Center would not have asked for her services unless it was absolutely necessary.

Shannon did not know the name of the man who was supposed to sit next to her at the bar and she had no idea what was on the pen that she was supposed to pick up after he left. Her job was to sit at the bar, have a drink, eat some dinner, and read the *Financial Times*. If he didn't show up by 1910, her orders were to leave.

By 1900, the glass windows that fronted the street were black, the Laogedou Sichuan Dish was nearly full, and there was no sign of her target. The noise level was deafening and the activity level bustling—perfect conditions for a handoff.

But her target was nowhere to be found.

By five minutes after seven, the seats at the bar filled up and Shannon was forced to move her handbag off the adjacent chair. She flipped the newspaper open and made a show of folding the pink pages so they would look like a flag to anyone sitting in the restaurant. She scanned the mirror for any sign of her target.

Nothing.

At ten minutes after seven, she called for the check and paid in cash. She donned her blazer, swung her handbag over her shoulder, and made her way to the door.

The air on the street was still and close, heavy with moisture. The few pedestrians that she saw had umbrellas in their hands, ready to unfurl at a moment's notice. As she turned to the left and started walking, the first fat drops of rain splashed onto the hot pavement.

Shannon removed a compact umbrella from her purse and snapped it open. Rain popped against the nylon shield. She quickened her pace, turned left at the first corner, then right at the next. The thunderclouds above the city let loose. Rain fell straight down, filling the air with the sound of rushing water.

The streets behind her were empty and any CCTV cameras in use would show shapeless black blobs, the faces hidden beneath umbrellas. By the time she reached the end of the block, her shoes were sodden and the gutters on the street flowed with water. Casually, Shannon removed the *Financial Times* from her purse and dropped it into a garbage can.

It was after 1930 when she reached her rental car. Despite the umbrella, she was soaked to the skin. She got behind the wheel, threw her wet blazer onto the passenger seat, and opened the messaging app on her mobile.

Great meetings today, she typed. *Lots of opportunity here. My morning meeting was canceled.*

The text bounced from the consulate in Guangzhou to CIA headquarters in Langley, where she knew the team at SAC was waiting. The only word in the message that meant anything was the word *canceled*. The code word meant that their contact did not show.

Shannon shivered. Her silk dress shirt felt slimy and cold against her skin. She started the car and turned on the heat. Rain hammered the windshield, sounding like the rattle of a snare drum.

Five minutes later, she had her response.

Great update. Call me soonest. News about your Aunt Martha.

Shannon sighed. The code word was *news* and it meant return to the consulate via an alternate route. She turned the windshield wipers on high and put the car in gear.

It was nearly five hundred kilometers back to Guangzhou. It was going to be a long night. Shannon checked her watch. If she hurried, she could make the nine p.m. ferry across the Qiongzhou Strait.

She steered onto the street and headed for the highway.

13

USS *Illinois*, 95 miles southeast of Hainan Island, South China Sea

Janet pulled up her collar and settled deeper into the oversized fleece. She thrust her icy hands deep into the pockets and hugged the soft jacket close to her body. She had on three layers, including the fleece, which was the warmest piece of clothing she owned, and she was still freezing.

She knew the chill was just a side effect of sleep deprivation. What she really needed was a hot shower and a good night's sleep.

That, however, was not going to happen anytime soon. For the last three days, the *Illinois* had been at modified general quarters and rigged for ultra quiet. With the exception of watchstanders, all crew members were confined to their racks. All other activities ceased unless deemed urgent by the XO. The galley served only cold food and hot drinks.

She could see the pent-up energy and the resentment in the faces of her crew. What had at first seemed like a chance to catch up on some much-needed sleep and goof off a few days ago now felt like punishment.

While her crew was mostly confined to their bunks, Janet and Tom Savarino both lost sleep. She and the XO divided the time into three-hour shifts, ensuring one of them was always in the control room. This close to the Chinese underwater test range, with a PLA Navy diesel-electric submarine in the area, they were at high risk of being detected. The difference between evasion and detection might be a split-second decision. Her stateroom was only a few steps away, but even that felt too far.

Janet had spent three years in command of the USS *Illinois* and she'd be damned if she'd allow a mistake in the last days of her time on board. Her mission was to record the next Chinese weapons test undetected, and she was not planning on leaving anything to chance.

The first twenty-four hours were the worst. Before the weapons test ship even left port, the PLA Navy established a blockade using two surface ships trailing towed arrays, running parallel racetracks along the perimeter of the underwater test range. A squadron of air patrol craft began dropping sonobuoys by the dozens so that the sea rang with their pinging. Another half dozen PLA Navy vessels were assigned to harass any US and allied warships in the vicinity, keeping them away from the test area, while also herding civilian shipping away from the range.

The PLA was taking every precaution to make sure that the guidance test of the new torpedo was clear of enemy listening devices.

In the first day, after the *Illinois* breached the blockade, her submarine had nearly been detected twice. Janet managed to evade her pursuers both times through the skillful use of the marine environment, which played games with underwater sound transmission. Ironically, between the Chinese surface ships and the marine patrols, there was so much interference in the water that the PLA had a difficult time distinguishing what was a real contact and what was an artifact of their own search efforts.

Janet allowed herself a satisfied smile. The *Illinois* was inside the PLA Navy's house now and the only thing that could detect her was their old friend Sierra 26, the *Changcheng* 346. She just hoped the Chinese wouldn't send out another of their boats to patrol the test area. Two Chinese submarines working collaboratively would be much harder to evade.

Her eyes found the sonar broadband display, where two bright parallel lines ran down the screen. The PLA submarine was at periscope depth, running her diesel engines.

"I'm ready to relieve you, ma'am." Savarino's deep voice startled Janet out of her reverie. She sprang to her feet to cover her surprise.

"Hey, Tom, has it been three hours already?" she said in a light tone.

"Feels like it's only been a week." She pointed at the bright lines on the waterfall display. "Two-six is still at PD. No other submerged contacts out there."

Savarino pinched his lip. "Do you think this is it?"

They'd been tracking the PLA submarine's movements and integrating their observations with the regular intelligence reports that the *Illinois* received every time they went to periscope depth to clear their own message traffic.

Judging by the satellite imagery and the captured enemy message traffic, the PLA had started a countdown twice in the past two days and then aborted. A weapons failure? An issue with the test range? No one knew for sure. The message traffic was encrypted, so the intel analysts were only guessing.

Janet shrugged. "All we can do is wait for the party to start."

"Get some sleep, ma'am," Savarino said quietly. "You look wrecked. I'll call you if anything comes up."

Janet nodded. Savarino was not given to exaggeration. If he was telling her she looked tired, then she probably actually looked like death warmed over.

She cleared her throat. "Officer of the Deck, I'll be in my stateroom. Address any questions to the XO."

Lieutenant Taylor gave her a worn smile. "Aye-aye, ma'am." He turned back to watching the sonar display. It seemed like all they'd done for the past week was stare at squiggly lines on a screen, waiting for the Chinese to do something.

It took all of three steps to go from the control room entrance to her stateroom. She entered, closed the door behind her, and sat on the edge of her bunk. Her body felt empty, jittery, as if the endless supply of adrenaline she'd been calling on to keep going had finally run dry. She was cold, hungry, and tired, but lacked the energy to act on any of those needs.

Sleep first, she decided. Janet reached for the speaker above her desk that let her listen to the activity in the control room. She clicked it on and turned the knob so that the voices were just barely audible. Then she zipped the fleece all the way up to her chin and lay back on the mattress. The reading light above her bed still burned, so she turned it off, plunging the room into darkness. The only illumination came from a thin line of light that showed beneath the door.

Over the speaker, the XO and Taylor were engaged in a muttered conversation. The voices settled into her ears, merging with her drifting mind.

Then Senior Chief O'Malley's voice rose above the murmur. "OOD, Sierra two-six has secured snorkeling."

Her mind registered the information, but her eyes stayed shut. Janet imagined she was in the control room of the *Changcheng*, watching her counterpart issue orders. She could tell by the way the submarine maneuvered that the commanding officer was more than competent. By rights, he should have had the *Illinois* when they'd lost the Narwhal and made such a racket in the water. Her successful escape owed as much to luck as to skill, but a clean getaway still counted as a win, however it happened. If the Chinese captain had gone active at full power even a minute earlier, he would have seen the *Illinois*.

I'm lucky, Janet murmured. She felt her lips move into a smile in the dark, then relax as she slept.

In her dream, O'Malley's voice said, "Officer of the Deck, I have a new sonar contact bearing due north, designated Sierra eight-six."

Then the sound-powered telephone next to her bed buzzed.

Janet dreamed she reached across and pulled the heavy black handset out of the cradle, held it to her ear.

"Captain."

"I think this is it, ma'am," Savarino said.

Janet levered herself off the bed. The room seemed to tilt. She caught the back of her armchair to steady herself, then pushed her body toward the door. Still not sure if she was dreaming or not, she stumbled the three steps to the control room.

A wave of chilled air hit her in the face. She wasn't dreaming after all. Janet strode to the sonar stack, joined Savarino behind O'Malley's broad back.

"Talk to me, Senior," she said, her voice still froggy with sleep.

The sonar chief's shoulders were rigid. He pointed to a bright spot on the waterfall display. "Convergence bounce, ma'am, about six minutes old." His face twisted. "Could be a launch. Not sure yet."

Fair enough, Janet thought. The launch platform was over 150 miles away. At that distance, depending on the sound conditions, you could set off a decent-sized bomb and they'd never hear it. All they could do was wait.

Minutes crawled by with no update on the sonar display. Janet tried to do the math in her head. The launch platform was about 150 miles away, on the northeast side of Hainan Island. If the weapon moved at the same speed as last time, it might take half an hour to get within sonar range of the *Illinois*.

One of the sonar operators tensed. O'Malley saw it as soon as Janet did. "Gimme a bearing, Luke," O'Malley said.

"Three-four-two, Senior," the young man replied.

O'Malley worked his own console, eyes closed, headphones clamped over his ears. A slow smile spread across his stubbled chin. "Captain, that's it. That's the Orca."

Ever since the intel reports identified the new Chinese torpedo as the Hu Jing, or killer whale, the crew had taken up the cause. Baloney sandwiches, long a staple in submarine cold rations, became "Orca meat" sandwiches. Crude signs showing an orca inside a circle with a slash were drawn in grease pencil on bulkheads around the ship.

Janet's pulse quickened, all vestiges of sleep gone. Now the Orca was back.

"Range to Sierra eight-six, Sonar?"

"Approximately four-two thousand yards, ma'am."

"Understood." Janet wheeled around, raised her voice. "Attention in control, we have sonar contact, designated Sierra eight-six, identified as the Chinese Hu Jing torpedo. You know the drill. We track and record every single movement this thing makes."

Janet heard O'Malley say something and she turned around. "What?"

The Senior Chief was shaking his head. "I'm clocking this thing at a hundred seventy-three knots, ma'am. That's as fast as a bullet train."

Janet did the conversion: Over two hundred miles an hour underwater was like something out of a science fiction novel. But they were seeing it in real time.

"Get the data, Sonar. We'll do the analysis later."

O'Malley nodded.

Ten minutes passed in electric silence as the watch team focused on the task. Janet sensed the quiet intensity with which the people around her worked.

"The rocket engine cut out," O'Malley announced. "Contact is slowing..."

Janet's gaze snapped to the sonar display, where the thick white line thinned to a wisp.

"Propeller noises," O'Malley reported, eyes closed, hands clamped over his headphones. "The weapon has transitioned to normal running."

"Any aspect change?" Janet demanded.

"No, ma'am."

Janet's entire body tensed. This was the moment of truth. If all they could do was drive the weapon to a point in the ocean, it was nothing more than a dumb bomb. If they intended to use it as a torpedo, it needed to run a search pattern.

"Weapon is turning," O'Malley called out. A pause, then the words Janet had been dreading rang out. "Active pinging. The weapon is searching."

"Captain," the XO called from the fire control stack.

Janet left the sonar operators and crossed to the fire control team. Three operators hunched over their workstations. Their job was to develop a track of the weapon. Savarino pointed to the display.

It was a snaking S-pattern, a textbook-perfect torpedo search routine.

Janet and the XO exchanged glances. It looked exactly like the search pattern of an American-made Mark 48 torpedo.

"Contact has ceased active search," Sonar announced. "Contact is turning."

Janet studied the changes on the lagging display. She didn't need O'Malley to explain what she was seeing: The torpedo was turning around.

"Steady on reciprocal course," Sonar reported. "They just did a one-eighty."

Janet tensed again. She picked up a spare set of headphones and slipped them on. The channel was already locked on the bearing of the Chinese torpedo.

She heard the buzzing whine of a normal torpedo, like a giant mosquito or a weed whacker. The noise abruptly ceased.

Janet held her breath. *One Mississippi, two Mississippi...*

The crackle of the ocean filled her ears, then a new sound drowned everything out as the rocket engine kicked back on. On the broadband display, the signal became a fat white line.

Janet went numb. She pulled off the headphones.

"Shit," the XO muttered under his breath. "They did it. They fucking did it."

Janet said nothing because there was nothing to say. The PLA Navy had a functional weapon.

14

CIA Headquarters, Langley, Virginia

The elevator doors opened on the seventh floor of the George Bush Center for Intelligence. Harrison stepped onto the expanse of plush blue carpet.

The floor was silent, the hallway in either direction empty, as he approached Don's office. It was just past six in the morning, early enough that Don's executive assistant wasn't even in yet. But the door to his office stood ajar and Harrison heard the murmur of voices inside. He knocked on the door.

"C'mon in, Harrison," Don called.

He pushed the door open to find Don Riley seated with Director Carroll Brooks in the sitting area of his office. The room was shadowy. Rivulets of rain streamed down the window behind them, distorting the view of gunpowder-gray clouds.

Don's hair was mussed and his chin shaded with gray stubble, making Harrison wonder if his boss had spent the night at the office. Carroll, on the other hand, was dressed to impress—a navy-blue pencil skirt and matching blazer, carefully coiffed hair, and flawless makeup.

The Director seemed to notice Harrison's assessment.

"I'm headed to the White House after this," she said curtly.

The Director didn't need to explain why she was headed to see the President. Twelve hours ago, news of the successful guidance test of the Chinese long-range torpedo had landed like a bomb in CIA headquarters. Information of that magnitude would be included in the President's Daily Brief, which would lead to pointed questions from the White House. Don's summons to his office before normal business hours was to help the Director get ahead of the problem.

Don lurched to his feet, empty cup in hand. "Coffee, anyone?"

Harrison shook his head. "I'm trying to cut back on caffeine, but I'll take a water if you have it."

Don shrugged, pointed to the refrigerator. When Harrison returned to the sitting area, he sat opposite Director Brooks. She studied him with a calculating eye. "What's the status of our source in the Advanced Weapon Division on Hainan?"

Harrison cut a look at Don, who shrugged.

"Tell her."

"Our asset was arrested," Harrison said.

The Director's sculpted eyebrows went up.

Harrison swallowed hard. "The official charges are for child pornography."

A look of disbelief crossed Carroll's face. "Kiddie porn? Are you serious? How did we not know that?"

Don scowled. "C'mon, Carroll, let's be real. We recruit flawed people to betray their country. This was a cold pitch on a new target and I was clear about the risks. We had no way of knowing about his predilections. Hell, it would've made our job easier if we had known."

The Director looked back at Harrison. "Please tell me we at least got the intel."

"No, ma'am," Harrison said. "We also have to assume he's burned us."

For a moment, Harrison thought Carroll Brooks might explode. Her jaw tightened and spots of color rose in her cheeks. Then she carefully lifted her coffee cup and took a measured sip, leaving a smudge of red lipstick on the white rim.

"I'm going to assume, Don, that the reason why you asked me here this morning is to present our Plan B."

Don leaned forward, elbows on knees, and looked at Harrison expectantly.

"That's your cue, my friend."

Harrison handed them both thin dossiers. The Director placed her unopened folder on the coffee table between them.

"Just talk to me."

He nodded, his throat suddenly dry. "We're targeting a mid-level software engineer. He's a programmer in the Advanced Weapons Development lab. A guidance systems specialist."

Don opened his dossier. "What's our angle?"

"Target is divorced and estranged from his wife. One child, a daughter, attending the University of British Columbia in Vancouver, Canada. The daughter's having issues in school. Normal stuff: bad breakup, absenteeism in class, that sort of thing. We've intercepted emails between father and daughter. Dad is worried."

"I don't see the play here," the Director said. "How do you exploit the father-daughter dynamic? Are you going to get him to travel outside of China?"

Harrison shook his head. "No, ma'am, we're proposing to meet him on his own turf."

Carroll held up a hand, turned to Don. "You want to operate inside the PRC? That's what you want me to take to the President?"

Don snapped his folder shut. "If you have a better idea, I'm open to it, Director. We tried the cold pitch, thought we had everything in hand, and that failed in spectacular fashion. We're back to square one and the clock is ticking."

The Director pinched the bridge of her nose. "Don, you do realize what you're asking."

It was a statement, not a question, and Harrison understood the Director's concern. The days of disguises and fake identities were in the past. Biometrics had changed everything in the spy business. You were who your biometrics said you were—and there was no way to hide it. Facial recognition, retina scans, palm prints, DNA profiling—these were unalterable features. The only way to be a field operator in the modern world was to be yourself, living a carefully constructed, legitimate life that would stand up to the closest scrutiny from foreign adversaries. Operators who possessed legends of this quality were rare and used accordingly.

"I do understand, Carroll, and I'm telling you that we don't have a choice."

The Director studied Harrison. "Tell me how this plays out."

"Our case officer goes in as a recruiter—happens all the time, even in China. She contacts the target, builds trust under the guise of offering him a job."

"And then?"

"The problems with the daughter ramp up. We already know that all travel for the weapons development group has been canceled until further notice, so he can't visit her. All Dad knows is what he's being told via email. It's not a pretty picture."

Don added, "If we've developed enough trust, Dad will need a solution. Our case officer will be there to provide one."

"I take it you already have someone in mind?" Brooks asked.

"We do," Harrison said.

"Who?"

Don told the Director.

Carroll Brooks stood, walked to the window. The rain-streaked glass distorted her reflection.

"We've spent years on her, Don. Think about what you'd be putting at risk."

"She's the best, Director. We need our best player on the field right now." Don's voice was gentle.

The Director turned from the window and walked to the door.

"Do it," she said, "but know this: If she gets burned, we're all finished."

15

Sanya, Hainan Island, People's Republic of China

Angelina-Marie Markov woke from her nap just as the setting sun touched the western horizon. An ocean breeze, heavy with moisture and the smell of salt, wafted against the gossamer curtains that framed the open balcony doors.

She stretched luxuriously and then rolled out of bed. The nap had been just what she needed. For the ten-hour flight from Sydney, she'd been in business class, but it had arrived in Shanghai at five in the morning. After a two-hour wait and a connecting flight to Sanya Phoenix Airport on Hainan Island, she'd needed to recharge her batteries.

Slipping on one of the plush white bathrobes that came with the executive suite, she stepped onto the balcony. Angelina-Marie rubbed her chin on the soft cotton. She could get used to this life—and the room was less than $300 a night, barely a quarter of what she'd expect to pay in Sydney. And this hotel looked practically brand-new.

The JW Marriott was located on a peninsula and her corner suite on the fifteenth floor gave her a commanding view of the world around her. To the east was Dadonghai Beach, where people the size of ants gathered their children and belongings after a day of sun and sand. To the west, the neon lights of a vibrant city sprang to life in the shadows cast by the setting sun. Beyond the buildings, the South China Sea stretched to the darkening horizon.

Her stomach rumbled. She hadn't eaten anything since a pair of steam buns in the Shanghai Airport this morning.

Angelina-Marie dialed room service, ordering a lobster risotto, a green salad, and a bottle of Chenin Blanc. While waiting for the food to arrive, she checked her email.

Her laptop was a new MacBook Air, stripped down to the basic functions needed to do her job: email, Word, PowerPoint. All the programs had associated directories filled with files that matched her job as Vice President of Talent Management for Odysseus Partners.

A knock at the door told her the food had arrived. A young man in a waistcoat and black pants parked a cart next to the open balcony door. With a flourish, he unfurled a white linen tablecloth, then presented the meal in spectacular fashion.

The lobster risotto was in a black half-moon-shaped dish that fit with a corresponding white dish containing her salad. The Chenin Blanc arrived in a bucket of ice, chilled to perfection. Lastly, the waiter lit a single candle and placed a white rose in a small vase. She tipped him like a foreigner and dug into her meal.

Darkness fell, the city lights offering a soft glow over the edge of her balcony. On the ocean, lights of distant ships crawled through the inky blackness.

Angelina-Marie checked her watch and sighed to herself. Time to go to work.

She showered quickly, then sat at the mirror, laying out her makeup. She was going for a very specific look tonight. Attractive, but not unattainable. Professional, but approachable.

From her Chinese mother, she'd received high cheekbones and fine features. From her Australian father, her height, athleticism, and brown eyes. Her skin was a beautiful compromise, a tawny color that glowed in the sun.

For tonight, she went light on foundation, used a touch of color to highlight her cheekbones, and just a hint of mascara to emphasize her eyes. She opted to wear her dark hair gathered at her nape in a loose chignon. A muted lipstick completed the ensemble.

Clothing was the next set of choices. Casual, she decided. A loose, cream-colored linen blouse that settled just below her hips complemented tight black leather pants and ankle-high calfskin boots.

Surveying the final result in the full-length mirror inside the closet, Angelina-Marie saw what she always saw when she studied her appearance. An outsider. Too Caucasian to be mistaken for ethnic Chinese and too Chinese to fit into the Western world completely.

She gave her reflection a dazzling smile. There were advantages to her mixed heritage. The otherness that she saw in her identity made her exotic in both cultures—a fact that she was counting on tonight.

Taking only a clutch purse, Angelina-Marie set out for the evening.

The Popcorn Self-Help KTV karaoke bar was a cozy establishment, not something that a tourist would find unless they had a local connection. When she arrived at nine thirty, the place was three-quarters full and there was a pleasant buzz in the air. These were regulars, and everyone seemed to know each other.

A couple occupied the small stage in the corner of the room, doing some serious damage to the English version of "Love Lifts Us Up Where We Belong." Angelina-Marie wondered if either had ever seen the movie *An Officer and a Gentleman*. It had come out a quarter century before either of these two had even been born.

Still, she observed, the meaning of the song seemed to cross the cultural and age gaps just fine. By the time she got to the bar, the couple had reached the climax of the song and looked like they needed a room.

She waited until the female bartender was free, then leaned across the bar. "I'm drinking rum and Coke all night, but make them with just Coke, no rum." She passed over a wad of bills.

The young woman expertly palmed the bills and announced. "One rum and Coke coming up."

Angelina-Marie, drink in hand, surveyed the room. The clientele was mostly young and male, with a high geek-o-meter score. She overheard snippets of work talk about programming languages and software architectures and knew she was in the right place. Now all she had to do was wait.

As the alcohol flowed, the room got louder. Crowds of young men, arms across each other's shoulders, laughed too long, too loud. A few tables of women and some couples balanced the audience.

A string of performers hit the stage, some of them not bad. It surprised her that many of them sang American songs from the eighties and nineties. That suited her fine. She'd brushed up on her karaoke skills before she left Sydney, and she had an arsenal of songs in multiple languages.

The evening crawled by. She worked her way through two more no-rum and Cokes and gently batted down a few clumsy advances.

At half past ten, her target showed up.

Chang Han was a little older than most of the crowd. She knew from his dossier that he was almost forty, but he looked younger. He was in decent shape and wore his hair long. He waved to a few friends as he made his way to the bar, but after he got a drink—Four Roses bourbon on the rocks—he sat by himself and pulled out his phone.

She watched him for the next half hour. He seemed to be there for the company. In between songs, he was on his phone, but when someone was performing, he watched them and clapped politely.

Angelina-Marie wondered if he was texting his daughter in Canada.

The young woman running the karaoke lineup caught her attention, indicating Angelina-Marie was next at the microphone. The young man onstage began an off-key Chinese love ballad. He was very drunk and his compatriots booed him, laughing. When he finished, he made a great show of bowing and passing the microphone to Angelina-Marie as if it were a sacred object.

She accepted, playing along as she stepped onto the tiny stage. A row of white lights glared down from the ceiling, making the audience indistinct.

"Good evening, everyone, I'm visiting from Australia," she said in Mandarin. "I'd like to sing a song that I think a few people in this room know something about."

The rapid-pulse bass line from Queen's "Under Pressure" pumped out of the speakers and Angelina-Marie was off. She loved to sing, and she cut loose, channeling her inner Freddie Mercury.

Her gaze penetrated the glare and she saw that Chang was watching her. She held his eyes for a split second, then broke away.

When she finished, the room erupted in applause. She clasped her hands to her chest, bowed, and stepped off the stage. She made her way through the audience, turning her hips to slide between tables, nodding thanks to well-wishers. She momentarily lost her balance when she passed Chang, placing her hand on the table and spilling his drink.

"Oh no," Angelina-Marie cried. "I am so sorry."

"It's no problem," Chang said, catching her arm so she could right herself. He had a pleasant voice, confident. "I was done anyway."

"Nonsense," Angelina-Marie said. "I insist on buying you a fresh drink. Please."

Chang Han shrugged. "Sure."

She picked up his glass and sniffed. "Let me guess. Bourbon. Four Roses."

Chang smiled. "Very impressive."

Angelina-Marie caught her bartender's attention and indicated two drinks. The woman winked back at her.

Chang pulled out an empty chair. "Please, sit."

Angelina-Marie put out her hand and introduced herself.

His grip was warm and firm. "You're a very talented singer, Angelina-Marie."

She feigned a blush. The drinks arrived and she toasted with Chang. "I normally don't sing in public, but after a few of these, I need to let off a little steam."

"Are you under pressure?" Chang quipped.

She slapped him playfully on the arm. "Stop!"

Now Chang blushed. "I'm sorry. I have a defective sense of humor."

"Oh, Han, I think it's cute," Angelina-Marie declared. She indicated a group of rowdy twenty-somethings a few tables away that were drowning out the performer. "Better than the alternative. In my job, I'm usually surrounded by guys like that."

"What do you do?" he asked.

She sighed. "It's boring. I'm a recruiter for a software company."

"Really? Which one?"

She told him and his face grew thoughtful. "I'm a software engineer."

Angelina-Marie looked surprised. "Really?" She lowered her voice, leaned in closer. "You seem so much more mature than most of the candidates I meet."

Chang laughed self-consciously. "Is that code for too old?"

Angelina-Marie held his eyes for a second longer than was necessary to make her point. "No, Han. It means I'm always looking for software developers with real experience." She paused. "If you don't mind me asking, what languages do you work in?"

Chang sipped his drink as he outlined his work experience. He spoke in clear terms, in a matter-of-fact voice. When he finished, Angelina-Marie opened her clutch purse and took out a card. "I'd like you to call me, Han. Tomorrow, if possible. I think you would make a great addition to our team."

"My job is very secure—"

Angelina-Marie cut him off, placed a warm hand on his forearm. "Call me. I can make it worth your while." She gave his arm a gentle squeeze, then stood and walked out of the club. She didn't look over her shoulder, but she could feel Chang's eyes on her back.

On the street, the air was cool, the sea breeze brisk. She hailed a taxi.

"JW Marriott," she said.

As the car pulled away from the curb, she sent a text to her best friend in Sydney.

Landed safely in Hainan. Hotel room overlooks the sea. It's fab.

The text hit the Sydney office cut-out. A bot processed the words, isolated the word *sea*, and sent an automated reply to Angelina-Marie.

Have a great night, honey, followed by a heart emoji.

Then the system sent a coded message to CIA Special Activities Center.

Contact established.

16

USS *Illinois*, 111 miles southeast of Hainan Island, South China Sea

Janet looked around the wardroom table at the ring of glum faces. One in the afternoon was rapidly becoming her least favorite hour of the day. For the last three weeks, she'd convened a daily department head meeting in the wardroom to keep tabs on the ship's readiness. After nearly four months of continuous sea duty, the *Illinois* and her crew were showing signs of distress.

The executive officer cleared his throat. "Chop, why don't you go first?"

The Supply Officer was a soft-spoken man with round glasses and short, thinning hair. As the only non-nuclear-trained officer on board, he received no end of ribbing from the rest of the wardroom, but Lieutenant Richard Stearns took it in stride. He frowned at his open laptop.

"We're down to our final supply of staples—flour, canned goods, and such. We've cut back on portions in the galley, but even with those measures, we're down to two weeks of food."

The XO scowled. "We could go to two meals a day," he ventured.

"There's another problem, XO," the Supply Officer said. "As of this afternoon, the soda machine is shut down. We're out of syrup—"

"Well, that's unfortunate." The XO's tone had a touch of sarcasm.

"I wasn't finished, sir."

The XO's face reddened. Aware that tempers were fraying, Janet stepped in.

"Finish your report, Rich," she said.

"We're almost out of coffee, ma'am."

Janet stared. "Come again?"

The Chop avoided her eyes. "I did inventory myself. We've got three cans of ground coffee left. At the rate we consume it, that's four to five days. I've already told the galley to go to half strength, but that only stretches our supply to a week or so."

Janet sat back in her chair. No soda was one thing, but the US Navy ran on coffee. The crew was on edge already. She could only imagine what things might be like if 120 people were simultaneously cut off from their caffeine supply.

She blew out a long breath. "On that note, let's hear from Engineering."

Lieutenant Commander Stuart McBain was a tall, thin man with a wispy beard and pencil-thin mustache. He offered a wan smile.

"We're holding it together back there, ma'am," he replied. "We made another temporary repair to the high-pac number two. As soon as we secure from ultra quiet, I've got a team ready to tear down the hydraulic system as we discussed yesterday."

"The high-pacs will hold, Eng?" the XO asked. Savarino was a former engineering officer and loved to get into the details. The high-pressure air compressor system was critical to submarine operations and ship safety. If both air compressors failed, the submarine would be forced to abandon the mission.

McBain nodded emphatically. "They'll hold, XO. Honestly, I'm more worried about aux seawater two. The water temperatures are rising. I need to run that pump."

The auxiliary seawater system on board the *Illinois* cooled non-reactor components. In the warmer waters of the South China Sea, it was often necessary to run both pumps to achieve the necessary cooling. One of the bearings on ASW pump #2 had deteriorated and the pump had failed its sound test. With a PLA submarine in the area, running the pump might give away their position.

"I think we can repair it at sea, Captain," the XO said. The engineer's face told Janet he did not share the executive officer's optimism. Just as she was about to intervene, the phone under the table buzzed. Relieved for the interruption, she extracted the handset from the cradle.

"Captain," she answered.

"Officer of the Deck, ma'am," came Lieutenant Taylor's voice. "We're at the rendezvous point and have the Narwhal on the locator beacon. Request permission to hover and recover the drone, ma'am."

She indicated with her eyes that Savarino should head to control to supervise. The XO got up and left.

"What's Sierra two-six doing?" she asked.

"Still at PD, snorkeling, Captain."

"Very well, OOD. I'm sending the XO up. You have permission to recover the Narwhal."

"Hover and recover, aye, ma'am." Taylor hung up.

Janet returned the heavy handset to its cradle and focused on the conversation. Out of the corner of her eye, she saw the ship's speed slow to a stop and felt the trim adjust as the *Illinois* hovered in the ocean.

Another ten minutes passed as the team dug into the details of the ship's functions. Navigator Jen Avery asked for a time window to recalibrate the ship's inertial navigation system and Janet gave her assent.

"Captain to Control." The words over the ship's intercom electrified the room. Janet pushed back her chair and headed for the door. Fifteen seconds later, she was in the control room. Savarino's face was pinched with worry as he nodded to Taylor to give the report.

"We were recovering the Narwhal and we lost contact with it," Taylor said. Janet's eye cut to the indicator board. The row of green was interrupted by a red circle indicating that the VLS tube was still open.

"Where is the Narwhal now?" she asked.

"We don't know, Captain," the XO said. "That's the problem. We think it might be stuck in the tube."

Janet cursed to herself. There was no camera or even a limit switch to tell her how far into the tube the drone had progressed. It was possible that the UUV was all the way in and just had a bad connection, but it was equally possible that the drone was stuck halfway inside. If she tried to shut the VLS hatch without knowing the exact position of the drone, it could be a patrol-ending disaster.

She ground her teeth together. When the *Illinois* returned to Pearl Harbor, she was going to have words with the engineers who had designed the UUVs and the deployment system. The entire design was fraught with single points of failure and now she was paying the price.

"OOD," the sonar supervisor reported, "Sierra two-six has secured snorkeling." A pause. "Hull popping noises, sir. He's going deep."

"What's the range, Sonar?" Janet asked.

"Five thousand yards, ma'am."

The XO drew close. "I think we need to put a diver in the water, Captain. Get a visual."

Janet bit her lip. The submarine had a qualified diver on board, but it was a young petty officer who had completed the Navy Dive School just before deployment.

"We can't do that here," she said. "We need to get off-station and regroup. Let's see if we can sneak out of here without attracting the attention of our Chinese friend."

This maneuver had all the makings of a disaster and Janet wasn't about to put that responsibility on a junior officer. She faced the OOD. "Lieutenant Taylor, I relieve you."

"I stand relieved, ma'am."

"Attention in control," Janet announced. "The captain has the deck and the conn."

As the watchstanders echoed her announcement, Janet took a steadying breath.

"Pilot, all ahead one-third," she said.

"All ahead one-third, aye, Captain. Engine room answers one-third."

Janet's eyes locked on their speed. The dial rested at zero. She felt the ship begin to gain headway. The dial stirred and began to rise. At two knots, she felt a shimmy.

"We're making noise!" the sonar supervisor reported.

"All stop, Pilot!"

"Answers all stop, Captain."

The speed dial fell back to zero.

"Ship is hovering, ma'am."

Janet's thoughts spiraled. One knot was bare headway, not even enough to overcome a strong current. Every minute they stayed inside the PLA submarine patrol area increased their risk of discovery.

The right answer was to eject the Narwhal and clear datum, but that meant their mission was over. Without the drones, there was no way to complete the task of mapping the underwater test range. The ship would be recalled.

"Sierra two-six, showing a change in aspect ratio. He's turning, ma'am."

"New heading, Sonar?"

"Stand by, Captain."

The clock ticked in her head. She watched the sonar display and came to her own conclusion.

"New heading is one-three-zero, Captain. He's coming our way, ma'am."

"Captain," the XO began, "I recommend that we—"

"I've got it, Tom," Janet said. "Pilot, make your depth six hundred feet. Quickly, but quietly."

"Six hundred, fast and silent, ma'am."

The depth gauge began to unspool as the submarine sank into the ocean. It took less than five minutes to arrive at depth.

"Six hundred feet, Captain."

"Very well, Pilot," Janet replied. "Weapons Officer, line up to eject the Narwhal. As soon as the drone is out, reestablish comms."

"Ready to eject the drone, Captain," Weps reported.

"Proceed, Weapons Officer."

She flinched as a burst of pressurized water forced the drone out of the VLS tube. "Narwhal is clear, Captain. Attempting to reestablish comms."

"Sierra two-six is three thousand yards away, Captain." The tension in the sonar supervisor's voice was evident. "They're altering course, ma'am. I think they heard us."

Janet cursed to herself. Of course, they heard her. The Chinese sonar team was as good as her own and she'd just popped a flare in the middle of the night sky.

"Very well, Sonar," Janet replied.

Very well, she thought bitterly. This situation was the opposite of *very well.*

"Weps," she said, "we need that link back."

"Working on it, Captain."

"Work faster."

"Sierra two-six is turning," Sonar reported.

Ranging maneuver, Janet thought. Exactly what I'd do. Once he has us, he'll go active and then we're screwed.

The gray box on the Narwhal display labeled LINK ESTABLISHED turned bright green. Janet's shoulders sagged with relief.

"We've got the drone back, Captain!"

"Program the drone to steer new course two-seven-zero, max speed."

"Yes, ma'am." The Weapons Officer followed her orders, but there was hesitation in his voice. "Ready with new course two-seven-zero, speed eighteen knots," he said. "The Narwhal is at less than ten percent battery, Captain."

"I understand, Weps. Execute."

"Aye-aye, ma'am," the Weapons Officer said. "Orders sent and received. New course—"

"Drone is cavitating," Sonar interrupted. "Sierra two-six can hear it, ma'am."

"I'm counting on it, Sonar," Janet said. "Pilot, come to new course zero-nine-zero, all ahead two-thirds."

The ship began to move in the opposite direction of the drone.

Seconds turned into minutes. The distance between her ship and the decoy lengthened, but the Chinese submarine had not changed course yet. Would the Chinese captain take the bait?

Janet closed her eyes, locking in the memory of this moment in her mind. This was it: Her last mission as captain of the *Illinois* was over.

"Sierra two-six is turning!" Sonar reported. "He's going active on the drone."

"Mr. Taylor," Janet said.

"Yes, Captain."

"You may relieve me now."

17

CNS *Changcheng* 346, 115 miles southeast of Hainan Island, South China Sea

Captain Kai felt the deck of his submarine level out under his feet as they reached their new depth.

"Captain," the watch officer reported, "steady on depth five-zero meters, course zero-one-zero, speed five knots."

"Very well," Kai mumbled, his attention focused on the tablet in his hand. His face was rigidly calm, but inside he raged.

He worked for idiots. How could they be so blind? There was an enemy submarine in these waters, and yet they wanted to recall his ship so that he could attend a classified briefing? They were deliberately ignoring his messages warning about—

Mao, he thought. Commander Mao was behind this. For him, a port visit was another opportunity to kiss some Party ass to further his career. This time, Kai vowed, the commissar had gone too far.

"Messenger," Kai snapped, "find Commander Mao and have him report to my cabin immediately. I want you to use those exact words. Do you understand?"

"Yes, sir." The young man departed at a run.

Kai headed for his stateroom, but a report from Sonar stopped him in his tracks.

"Submerged contact bearing one-five-zero!"

Kai leaped toward the sonar stack. "Show me."

"It's that tonal, sir," the sonar supervisor reported in an excited voice. "The same one."

"Yes," Kai hissed. A punch of excitement surged in his chest. He was right. Again.

The signal amplitude wavered.

"Watch officer," he demanded, "where's the layer?"

"Eight-zero meters, Captain."

"Make your depth one hundred meters, steer new course zero-nine-zero. Speed ten knots."

The ship banked gently into the turn and headed downward.

The door to control opened and Commander Mao strode in. Kai could tell by the clip of his boots on the deck that he was annoyed at the peremptory summons by an officer of the same rank.

"I'm here, Captain," he said, acid in his tone, "as directed."

"Not now, Commander," Kai snapped.

The ship steadied on the new course and depth. Kai watched the narrowband frequency display. A sharp signal spiked above the background noise. It was clear and strong.

"I've got him, sir!" Sonar reported. "It's him. It's the same frequency."

"Range?" Kai demanded.

"Between four and eight thousand meters, sir. Best guess. I need another leg to give a more accurate range estimate."

Kai nodded. Bringing the ship to a new heading would give the sonar system another set of bearings to triangulate the enemy's position, but it would take time, and this target had a way of disappearing on him.

"Line up for active sonar transmission," he ordered.

"Captain Kai," Mao said immediately, "can I speak with you privately, sir?"

Kai wanted to punch the bulkhead in frustration. Why was this man always in his way?

He spun and stepped close to the political officer. "What?" His voice was sharp with anger.

"Your decision to use active sonar the last time was met with a reprimand, Captain." Mao was doing his best to be reasonable, even Kai could see that, but that only raised his frustration level.

"If I can prove there is an enemy submarine in our waters, then I am willing to risk disapproval from my chain of command."

"I am not," Mao shot back, "and you've been ordered to consult with me on these matters."

Kai's pulse hammered in his ears. Technically, Mao was correct, but *consult* could mean a lot of things.

"Captain," the watch officer asked, "I recommend new course two-one-zero to triangulate the contact's range."

Kai held Mao's gaze until the political officer looked away. He kept his voice low and steady. "I intend to confirm the range to the enemy submarine, then use active sonar to drive it out of our patrol area. Do you concur, Commander?"

Mao nodded curtly. "I concur, sir."

The submarine changed course again and the towed array lost the signal. That was normal, Kai knew, but it was disconcerting all the same. How many times had he detected this intruder and failed to prosecute the target?

Not this time, he vowed. With Commander Mao to witness it, he would prove once and for all the existence of an enemy submarine in their waters. And then his chain of command could take their reprimand and shove it up their—

"Contact regained." The sonar supervisor broke his train of thought. "Strong signal, sir."

"I've got you this time," Kai whispered. He stole a quick look at Mao and was gratified to see the political officer following the action closely.

"Range to target, three thousand two hundred meters—" Sonar said, then stopped. "Transient! Bearing one-one-five, correlates with the contact."

Kai reached for the headphones. "Play it back," he ordered.

He closed his eyes as he listened. A scraping noise, then a whoosh sound.

"Steer new course—" he began, but Sonar interrupted him.

"Contact is moving away at high speed, sir! Contact is cavitating."

Kai grinned. He had them now—and they knew it. They were trying to run away.

"Contact is on course two-seven-zero, speed nineteen knots, sir."

Kai's smile grew. They were headed *toward* the underwater test range. He had them boxed in now.

"Watch Officer, steer new course two-seven-zero. Line up to go active."

He watched Mao out of the corner of his eye. The political officer frowned, but he did not object.

The ship steadied on its new heading.

"Standing by for active transmission, Captain," Sonar reported.

"Transmit," Kai said. "Full power."

He licked his lips as he waited for the sonar display to update. He scanned the screen for the telltale bright blob of reflected energy from a seven-thousand-ton metal object in the ocean ahead of them.

There was nothing. Not even a blip.

"Transmit again!" he ordered.

Another fifteen seconds evaporated.

The ocean was empty.

"We lost the contact, sir," Sonar reported.

"Define *lost*," Kai said.

"It's not there, Captain...It's...gone." The young sailor looked shaken.

Kai felt his cheeks flush with hot shame. He'd been played again. He'd followed a false signal, probably a drone or a countermeasure. The enemy submarine—the real target—was miles away by now.

"Captain." Mao's voice was cold. "I would like to speak to you in your stateroom. Now."

18

Wujistan City, Hainan Island, People's Republic of China.

Angelina-Marie arrived at the restaurant early. The lunch rush was over, so she had her pick of where she wanted to sit. She selected a table for two in the corner of the room and seated herself with her back to the wall, facing the entrance.

She'd chosen her outfit carefully. Blue pantsuit, pale yellow blouse with a high neckline, and a bright yellow scarf to tie back her hair. Her manner of dress in the karaoke bar had been designed to get her noticed. The goal of today's ensemble was a professional appearance. She was here to recruit Chang, not sleep with him.

She opened her laptop and pretended to be absorbed in her work. That was how Chang Han found her when he arrived ten minutes late, red-faced and panting.

"I'm so sorry to have kept you waiting," he apologized.

Angelina-Marie smiled as she stood and held out her hand. "No problem, Han. I was just catching up on some email. The boss always wants to know what I'm doing every minute of the day. He thinks I can't do my job without him." She lowered her voice. "I think the opposite is true."

Chang nodded. "I know what you mean. I had to practically beg my boss to take a late lunch." He pulled a thumb drive out of his pocket. "Before I forget."

Angelina-Marie made a show of accepting the device. "So soon? I just sent you the technical challenge yesterday."

Chang ducked his head in modesty. "It wasn't really much of a challenge."

"Well, then, let's just check it out right now, shall we?" Angelina-Marie inserted the thumb drive into her computer. While she uploaded the code into a program to check his work, she also downloaded spyware onto the device. From now on, she would have a record of every computer to which the thumb drive was connected.

The checker program completed the assessment, and she swiveled her laptop around to show him a perfect score.

Chang shrugged. "Like I said, it wasn't that hard."

Angelina-Marie poured on the praise. "That's not true, Han! We give this test to hundreds of software engineers every month and most of them either fail or turn in some AI-generated crap. Very few people get a perfect score." She grinned at him, touched his arm. "I think we have a lot to talk about."

Chang ducked his head again. "I have an unfair advantage. The test was very similar to what I do for work."

You certainly do, Angelina-Marie thought. The test was to write a mapping protocol for robotic surgery. A 3D mapping challenge, not unlike what might be used to guide a torpedo in the ocean.

"You write software for medical devices?" she asked.

Chang lowered his voice. "I write software for guidance systems."

"You mean like air traffic control?"

"Not exactly," Chang replied, his voice dropping to a whisper. "Navy weapons systems. Confidential material mostly."

Inside, Angelina-Marie celebrated at this display of trust. Outwardly, she let her eyes widen and she sucked in a breath. "Say no more," she whispered back.

She could almost see Chang's chest puff up a little.

"How long did it take you?" she asked, to change the subject. "I want to make sure you're paid fairly."

"Paid?" Chang frowned. "I thought this was part of the technical assessment."

"It is, normally," Angelina-Marie said, "but you're not an ordinary candidate, Han. Someone with your experience deserves to be fairly compensated for their time."

She named an hourly rate that was at least double what he made at his job. "Is that a fair number for you?"

Chang gaped. "I—I, yes, of course, but this is all moving very fast."

"I don't want you to do anything you're not comfortable with, Han," she said soothingly. "We'll go at your pace. I'll give you an assignment and you can work on it as you have time. Consider it a side business doing consulting work. Nothing to do with your regular job, okay?"

She reached into her purse, extracting an envelope. "I don't have your payment details yet, so I assume cash is okay? Just for today?" She smiled reassuringly. Getting a recruit to accept that first gift was a big step.

Chang took the envelope, cracked it open. "Sure," he said, but his voice wavered. She wondered if she'd pushed him too far. Time to change the subject.

"That's enough work talk," she announced. "The food is here, and I want to get to know you better."

Under the guise of clearing the table for the approaching waiter, she placed her phone on top of his and moved both devices, along with her purse, to the chair next to her. On her laptop, she saw his phone register on the screen. She tapped a key to initiate the spyware installation.

"Oh, look at this feast," she exclaimed. She over-ordered to make sure the table was crowded with dishes. Like most people, Chang looked uncomfortable without his phone at hand, so she went into distraction mode.

With chopsticks, she picked a steaming shrimp off the tray and placed it on his plate. "You must try this, Han. It is *amazing*."

She followed the shrimp with another delicacy, then another. All she needed to do was keep him away from his phone for three minutes.

"Tell me about yourself, Han," she said. "Are you married?"

Chang's face clouded. Angelina-Marie put a hand over her mouth. "I'm sorry, did I say something wrong?"

Chang gave a nervous smile. "No, it's just…I'm divorced. It was an ugly breakup. She was cheating on me…" He looked searchingly into her face. "I don't know why I'm telling you this, but I feel like I can trust you."

Angelina-Marie's eyes moistened on command. "That's so sweet. I can't imagine any woman would betray you like that."

Chang toyed with his food. "It's been hard, but it's been harder for my daughter."

"You have a daughter? How old? Let me guess…twelve, right?"

Chang smiled. "I guess I'm older than I look. My daughter is twenty."

"Twenty? Do you have a picture?"

"On my phone."

Angelina-Marie removed his compromised phone from the chair and handed it back to him. Chang pulled up a picture of a young woman with a round face and shy smile.

"She has your eyes," Angelina-Marie said. "Kind eyes. What's her name?"

"Cassandra. Cassie, we call her. She insists that we use her English name now, because she's in school in Canada."

"Canada, really? Where in Canada?"

"She's in Vancouver," Chang replied with a note of pride in his voice. "At the University of British Columbia."

Angelina-Marie touched his arm. "What a coincidence. We have an office in Vancouver. If you worked for us, you could visit her on business trips."

Chang's eyes softened. "I would like that, but my work is here."

"Is your work that important, Han?"

"I work in a very small group," he replied. "I'm a critical team member."

"But you must have vacation time, right? Your boss could handle the work."

Chang laughed. "If you gave my boss the same test you gave me, he would have failed."

"No," Angelina-Marie teased.

"Yes." Chang's face went serious. "We have a very important test coming up and my boss is freaking out." He lowered his voice, laughing. "He has no idea what he's doing. I'm going to have to hold his hand the whole time."

"Really?" Angelina-Marie breathed. "It sounds like you're the man in charge. Maybe you should be the boss."

Chang shook his head. "I wouldn't want his job for anything. Too much pressure, and the politics." He rolled his eyes. "I'm happy to be the man behind the man in charge."

She placed another shrimp on his plate. He nodded his thanks and chewed thoughtfully.

"Your company has an office in Vancouver?" he said, his voice wistful.

"We do."

"And you think it's possible I could get a job there?"

Angelina-Marie put a hand on his forearm again and squeezed gently. "For you, Han, I think almost anything is possible."

19

Beihai, People's Republic of China

Yan Yuxuan's mobile phone pinged. His gaze cut from the spreadsheet he was studying to the phone's screen. He blinked as if the act of opening and closing his eyes would make the alert from his credit card company disappear.

A charge for 490 euros from a company called Fratelli Rossetti in Milan, Italy.

The purchase wasn't a scam, of that he was certain. His wife was in Milan on holiday with her sister. Before she left, he'd begged Bao to go easy on the credit card, but she'd just laughed and kissed him like she always did when she was planning to ignore him.

"Yuxuan," she cooed at him, "I'm investing in our future."

He turned to the internet to see what kind of "investment" she'd made at Fratelli Rossetti. Yan felt his whole body tighten with anger when the results of the search engine populated the screen.

Shoes? She'd spent almost five hundred euros on fucking shoes?

Rage at her thoughtlessness bubbled inside him. He needed to move, to burn off energy. He seized his hardhat from the credenza and stormed out of his office.

"Supervisor Yan!" his assistant called to his back. "There's a new work order I need you to approve."

He did not turn around. "Not now, Tan. I'll do it when I get back."

Yan exited the building, slid behind the wheel of a waiting golf cart, and sped off. The work of the Guangxi Beihai Tongda Ship Factory buzzed around him. For years, the site had been a sleepy shipyard for small break-bulk freighters, but a partnership between the PLA Navy and GBT's parent company, Feng United Enterprises, poured money and resources into the business. GBT was now one of the fastest-growing, most modern shipyards in all of China.

He drove past the hull of an oil tanker under repair—the sixth one they'd serviced this quarter—and entered the secure area of the shipyard dedicated to supporting the PLA Navy. He had three projects underway here. Two late-model frigates were pierside for a three-month refit and a guided missile cruiser occupied the drydock. A fourth ship, a PLA Navy destroyer, was anchored in the harbor waiting for a berth at the pier to open up.

The PLA Navy contracts added stability to the business. The military paid on time and they were clear about their needs. In contrast, with commercial refit contracts, everything was a negotiation.

He pulled into the parking spot labeled SHIFT SUPERVISOR and set the brake, his hands still clenched around the steering wheel. Exercise. He needed exercise.

Yan planted the white hardhat on his head and pulled on the fluorescent yellow safety vest. After only a few steps, he saw out of the corner of his eye the pear-shaped form of Li Jian bearing down on him. Yan pretended he didn't see the man, increased his pace.

"Supervisor Yan," he called, "I didn't expect to see you this morning. What a pleasant surprise."

Yan sighed and slowed to allow the man to catch up to him.

Sweat bathed Li's doughy face. "Can I help you, sir?" he asked in an oily voice.

Yan shook his head. "Just wanted to see how the drydock preps were coming along," he lied.

"I can file a full report for your review—"

"I wanted to see the work for myself," he snapped. "I'll read your report when it comes in. Thank you." He turned and walked off.

He hated how the rest of the staff treated him, and Li was the worst. As the youngest supervisor in the shipyard, he knew what they said about him: His father-in-law got him the job. He didn't earn the position.

A title on a business card was one thing, but pay was linked to seniority. As the youngest supervisor, he was also paid far less than his colleagues.

And my wife spends money like I'm the Party chairman, he thought savagely.

It wasn't really Bao's fault, he knew. It was her bitchy sister. A year younger than Bao, Ling had spent her entire life in competition with her older sister. Bao was always more beautiful, more delicate and graceful. Bao outdid her younger sister in everything...except marriage.

Yan's walking pace increased.

Ling had landed a young man whose family was even more entrenched in Party politics than her own. He was the deputy assistant to the governor of a province in western China, and if his wife was to be believed, his star was on the rise.

Every time they met, his brother-in-law had a new car, a new watch, a new designer suit. New stories about the politicians he'd dined with and the deals he'd signed for his boss.

It was mostly bullshit, Yan suspected, but it had the desired effect on his wife. For the first time in her sheltered life, Bao was second to her younger sister—and it drove her insane.

Bao tried to keep up with her sister, posting on social media about her new clothes, new furniture, new cars—and Yan was left to pay the bills.

He and Bao fought about money all the time. She begged him to ask her father for a loan. He refused. Instead, he dipped into savings month after month. He tried to explain that she was slowly bankrupting them, but Bao either didn't care or was powerless to stop her ruinous habits.

When she proposed a trip to Italy with her sister and brother-in-law, Yan refused. Too expensive, he'd said.

Then his ever-helpful brother-in-law intervened. Bao would be listed as part of the trade delegation, so her ticket and hotel were paid for by the Party.

Yan had no choice but to relent, knowing all the time that it would be a financial disaster for him. The only thing worse than having two sisters trying to keep up with each other's purchases on social media was having them do it in person.

And he was right. In the first day, she'd already spent five hundred euros on *freaking shoes*. This trip was shaping up to be a credit card death match.

Yan watched with satisfaction as a large gray box gracefully touched the deck of a pierside warship and workers swarmed over the new installation. No matter what anyone said, he was good at his job. His projects came in on time and on budget, always. That didn't happen by accident. It happened because he got involved in every detail of every job and headed off the problems before they became expensive mistakes.

Sweat bathed his face, but his mental burden felt lighter as he returned to his golf cart and drove back to the office. He placed his hardhat on the credenza, angled so that the block letters SUPERVISOR YAN faced the door. Any visitor could see he was a man of action who spent his time out on the job.

A careful tap at the door.

"Come in," he called.

Tan entered timidly. The young man was willowy and pale. He half bowed when he presented a manila folder.

"I thought you should see it right away, sir."

Yan opened the folder, scanned the first page. He frowned. "When did this arrive?" he demanded.

"About an hour ago," his assistant whispered. "It arrived by Navy messenger."

Yan remembered now. Tan tried to stop him when he went out to cool down.

He dismissed the young man, read the work order all the way through. Then called up the long-range work schedule.

Yes, there it was, on the plan for late September. He compared the details.

Relocate a *Luda*-class destroyer from the decommissioned fleet pierside.

Strip her for parts, salvage electrical conduits, remove all fuel, and install a sensor package.

It was six weeks' worth of work, already planned for and budgeted—for September. This was May. And they wanted the work done in half the time, which would require round-the-clock staffing and eye-watering overtime pay. He rubbed his mouth, trying to push back the nausea that rumbled in his gut.

This was a disaster. His work plan, his budget, everything was ruined. Even if he could convince the Navy to allocate extra money to expedite the work from six weeks to three, they would not compensate his section for all the other jobs he'd have to push back.

Why were they doing this?

He went back to the work order. The answer was in the last paragraph on the last page.

Hull Six of the decommissioned Luda-class will be the target in a live-fire test on or about July 1st.

Yan laughed at the irony. He was expediting work on a decommissioned ship, just so the Navy could blow it up.

His phone pinged and he glanced at the screen. His fingers clenched around the device, wanting to throw the phone at the wall.

A new credit card charge for 350 euros.

As he stared at the phone, a new text arrived. A picture of Bao, the perfect oval of her face smiling up at him. The brim of a sleek hat, dark blue with a curving feather, slanted down over one eye. A string of emojis followed.

Yan wanted to be sick. He was dealing with a professional disaster, and his wife was buying fucking hats in Italy. Hats that he could not afford.

He leaned back in his chair and closed his eyes, his mind already planning the new work schedule. He would find a way to make it work. He was good at his job.

His personal finances? That was a different story. He was out of options. Bao would not stop spending, and he was powerless to make her. He would have to go to his father-in-law for a loan after all. The shame of it made him sick to his stomach.

A new thought occurred to him. Yan spun his chair around so that he could look out over the shipyard.

He was having dinner with Tony next week. Tony, whose real name was Tian, had been his college roommate. He worked in finance now as an analyst. The job paid well and he always bought dinner when they went out. More than just dinner. Tony usually brought him a gift. A bottle of fine wine, a watch, a Montblanc pen.

When Yan protested, Tony waved him off.

"It's a business expense for me," he explained. "I'm an analyst and I consider you a trusted source. You're earning this gift, Yuxuan."

It seemed odd to Yan. After all, what he told Tony was public information. Well, mostly public. The PLA Navy schedules were technically confidential.

A few months ago, Tony started giving him cash when they met, instead of gifts. "I'm paying for information, Yuxuan. It's company policy."

Yan took the cash reluctantly, but he took it. With Bao's spending habits, he needed every yuan he could lay his hands on.

Last time they'd met for dinner, the envelope from Tony had been heavier than usual. His friend leaned across the table, lowering his voice.

"I know we meet once a month, but if you ever have new information, call me immediately. My clients will pay big-time for breaking news." He winked, then said again, "Big. Time."

Yan looked at his computer screen at the now-obsolete work schedule, then at his phone where Bao made a kissy face at him beneath that ridiculous, super-expensive hat.

This was new information. Maybe Tony would be interested.

He picked up his phone and sent a text to his college roommate.

Drinks tonight?

The phone showed the text had been delivered and Tony was typing a response.

Normal place at 7. See u then.

Yan put his phone face down on the desk, then faced his computer. He had a schedule to revise.

20

CIA Special Activities Center, Langley, Virginia

As usual, Bob James had not arrived with good news.

Harrison studied the satellite image on the screen at the front of the secure conference room, trying to quell the sinking feeling in his stomach.

The retired submarine captain turned analyst used his laser pointer to draw a box amid a tangle of smokestacks, decks, and shipyard equipment. "You're looking at a top-down view of the Beihai shipyards, north of Hainan Island, on the mainland. This is an old *Luda*. She's being prepped for a SINKEX on an accelerated schedule."

Harrison looked across the table to Michael Goodwin for a translation. "The *Luda* is an older class of PLA Navy destroyer. Just like us, the Chinese keep decommissioned ships in floating storage. This one has been pulled out of mothballs and is being prepped to serve as a target for a live-fire exercise."

Harrison had known Michael for many years. The former naval officer was an Annapolis graduate and computer expert, with a unique gift for pattern recognition. Michael, along with Janet Everett and another midshipman, had been pressed into service by Don Riley for a covert operation in North Korea even before he graduated from the Naval Academy.

After he received his commission, Michael had been one of Don's first recruits for the new Emerging Threats Group, which was where Harrison had first met him. When Harrison was tapped to run the Special Activities Center, he immediately asked Michael to join his leadership team.

Harrison turned his attention back to James. "You said accelerated. How much has the schedule moved up?"

"They were originally scheduled to start work in September. They've moved it up to May and put it on the fast track. Our source says the PLA Navy wants it ready by the end of June."

Harrison rubbed his chin, feeling the bite of whiskers on the back of his hand. "And the live-fire exercise is for the Hu Jing, the new torpedo?"

"I'd bet my paycheck," James said.

"How good is the intel?"

"We have a shipyard supervisor on the payroll—the China shop is top notch," the retired Navy commander replied. "The intel is good."

Harrison sat back in his chair. A Chinese live-fire test for a game-changing naval weapon taking place on the July Fourth holiday. That couldn't be an accident. The Chinese were looking to send a message, a nice *up yours* to President Cashman on the anniversary of the nation's independence.

As if reading Harrison's thoughts, James continued. "The other weapons tests we witnessed, the propulsion test and the guidance test, were conducted in secret. The Chinese ran them on their underwater test range so that they could track the torpedo."

James paused to make sure he had everyone's attention. "A live-fire exercise is a public event. You have to put out a Notice to Mariners to make sure no one gets close to your target. The Chinese won't mess with that process. It's too dangerous.

"Back in 1988, the US Navy thought they'd cleared the range for a live-fire test of a Harpoon anti-ship missile. Except they hadn't: An Indian merchant ship steamed into the area. The guidance system spotted the Indian ship instead of the hulk, veered off target, and struck the merchant ship. Thank God there wasn't a warhead on the missile, but it was bad. The Chinese want this test to go off flawlessly and the South China Sea is a heavily trafficked waterway. They will let the world know what's going on, which gives us an advantage."

Harrison felt a stirring of hope. "I could use some advantage, Commander. Explain."

James puffed up a little when Harrison used his retired rank. "You have to sink the hulk in deep water." He pulled up a large-area chart of the South China Sea. "Also, even though the Chinese don't give a rat's ass about the territorial claims of their neighbors, they'll want to avoid a political spat messing with their moment of glory."

He indicated with his laser pointer an area to the northwest of the largest Philippine islands and directly south of the island of Taiwan. "Someplace like here. Deep water, out of the shipping lanes."

"Why not the underwater test range?" asked Harrison.

"They won't want to clutter up their test range with a shipwreck," James said. "Besides, they'll want Taiwan to see what's going on. This is a coming-out party for the Hu Jing. They're announcing to the world that they have a new weapon and they know how to use it."

"So let me make sure I understand the process." Harrison got to his feet and approached the screen. He pointed to the deep water south of Taiwan. "The target ship—the hulk, you called it—is here, and the launch platform is where?"

James used his laser pointer to indicate water to the southwest. "Somewhere around here. Probably about two hundred miles away."

Harrison nodded. "The launch platform shoots the torpedo, and it drives in at high speed, then it slows, does the search pattern, and rams into the hulk. Big explosion and pop the champagne?"

James shook his head. "Modern torpedoes don't use contact detonation. They are designed to home in and detonate underneath the target to create a big bubble in the water." He held up a pencil and used his finger to pantomime an explosion underneath.

"Modern ships are heavy," he continued, "but the weight of the ship is evenly distributed along the length of the keel when it's in the water. If you make a big hole in the water beneath the ship, you mess with that even distribution. The bow and stern are still supported by water, but the middle...nothing there." Holding the pencil by both ends, he snapped it in half. "The keel snaps, splits the ship in half. Very effective."

"So what is our best chance to compromise the weapon?" Harrison asked. "During the search phase, when the torpedo homes in on the target?"

James rolled his eyes, a rare break in his professional demeanor. "Sure, if you can figure out how to do that." His words were heavy with sarcasm. "We're talking about a live warhead on an active test range, Mr. Kohl."

Harrison hesitated. Commander James hadn't been read into the full program. He didn't know about their asset inside the Hainan weapons lab.

"Suppose," Harrison began, "that I had someone with access to the computer software code in the guidance system. What would be the best way to make the test fail?"

James ran his hand over his crew cut as he thought through the problem. "The code for the guidance system would be checked, double-checked, and then checked again, so trying to hardcode a fault into the programming would be impossible."

Harrison winced.

"But"—James held up a finger—"all is not lost. Just before you launch the weapon, you have to download instructions. Remember how this torpedo works: It drives at high speed on a programmed heading, then slows down and executes a search pattern. If it finds the target, it goes into kill mode. If it *doesn't* find the target, then it repositions and searches again. It keeps doing that until it either finds the target or runs out of fuel. All of those variables need to be sent to the weapon before you launch it. The person downloading the final guidance system parameters is the last person to touch that torpedo."

"Can we just get this guy to put in an instruction to make the torpedo blow up after they launch it?"

James was deep in professor mode now. "You could do that," he said conversationally, "but your guy would end up in front of a firing squad in about fifteen minutes—which is how long it would take him to confess the entire story to the Ministry of State Security. If the Chinese know it was sabotaged, they'll just run the test again."

"I suppose you've got a better idea," Harrison said.

Bob James studied the chart of the South China Sea for a long moment.

"Actually, I do." James flipped the laser pointer in his hand absently. His voice had a thoughtful quality. "If you've got a man on the inside who has a chance to mess with the launch parameters on the new torpedo, then I say we swing for the fences."

"Which means what?" Harrison asked.

James grinned wolfishly.

"Let's steal the torpedo."

21

USS *Illinois*, 180 miles southeast of Hainan Island, China

Janet lay back on her bunk, staring at the ceiling of her stateroom and waiting for the call from the control room. She wasn't tired. Since they'd cleared their assigned patrol area near the Chinese underwater test range over twenty-four hours ago, she'd managed to catch up on her sleep.

What the hell is taking them so long to send us new orders? she wondered. US Navy bureaucracy was one thing, but this was too much. Their last remaining Narwhal was lost. They were almost out of stores. As much as she hated to admit it, their mission was over. The only thing left to do was to send them home.

Instead, the *Illinois* had been told to wait for further orders. For the last twenty-four hours, the submarine bored holes in the ocean at constant depth and speed, changing course only when they reached the edge of their assigned patrol area. Every six hours, they broke the monotony by making a trip to periscope depth to retrieve their message traffic.

Janet had little doubt that the *Illinois* would be ordered back to their homeport of Pearl Harbor. God knows this crew has earned it, she thought. They'd performed above and beyond her expectations. The loss of the

Narwhal was not their fault. The drone had never been designed for the number of duty cycles they'd put it through.

But pride in her crew inevitably gave way to sadness, as it always did with her. Orders for home meant that her dream job was coming to an end. It was time to turn over her ship to a fresh commanding officer and move on to her next challenge.

She'd toyed with the idea of asking to go back to work for Don Riley at the CIA but dismissed it. The submarine force was her home, where she belonged. Her next job would not be as exciting as being a submarine captain, but it would be just as important. They'd likely give her some staff assignment first, let her mark time for two years, then she'd screen for major command—maybe commodore of a submarine squadron.

She felt the bow of the submarine angle upward. Her eye watched the depth gauge as it settled on 150 feet. No sloppy fluctuation around the depth, just bang on target. She smiled to herself. This was a professional crew that knew how to do their jobs.

The ship began a slow turn to port, heeling slightly as the Officer of the Deck cleared baffles. The submarine steadied on a reciprocal course as the sonar team used the towed array to search the surrounding ocean for enemy contacts.

She let five minutes pass, then sat up. The phone next to her bunk buzzed and she picked it up.

"Captain."

"Officer of the Deck, ma'am. Steady at one-five-zero feet, speed six knots, course one-eight-zero. Request permission to make a trip to PD."

"Take the ship to periscope depth," Janet ordered. "Clear message traffic."

"PD and clear traffic, aye, ma'am."

Janet looked at herself in the mirror. Her eyes were still puffy from sleep. She splashed water on her face, smoothed her hair back, and remade her ponytail. She scowled at her image. When she got home, she was going to spend about a week in the most expensive spa she could find and get every treatment on the menu. Twice.

As she left her stateroom, the bow angled upward. Janet let herself into the control room.

"Captain's in control," the Pilot announced.

"As you were," she said quickly.

She remained in the doorway, watching the team at work, absorbing the sounds of *her* control room on *her* ship. How many more of these opportunities would she have before they arrived back in Pearl? Fifty? A hundred? The empty feeling gnawed at her. Whatever the number, it would not be enough.

"Pilot, make your depth five-zero feet," ordered the OOD.

As they went shallow, the ship rocked gently from the wave action on the surface of the ocean.

"Raising the photonics mast," the OOD announced. He controlled the direction of the optics using a joystick on the panel, slowly rotating the field of view through 360 degrees.

"Mast is clear," the OOD said. She watched as he did a full rotation. "No close contacts."

"Steady on five-zero feet," the Pilot said.

"No close radar signatures detected, OOD," the fire control tech reported.

"Very well, Fire Control." The OOD made a slower sweep around the submarine. It was nighttime and the glow of a half-moon silvered the surface of the water. The OOD switched to infrared and continued searching the horizon. He raised the communications mast.

"Radio, Conn, SATCOM mast is up. You have permission to transmit."

"Conn, Radio, transmitting." A bleep of electromagnetic noise interrupted the static playing over the intercom. In that brief burst, the ship sent hundreds of unclassified emails from the crew as well as the encrypted ship's message traffic and received the same from the satellite.

"Radio?" the OOD said after a full minute passed. "Are we good?"

"Conn, Radio. Yes, sir. Message traffic downloaded and verified. Be advised we have flash message traffic for the captain."

"Very well, Radio." The OOD cast a look at Janet. "Lowering SATCOM mast."

"Go deep, Mr. Taylor," Janet ordered.

"Pilot, make your depth three hundred feet."

"Three hundred feet, aye, sir," the Pilot echoed. The deck angled down.

The Radioman appeared on the other side of the control room, carrying a tablet. The third-class petty officer was a twenty-year-old redhead from Iowa with a fringe of ginger fuzz covering his freckled cheeks.

"Thank you, Morgan." She tried to appear calm as she unlocked the tablet. Now maybe she'd find out why they'd been waiting so long for their orders.

She scanned the flash message, her face still. But inside, she felt a jolt of excitement.

Proceed to Subic Bay at best possible speed. Take on stores and effect critical repairs.

So far, so good. She'd expected to be routed to Yokosuka, Japan, for stores, but Subic was another option. Then her eyes fixed on the line:

Prepare to put to sea within 72 hours. New orders to follow.

She forced herself to read the message again, looking for clues in the spare bureaucratic language. The sense of urgency was there. Best possible speed, emergency stores, and the magic phrase, *put to sea within 72 hours.*

It seemed that their mission was not over.

Don't assume, she warned herself. One step at a time, and step one was organizing the crew to make sure they got the most out of a short port call.

When Janet looked up, she saw the entire control room was watching her. She tried to divine the emotions behind the faces. Were they anxious to go home or eager to finish the job?

"Officer of the Deck."

"Ma'am?"

"Pass the word on the 1MC. All officers not on watch, report to the wardroom."

22

Hainan Island, People's Republic of China

Angelina-Marie arrived an hour early for her meeting with Chang Han. Following her initial contact with her target, she'd scouted the island for suitable meeting locations, looking for places where they could have a private conversation in a public setting and she could maintain good sightlines of the interior at all times.

Today's meeting location was the Prince Edward Road Beer Square in Ling Tao Village, a touristy faux-British pub about twenty minutes from the naval base where Chang worked. At three in the afternoon, the place was only half full of families and couples on vacation, but she'd done her homework. Within the next hour, it would fill up. No one would take any notice of the couple sharing an after-work drink.

She secured a table for two along the back wall, underneath a weathered metal sign that read *Guinness Is Good for You*. From this spot, she had a clear view of the door and a good angle on the mirror behind the bar. The rear entrance was down the hall, past the restrooms.

Angelina-Marie ordered a Heineken Zero and settled down to wait.

This was her fourth meeting with Chang Han and all signs pointed toward a strong possibility for a successful recruitment. He was now accepting money without hesitation for the "tests" that Angelina-Marie was assigning to him. At each successive meeting, conducted at a different location each time, he increasingly opened up to her about his personal life.

His ex-wife sounded like a real piece of work. She still lived in Shanghai, near her family and childhood friends. Their daughter, Cassie, was an unplanned pregnancy in graduate school that led to a hasty, and ultimately doomed, marriage. They'd stayed married for their daughter's sake, but when Chang's work brought him south to Hainan Island, wifey put her foot down. She was not moving out of Shanghai and neither was his daughter.

Chang took the job anyway. Two years later, as soon as Cassie left for college, the wife had filed for divorce. He complained bitterly that she'd had affairs throughout their troubled marriage while he stayed faithful, but he was grateful that his wife's family had the money and connections to get his daughter into a good school in Vancouver.

But now that Cassie was running with the wrong crowd—Chang blamed his wife for setting a poor example—he was worried. Angelina-Marie let him talk and then verified everything he told her against the facts.

Even in China, the CIA had an excellent capability for checking on the minutiae of a person's life. Every detail Chang shared with her, no matter how small, was checked. In the world of human intelligence, asset validation never stopped. If Chang lied, she needed to know how and why.

His story was mostly true. Chang hadn't been quite the honorable Boy Scout he claimed. They'd cracked his phone and discovered an on-again, off-again sexual liaison with his landlord's wife that had been going on for the last few years. The arrangement seemed less like an affair and more like an occasional hookup. His relationship with his daughter seemed strained but genuine, and his worry was real and valid. Cassie was indeed headed for trouble.

Angelina-Marie had been a case officer for ten years. She was pleased with her progress with Chang. Given six months, she was confident she could develop him into a valuable long-term asset. Unfortunately, she'd just learned that Harrison Kohl had a much shorter timeline in mind.

As she did every day, Angelina-Marie texted with her pseudo bestie back in Sydney. The texts were inane blather between friends, full of inside jokes, emojis, and keywords that only had significance to their intended recipient in Langley.

When she texted about the amazing lobster dinner the previous night, she was telling Harrison that she'd completed her scheduled meeting with Chang.

When he texted back that he wanted to go to a *football game* when she returned, she was getting new instructions. When the orders arrived, coded inside a picture in her email, she had to read them three times before she believed what she was being directed to do.

She accepted her drink from the waitress and took a contemplative sip. Although he didn't know it yet, today was going to be an inflection point in Chang's life.

She'd been briefed on the new torpedo as part of her mission prep, but what Harrison wanted from Chang at this point in his recruitment was high risk. She might be able to get him there eventually, but in the timeframe Harrison wanted? If Chang had any sense at all, he would run—not walk, *run*—as far away from her as possible. And maybe even drop a dime on her with the authorities to cover his ass.

That's why they pay me the big bucks, she thought.

Angelina-Marie tried to be objective about the problem. Chang was no dummy. He knew there was something off about their relationship, but he kept coming back and he kept taking her money. It wasn't the promise of sex. Angelina-Marie was an attractive woman, and she'd used her femininity to get his attention in the karaoke bar, but after that, she'd kept it strictly professional. He'd followed her lead.

It wasn't really money either. Chang made a good salary and had savings. He could easily afford a better apartment or car, but he chose to live frugally. He didn't have a problem accepting her money, but he didn't need it either.

Which meant Chang had other motivations. Cassie was a genuine source of worry, but for all his concern, he hadn't done much except talk to her every week. She'd been in Canada for two years, and although he had the means to travel, he had not visited her.

She suspected Chang was a closet bad boy. He'd told her that he loved spy novels and movies. The review of his phone confirmed that love was real.

At some level, Angelina-Marie realized, Chang knew what she was and the whiff of danger attracted him. She just hoped he didn't freak out when fantasy turned into reality.

As if on cue, Chang entered the bar. She waved to get his attention and he made his way across the rapidly filling space. Angelina-Marie got up and shook his hand. She hesitated, then hugged him. She was mostly sure his interest in her wasn't sexual, but it wouldn't hurt to butter him up for what was about to come.

He seemed momentarily flustered by the unexpected close contact. Angelina-Marie flagged down the waitress. Chang ordered a Heineken and she indicated another Heineken Zero.

"First things first," she said, sliding an envelope across the table. "Your work, as usual, was flawless. We are very impressed." She paused, winking at him. "I hope we can talk about next steps today."

Chang smiled back at her. "I'd like that."

Be careful what you wish for, she thought.

The waitress arrived with their drinks. Angelina-Marie held up her sweating glass. "To the future."

"To the future," Chang agreed.

They drank.

"How's Cassie doing?" Angelina-Marie asked, a note of concern in her voice. "Better, I hope?" She knew the answer already, but this line of approach would help to frame his options more clearly.

Chang frowned at his beer. "She says she's doing better, but I'm not sure I believe her."

"Would it help if we got her an internship at the Vancouver office this summer?"

Chang looked up, surprised, hopeful. "You would do that?"

Angelina-Marie held his gaze. "If it will get you on board our project, I will absolutely make that happen."

"That...that would be great. She needs a new circle of friends, I think."

"And what about you?" Angelina-Marie pressed. "How's work?"

Chang rolled his eyes. "Crazy. The only way I could take off early was if I promised my boss I'd come back this evening."

"They work you too hard," Angelina-Marie said. "Are they short-staffed or something?"

"There's a big test coming up in a few weeks. My boss is freaking out. The guy is in over his head."

"But he has you."

"Exactly, but I'm tired of carrying his sorry ass."

"You deserve to be recognized for the great work you do."

Chang blushed. Angelina-Marie sipped her beer. This was the moment, she decided.

"What's the test?" she asked in a casual manner. "It sounds important."

Chang looked up. "It's...um." She saw the shift in his eyes. He knew what she was asking.

"I know what you do, Han," she said gently.

The engineer surprised her. "I've been trying to figure out if you work for the MSS and this was some sort of sting operation. It isn't."

A statement, not a question.

"I don't work for the MSS."

Chang toyed with his beer glass.

"How much do you know about what I do?"

Angelina-Marie hesitated. Up until now, everything was hypothetical, her cover intact. The next step meant admitting she was a foreign operative on Chinese soil. Her mind ran through the risks—and there were many—but her instinct told her she could trust him.

"I know you're a software engineer on the guidance system for the new long-range torpedo."

Chang stiffened in his chair, then drained his beer.

"How? How do you know that?"

Angelina-Marie channeled calm and tranquility. If he was going to bolt on her, this was the moment.

"How I know doesn't matter, Han. It's true, right?"

Chang waved at the waitress, held up his empty glass. When he looked at Angelina-Marie again, his eyes were hard. "It's true."

Angelina-Marie relaxed. The trust was still there. Hanging on by a thread, but still there. Rapport always took a hit when you crossed into this phase of a recruitment. A short-term loss of trust after the reveal was to be expected, but she was pushing her luck to the limit by moving this fast.

The fresh beer arrived and he drank again. His Adam's apple kept bobbing even after he stopped drinking and his eyes cut around the room. Angelina-Marie put her hand on his forearm.

"Take a beat," she said. "Gather yourself. Think about Cassie. Think about how much I can do to help her, and to help you."

She watched his death grip on his beer glass ease at the mention of his daughter. A useful data point.

They sat in silence for a full minute. The next move belonged to him. Angelina-Marie needed him to take that next step willingly.

Chang stared at the table, lost in thought. The internal struggle was plain on his face. She could imagine the battle going on inside his head. Then his shoulders dropped, and he sat back in his chair. Chang slid the beer glass aside, clearing a lane between them.

"What do you want me to do?"

23

Lagonoy Gulf, The Philippines, 5 miles west of Catanduanes Island

From the bridge of the thirty-meter luxury catamaran SS *Arrogant*, Claude Buettner surveyed his domain. Outside the windows of the air-conditioned bridge, the late afternoon sun turned the Lagonoy Gulf into a sea of beaten brass.

He raised a pair of field glasses to his Ray-Bans and scanned the horizon. Two miles out, a fishing charter skipped across the waves. The triangular sails of two sailboats were hull down to their northwest. In the east, the hazy green bulk of Catanduanes Island rose from the sea. To the west, the forested hillside rose toward Mount Malinao.

He continued his methodical scan until he had the *Arrogant*'s diving launch in his field of view. The launch had a canvas canopy, bench seats, and racks for compressed air tanks, with enough space for twelve divers. The red-and-white diver-down flag flapped in the breeze, warning nearby boats that they had divers in the water.

As Claude watched, a head bobbed to the surface. Roger, the dive-master, stepped to the back of the launch to help the diver out of the water.

The diver climbed the ladder, stripping off mask and snorkel, and shimmying the wetsuit down to reveal an emerald-green bikini top. She shook out a mane of dark red hair.

"Ah," Claude muttered to himself, "the lovely Marta."

Their typical clients fell into buckets: serious photographers after the marine life, unserious social media influencers after more followers, Old Money (trust fund babies), and New Money, usually tech bros. The only things these disparate groups had in common were an excess of disposable income and free time.

Marta was the rare exception to the rule. She was, as Roger put it after her first evening on board: fifty, fit, and fabulous. She was traveling the world solo, a free spirit gathering life experiences—and probably breaking a few middle-aged hearts along the way.

Marta and Claude made a connection the moment he welcomed her on board.

"*Arrogant* is quite a name for a ship, Captain Claude," she said by way of greeting, a hint of mockery in her tone. She shook his hand, her touch electric on his skin.

"I didn't name her, ma'am. The owners did. I'm just a humble servant."

Marta arched an eyebrow, but kept his hand in hers. "Servant, eh? I don't believe that for a moment, Captain. Who are your owners?"

"You wouldn't believe me if I told you." Claude laughed. He moved to greet the next guest before she could press the point.

He was telling the truth: She probably wouldn't believe him. Officially, the SS *Arrogant* was owned by a shell company, Tortuga Enterprises, based in the Caymans. If a dedicated investigator dug deep enough, he would find another level of financial subterfuge, and then another. The true owners had gone to great lengths and significant expense to conceal their identity.

Claude watched through the field glasses as more heads bobbed to the surface and the rest of the divers started to clamber aboard the launch. Marta was laughing at something Roger said, leaving Claude with a twinge of jealousy.

Technically, there was no rule against sleeping with the clients, but Claude had always steered clear on principle. Marta might be the one to change his mind. This was day three of a five-day excursion, so if he was planning to make his move, he'd better get going.

Not a good idea, old son. Then again, he told himself, how often did he cross paths with a woman like Marta?

He pulled the ship-wide walkie-talkie off his belt.

"Helen, looks like Roger will have the guests back in the next fifteen minutes."

"I'll throw another shrimp on the barbie, Cap'n," Helen replied with a fake Australian accent.

Claude rolled his eyes. "Stick to killing people with a handgun instead of humor, Helen. I think you'll have a higher success rate."

"Arsehole," she snapped back in her faux Australian brogue. "No Foster's for you, mate."

Like the rest of the crew, Helen, the chief purser, was former military, an Army Ranger with two combat tours. The crew had been required to remove any military-related tattoos before joining the program, but not all identifying features could be hidden. Helen never wore a bikini because of the scars on her stomach and torso: a knife wound and a bullet hole.

He took one last look at the dive launch. Roger had all the guests back on board and was pulling up the anchor. Claude stowed the field glasses and left the bridge.

The spacious main deck of the *Arrogant*, one level above the waterline, ran almost the entire length of the ship. The teak wood flooring glowed from regular cleaning. The main dining table, an expanse of glass capable of seating twenty people, was laden with food: cheeses, sushi and grilled lobster, crusty breads and fresh fruit. From behind the bar, Helen polished a glass like she was trying to extract a confession.

Claude nodded in satisfaction. All was in order. He walked the length of the deck, used his knee to nudge one of the plush leather armchairs closer to its neighbor.

"Don't mess with my furniture," Helen called.

Claude flipped her the bird over his shoulder.

"Save it for Marta, old man. You're going to need all your strength for that one."

"Don't listen to that nasty woman, boss. I think you carry your dotage well," said Neil, carrying a bucket of ice to the bar. "I look up to you as my father, aged and wise."

In the ship's uniform of white shorts and blue polo, Neil Vasquez looked like a South Seas deity. His chiseled torso and muscled legs looked as if they were carved out of mahogany. The former Navy SEAL and ship's comms specialist carried the full five-gallon bucket like it was empty.

"Anything in message traffic I should know about?" Claude asked.

Neil shook his head. "Normal bullshit."

Claude heard the launch come alongside. He strode down to the fantail to meet the guests and was greeted with a wave of animated chatter.

He appreciated the post-dive excitement. Claude had been diving for more than thirty years, both in the military and out of it, and he never tired of seeing life beneath the waves or sharing it with others.

As Roger maneuvered the launch broadside, Claude caught the stern line and secured it to the cleat while Neil attended the forward line.

Marta held out her hand. Her touch was like a spark on his skin. As she stepped onto the deck of the *Arrogant*, she leaned into him, placing her palm on his breastbone.

"Always the gentleman, Captain Claude," she murmured. "Do you ever get tired of it?"

Claude was acutely aware of her hand, still chilled from the water, on the bare skin of his chest. The skimpy bikini was the exact shade of her eyes.

"I never forget my place, ma'am."

She chuckled. "Make an exception, Captain. For me."

He watched her walk away.

Roger put a hand on his shoulder. "Still waters run deep, Captain."

"I'm a good swimmer, Roger." Tonight was the night, he vowed to himself.

The group migrated to the bar where Helen was slinging drinks like a pro. Margaritas, martinis, Manhattans, and mojitos appeared in the hands of their guests as if by magic.

Claude got two glasses of chilled Albariño—Marta's drink of choice—and scanned the deck for her. She emerged from the stairwell, wearing a clingy sundress over her bikini. She'd run a brush through her damp hair and gentle curls spilled across her shoulders. It was amazing to Claude how she'd put on more clothes and somehow looked even sexier.

Marta's eyes found him, then dropped to the two glasses of straw-colored wine. She gave him a slow smile as they walked toward each other.

This is happening, Claude thought. All systems are go for launch.

Neil intervened when he was six feet away. "We got a ping, Captain."

A *ping* meant high-priority message traffic was waiting for his action.

Neil scanned his face. "Helen did not put me up to this, sir. It's real."

Claude handed both glasses to Neil. He looked over Neil's shoulder into Marta's questioning gaze. "Duty calls, ma'am," he said with false cheer. "Hopefully, I can join you for dinner this evening."

"I look forward to it," she called after him.

He turned and marched to the stairwell. He locked his stateroom and sat down at his desk, drumming his fingers as he waited for his laptop to boot up and connect to the ship's Wi-Fi. His email started to download. He scanned the subject lines for the *Arrogant*'s keyword identifier and selected the message.

It was an ad for an online magazine about charter fishing, something that might just as easily have gone to the spam folder. He pulled up a decryption program from the partitioned section of his hard drive and clicked on the icon.

It took thirty seconds to convert the email into a military-style message format. His eyes caught on the sender: the CIA Director of Operations.

He sat back in his chair, his pulse quickening. Don Riley himself was sending direct tasking to the *Arrogant*, otherwise known as Feisty Minnow Unit 74.

The Feisty Minnow program was a fleet of civilian ships scattered around the world, staffed by Agency officers and former military. The ships were outfitted with a range of concealed sensors that allowed them to capture communications, electronic intelligence, and acoustic data as well as photographs.

Posing as civilians, they sailed inside territorial waters and into ports of all nations, friendly or unfriendly to the United States. Twenty years ago, Claude knew, Feisty Minnow had been Don Riley's pet project and the covert fleet had expanded to include dozens of luxury yachts, high-end sailboats, and catamaran diving charters like the *Arrogant*.

On very rare occasions, an intelligence collection platform was called on to assist in a covert action. Claude scanned the message.

This was one of those times.

Unit 74: Cancel current cruise and all further obligations for next 30 days. Disembark civilians at nearest port. Proceed at best possible speed to Puerto Real for embarkation of new team. Details to follow. Advise ETA Puerto Real soonest.

Claude looked up at the ceiling. Puerto Real was two hundred miles to the north. The nearest port to disembark their passengers was Sabang, only about twenty miles to the northwest.

The bigger issue was that they still had two more days on the charter. But his orders were clear: Dump the civilians and haul ass north.

He pulled the walkie-talkie off his belt.

"Captain to Helen."

"Yeah, boss."

"I need to see you in my stateroom." He kept his tone neutral, but Helen got the message.

Two minutes later, she was reading their new orders. She let out a low whistle. "I smell action ahead, matey," she said in her fake Australian accent, then caught herself when she noted the serious look on his face. "Sorry."

"Any ideas on how to get our customers off the ship without creating unnecessary suspicion?" he asked.

Helen puffed out her cheeks as she thought. Her face brightened. "I predict we're going to have an electrical fire in the galley. Lots of flash, lots of smoke, very scary. The really bad news is that the galley will be out of commission and our reefer damaged. No way to feed them." She frowned at Claude. "I'm very sorry, Captain, but we're going to have to head to port tonight."

Claude cracked a smile. "That'll work. Make it look convincing, but not too many heroics. I know how you get."

"I'm offended by that remark, sir."

Claude ignored her, his mind already on his next task. “Give it an hour or so, okay? Let them finish their drinks before we ruin their evening.”

Helen grinned and saluted. “Aye-aye, Cap’n.” The Australian accent was back.

As the door closed behind her, Claude leaned back in his chair, his thoughts drifting. He sighed, filing the mental image of the lovely Marta under “what might have been.” Then he leaned over his computer to compose a reply to the Director of Operations.

24

USS *Illinois*, pierside Subic Bay Naval Base, Luzon, The Philippines

"Make a hole! Captain coming through."

Janet couldn't identify which member of her crew had shouted the warning, but she was grateful all the same. Since they'd arrived in port, the number of bodies on board the *Illinois* had more than doubled as a cadre of maintenance teams worked around the clock to effect urgent repairs. Janet and her crew were determined to make the most of their seventy-two hours in port.

Three shipyard workers carrying tool bags flattened themselves against the wall as Janet shouldered past them. Whatever her new orders were, they came with some high-level support. A team of two dozen maintenance techs from Pearl Harbor Naval Shipyard had been waiting on the pier for the *Illinois* when they arrived in Subic.

She stepped through the hatch into the engine room. The space was stuffy, the air sharp with the smell of burnt metal from welding. She passed a team of maintenance techs kneeling next to a dismantled high-pressure air compressor and another group replacing lagging over steam piping.

She swung down a ladder and traveled deeper into the bowels of her ship in search of the engineer. She found McBain on his hands and knees, shining a penlight into an open pipe the size of a manhole cover. A huge gray pump, the size and shape of an oil drum, hung on a chain hoist a few feet away.

"Sir," one of the chiefs prodded the engineer. "Captain's here."

The engineer got to his feet slowly. His complexion looked waxy and damp and his eyes were red. Janet wondered when he'd last slept.

"How we looking, Eng?" she asked.

He gave her a wan smile. "We'll get there, ma'am."

Janet looked around dubiously. "Do you need more help? I can get more manpower if you need it."

He shook his head. "I have more bodies than I can use now." He gestured at the pump suspended in the air over the deck. "Once we get this buttoned up and sound-tested, we'll be in good shape."

She drew him aside. "I love the ambition, Stu, but I intend to leave tomorrow night. If you've bitten off more than you can chew, tell me now and let's fix it together."

McBain frowned. "I've got it, Captain. You have my word."

Janet realized she'd gone too far. Like so many high-performance submarine captains, she sometimes fell prey to micromanagement. She opened her mouth to apologize, but the engineer beat her to it.

"I understand the concern, ma'am," he said with a tired smile, "and we'll be ready to take the reactor critical by lunchtime tomorrow. I'll stake my paycheck on it."

Janet laughed. "That won't be necessary, Engineer. Carry on."

The speaker above her head blared to life. "Captain, Topside."

She found the nearest sound-powered phone and picked up the heavy black handset.

"Captain."

"Captain, Petty Officer Wilson on topside watch. You have three visitors, ma'am."

"Who are they?"

"The gentleman didn't want to give me his name. He asked to speak to you in person."

"Civilian or military?"

"They're all in civilian clothes, ma'am."

Janet pinched the bridge of her nose. She did not need this today. "I'll be right up."

If it was warm in the engine room, the atmosphere topside was liquid heat. The sun blazed down like a living thing, and after breathing cool, conditioned air for the last four months, the humid tropical climate of the Philippines felt like she was breathing underwater.

Petty Officer Wilson saluted as she approached the brow connecting the deck of the submarine to the pier. He pointed to three men standing on the pier.

"That's them, ma'am."

The three men were all dressed in civilian clothes and wore ball caps and sunglasses. They faced away from her, their heads together in conversation. Beyond them, the pier was alive with activity. Forklifts raced along, sailors and shipyard workers hurried past. A crane trundled by, men in yellow safety vests clearing the path. This was the most isolated and secure pier in the base. Armed speedboats patrolled the adjacent waters to ward off civilians who wanted to get a closer look at a US Navy submarine.

"I think I recognized one of them, ma'am, but he wouldn't give me his name. Kinda weird," Petty Officer Wilson said.

"Thanks. I'll take care of it, Wilson." Janet stepped onto the brow, saluted the American flag flying from the flagstaff at the rear of the submarine. Her heavy work boots clanged on the steel surface as she approached the knot of men.

"Can I help you, gentlemen?" she called as she neared the end of the brow.

The tall man on the end turned around and removed his sunglasses. Janet realized she was looking at Rear Admiral Spooner, Commander, Submarine Forces Pacific, better known as SUBPAC. Her hand started to come up into an automatic salute, but he stepped forward and held out his own hand.

"Don't salute, Captain. I'm not supposed to be here."

She shook his hand, suddenly realizing that she looked like a hot mess. Her coveralls were filthy, her work boots grimy, and she couldn't remember the last time she'd showered. Thank God she'd tucked her hair up into her ship's ball cap; otherwise, she'd look like the Wicked Witch of the West.

Spooner, on the other hand, looked cool and collected. He wore a blue polo, tan chinos, golf shoes, and a snow-white ball cap.

"I'm supposed to be golfing right now. There's another guy dressed the same as me out on the course, just in case anyone's watching."

"Yes, sir." Janet didn't know what else to say.

"Allow me to introduce my compadres, Captain." He indicated a sweaty man, early sixties, dressed in khakis and a polo. "This is Bob James, retired O-5, former submarine commander."

James's grip was sweaty but firm. "Big fan of your work, Commander Everett."

She turned to the final man and realized she knew him. "Harrison! What are you doing here?" She hugged him without thinking.

"Seems you two are acquainted," Spooner said dryly. "I'm guessing this is another service record redaction, Commander Everett?"

Janet flushed. The gaps in her service record from her time with the CIA were a regular source of irritation to her chain of command. "Something like that, sir."

She led the trio across the brow and spoke to her topside watch. "List these gentlemen down in the logbook as my guests, no names are necessary. Where's the XO?"

"He left about an hour ago, ma'am, headed for the maintenance depot office."

Janet nodded. "Send a messenger to find him and tell him I need him back here on the double."

She led her guests to the forward hatch and swung down the ladder. When the three men climbed down, she led them into the control room. Senior Chief O'Malley was supervising sonar diagnostics. She called him over.

"Gentlemen, Senior Chief O'Malley is the brains behind our crack sonar team." She noted how the comment sparked interest from Commander James. "He's going to escort you to the wardroom. I'll join you in just a moment."

Janet raced to her cabin and slammed the door behind her. She stripped off her coveralls and boots while running water in the basin. After splashing water on her face, she tamed her hair into a ponytail and painted her underarms with deodorant. A fresh pair of uniform khakis and polished black shoes completed the transformation. The whole evolution took less than three minutes.

Thank the sweet Lord for uniform races at the Naval Academy, she thought as she opened the stateroom door.

She needn't have worried. In the wardroom, O'Malley was deep in conversation with her visitors about the frailties of the Narwhal underwater drone design. Rear Admiral Spooner was writing in a small notebook.

"Thank you, Senior Chief," Janet said pointedly. "I'll take it from here."

As O'Malley got up to leave, James rose with him and pumped his hand. "Excellent work Senior Chief. Some of the finest intel I've seen in my entire career."

Janet stared at the retired submarine commander. Something about him seemed familiar.

"Commander James," she said, "this might be a personal question, but do you have a brother in the Navy?"

James offered a rueful smile. "That would be Wild Bill, my ne'er-do-well younger brother. Mom's favorite. How do you know him?"

"We've met," Janet said vaguely.

"Ah, I get it," James replied with a wink. "Above my paygrade."

Thankfully, the door to the wardroom opened and Tom Savarino burst in. Sweat poured off his red face and darkened the collar of his khaki uniform. He worked to catch his breath. "Sorry I'm late, Captain." He caught sight of Spooner and stopped. "Admiral, I didn't—"

Spooner extended his hand. "Have a seat, XO, before you fall down. This heat is nothing to mess with. Especially after you've been submerged for as long as *Illinois* has been on station."

The XO collapsed in a chair, mopping his face with a handkerchief. Janet buzzed the galley and ordered the room secured for a confidential briefing.

"Let's get to it," Spooner said. "I'm here today because Mr. Kohl and his... *organization*"—Janet caught the XO's inquiring look and she gave a slight shake of her head—"have requested the services of the *Illinois* for a very sensitive operation."

Janet suppressed a thrill of excitement. Their mission was not over yet.

"I see you're smiling, Commander Everett," Spooner continued. "After you hear what these gentlemen have in mind, you might not be so pleased with yourself."

Janet tried to hide her grin and failed. "Sorry, sir. What is the mission?"

"Your work monitoring the Chinese Hu Jing torpedo has been invaluable, Janet," Harrison said. "Without your intel, we probably wouldn't even know this weapon existed, much less be in a position to do something about it."

"That's kind of you to say, but it was mostly right place at the right time for us."

"Well," Harrison said, "there's more work to be done. Our intel says the Chinese are planning a SINKEX in the next few weeks. According to Commander James, if the live-fire test is successful, it will have serious implications for the next-generation Chinese submarine. I don't think I have to tell you that it would be a disaster for our position in this part of the world."

"You want us to gather intel on the live-fire test?" Janet asked.

"Think bigger," Harrison said.

Janet and her XO exchanged glances. "Do you have a way to disrupt the test?"

"Bigger." He let the silence hang for a few beats.

"I'm not sure what to say, Harrison," Janet replied finally.

"We want you to help us steal the torpedo."

"That sounds..." A river of words ran through Janet's head: *ridiculous, dangerous, colossally stupid*. She settled on, "Audacious. I can't wait to hear your plan."

Harrison turned to Bob James.

"Commander, you have the floor."

25

Yulin Naval Base, Hainan Island, China

Captain Kai Jun had never seen security on the Yulin Naval Base so tight. Even as a submarine commander, he had to park off base and take a bus to the briefing building in the Advanced Weapons Division.

He sweated as he waited in line outside the secure conference room, a red visitor's badge clipped to the pocket of his summer dress uniform. After weeks at sea, wearing a loose underway jumpsuit and living in a cool, climate-controlled atmosphere, the uniform felt restrictive.

But even that discomfort could not dim his enthusiasm. He took a seat in the small auditorium next to his political officer. "Commander Mao, good morning."

Mao returned the greeting, then leaned toward him. "I think you can see now how important this weapons test is to the Navy," he murmured.

"Agreed. I'm pleased I was able to advise the admiral about the imminent threat to the test plan."

The imminent threat was the USS *Illinois*, a United States Navy *Virginia*-class submarine, the most advanced underwater platform in the world. Finally, he had uncovered the identity of the enemy submarine patrolling the waters surrounding the underwater test range.

While reviewing the latest intel updates, he came across a report from a source inside the Philippine Navy Base in Subic Bay, corroborated by satellite imagery. The USS *Illinois* had arrived in port unannounced for repairs and stores. He was certain that was the submarine he had been chasing for weeks—it was the only logical conclusion. The other US Navy submarines in the Pacific Ocean were all accounted for, except for the *Illinois*.

As usual, his political officer disagreed. "The fact that a US Navy submarine pulled into a Philippine base in the South China Sea does not prove anything, Captain."

"We had contact with—"

"You had *intermittent* contact with a subsurface object that *may* have been a submarine. In fact, your unauthorized use of active sonar proved conclusively that the last contact was most definitely not a US Navy submarine," he shot back.

"It was a decoy," Kai sputtered, but Mao turned away, a superior look of disdain on his patrician features.

It didn't matter what Mao thought. Kai was right, and he knew he was right. He was so sure that last night he'd drafted another message to his chain of command and sent it off without Mao's approval.

He was justified in going around the political commissar. His superiors needed to know that the secrecy of their weapons testing might already have been compromised. For almost two months, he'd been telling them that there was an enemy submarine in the area, and they hadn't believed him. But now, finally, he knew the identity of the submarine. There was no way that the port visit of the *Illinois* was a coincidence. That was the submarine he had been tracking.

He wondered what the captain of the *Illinois* was like. He knew that American submarines didn't have political officers on board. For them, the word of the commanding officer was final—no second-guessing, no meddling.

That must be nice, he thought.

Still, he wondered why he had not received a reply to his urgent report. To be honest, Kai felt like he deserved a commendation for his dogged pursuit of the truth. But he'd settle for an acknowledgment. He wondered if they were waiting to mention his discovery at today's briefing. *That* would be a just comeuppance for Mao.

He surveyed the audience. Most of the three dozen people in attendance were commanding officers and their political counterparts, like he and Mao, but there was also a sprinkling of civilian engineers and technocrats.

A call to attention rang out from the back of the room. Everyone rose to their feet and Rear Admiral Chin, Director of PLA Navy Weapons Testing, walked to the lectern next to the projection screen.

Waddled was more like it, Kai thought. Chin was a large man, with a belly that strained against the fabric of his summer white uniform. Despite the air conditioning, his round face was bathed in sweat. The fleshy folds held what Kai guessed was a permanent scowl. A pair of black, beady eyes scanned the audience.

"Take seats," he barked.

Despite his prickly personality, Rear Admiral Chin knew how to deliver a professional briefing. Using a projected image of the South China Sea, he quickly outlined the live-fire test.

Kai was surprised to see that the test would be conducted to the north and east of Hainan Island, well away from the shipping lanes. The test barge containing two Hu Jing torpedoes—a primary and backup unit—would be located 180 nautical miles southwest of the target, which would be set adrift in deep water a few hours before the test.

Chin scanned the audience for questions, then put up a slide that read: Security Measures.

Kai sat up straighter in his seat. This is where they would announce his discovery of the enemy submarine.

Chin described the plans to release a public announcement, called a Notice to Mariners, a week before the exercise to warn commercial shipping away from the test area.

"When the warning to navigation is released," Chin stated, "it will be the first time the world will hear about the Hu Jing torpedo. We must be on our guard to keep enemies of the Chinese State away from this test."

Wait, Kai thought, the Americans already knew about the torpedo. They had seen at least one of the previous tests. He raised his hand.

"Put your hand down," Mao hissed.

But Chin had seen the movement. He swung around until his belly faced Kai. "Yes, Commander? You have a question."

Kai stood. "Commander Kai Jun, Captain of the *Changcheng* 346, Admiral. I reported an American submarine in my patrol area a few days ago. I believe they have been monitoring our previous tests."

A ripple of irritation crossed Chin's fat face. "I've seen your report, and we are unable to corroborate your theory. Our intelligence service has deemed your report without merit."

Kai felt a hot flush creep up his neck as the other commanding officers stared at him. "But, Admiral—"

"That will be all, Commander."

Kai dropped into his chair. Mao looked away with an expression on his face that Kai could not read. Anger, disgust, or maybe just pity.

He stared at the screen without comprehending what he was seeing. He heard the name of his submarine being called. He forced himself to focus.

The screen showed a ring of surface ships forming a semicircle around the launch platform, then another inner ring of three submarines. He searched for his ship and could not find it. His eyes traveled up the screen to the target hulk, then beyond. Finally, he found the *Changcheng* 346.

Almost one hundred kilometers past the target was a ring of pickets: three surface ships and his submarine. Their job was to make sure that stray surface ships did not wander into the test area. They were babysitters. Kai felt like he'd been punched in the gut. The only way he could be farther from the action was if his ship stayed in port.

This has to be a mistake, he thought. His ship deserved to be part of the protection detail around the launch platform. That was where the American submarine would be. He needed to be *there*.

Kai started to raise his hand, but Mao clamped a hand on his wrist.

"Don't," he snapped. "Haven't you done enough damage already? Do you want to get us both court-martialed?"

Kai shook off his grip but kept his hand down.

So that was it. He was being punished for telling his chain of command the truth that they did not want to hear. He stared at his shoes, his face burning anew.

The rest of the briefing passed without Kai hearing a single word. A voice called the room to attention, and he stood mechanically. Rear Admiral Chin stomped out and the meeting broke up.

Kai sat back down. The room emptied until only he and Mao remained.

"Are you happy now?" Mao asked, acid in his voice.

"It was the truth, I know—"

"Are you really that naïve, Jun?" Mao used his first name to jolt Kai out of his stupor. Kai looked up. Mao's normally calm face was alive with anger.

"Are you that determined to ruin your reputation—and mine?" he snarled. "Can you not think for just one second about how your actions will impact others? Did it ever occur to you that that fat fuck didn't want to hear that an American submarine has been present the whole time they've been testing the new weapon?"

"But—"

"But what?" Mao thundered, on his feet now. "What is he supposed to do with that information? Does it change anything? No, it just makes him look bad to his boss." He leaned in until Kai could feel the man's breath on his face.

"Instead of being right, learn how to be effective, *Captain*."

Kai felt the insult in the words as surely as if he'd been slapped. He stormed to his feet. "I'm going to see Admiral Chin."

Mao looked at him with undisguised pity. "No, you're not."

"You can't stop me!"

Mao bared his teeth in a tight smile. "I can and I will. If you attempt to see Rear Admiral Chin, I will see that you are relieved of duty."

Kai felt his stomach drop. Could Mao do that? He wasn't sure, but he also didn't want to try it.

A surge of fresh anger consumed him. It was always the same in China. Mao was connected. Friends in high places, cousins and relations everywhere, while Kai had nothing but hard work and love of his country. His fists went tight; his body trembled.

Mao saw the reaction, raised an eyebrow as if taunting him. The air between them sang with Kai's anger.

Mao cocked his head like he was looking down at a dumb animal. You are nothing, his look said to Kai.

"Good day, Captain."

The political officer spun on his heel and stalked away.

26

Cagayan Port, Mindanao, The Philippines

Commander Mike Ferrell, captain of the USS *Kansas City*, studied the three men seated in his wardroom. The situation he found himself in was so strange as to be surreal.

Fifteen minutes ago, he'd been going about his morning in-port routine. He liked to spend at least an hour touring the ship, keeping up on maintenance and making sure his crew knew that the Old Man was watching. At thirty-nine, he certainly didn't feel old, but when he thought about his small crew—average age of twenty-three—he knew he seemed ancient to them.

Midway through his tour, he'd been summoned to the quarterdeck to meet visitors who refused to give their names to the petty officer on watch. Annoyed, Ferrell made his way down to the hangar underneath the main deck. The quarterdeck watch pointed out three men waiting at the bottom of the ramp that connected the hangar to the pier.

Although he'd never met them in person, Ferrell recognized two of them by sight. Major General David Holahan would have looked like a Marine if he was dressed in a gorilla suit. The Director of Operations for the US Indo-Pacific Command had a ramrod straight posture, a high-and-tight haircut, and wore his civilian clothes like a uniform. Rear Admiral Rob Beer, N3, Director of Operations for the entire Pacific Fleet, stood next to Holahan. Both men wore polo shirts and chinos, more suitable for the golf course than a visit to a US Navy warship.

Ferrell paused, not sure what to do. A visit from two flag officers to his command was cause for days of cleaning and briefing all the way up his chain of command. And yet they were here. On his quarterdeck. In civilian clothes.

"At ease, Ferrell," Holahan called, holding out his hand as he climbed the ramp. "We're just a couple of civilians looking for a tour."

"A tour, sir?" Ferrell shook the proffered hand, then shook Beer's hand as well.

"Maybe we could take this inside, gentlemen?" said the third man, who had not introduced himself. "And we'd prefer our names were not listed in the ship's log, Commander."

Ferrell cut a look at the senior officers, who nodded.

"Understood." Ferrell led them into the hangar deck past the hull of an unmanned surface vessel that was the heart of the mine countermeasures mission package. The rest of the MCM was stored in shipping containers. He noticed the senior officers eyeing the installation and wondered if they'd ever been aboard an LCS before.

He sighed to himself. The littoral combat ship development program was long considered a black eye for US Navy procurement.

Divided into two hull variants, one a traditional steel monohull and the other an aluminum trimaran hull, which included the USS *Kansas City*, the ships were envisioned to be high-speed, high-maneuverability platforms, able to operate in shallow water and equipped with modular mission packages that could be loaded on and off as needed.

On paper, the platform addressed a long-overdue need for the United States Navy. A low-cost, easy-to-maintain platform, with superb mission flexibility. The reality was much different. Cost overruns, design flaws, and a failure to develop the necessary mission modules created a fleet of almost thirty ships with an uncertain future.

The *Kansas City* was armed with mostly defensive weapons. Against air attacks or any enemy platform larger than a small destroyer, the ship was outgunned.

For all its flaws, Ferrell loved his command. There were issues, but there were issues on every warship he'd ever served on. It was easy to criticize without understanding first. The *Kansas City* was by far the most maneuverable and fastest warship he'd ever had the pleasure of piloting. Still, even Ferrell could see that the LCS was a ship in search of a mission.

Ferrell snagged the arm of a passing petty officer. "Hellmann, find the XO and have him join me in the wardroom ASAP."

The young man eyed the visitors. "Aye-aye, sir."

Ferrell showed his guests into the wardroom. "Coffee, gentlemen?"

The two flag officers accepted, but the third man asked for a club soda. Ferrell sent out to the mess decks for the drink.

The man finally introduced himself as Harrison Kohl, but didn't elaborate beyond his name. Kohl was medium height with a slight build. He wore his graying hair short and his cheeks had a few days' worth of stubble. It didn't look like Kohl was getting much sleep.

Definitely not military, but Ferrell noticed how the two senior officers seemed to defer to him. CIA, he decided, which piqued his interest. What did the CIA want with his ship?

Lieutenant Commander Carlston McKenzie arrived, and introductions were made. McKenzie was a six-five Minnesota kid who looked younger than his thirty-four years and had somehow retained an aw-shucks sense of wonder at his place in the world.

The XO's eyes widened when he realized who their visitors were.

"Sorry about all the cloak-and-dagger stuff, Commander," Holahan began, "but we've been tasked to deliver orders in person about a highly classified operation." The Marine couched his words carefully.

"Of course, sir," Ferrell said, his voice neutral.

"In the next twenty-four hours," Holahan continued, "you will receive orders to lead a small surface action group on routine maneuvers. You will be the SOPA over the USS *Oakland* the USS *Mobile*."

Ferrell sat up straighter. The LCS was normally tasked as part of a larger group of surface ships, commanded by more senior officers. Acting as senior officer present afloat in command of his own surface action group was a first for him.

Admiral Beer unfolded a chart on the table. He rested his finger west of Palawan Island, a long, thin piece of land that served as the westernmost boundary for the Philippines' home islands. Beyond Palawan were the Spratly Islands, the most contested bits of land in the South China Sea.

"We want you operating in this area. You can expect the normal complement of Chinese ships—Navy, Coast Guard, and the fishing boat militia. We want them to get a good eyeful of you, but stay away from the Chinese-claimed areas. Don't do anything to provoke them." He cut a look at Kohl. "Yet."

"Yet?" Ferrell repeated.

Holahan picked up the narrative. "While at sea, you're going to receive orders to escort a Philippine resupply mission to Second Thomas Shoal."

"Okay," Ferrell said carefully, keeping his expression neutral.

For the last twenty years, the Chinese had systematically occupied small atolls in the Spratly Islands, all claimed by the Philippines and well within their two-hundred-nautical-mile exclusive economic zone. Over time, the Chinese turned the bits of reef into reclaimed islands, dredging harbors, building airstrips, and erecting barracks. Today, these former atolls were fortified military bases, armed with surface-to-air missiles and bristling with radars.

Despite rulings by international courts and centuries of precedent, Beijing now claimed the islands and the surrounding waters as Chinese territory—and asserted their right to defend that territory. It was the major source of tension in the region.

Except at Second Thomas Shoal.

On that scrap of land, the Philippines had given the Chinese a taste of their own medicine. In 1999, the Philippine Navy intentionally grounded a World War II–era US Navy amphibious landing support ship on the reef. The *Sierra Madre* now served as a lookout post for the Philippine Navy, with rotational crews keeping an eye on their Chinese neighbors.

As tensions mounted between China and the Philippines over claims to the Spratlys, the Chinese had grown increasingly aggressive toward the routine resupply missions to the *Sierra Madre*. It was now common for the

Chinese to harass the Philippine Navy with water cannons and ship-on-ship contact, known as shouldering.

To date, the US Navy had offered only diplomatic support against the Chinese aggression. Apparently, that was about to change—and Ferrell was the tip of the spear.

"An operation like that is bound to provoke the Chinese, sir," Ferrell probed.

"Agreed," Holahan replied in a matter-of-fact voice, and Ferrell noted the faint smile. "The Chinese will not be happy, Captain."

Beer interjected. "You'll have airborne support from two Poseidon maritime patrol aircraft as well as high-flier UAV coverage. In addition, the USS *Carl Vinson* will be transiting the Strait of Malacca. Her strike group will be about five hundred miles south of you, but her air wing will be on alert."

"That's a lot of firepower, sir," replied Ferrell cautiously. "What level of resistance can I expect from the Chinese?"

"Assume the worst," Beer said with a thin smile. "This resupply mission is of critical importance. It must go through, Captain. We're counting on you."

Ferrell remained silent, looking back and forth between the two senior officers. He knew a setup when he saw one and this plan smelled. There's a reason they're called orders, he told himself.

Ferrell hesitated. "Can I ask why now, sir?" The question bordered on impertinent, but he was the one going toe-to-toe with the Chinese fleet.

The two flag officers looked at Kohl, who did not seem perturbed by the increased attention. "I understand these ships are fast, Captain."

Ferrell got that surge of pride he always felt when someone complimented his command. "Fastest thing on the water, sir. We can do over forty knots flat out."

"Good," Kohl said. "Your operating area is a hundred miles away from Second Thomas Shoal. When you get the call to escort the Philippine resupply mission, I want you to haul ass. I want you to bear down on the Chinese like the hounds of hell."

Ferrell grinned in spite of himself. "You want us to make a real statement."

Kohl returned the smile, but it was cold. "Absolutely. I want the phones in Beijing to ring off the hook. I want the Chinese defense minister and the foreign minister to collectively shit themselves. Can you do that, Captain Ferrell?"

Ferrell's grin got wider. "I can, sir."

"Standard rules of engagement apply, Ferrell," Holahan added.

"We're done here, gentlemen," Kohl said. "Thank you for your time, Captain. Remember: hounds of hell. When I give the word, I want every eyeball in the South China Sea on you and what's going on at Second Thomas Shoal."

Minutes later, Ferrell and the XO watched the three men stride down the pier.

"Who was that Kohl guy?" McKenzie asked.

Ferrell sighed, then punched the XO's beefy shoulder. "If I told you that, Carlston, I'd have to kill you."

27

Lingshui, Hainan Island, China

"I can't do this," Chang Han said when Angelina-Marie opened the door of the hotel room.

It was raining outside and the man was soaked to the skin, his dark hair plastered flat against his scalp. Beyond his bedraggled state, he looked undeniably terrible. Dark circles under his eyes and sagging shoulders spoke of a man who'd not had a good night's sleep in weeks.

She took him by the arm and gently guided him inside the room. She pointed at the bed. "Sit."

He followed her command, leaning forward with his elbows on his knees, head hanging down. "The ship sails tomorrow. The weapons are already loaded." His voice cracked and she thought he might start weeping. "I don't think I can do this. I want out."

Angelina-Marie got a towel from the bathroom and handed it to him. "Here. Dry yourself off."

As he listlessly ran the towel over his wet hair and face, she busied herself arranging the takeout food from a nearby restaurant. Rich smells filled the small kitchen area.

She went back to the bed and put a hand on his shoulder. "Come and eat something."

"I'm not hungry."

"When was the last time you ate a real meal?"

Chang shrugged. Angelina-Marie pulled him to his feet and steered him toward the table. Not knowing what he liked to eat, she'd overbought. There was a local soup, a spicy crab dish, moo shu pork, and a burger and fries.

Chang sat down and started eating the soup. "It's good," he said. "Thank you." The genuine appreciation in his voice was unmistakable.

Angelina-Marie got two beers from the fridge and sat across the table from him. "You need to take care of yourself, Han." She kept her voice gentle but firm. "If you act like a crazy man, someone will take notice. We don't want that."

Chang, still bent over his soup, nodded. He reached out and snagged a handful of fries. "I'm sorry," he mumbled.

The food seemed to be having a positive effect on his blood sugar and his mood. Angelina-Marie breathed a sigh of relief. "How are you sleeping?"

Chang stopped chewing. "Is that supposed to be funny? I'm committing treason. How do you think I'm sleeping?" The edge of panic was back in his tone.

Don't react, she thought. Stay calm.

"I'll give you something to help you sleep," she said soothingly.

Chang lowered his eyes. "Sorry." He looked out the rain-streaked window, pondering. "I'll be fine. It's just...stressful."

This was going too fast, but she had no choice. Their time was up. He was leaving tomorrow and it was her job to get him ready.

This was their third and final meeting before Chang put to sea on the weapons test barge for the live-fire exercise. All three meetings had taken place in different hotels. Angelina-Marie selected locally owned, lower-class establishments that catered to people traveling on a budget—places that would accept cash and were less likely to have working surveillance equipment.

Long meetings like this one were a risk, but she needed uninterrupted time to interview and prepare the guidance systems engineer for the task ahead. If they were discovered, their cover story was that they were having an affair and trying to keep it on the down-low, hence the shabby accommodations.

In the first meeting, she'd interviewed Chang extensively on the guidance system software, asking him to reproduce as much of the code as he could from memory and explain the software architecture. Then she went through the procedure of downloading instructions to the Hu Jing torpedo. The process was straightforward: just before the torpedo was loaded into the tube, a laptop, connected to the weapon by an umbilical, was used to input and download final launch parameters. On an actual submarine, the combat systems computers would do that automatically, but this was a testbed.

The torpedo was assigned a heading and a runtime. When the initial run was complete, the weapon entered a predetermined search pattern. After a set period of time, if the target was not detected, the torpedo executed another high-speed run on a new heading, then slowed and repeated the search pattern. The process repeated until the weapon either found the target or ran out of fuel.

Modern torpedoes were connected back to the launch submarine platform by a wire through which the weapon could be steered or the parameters updated. Because of the high-speed rocket motor and the distances, there was no wire guidance capability on the Hu Jing. Once the weapon was launched, there was no way to recall it or to change parameters.

That was the flaw in the system that they wanted to exploit.

For the past two weeks, Chang reported that his boss had begun practicing final weapons parameter uploads on a dummy torpedo. Gang Wei was obsessed with making sure that their part of the test went flawlessly, and he insisted they practice every single day.

Here was where they got their first big break. His boss had decided that Chang was to do the data input for the torpedo testing. Angelina-Marie had been racking her brain for a way to get Chang into the driver's seat for the test, but she needn't have worried. Han's boss had done it for her.

In their second meeting, Angelina-Marie had a list of detailed follow-up questions and spent hours walking through every detail of the download procedure to the point where she probably could have performed the exercise herself. At the end of the long night, Chang asked her the obvious question: If they're watching me, how am I supposed to input phony launch parameters?

She didn't have an answer for him then, but she did now.

She let him finish his beer as she cleared the food away and set up their dummy laptop. She ordered Chang to walk her through the download procedure, mentally checking off the steps in the process.

Chang looked up at her. "Now what?"

Angelina-Marie went to her purse and pulled out a Huawei mobile smartphone. "This is your new phone, Han."

Chang turned it over in his hand. "It looks just like my phone."

And it was, right down to the scratch on the right corner and the chip out of the protective glass. The icons on the home screen were all arranged exactly the way his old phone was set up and the data was already synced.

Angelina-Marie took his old phone and slipped it into her purse.

"Open up the photos app," she said. "The pinned photo is a picture of Cassie. Click on it, then close the phone and put it in your pocket."

Chang did as he was told.

"Now, I want you to go back to the torpedo download procedure."

Chang returned to the launch parameters input screen and cleared the data.

"Enter the data normally."

Chang typed in a heading and a runtime for the high-speed torpedo and hit return. The computer screen cleared, and a dialogue box appeared that read, *Ready to upload?*

Angelina-Marie pointed at the top of the screen. "Click on the battery icon."

After Chang followed her instructions, she said, "Now go back to the launch parameters screen."

Chang hit the back button. The parameters were all different. He sat back in the chair. "What just happened?"

"Your phone overwrote the launch parameters," Angelina-Marie said.

"You mean there's spyware on my phone? What if someone finds it?"

"They won't find anything," Angelina-Marie said.

Chang looked doubtful. His face folded into a frown.

"My people know what they're doing, Han," she said, her voice slipping back into a soothing tone. "Someone could tear this phone apart and they wouldn't find anything wrong with it."

Probably a lie, but she needed to stop him before Chang spiraled down another mental rabbit hole.

She plucked the phone from his hands and called up his daughter's picture.

"Look at her," she ordered. "I want you to really see her. She is your North Star. She is the reason why you're doing this. When you're out there in the torpedo room on the test barge, you're going to call up this picture.

"Once you click on Cassie's picture, the transmitter stays on for five minutes. That's it. Once the test is over, you can throw the phone overboard for all I care."

Chang stared at the screen with his daughter's picture. Angelina-Marie noticed he was starting to breathe faster. She slid her arm around his shoulders.

"Close your eyes, Han," she whispered.

He stared as if he hadn't heard her.

"Close. Your. Eyes." Gentle but firm.

He slammed his eyes shut, breathing faster now.

"Deep breath," she said. "Deeper...Now hold it...Let it out slowly." She did the same. "One more time."

The rigidity in his shoulders softened.

"Good," she said. "Now, I want you to picture being in the airport in Vancouver. Cassie is waiting for you. Can you picture it?"

Chang nodded.

"She sees you. Her face lights up. She's so happy to see her father. She runs to you and gives you a big hug."

Chang's shoulders started to shake. Tears leaked out of his eyes.

"Open your eyes, Han."

Cassie's picture. He stared at his daughter's image.

"Better?"

Chang nodded.

"Good," Angelina-Marie said with a stern note in her voice. "Now, let's run the procedure again."

28

Maconacon Port, The Philippines

From his vantage point on the bridge of the SS *Arrogant*, Claude Buettner watched the supply barge head back to the dock. The sound of Helen shouting profanity-laced directions about where to store the supplies floated through the open window.

Claude had no idea where she was going to store that much food. They'd taken on enough supplies to feed a small army for weeks. She'd figure it out. Lord knew she had enough manpower that she could remodel the ship if she chose to.

In Puerto Real, they'd taken on fifteen men and a mountain of equipment. Their cover story was that they were filming an underwater documentary about the vanishing ecosystem in the Philippines.

In reality, he'd taken on a squad of US Navy SEALs from SEAL Delivery Team One in Hawaii, three EOD technicians from Guam, and three US Navy salvage divers from Japan.

And all their equipment. SCUBA and closed-circuit dive systems, underwater cameras and lights. He noticed their wetsuits were 6mm material, overkill for this part of the world, unless you were planning to stay in the water a very long time. There were also at least two dozen sealed black

Pelican cases that immediately disappeared into the well between the twin catamaran hulls.

In Claude's view, they'd brought on enough gear and expertise to raise the *Titanic*. Twice.

For the last ten days, he'd been ordered to bolster their cover story by running daily dive excursions for his "guests." The passengers dove in three independent teams, each with their own gear and training routine.

What were they training for? Claude had no idea, and so far, no one had seen fit to clue him in.

So, he played skipper to a bunch of hyper-fit special operators who viewed their time on board his ship as a mini vacation.

That wasn't exactly true, Claude thought. The teams executed their daily training routine with focused professionalism, but once their work was over, they transformed into children. Extremely fit, ravenous children. The main deck of the ship now resembled a frat house, complete with weight sets, wrestling mats, and a grill that always seemed to have at least one steak on it. There were endless push-up contests, arm wrestling every hour on the hour, and round-the-clock practical jokes.

When his guests were off duty, Claude felt more like Mr. Conductor of the Greater PI Booze Cruise than a highly trained clandestine operator of a covert CIA vessel.

He tried to cut them some slack. They were never destructive and never put his ship or crew in physical danger. He knew they needed to blow off steam to stay sharp for their mission—whatever it was—but his patience was not bottomless.

And the food. It seemed to evaporate whenever they were around. If they weren't training, they were eating. After only a week at sea, Claude had to put in a request to resupply, which was why they were in Maconacon now.

Helen appeared in the doorway of the bridge.

"That's the last of it, Captain," she said. "I don't know where we're going to put it all, but at least we've got it on board."

Claude sighed. "The way these animals eat, it won't last long."

"Buck up, little buckaroo." Helen punched him on the arm. "Isn't it nice to have some new blood on this tub of ours? You feelin' your age there, old man?"

"Bite me."

Helen gave an exaggerated hair toss. "You're old news, Claude. I can have my pick of the fleet down there."

They laughed together. They both knew Helen had about as much interest in the gun show on the main deck as she did in collecting rocks. Something out the window of the bridge caught her attention.

"Heads up, Skipper. Looks like we've got an inbound."

Claude picked up the field glasses. A banka, the local name for an outrigger, was approaching the *Arrogant*. About five meters long and equipped with an outboard, these boats were common in the small port towns around the region.

Claude focused on the lone passenger. He stood in the bow, one foot on the gunwale, with a pose like George Washington crossing the Delaware. A white guy in the tourist uniform of green cargo shorts, Hawaiian shirt, sandals, ball cap, and Ray-Bans.

"Not another one," Claude muttered.

"He's not bunking with me," Helen said as she left the bridge.

Claude hustled down to the fantail, arriving just as the banka drew up to the *Arrogant*'s stern. The passenger, carrying a backpack and a small duffel, deftly stepped from the moving boat to the teak freeboard deck at water level. He waved to the pilot as the water taxi motored away.

He offered Claude a casual salute. "Permission to come aboard, Captain."

"What if I say no?" Claude asked.

The man removed his ball cap to reveal a full head of sandy-colored hair that touched his ears. He scratched his three-day growth of gray stubble. "Well, it's a helluva swim back to shore, but I reckon I could make it."

"Come aboard," Claude grumbled.

The man mounted the ladder with a light step. He removed his sunglasses and held out his hand. "Bill James. You must be Captain Claude."

Claude shook the man's hand. "Claude Buettner, Bill. They tell me I'm in charge, but..."

"My kids giving you trouble?" Bill's gray eyes sharpened.

Before Claude could answer, he heard one of the SEALs exclaim, "Wild Bill's here, guys!"

Bill slapped him on the shoulder. "Don't let the call sign fool you, Claude. I'm a reasonable guy, I swear. Hey, let me say hi to the fellas. Can we regroup in ten?"

"I'll be in my cabin."

As Bill James waded into a melee of back slaps and fist bumps, Claude caught the arm of one of the operators. Johnny Bravo, so nicknamed for his spiky blond hair, turned around.

"'Sup, man?"

Claude nodded at James. "Who's he?"

"Wild Bill? He's the CO of SDV Team One. Awesome dude. Total operator."

Claude was impressed. The unassuming, last-minute visitor was the commanding officer of SEAL Delivery Vehicle Team One, based in Pearl Harbor. The SDV teams specialized in delivering operators to target beaches from long ranges, often in unfriendly waters and using advanced platforms like minisubs.

Claude reassessed the situation. If the CO of one of the premier SEAL team units in the world was on board his ship, that was a huge deal. He was undoubtedly here to take operational command of their mission, whatever it was.

He hustled back to his stateroom and executed a quick cleanup before Bill arrived. Exactly ten minutes after he'd left the main deck, there was a knock at his door.

"It's open."

Claude held up his hands as the Navy SEAL entered. "Look, I didn't know—"

Bill cut him off. "I think I owe you an apology, Captain. My guys can be a handful. I told them to take it down a notch."

"Thanks," Claude said.

"Another thing," he continued. "I can see you're already short on berthing. The last thing you need is me throwing the plan into disarray. I'm a low-maintenance guy. I have a bivy sack with me and I'm happy to sleep on deck."

"Commander, I—"

James held up a hand. "It's Bill."

"Not Wild Bill?" Claude asked.

The SEAL offered a ghost of a smile. "That was a long time ago. I'll tell you the story once we get to know each other a little better."

"I'd like that."

"Enough chitchat, Captain," Bill announced. "You have new orders. Can I use your laptop?"

Claude passed him the computer. Bill logged into his email account, retrieved a classified message, and entered his identifier to allow the decryption program to run. He passed the laptop back to Claude.

Proceed north along the east coast of Luzon, then into Babuyan Islands for a chartered dive excursion. Maintain cover, loiter on NW side of islands. Report exact datum and status every 12 hours. DTF.

"Details to follow," Claude said with a tinge of bitterness. "I feel like a tour bus driver."

"Delta Tango Foxtrot," Bill said in a sympathetic tone. "I'm pretty sure my first wife wrote that at the bottom of her Dear John letter."

Bill sprang to his feet. "If you don't mind, Captain. I'd like to run some training exercises on my guys tonight. Can you stop to let us play at maybe two a.m.?"

"It depends," Claude replied. "What can you tell me about our mission?"

Bill grinned. "Captain, you wouldn't believe me if I told you."

29

Special Activities Center, CIA headquarters, Langley, Virginia

Harrison Kohl sensed the change as soon as he entered the Operations Center in the secure basement area. The air-conditioned space felt charged with the excitement of a pending operation. People sat up straighter at their workstations, looked more alert.

He knew that feeling. He'd lived those moments where he was part of a team, part of a critical mission. Finally, after months of planning and positioning, the moment had arrived.

It was showtime.

Michael Goodwin stood at the supervisor's desk directly behind a row of six workstations. The front of the room was dominated by a wall screen showing a large-scale view of the South China Sea. Michael, deep in conversation with Bob James, turned when he heard Harrison enter.

James looked as if he still hadn't gotten over jet lag from their whirlwind tour of Southeast Asia. Harrison had felt the same way a few minutes ago, but the energy in the ops center gave him a new sense of vitality. A not-so-subtle reminder to himself of how much he missed field work.

The pair looked mismatched. Michael was tall and dark-skinned with broad, muscled shoulders. James was thin and pale, stooped with fatigue. Harrison gave them both a nod in greeting.

"Sitrep, please, Michael."

"As of 0500 local yesterday, the target hulk was towed out of the shipyard. We're tracking them on an overwatch drone with occasional satellite imagery backup shots. We estimate it'll be in position by this time tomorrow."

"The torpedo launch platform?" Harrison asked.

"It left port yesterday afternoon under heavy escort. Angelina-Marie confirmed that our asset is on board. He has the phone with him and it's active. We can track it."

Harrison nodded.

"She said she drilled him on how to use it," Michael continued, "and he's set."

"How did she describe his mindset?"

Michael shrugged. "Nervous, determined, shitting his pants—pick your descriptor. It's a lot of pressure for an asset that hasn't been active that long. She's got him trained and in position. The rest is up to him."

So it is, Harrison thought, but Chang Han was just one link in a chain of events that had to go flawlessly for them to pull off this heist. If it worked, this one would go down in the top-secret history books as an unparalleled victory.

If it failed...Well, he'd worry about that when it happened.

"What's the window on the Notice to Mariners?" he asked.

"Live-fire testing will commence anytime between 0600 tomorrow through the rest of the week," James answered. "We're launching all the normal protests, but the Chinese are ignoring them, as per usual. They've been exceptionally aggressive about clearing the test area. Three PLA Navy destroyers are pushing any stray ships away from the area we believe will be the release point for the target hulk."

"The security around the launch platform is insane," Michael added.

He zoomed to the southeast of Hainan Island, down toward the Paracel Island chain. Dots of white on the screen became the bullet-shaped hulls of warships as the resolution sharpened. Harrison did a quick count and let out a low whistle.

"Eighteen surface ships?"

"Even if we wanted to monitor the launch platform directly," James said, "we'd never get within fifty miles of it."

"How many submarines?" Harrison asked.

Bob James grimaced. "Well... That's the tricky part. Three put to sea last week and there were at least two on patrol already, so five that we know about. My guess is that they'll concentrate them around the launch platform."

"Okay," Harrison said. "Show me our assets."

Michael called to one of the operators and the screen shifted again. Two blue dots showed up in deep water south of the Pratas Islands, north of the exercise area. Each blue dot had a small arrow pointing southward, an indicator of course and speed.

"The *Illinois* is in the lead, positioned about eighty miles north of where we expect the target hulk to end up," James continued. "The *Agamemnon*—that's the UK sub—is the other asset. She's there to guard Commander Everett's six o'clock and run interference, if necessary."

Michael shifted to the east where another blue dot nestled among the jumble of the Babuyan Islands in the waters above the main islands of the Philippines.

"*Arrogant* is on station. The teams are prepped and ready. We'll move her into position when the target hulk is cleared for action." Harrison's gaze lingered over the tiny dots of land that peppered the satellite image. Too many to count, each one an atoll or a bit of exposed reef in the turquoise sea.

"What about our Commander Ferrell?"

Michael called out again. The image shifted to the south and sharpened. Harrison could tell from the data at the bottom of the screen that they were getting a live feed from an overwatch drone. He was taking no chances with gaps in satellite coverage.

The hulls of three ships in an echelon left formation, white wakes streaming behind them, maneuvered around the southern end of Palawan Island.

"Commander Ferrell is playing his part like a champ," Michael said. "They're staying away from the Chinese-held islands, and so far, the

Chinese are watching from a distance. They've got a lot of hardware in the area. Let's hope they play nice when things heat up."

Harrison nodded. Understatement of the year. "What about the supply convoy?"

"The Philippine ships are ready to go, waiting north of Naval Station Carlito Cunanon on Palawan Island. The Philippine foreign minister and the US ambassador in Manila are standing by to call on the Chinese embassy to alert them of the Second Thomas Shoal resupply mission."

"Angelina-Marie?" Harrison asked finally. "What's her status?"

Michael checked his watch. "As of an hour ago, she was on a plane back to Sydney. We received a text from her with the requisite code word for all clear."

Harrison blew out a breath, feeling—and enjoying—the familiar tension in his stomach. The chessboard was set. The game was about to begin.

"Mr. Goodwin," he announced in a voice loud enough for all to hear. He saw cocked heads, straight backs. They knew what was about to happen.

"Sir," Michael replied, coming to attention. As a former naval officer, old habits die hard.

"Start the mission clock," Harrison ordered. "I want the ops center fully staffed around the clock and status briefings every six hours. Call me if anything changes. Once this thing kicks off, we're going to be busy." He grinned at Michael. "Let's go steal a live torpedo."

"Aye-aye, sir."

30

USS *Illinois*, 87 miles south of Pratas Island

"Steady on new depth one-five-zero feet, Officer of the Deck."

"Very well, Pilot," Lieutenant Taylor responded.

Janet listened to the exchange, trying to keep her impatience in check. She'd had commanding officers who snapped and snarled at their crew, insisting that everything happen *now, now, now*. She'd told herself time and again that she would not be that kind of CO.

But for the love of Christ, this was just taking too damn long.

"OOD, where's my message traffic?" Janet regretted the tone as soon as the words left her lips. Taylor's head snapped up. He motioned for the messenger to go to Radio.

"Sorry, ma'am," he apologized. "I'm on it."

Janet gave him a curt nod, hugged her arms tighter across her chest. She resisted the urge to pace. It was just nervous energy, but she was handling this all wrong. She knew that her team would look to her for cues about how to react. She needed to model calm and professional.

And that was hard, given her situation. Risky didn't even begin to describe what they were asking her to do: put her submarine in the path of a torpedo. A torpedo with a live warhead.

Harrison Kohl made assurances to her that they had a man on the inside. They knew the track of the incoming weapon and the warhead would be disarmed, but Janet wasn't born yesterday.

That was the *Plan*. But anyone who'd spent more than five minutes in the field knew that the *Plan* never survived first contact with the real world. The difference between success and failure came down to people and the actions those people took after the *Plan* went out the window.

Those people were Janet and her crew.

Nevertheless, she'd accepted the mission. Technically, she'd volunteered for the mission, but refusal never really crossed her mind. She knew better than anyone what a successful weapons test for the Chinese meant to US national security. Hell, that's why Harrison chose her in the first place. He *knew* she would never say no.

Where the hell was her message traffic?

"Captain," Lieutenant Commander Avery called from the central navigation plot, "I have the intel update coming through."

Janet strode to the horizontal plot in the center of the control room just as the display was updating with new information. Boxes representing their assigned waterspace appeared over the topographical display of the seafloor. Red triangles indicated PLA Navy surface ships. A bright red square indicated where they expected the target hulk to be released.

Avery indicated the row of four red triangles arranged in a loose semicircle around the target hulk. "It looks like this is their picket line. It's"—she paused to check the range—"about fifty miles north of the target."

Their waterspace assignment had been expanded to well inside the PLA picket line. "They've opened up new water for us, ma'am. It goes active at midnight."

Janet nodded. For the last two days, they'd hung back while the Chinese Navy sanitized their test area. Surface ships, with active sonars banging away, had run patrols back and forth. That action ceased at sunset and the ships were now on station for the live-fire exercise.

"How many PLA submarines are active?"

Avery made a face. "Three that they know about and probably two more."

"Let me guess," Janet said, "Intel has no idea where they are."

Avery shook her head. "They speculate that the subs are patrolling near the launch platform."

Janet puffed out her cheeks as she thought. Waterspace management for five submarines around a fixed point in the ocean would be a nightmare. No planner in his right mind would put a submarine in the path of the torpedo test, which made the restrictions even tighter. She could see patrol areas for three, maybe four units, which left at least one Chinese submarine unaccounted for.

She surveyed the screen. Thousands of square miles of open water. Would the Chinese assign a submarine to the picket line? She had to assume they would, which meant she had to be on her guard when she advanced toward the target hulk.

Janet took comfort from the fact that the *Agamemnon* was watching her back. If this mission turned out to be a success, she'd owe that skipper a nice bottle of scotch.

"Captain?" It was Taylor with the message tablet. "Sorry about the delay, ma'am. There's an eyes-only at the top of the queue."

The message, from mission control in Langley, was barely two lines long.

Illinois and Agamemnon authorized to move into position. Exercise extreme caution. Weapons free. DTF.

DTF. Details to follow. Rapidly becoming her least favorite acronym in the world.

Those two simple lines directed Janet to take her multi-billion-dollar submarine and 119 souls into the belly of the beast. Into the path of a live torpedo.

"Officer of the Deck," she called.

"Captain."

"Rig ship for ultra quiet. Make depth five hundred feet, speed five knots, new course one-eight-zero."

She listened to the repeat back and watched her crew execute the same maneuvers they'd done a thousand times on this long deployment.

Quiet, competent, professional.

She got that swell of pride in her chest again. That mental reminder to savor this moment. Right here, right now. This moment might be the apex of her professional life experience.

The deck angled down. "Rig ship for ultra quiet," sounded over the 1MC ship-wide intercom.

Janet walked over to stand behind Senior Chief O'Malley, who was standing watch as sonar supervisor. She didn't say anything; she didn't need to.

O'Malley turned in his chair, shifted the headphones off one ear. "If he's out there, I'll find him, ma'am."

Janet patted his shoulder, then left the control room. She entered her stateroom and lay down on her bunk, fully clothed. The intercom above her head was switched to the control room, the volume turned low.

Captain Janet Everett closed her eyes.

31

CNS *Shinyan*, 145 miles east of the Paracel Islands

1945 China Standard Time

Chang Han had worked for the Advanced Weapons Development lab for nearly five years. In that time, he'd been to sea six times and he'd never been seasick. Not even once.

But now, in the makeshift torpedo room of the *Shinyan*, his stomach did acidic somersaults. He covered his mouth and released another burst of sour gas. A fresh wave of sweat bathed his face.

Gang Wei, his boss, leaned close. "Are you feeling okay, Han?"

Chang attempted a weak smile. "Fine, sir."

Gang nodded, went back to listening to the test director, who was standing in the wide alley between the two massive Hu Jing torpedoes. In a few minutes, they'd do a final walk-through of the launch sequence.

The *Dahua*-class weapons testing ship had been designed to serve as an evaluation platform for new missile systems, radars, fire control systems, and guns. In other words, all things above the waterline of the ship.

Chang wrapped his arms around his aching midsection. Whoever decided that the *Shinyan* would make a good torpedo test platform was a sadist, he decided.

The designers had essentially removed the forward third of the ship's interior below the waterline and replaced it with a torpedo room. Instead of a bow-mounted sonar, the *Shinyan* now had a single torpedo tube the size and shape of a sewer pipe jutting into the water ahead of them.

The *Shinyan* had reached their destination just after the evening meal, which Chang had not eaten. Just the smell of food sent his stomach into spasms. The ship did not anchor. Instead, it rolled gently in the waves of the South China Sea.

Here, in the torpedo room, in the bow of the flat-bottomed barge, the mild rocking felt exaggerated to Chang. His vision swam as he tried to focus on Mr. Li addressing the group of engineers.

Chang rested his cheek against the cool skin of the Hu Jing torpedo. Even through his pain and stress, he still felt a deep sense of pride for this weapon he'd helped to create.

The Hu Jing was just over a meter in diameter and as long as a Hainan city bus. For the test, the two torpedoes were given stylized paint jobs. The one against his cheek had the image of a red dragon in motion, teeth bared, launching forward. The torpedo across the aisle had a similarly artistic tiger.

A young, enlisted man dressed in the PLA Navy underway uniform pushed through the knot of engineers to Mr. Li, handing the test director a folded note. When Li read the paper, his face drained of color. "He's coming here? Now?"

The messenger nodded.

Li clapped his hands. "We'll reconvene here in half an hour. Thank you all."

He pushed through the men toward the exit. As he passed, Chang followed in his wake, sprinting to the nearest head. He pushed open the door of a stall and vomited into the bowl.

He knelt on the floor of the bathroom, staring into his own sick. Hot tears burned his eyes. Why was this happening to him? Why now?

Get a grip, he told himself. You have a job to do. For Cassie.

Chang got to his feet, staggered to the wash basin and splashed cold water on his face. He barely recognized his reflection in the mirror. Dark circles under his eyes, hair limp and greasy, sallow skin. He pulled a bottle of motion-sickness pills from his pocket and poured out a handful. He chewed them.

Chang made his way topside, stepping into a breezy, cool evening. He leaned against the railing, letting cool air wash his overheated body. The chill on his skin felt good. His stomach was calm, finally. Maybe he just had to get it out of his system.

A sound reached his ears, a steady *chop-chop*, rapidly growing louder. The navigation lights of an incoming helicopter buzzed by the *Shinyan* fore to aft, then swung in a wide circle and approached the helo pad on the stern.

Chang made his way aft along the weather deck to find the rest of the test engineers gathered to watch the helicopter land. The aircraft touched down and the side door rolled open. A PLA Navy commander leaped to the deck, then immediately turned to help a heavyset man with the gold braid of an admiral on his epaulets descend to the deck.

Chang found Gang in the crowd. His boss wore a wide grin.

"Who is that?" Chang asked.

"Rear Admiral Chin," Gang answered without turning. "The admiral in charge of all weapons systems procurement for the entire Navy." Gang's voice had a wistful quality. "He's here."

Chang watched the man walk under the whirling rotors. He didn't stoop like most people did involuntarily, but that was probably because he couldn't bend at the waist. Behind him, the helo pilot increased power and the aircraft took off again.

Silence settled over the group as Mr. Li went out to greet his visitor. Chang could hear the man's voice saying how pleased he was that the admiral could find time in his busy schedule, blah, blah.

Chin's fat face was sweaty, making the deck lights shine on his skin. "I want to see the installation," he announced without breaking stride. Mr. Li followed in his wake without taking a breath in his running commentary. The rest of the engineers formed a long procession behind them.

When they reached the torpedo room, Chang was at the back as Mr. Li conducted the walk-through for the benefit of their new visitor. He had his laptop under his arm, ready for when Li called for him.

Chang had scouted the torpedo room as soon as he arrived on board.

The guidance system for the torpedo was just behind the blunt nose of the weapon. A rolling desk, where he would connect the laptop to the torpedo, was already in place. The silver umbilical cord used to connect his computer to the torpedo was coiled neatly on the desk.

Mr. Li indicated the floor between the two torpedoes where the group was assembled. "Beneath the deck, Admiral, is the transfer mechanism for the torpedo. The weapon is moved sideways onto the slide, then shifted forward." He pointed at the torpedo tube door. "Just before we load the weapon into the torpedo tube, we have to update the guidance data. That will be done by Engineer—"

Gang, who was standing next to Chang, raised his hand. "By me!" he shouted. Gang seized the laptop from under Chang's arm and pushed forward toward the admiral.

"Engineer Gang Wei, Admiral." Gang's voice was smooth, his smile confident. "Director of the Guidance System Development Team. I will be handling the pre-launch updates personally, sir." Dressed in a pressed short-sleeve shirt and dark pants, with his hair carefully combed, he looked every inch the competent technocrat. Even Rear Admiral Chin's fleshy face seemed to soften.

Gang led the admiral to the umbilical station, where he opened up the laptop. Chang watched in horror as his entire plan evaporated before his eyes.

Although Gang's demonstration lasted only a few minutes, it seemed like an hour to Chang. His boss returned to Chang's side, positively glowing with pride.

"That went very well," he whispered to Chang.

"But I was supposed to—" Chang began.

"Do you think I'm going to pass up this opportunity for face time with the *admiral*?" he said the word *admiral* like he was in church. "That man is in charge of tens of billions in spending every year. *Tens of billions.*" His eyes shone, then he seemed to see Chang for the first time. "You look a mess, Chang. Until you change your shirt, I don't want you to be seen by the admiral."

"But I did all the training," Chang tried again. "What if there is a problem tomorrow?"

Gang sneered. "C'mon. This is a few simple keystrokes. I've seen you do it a thousand times."

"But what about—"

Gang seized his arm and dragged him to the back of the torpedo room out of earshot of the briefing.

"I am in charge of the testing tomorrow. I will be the one in front of the admiral. Is that clear?"

Chang nodded.

"Good. Now, go get cleaned up before the admiral sees you. You're a disgrace."

Chang looked down at his shirt to see a line of dried vomit on the fabric. He left the torpedo room and, after fifteen minutes of searching, found his bunk. He got a towel and soap and went to the head. He stripped down, turned on the shower and stood beneath the spray of hot water.

His stomach felt fine now, but his heart raced, and his pulse hammered in his ears. He pressed his forehead against the stainless-steel wall of the enclosure.

Think, he ordered himself. Of all the scenarios he'd discussed with Angelina-Marie, they'd never thought of this one. What was he going to do?

Gang Wei was an ass-kisser and Rear Admiral Chin's backside was the most important ass in a thousand miles. There was no way he'd be able to stop Gang from running the guidance computer...

He fantasized about pushing his boss into the ocean. That wouldn't work, he reasoned. Someone might see him or realize he was gone. It needed to be more subtle than that.

He heard a toilet flush and the idea appeared in a flash. Chang turned off the water, grabbed his towel, and swept the shower curtain aside. A young man, his face puffy with sleep, stood in the middle of the room, scratching himself.

"Where's the infirmary?" Chang said.

32

USS *Kansas City*, 2 miles west of Canipaan Bay, Palawan Island, The Philippines
0445 China Standard Time

Commander Mike Ferrell, captain of the littoral combat ship USS *Kansas City*, could not sleep. Normally, he was lights out as soon as his head touched the pillow, especially at sea, where the gentle rocking of the waves and thrumming of the deck plates made for a drowsy combination.

He recalled a saying he'd learned as a midshipman: "When at sea, eat until you're tired, and sleep until you're hungry." It was a mantra he and his fellow mids tried to live by on their summer training cruises. Eventually, they'd all grown up and assumed their responsibilities in the world. Still, for Ferrell, he never slept better than when he was at sea.

But not this night.

At five minutes to five, he gave up the battle. He showered, donned a fresh uniform, and made his way onto the bridge. Lights of the instrument control panels and computer screens illuminated the faces of the watch-standers in the predawn gloom.

"Captain on the bridge." The messenger of the watch jumped to his feet when Ferrell appeared in the doorway.

"As you were," Ferrell said. He crossed the space and stood behind the Officer of the Deck, who occupied the pilot seat of the ship's controls.

The littoral combat ships were unlike any other ship in the United States Navy. On this modern bridge design, the OOD manned the helm and piloted the ship while the Junior OOD acted as an air traffic controller for the remaining thousand details of running a warship. The Readiness Control Officer, the equivalent of an Engineering Watch Officer on any other platform, manned a computer console in the rear of the large bridge space. Depending on the tactical situation, the other four computer workstations on the bridge could be manned. All were configured to be interchangeable between all the bridge functions: navigation, fire control, radar, engineering, and communications.

"Morning, Captain," said Lieutenant Jack Ryder, the OOD. On the center console next to his chair were four adjustable dials that represented the four engines of the ship. The *Kansas City* had no rudder. Instead, she used directional waterjet propulsors to change course and speed. The innovative design allowed the ship to literally do donuts in the ocean, if necessary.

A quick glance at the control panel told Ferrell all he needed to know. Only two of the ship's propulsors were operational and ganged together for normal steaming.

"Six knots to nowhere, sir," Ryder reported. "Steady on course zero-one-zero with *Mobile* leading the parade."

Ferrell walked the bridge slowly, greeting the watchstanders and checking the screens. The radar picture showed the *Mobile* five hundred yards ahead, the *Oakland* the same distance behind them. The only other contact in range was a container ship fifteen miles to the west.

He scanned the message traffic. At the head of the queue was the PLA Navy Notice to Mariners that had gone into effect at midnight for the next five days. The positioning of the live-fire exercise area was playing havoc with traffic in the shipping lanes. Just like the Chinese to treat the entire South China Sea as their personal playground.

The next message was from PACFLT, advising that a resupply mission to the *Sierra Madre*, the Filipino hulk grounded on the Second Thomas Shoal, was leaving port north of their position.

His JOOD was Lieutenant Junior Grade Jess Harper. He showed her the message. "Do you have a satellite track on this convoy?"

"I've got something better than satellite, sir." She called up the high-resolution video feed from the MQ-4C Triton, a US Navy version of the Global Hawk Unmanned Aerial Vehicle. "We have live coverage, sir."

The screen showed three ships in echelon left formation, plowing through a dark ocean. The large supply ship stood between a Philippine Navy frigate and a small patrol craft as escorts.

"What's the Chinese Coast Guard doing?" Ferrell asked.

The PLA Navy warships tended to stay out of the skirmishes around the contested areas in the Spratlys, leaving the job to the Chinese Coast Guard and fleets of fishing vessels that formed a sort of seaborne militia. Keeping naval combatants out of the mix made it much more difficult for the government of the Philippines to accuse the Chinese of open military harassment. By using Coast Guard vessels, the Chinese were able to claim they were protecting fishing areas or policing unsafe maritime practices. It was classic hybrid warfare, pressuring her opponents just below the threshold of military engagement.

Harper shifted the Triton's video image. "They're rolling out the welcome wagon. Four Chinese Coast Guard vessels against two Philippine Navy escorts and the resupply ship. Not good odds."

Ferrell stepped out onto the bridge wing. The cool morning breeze washed over his face.

Over the last year, the Chinese had been steadily ramping up pressure on the Philippine resupply missions. While the diplomats argued, the situation at sea got dicier. There had been close calls, including aggressive "shouldering," where a Chinese Coast Guard ship attempted to bump a Philippine ship off course. There was even an incident where Chinese "fishermen" boarded a Philippine fishing vessel, beat up the fishermen, then sank their boat in international waters.

Injecting three US Navy warships into this resupply mission was like playing with matches in a haybarn.

With what he'd seen on the screen, Ferrell figured the Philippine supply convoy was just under a hundred miles away. At top speed, his surface action group could be there in two hours and change.

The Philippine resupply mission consisted of a supply ship and two combatants: the *Juan Magluyan*, a patrol craft, and the frigate *Antonio Luna*. Together, these ships were no match for four modern Chinese Coast Guard ships. The situation as it stood now would give them no cause for alarm. The Chinese were used to having overwhelming force against the much smaller Philippine Navy.

But what was going to happen when three state-of-the-art US Navy warships joined the party? Five combatants to four Coast Guard ships were not odds that the Chinese were used to dealing with.

What happens then? he wondered. Would the Chinese back down?

He didn't think so.

The hazy horizon grew brighter and the sun breached the line between water and sky. Deep, molten orange promised a sweltering day on the ocean.

He borrowed a pair of binoculars from the lookout and spied on the *Oakland* to their stern. Ferrell half hoped Captain John Hibbard might be making his morning rounds. Hibs had been a year behind him at the Academy, and they'd been friends for years. He'd wanted to warn his fellow captains about the danger they might be sailing into, but the mysterious Mr. Kohl from the CIA had been explicit: He was to tell no one about their mission.

Ferrell tried to make up for it by pushing the three-ship SAG hard during the past week at sea. Close formation maneuvers, gunnery exercises, combined fire control drills. He knew if Hibs were standing next to him, he'd be giving Ferrell all kinds of shit about how the power of his SOPA designation had gone to his head.

The LCS platform was not designed as a heavily armed combatant. The original platform armament was primarily defensive in nature, including four .50 caliber machine guns, an eleven-shot SeaRAM point defense system, and a 57mm naval gun mounted on the raked bow of the ship.

In the past year, all three ships in Ferrell's SAG had been outfitted with the Naval Strike Missile package, their first and only long-range offensive weapon. Two NSM box launchers, each carrying four missiles, were installed behind the naval gun on the bow. The NSM gave the *Kansas City* and her sister ships the ability to strike targets up to a hundred miles away.

He swung the field of view across the horizon, coming to rest on the lead ship in the column. The USS *Mobile* had been in the region only two months. It was her new captain's first deployment.

He didn't know Commander Elizabeth French well—they'd only met a handful of times—but she seemed competent enough. Ferrell had known the outgoing captain of the *Mobile*, and he was a good leader. The crews on littoral combat ships were small, which meant that every man and woman on board needed to be on their game. The crew of the *Mobile* was solid. If Captain French trusted her crew, she'd be okay.

To his surprise, he saw the bridge door on the *Mobile* open and French stepped out. Like him, she held binoculars and scanned the horizon. As she turned toward him, Ferrell raised his arm in greeting. She returned the gesture.

Ferrell smiled to himself. He'd like to call up Hibs right now. Tell him to get his ass out of the rack and do his job. A brand-new captain was showing him up.

On that pleasant thought, Ferrell departed the bridge and went to the wardroom for breakfast. He ordered his usual: coffee, two eggs over easy, a pair of sausage links, and a side of rye toast. He switched on the radio and tuned it to stream Minnesota Public Radio. No matter where he was in the world, he liked to keep a connection to home. It made him smile to hear about drought conditions in the Arrowhead region while he was sitting in a monsoon in the Philippines.

Executive Officer Carlston McKenzie, his dark hair still wet from a shower, entered. "May I join you, Captain?"

Like him, McKenzie was a Minnesota native. He often wondered what the odds were of two guys from Minnesota becoming the CO and XO of a US Navy ship.

Ferrell dug into his meal, nodded his approval. The XO's usual breakfast order appeared less than a minute later. Three eggs, six sausage links, four pieces of toast, and a side of oatmeal.

"Where do you put it all?" Ferrell asked.

McKenzie grinned as he ran a hand down the front of his big-and-tall uniform. "This doesn't happen by accident, sir. You have to feed the beast."

Ferrell was still chuckling when he heard a knock at the wardroom door.

"Come," he called.

The messenger appeared, carrying a tablet. "Officer of the Deck sends his respects, Captain. P4 message for you, sir."

Ferrell took the tablet and dismissed the messenger. McKenzie eyed him as he unlocked the tablet. The message addressed to Eyes-Only, Commanding Officer USS *Kansas City*, was all of two lines.

At 0800 local, proceed to intercept and support PI resupply mission at Second Thomas Shoal. Max speed authorized. Rules of engagement apply.

"Is that what I think it is, sir?" McKenzie asked.

Ferrell locked the tablet.

"Finish your breakfast, Carlston. It's gonna be a long day."

Ferrell put a forkful of eggs in his mouth. They tasted like cardboard.

33

SS *Arrogant*, Iroo Island, The Philippines
0615 China Standard Time

Claude Buettner opened his eyes. Sunlight reflecting off the water played on the teak ceiling of his cabin. A gentle breeze, laden with moisture and salt, pulsed through his open window.

He sat up in bed. As a light sleeper, Claude had been woken before dawn every day since the SEAL team had arrived on board. His visitors were young and full of life. At every hour of the day or night, there were at least a few of them exercising or just grab-assing around his ship.

But this morning was calm, quiet. He sniffed the air. The grill wasn't even lit.

What the hell was going on?

Claude swung his feet to the deck and into a pair of waiting sandals. He snagged a polo shirt off a hook and pulled it on as he headed for the bridge.

The *Arrogant* rode lightly at anchor in a lagoon formed by a pair of atolls that curved together in the shape of a heart. Surf broke gently over black rock a hundred meters away. From the top deck, he could see giant trevally patrolling the edge of the reef and a school of yellowfin tuna cutting through the crystal-clear waters.

One of Bill's men was manning the bridge. He had Claude's field glasses in hand, scanning the horizon. On the chart table, a compact comms set showed an array of red lights.

"Morning, Captain," the man said brightly.

"Morning." He tried to remember the guy's name and gave up. "What's going on?"

"Wild Bill has me on comms watch. I figured I'd double as a lookout while I'm at it."

Claude grunted an acknowledgment, taking a closer look at the radio. Secure laser comms meant they either had a dedicated satellite link or there was an overwatch drone in the sky above them to act as a relay.

"Anything I can do for you, sir?" the young man asked politely.

"Where is everyone?" Claude asked. "It's so damn quiet this morning."

"I expect they're getting ready, sir."

"Getting ready for what?"

He smiled. "I wouldn't know, sir. You'd best talk to Wild Bill. I'm just a mushroom."

Claude stared blankly. "Mushroom?"

"They keep me in the dark and feed me shit." The kid delivered the quip with the joy of a preschooler telling a knock-knock joke.

"I guess I asked for that." Claude needed coffee, stat. The lookout's laughter followed him off the bridge.

When he walked out on the main deck, Claude had to pause to take in the view. The furniture was neatly stacked out of the way, leaving the full length of the *Arrogant* as a long open space. The Navy SEALs and the other operators were set up in three teams, each man bent over his gear. Apart from occasional murmurs of conversation, the space was as quiet as a high school study hall. Claude even heard a fish leap and then splash back into the water.

The long glass dining table had been relocated to the rear of the deck, close to the stern. Bill James had his hands on either side of a large military-grade laptop and he leaned in close, studying the screen. He looked up as Claude approached, his eyes bright.

"Captain, top of the morning to you, sir. I hope we didn't wake you."

"The silence is deafening," Claude deadpanned.

Bill chuckled. "Our attention is focused on the matter at hand. No time for horseplay when there's work to be done."

"So, today's the day?" Claude asked.

The SEAL commander shrugged. "That's not really up to us. We will respond as needed to an emerging situation."

"I see." Although Claude didn't really see anything.

"I am going to need your assistance today—"

Claude held up a hand. "Coffee first, Commander."

"Good call," Bill responded. "Drake!"

"Sir." A muscled young man stood up.

"Two coffees, please, young man. Black and bitter. And be sure to give Helen my best regards."

"Right away, sir." Drake hotfooted his way across the deck.

Claude rubbed a hand over his face. What the ever-loving *fuck* was going on? Yesterday, his ship was like *Animal House* afloat and today it was school in session with Wild Bill as the respected headmaster.

Drake was back with the coffee. Claude mumbled his thanks and sipped. Even the coffee tasted better this morning.

Bill swung the laptop screen so that they could both see it. Claude studied a high-resolution video image of the *Arrogant* at anchor in the lagoon. He looked up.

"You've got an eye in the sky."

Bill offered a tight smile. "We have considerable assets at our disposal for this operation, Captain." He expanded the field of view to show the western edge of the Babuyan Islands. Claude checked the scale of the image and saw he was looking at a twenty-mile stretch of ocean. At this scale, the *Arrogant* was a speck. The atolls and small islands looked like scattered bits of black ringed with pulsing white surf.

"I'm expecting a call this morning," Bill continued. "When we receive that call, I want to position a line of hydrophones along this axis." He used the cursor to draw a shallow arc facing away from the islands, toward the open South China Sea.

"Hydrophones," Claude said. "You're serious?"

Bill ignored the sarcasm. "I want to position them about one every two miles. I also have a few handheld jobs that we put over the side of the dive launch and this ship. Let's say we pre-position the dive launch here, the *Arrogant* here, and the zodiac here." Bill's finger touched the screen in three places.

"What zodiac?" Claude asked.

Bill jerked his thumb over his shoulder. Claude walked to the stern railing and looked down. A brand-new four-meter inflatable zodiac with an electric outboard was tied to the stern of his ship.

Behind him, Bill said, "We like to have options."

"Commander, when are you going to tell me what's going on?"

Bill gave him that irritating grin that told Claude he was not going to answer the question. But the man surprised him again.

"I'm not authorized to brief you on this mission, Captain. However, I assure you, you have enough open-source information in your possession to figure it out on your own." He held up his empty coffee cup. "Another?"

Claude nodded, handed his cup over. Drake leaped to his feet, but Bill waved him down. "I've got this one, young man."

The SEAL strolled away.

Claude stared at the computer screen, trying to puzzle out the problem. Bill wanted to set up a line of hydrophones, which meant he wanted to track a submerged object. What other open-source intel did he possess?

Then it hit him. There was a Notice to Mariners about a Chinese live-fire test. He closed his eyes, struggling to recall the details.

A SINKEX was starting today...a missile test? No, an underwater weapons test, so a torpedo.

He expanded the field of view on the screen, vaguely remembering the size of the exclusion area. It was at least a hundred miles away in deep water. Much too far for a torpedo to travel.

"Any questions, Captain?" Bill handed him a fresh cup.

Claude took it, still focused on the screen. "I assume with that many hydrophones, you're looking for some pretty big fish."

The Navy SEAL's eyes flashed with humor.

"We're looking for Moby Dick, Captain."

34

CNS *Changcheng* 346, 83 kilometers south of Pratas Island
0817 China Standard Time

Captain Kai Jun hunched over one of the monitors in the control room. He turned up the collar of his warmest sweater and tucked his hands into his armpits. All day long, he'd been unable to get warm.

At periscope depth, the room swayed gently. He closed his eyes, listening to the comforting sounds of the control room. *His* control room.

Kai had been a fighter all his life. Through grit and hard work, he'd risen through the ranks in the PLA Navy. Not a single thing in his career had been handed to him because of who his father was or what school he'd attended. He earned every promotion, every posting, every ribbon on his chest.

At every new assignment, he'd had to prove himself all over again. It wasn't enough to be good. He had to be better than his peers to get the same respect—and he'd done it over and over again. Willingly. Gladly. And those years of dedication paid off when he was awarded command of one of the People's Liberation Army Navy's finest submarines.

And for what? he wondered. For the first time in his life, Kai could not summon the energy to fight. For the first time in his life, he was beaten.

"You disrespected me and my position as your commissar, but I saved you," Mao said with venom in his voice, his sharp jawline tight with anger. "I saved your ass, Captain."

Kai opened his eyes again if only to dispel that shameful scene from his mind. The monitor in front of him mirrored the view from the periscope. The watch officer paused his sweep to focus on a thin line poking above the horizon to the west. He switched to high magnification and the line transformed into the superstructure of a Chinese warship.

The CNS *Zunyi*, one of the newest Type 055 destroyers, was flagship for the line of four picket ships posted fifty miles to the north of the target hulk. The job of the pickets was to ensure no enemy ships got near the target hulk, and to keep merchant shipping out of the live-fire area. They tracked every surface ship and aircraft on radar and hammered away with active sonar to scare off any submarines.

The water was so full of sound energy that it was difficult for his sonar team to do much of anything.

It was depressing to realize that his presence here was pointless. One of the finest submarines in the Chinese fleet relegated to guard duty.

Degrading, Kai thought, but that was probably the point. He'd embarrassed the admiral by implying that the security around the underwater test range was inadequate. Always the overachiever, Kai had even managed to embarrass the same admiral *twice*.

And for his troubles, he was on the sidelines of the most important weapons test in PLA Navy history.

I saved your ass, Captain. The political officer's words gnawed at Kai. The very idea that he owed anything to that self-satisfied prick made him want to scream.

"Captain." The voice of the watch officer roused him from his reverie. The man sounded tentative. Everyone around him sounded tentative. Did they really think that their commanding officer was that fragile?

"What?" he snapped.

The young officer handed him a tablet. "Message traffic received, sir. Request permission to go deep and resume our mission."

"Permission granted," Kai grated out.

Our *mission*, he thought darkly. Our *mission* is to sit around with our thumbs up our asses and bore holes in the ocean.

Kai scanned the first message on the tablet. It was a regurgitation of their orders. The *Changcheng 346* was to provide "escort duty" to the *Zunyi*. It made him want to gag. Escort duty?

He thrust the message tablet at the nearest body and stalked out of the control room. Entering his stateroom, he rested his back against the closed door. A great weight seemed to settle on his shoulders. He was exhausted.

Kai lay down on his bunk fully clothed and closed his eyes. The deck angled down as they went deep. Kai did not bother to check the indicators on the wall of his cabin. The watch officer could handle it.

For the first time in his career, he wondered if he should just resign his commission and go home. The thought was almost too much to bear.

A knock at the stateroom door. Kai sighed. The only person who would bother him now was Mao and there was no way he'd give that asshole the satisfaction of seeing him this low.

"I'm not in the mood, Mao," he called out. "Another time."

"It's not Commander Mao, sir," came a tentative young voice.

With an effort, Kai sat up and swung his feet to the floor. He drew a deep breath and straightened his spine.

"Enter." It came out much more harshly than he'd intended.

The door opened to reveal the messenger of the watch. The young man was probably seventeen, and so new on board that the only duties he was qualified for was to carry messages and get coffee.

His voice quavered as he delivered his message:

"Sir, the watch officer sends his respects. He requests your presence in the control room, sir."

"Why?" Kai snapped.

"I—I don't know, sir. Something on sonar, I think."

Sonar? Kai frowned. "I'll be there in a minute."

The messenger practically launched out of the doorway in his haste to get away.

Kai got to his feet and ran water in the wash basin. He avoided the face that stared back at him in the mirror. The face of a loser.

He splashed water on his face and combed his hair, then reentered the control room.

"What is it, Watch Officer?" he said, feeling his impatience bleeding into his voice.

"Captain, I know this is no longer part of your standing orders, but we've picked up the tonal again, sir."

"What tonal?"

"The same one we were tracking at the underwater test range, Captain."

Kai blinked at him. Not possible, he thought. This is some kind of cruel joke. But, in spite of his skepticism, he felt the weight on his shoulders shift ever so slightly.

"Show me," he ordered.

The sonar supervisor took over, calling up a screen that showed a frequency spectrum. The sonar computer processed all the sound in the ocean into discrete frequencies, displaying the results in a squiggly line that ran across the bottom of the screen, like the teeth of a saw blade. Every now and then, a spike poked above the line.

"We still have the old search parameters loaded into the system," the sonar chief said, "so we got an alert when this showed up." He scrolled backward until Kai could see a spike reaching above the noise and staying there.

"We had it for about five minutes, then we lost it in the baffles."

Kai put his hand to his face. He wanted to slap himself to prove that he wasn't dreaming, but he held back. Instead, he snapped his fingers. "Show me the last thermocline data."

The watch officer handed him the paper readout. Kai traced the line on the graph.

A layer at one hundred meters. His eyes cut to the depth gauge. They were at seventy-five meters.

"Give me an intercept course, Sonar, to put that frequency on our beam."

"One-eight-seven, Captain," the sonar chief replied immediately.

"Watch Officer," Kai said, "steer new course one-eight-seven, speed ten knots, and depth one-two-zero meters."

The control room sprang into action. The ship made a wide turn, angled down. Kai stood at the sonar display, waiting for the screen to update.

The door to the control room opened. Kai did not need to turn around to know it was Mao.

"Captain Kai." Mao was right behind him, his voice low and even. "Why are we headed away from the flagship? Our orders are to stay within underwater comms range of the admiral."

"Incorrect, Commander." Kai kept his eyes on the screen. He would not give the political officer the satisfaction of seeing his face. "Our orders are to escort the flagship, which means we are free to operate in our assigned patrol area to fulfill our duties."

"Captain," Mao said. Kai could hear the tension in the man's smug voice. "I *suggest* that we—"

"Quartermaster," Kai interrupted. "Are we operating within our assigned area?"

"Yes, Captain."

"Thank you, Quartermaster." Kai turned to face Mao. The man's dark eyes showed anger at the snub. Good, now you know how it feels, asshole.

"Your suggestions are noted, Commander. Now, please leave my control room. I have work to do."

He turned back to the sonar display.

"Towed array is stable, Captain," the sonar supervisor reported. "Gathering data now."

"Very well." His eyes locked on the squiggly line.

The USS *Illinois* was out there—and he was going to find her.

35

CNS *Shinyan*, 122 miles northeast of the Paracel Islands
1010 China Standard Time

Chang Han's hands shook as he opened the laptop computer on the worktable next to the massive Hu Jing long-range torpedo.

Behind him, his boss, Gang Wei, was telling an off-color joke to a gaggle of junior engineers. Chang had heard the joke before. It was the one Gang used when he wanted to seem like he was one of the guys.

Over the course of a sleepless night, he'd considered every possible option to convince Gang that he should allow Chang to upload the launch parameters to the torpedo. It was useless. His boss had a penchant for kissing up to his superiors and Admiral Chin was as senior as they came.

At 0500, as the new watch section was getting ready for the day, Chang went to the infirmary. He asked the corpsman on duty for a dose of magnesium citrate. The corpsman tried to give him a pill, but Chang insisted on the magnesium citrate because he knew it was a clear liquid.

He searched the mess decks for Gang, but his boss was sitting at a full table surrounded by other members of the test team. Gang saw him waiting and called him over.

"Are you eating breakfast this morning, Chang?"

"No, sir, I'm not hungry."

"Good," Gang replied. "I want you to go to the torpedo room and set up the workstation. I want everything perfect for the test."

"Yes, sir." Chang eyed his empty coffee cup. "Can I get you more coffee?"

Gang's eyebrows quirked up. "Thank you, Chang. That's very kind of you."

Chang reached for the cup, but one of the junior engineers grabbed it first.

"I'll do it, Mr. Gang. I'm getting more coffee already," he said brightly.

Chang just stood there, outstretched arm, hand empty, like an idiot.

Gang eyed him. "Was there something else?"

Chang shook his head and left.

In the torpedo room, the technicians were hard at work. They had removed the deck plates between the two torpedoes to reveal a hydraulic lift. They transferred the torpedo laterally, from the storage position to the center lift, then shifted it forward. The torpedo was now positioned along the centerline of the ship, in front of the open torpedo tube. Chang could see the backside of a technician doing a physical inspection of the tube.

He skirted the workers and made his way to the workstation at the front of the torpedo. It was a variable-height desk, with a power strip and a cradle holding the bulbous end of the umbilical cord that would connect the computer containing the launch parameters to the torpedo.

Behind him, Gang began telling another anecdote to a rapt audience. Chang knew his boss was a creature of habit. He drank two cups of coffee at breakfast, then switched to tea for the rest of the day. He only drank his tea from a large ceramic mug that he had purchased on one of his trips around the country. Also, he only drank a certain type of rare tea that was hand-picked by eunuchs and carried to market on specially bred yaks...or some such shit. Chang had been listening to the man bloviate for so long that he'd blocked the details out of his mind.

None of this mattered unless he figured out a way to put that laxative into his boss's tea. As he fiddled with the desk, inspiration struck.

Chang waited for a break in Gang's monologue. "Excuse me, sir."

Gang turned, annoyed that Chang had interrupted his flow. "What is it?" he asked in a brusque voice.

Gang looked every inch the competent professional. His white polo shirt gleamed, and his khakis were not only wrinkle-free but had a knife-edge crease. Chang, on the other hand, looked like he hadn't slept—which he hadn't—and appeared to be wearing the same clothes as yesterday, which he was.

"I'd like to adjust the desk height for your exact needs."

Gang's gaze shifted to the variable-height desk, and his face broke into a smile. "Good thinking, Chang. We want everything to be perfect."

He crossed to the desk. Placing the tea mug to the right of the laptop, he held out his hands as if he were typing. "Let's raise it about five centimeters."

"Yes, sir." When Chang reached for the controls, his elbow knocked over the mug of tea. The liquid splashed away from the laptop.

"You idiot!" Gang shouted. "That mug is very valuable. It was a gift from..."

But Chang wasn't listening. He snatched up the mug on the pretense of mopping up the spilled liquid with his handkerchief.

"I am so sorry," he said. "Let me get you more hot water, sir."

"Give me that." Gang reached for the mug, but Chang evaded his grasp, stepped around him.

"I was clumsy. Let me make it up to you, Mr. Gang." He half bowed as he walked away, mug in hand. There was a hot water station set up in an alcove just outside the temporary torpedo room.

Adrenaline flooded his veins, causing Chang's hands to shake so hard that he had to put the mug down for fear he would drop it.

Get a grip. He clenched his hands into fists.

The stainless-steel infuser lay at the bottom of the mug. He knew that Gang often refilled the mug without replacing the tea leaves in the infuser. Chang drew the clear plastic bottle out of his pocket. He had no idea what an effective dose was or how much he could put in without Gang tasting it. He dumped the entire bottle into the mug and filled it with water. He sniffed the tea. It seemed fine to him.

When he returned to Gang, he lowered his eyes as he handed him the mug. "I'm very sorry, sir."

Gang sneered at him, then turned back to a conversation with another engineer.

"Chang!" he snapped.

Chang stiffened, his heart racing. "Yes, Mr. Gang."

"Fix the desk. Up five centimeters."

Chang felt like he was going to faint. "Right away, sir."

Out of the corner of his eye, Chang watched Gang take a sip of the drugged tea and make a face. "The water on this ship tastes like shit," he said to the engineer, then started to talk about his special blend of tea.

Admiral Chin arrived in the torpedo room at 1130 with an entourage that included a still photographer and a videographer. The admiral's body was stuffed into a pressed dress uniform. The fat folds of his neck lapped over his tight collar.

Mr. Li, the test director, rushed forward to greet the VIP, gushing praise. Chin waved him away with a curt, "Proceed."

The mechanical team stepped forward. Two engineers ran through a checklist. It was all for show. The team had already been over the torpedo twice and a cleaning crew had polished the paint until it gleamed.

Chang checked his boss's face for any sign of discomfort and saw nothing.

The test director accepted the completed checklist, making a show of reviewing the document and affixing his signature.

Chang checked his phone. It was 1145.

"With your permission, Admiral," Mr. Li said. "We will download the final launch parameters into the torpedo and then load the torpedo into the tube."

Mindful of the camera, the admiral gave a grave nod for posterity. Everyone gathered around the desk where Gang stood. Chang touched the picture of Cassie, then pushed through the crowd to stand next to the desk. If Gang took ill at the last moment, he might still be able to salvage the situation.

Gang looked at him with a baleful glare. "Move."

"But, sir, you may need assistance with the program."

Gang's face flushed deep red. He put his palm on Chang's chest and pushed him back. He turned to the admiral. "Would you like to observe, sir?"

Chang was shunted aside unceremoniously as the admiral bellied up to the desk.

Gang wore his studious engineer persona as he spoke with the admiral. He tapped on the keyboard, then held his index finger up in dramatic fashion.

"The launch parameters are checked and entered, Admiral Chin. Do I have your permission to upload them to the weapon?"

Chin's fat face creased into a smile. "You may proceed, Engineer Gang."

Chang wanted to throw up. Gang was probably creaming his pressed khakis over the fact that Chin knew his name.

The finger descended.

Chang barely registered the rest of the test activities. The torpedo entered the tube, the door clanged shut. There was a lot of noise as the tube was flooded with seawater and pressure equalized with the ocean, then the outer tube door opened.

The test director had arranged for a big red ceremonial launch button for the admiral to push. There was a great pumping *WHOOSH* sound as the massive torpedo was forced out of the tube. Chang's ears popped.

A technician called out, "Torpedo booster on!" and a great cheer went up in the gathering. High fives, fist bumps. Even Admiral Chin smiled and shook the test director's hand.

Chang sagged against the bulkhead. He had failed. He would never see Cassie again. His stomach turned sour. All that risk, for what?

"Time to transition: sixty-three minutes," the technician announced.

In a little over an hour, the torpedo would switch to search mode, find the target, and explode.

36

USS *Illinois*, 98 miles south of Pratas Island
1215 China Standard Time

Lieutenant Commander Savarino reeled off the sonar contacts. There were four, all PLA Navy surface ships, the closest over eight thousand yards away. The rest were arrayed in a picket line to the southwest.

Janet cursed to herself. Surely the Chinese would have at least one submarine in the northern picket line to protect the live-fire test, but where was it?

She cut a look at Senior Chief O'Malley, who gave a slight shake of his head. If there was an enemy submarine out there, he hadn't found it.

The XO concluded his contact report. "Request permission to take the ship to PD and retrieve message traffic, Captain."

Janet rolled her neck, trying to release some of the tension. It felt like her shoulders were trapped in a vise.

To minimize their exposure while on station, the *Illinois* trailed an antenna capable of picking up VLF signals. The only problem with VLF was the slow transmission time, so messages were typically only a few characters long. XPD, the message they'd received thirty minutes ago, meant "proceed to periscope depth to receive message traffic."

In contested waters, there were a hundred ways a trip to periscope depth could go wrong. A high-definition radar might detect the exposed mast. In light seas, a passing marine patrol aircraft or a drone might see the feather of water left by the submarine's periscope. Even worse, the airborne asset might see the shape of the submarine in the crystal-clear waters of the South China Sea.

She leaned over the broadband sonar display as if searching for something her expert team had not detected in the noisy ocean, but there was no new information there. She gripped the edge of the console until she felt the muscles of her forearms quiver with the effort.

As if to emphasize the danger, she allowed the silence to lengthen and the tension to spike.

Janet straightened her spine, turning to face the watch team. Savarino was an expert ship handler, every bit as good as she, and Senior Chief O'Malley was in place as sonar supervisor. The ship's chief radioman joined them. This was her A-Team.

"This needs to be the fastest trip to periscope depth you've ever made," she said. "We are in enemy territory. I want the absolute minimum exposure time on any masts."

Savarino nodded. "Understood, ma'am."

"Radio," she turned to Chief Tyndale. "You have permission to query the satellite as soon as the mast is clear. I want the intel snapshot and that message that's waiting for us. I don't care about anything else."

Tyndale was an experienced hand. "Yes, Captain."

"Very well," Janet said. "XO, the ship is yours. Let's go get our orders."

"Aye-aye, ma'am." Savarino took charge. "Pilot, make your depth five-zero feet."

"Five-zero feet, aye, sir." The deck of the ship angled up slightly.

Savarino flipped a switch on his control panel. "Raising the photonics mast." Using the joystick, he began a slow rotation of the field of view.

The picture was dark, but as they drew near the surface, the color of the water lightened. The mast broke the surface, revealing calm seas, clear skies, and bright sunshine.

Janet cursed to herself. This was perfect weather for them to be spotted from the air.

"Scope is clear," the XO called out. Over the intercom, the chirp of surface search radars made Janet's skin crawl. She'd expected a lot of electromagnetic noise and she was not disappointed.

The XO made a deliberate 360-degree rotation. "No close contacts." He toggled the panel. "Lowering the scope." He touched a button on the panel. "Setting a one-minute timer. Raising the SATCOM mast." He raised his voice. "Radio, Conn, you are clear to transmit."

"Conn, Radio, transmitting."

Seconds passed.

"Radio," Savarino said. "What's the status?"

"Incomplete download, Conn. Request permission to query the satellite again."

Janet nodded curtly. An incomplete download was not unusual, but if any sensors nearby had detected the first transmission, a second burst could pinpoint their location.

"Radio, Conn, transmit."

"Conn, Radio, aye." Three heartbeats passed. "Download complete."

"Get us out of here, XO," Janet said.

"Pilot, make your depth one-five-zero feet," Savarino called.

Janet checked her watch and breathed a sigh of relief. The whole evolution, from mast up to mast down, had been less than two minutes. She hoped that was good enough.

"Conn, Radio, sending the intel update to the nav plot now."

Janet gathered next to Navigator Jen Avery and the XO. The screen updated slowly. The picture that emerged had obviously been pieced together from a combination of high-flying overwatch drones and satellite coverage.

The *Illinois* showed as a blue dot at the top of the screen. A second blue dot, the *Agamemnon,* showed twelve thousand yards to their north. Four red triangles, the designator for hostile ships, curved away behind them and to the west. The target showed as a red X in the center of the screen. At the bottom of the display, a hornet's nest of red triangles clustered.

"Holy cow," Avery said, "there has to be two dozen PLA ships around the launch platform."

There were no submarines listed because no one knew where the submarines were. Ten years ago, Janet never would have worried about being ambushed by a Chinese submarine. In this moment, she couldn't stop thinking about it.

Chief Tyndale brought the message traffic into control.

Janet accepted the tablet and unlocked the device. A priority message waited at the top of the queue. It had been routed through SUBPAC, but she could see by the designator that it had originated in Langley.

Geronimo 1201 local. At waypoint est 1325. Proceed to tgt. Weapons free.

Janet showed the message to the XO and the Navigator. "The Chinese have launched," she said. "Where's the waypoint?"

Avery worked the controls. A dotted line extended from the cluster of red triangles to the target hulk. It passed the target, extending to the north.

The Navigator pointed to where the track made a sudden right-hand turn. "There's the projected waypoint, ma'am." Janet could feel how the word *projected* carried a lot of weight in that statement.

The waypoint on the display was a guess, plain and simple. They were dealing with a weapon that traveled almost five times faster than her submarine, which meant a lot of room for error. If it left the target hulk even a degree or two off the projected course, it could be miles off target at the waypoint.

Janet blew out a breath. She was about to put her submarine in the path of a torpedo that moved at two hundred knots—and it was carrying a live warhead.

This could end very badly.

"Recommended course and speed to intercept the waypoint is..." Avery read the information off to the XO.

This is reckless, Janet thought. This is insane...and this is the mission.

"Captain," Savarino said, "request permission to proceed to the rendezvous."

The XO was every bit as conflicted as she. Excitement and concern were at war on his features. She needed something to ease the tension.

Savarino was a huge Trekkie in his off time. He'd even shown up to a Halloween party in a complete *Star Trek* red shirt uniform.

Janet popped an eyebrow up.

"Make it so, Number One."

37

USS *Kansas City*, 42 miles east of Second Thomas Shoal, Spratly Islands, South China Sea
1220 China Standard Time

At forty knots, the *Kansas City*'s trimaran hull rode high in the water. Wind screamed outside the open bridge doors. Under his feet, Commander Mike Ferrell could feel the power of four engines churning the ship through the ocean.

He glanced over his left shoulder to where *Mobile* and *Oakland* matched their speed in an echelon formation. The sight filled him with pride. He didn't care what the pundits said about the LCS platform. He loved these ships with all his heart.

Although the speed and maneuverability were two of the platform's best features, it was rare to make a high-speed run on four engines. At top speed, the littoral combat ships guzzled fuel, so they normally operated only two engines at a conservative twelve knots or so.

For his chain of command to authorize a multi-hour, high-speed run for all three ships meant that someone all the way back in Washington had signed off on this mission. Ferrell would be a fool if that didn't worry him a little.

"Philippine supply convoy bearing two-seven-zero, range nine thousand yards, Captain," the radar operator reported.

"Very well," Ferrell replied. He raised the binoculars to his eyes and searched the hazy, sun-drenched horizon. A bump on the fuzzy line between water and sky resolved into the superstructure of the Philippine Navy frigate *Antonio Luna*. The other escort ship, the *Juan Magluyan*, a patrol craft, was not visible. He could just make out the superstructure of the large supply ship behind the *Luna*.

"I have a visual on them," he called out. "Officer of the Deck, slow the SAG down to ten knots."

He listened to the OOD make the call to alert the surface action group, then give the order to execute the speed reduction.

The *Kansas City* settled into the water as she lost speed. The roar of the wind died away.

Ferrell grabbed the VHF handset. "Supply convoy, this is US Navy surface action group Tango. We have been ordered to provide you with an escort. Over."

The response came immediately, and Ferrell could hear a note of relief in the man's voice. "Tango, this is Philippine supply convoy en route to Second Thomas Shoal. Your escort is most welcome. Over."

"Happy to be here," Ferrell replied. "Maintain course and speed. We'll take station behind your formation."

"Roger that, Tango. Maintaining course and speed."

Ferrell spent the next sixty minutes coordinating his SAG until the three littoral combat ships sailed in a wedge formation directly behind the supply convoy. He wondered how the Philippine captains of the three ships felt about the US Navy presence in their operation.

He knew if the roles were reversed, he'd be irritated by outsiders appearing out of nowhere. But his orders were clear: Escort the Philippine supply mission as part of a freedom of navigation operation into the contested waters around the Second Thomas Shoal.

Ferrell had been involved in several FONOPS during his time in the region. The Chinese claimed—falsely—that the atolls they had seized and turned into military bases were sovereign territory of the People's Republic of China. Therefore, the reasoning went, they were entitled to a twelve-nautical-mile territorial boundary around their territory.

Since no one recognized the Chinese claims, the US periodically sent ships or aircraft inside the twelve-mile boundary. These freedom of navigation operations had become more hazardous as the Chinese military presence increased in the region.

Nowhere was this harassment more intense than at Second Thomas Shoal. As the Philippines continued to press forward with their supply missions, there had been minor collisions, but no full-blown military engagements. So far.

Today might be the day, Ferrell knew. This was the first time US Navy combatants had been assigned to escort a Philippine supply mission. This was more than a FONOP, this was a deliberate provocation of the Chinese claims.

Ferrell checked on his sister ships. *Mobile* steamed eight hundred yards off his starboard quarter and *Oakland* mirrored her position on the port side. The supply convoy ran 1500 yards ahead of them with the supply ship steaming between the two Philippine combatants.

He focused on the bridge of the *Oakland*, where he thought he could see Hibs on the bridge wing. Ferrell felt an urge to go outside and wave to his old friend, but he killed the idea in his mind. There would be time enough when the job was done. He chuckled to himself. The story of today would be told and retold over many beers back in port, and it would only get better with age.

Ferrell studied the radar picture. He would have liked to tighten up the formation, but he didn't know anything about the skill level of the Filipino crews. The last thing he wanted was a self-induced accident because he was crowding the field. Better to leave some room for now.

He used the cursor on the radar screen to get a distance to Second Thomas Shoal.

Just over thirty miles away now. At their current speed of ten knots, that meant they'd be hitting the Chinese resistance in less than two hours.

Might as well get this over with, he thought.

"OOD," he called out.

"Yes, Captain."

"To all units, increase speed to twelve knots. Maintain formation."

38

CNS *Shinyan*, 122 miles northeast of the Paracel Islands
1257 China Standard Time

The only thing keeping Chang Han on his feet was the bulkhead. His back was pressed against the cold gray steel, his shoulder wedged into the corner of the torpedo room.

In his mind, he kept coming back to all that had led to this moment. This *failure.* When he considered the risks he'd taken, it made him cold inside. He'd tried to betray his country. Chang knew what the MSS did to spies...and their families.

Stupid, foolish, selfish man, he thought. And for what? In the end, after all that planning, you were outmaneuvered by your blowhard of a boss who wanted to kiss the admiral's ass. Some super-spy you turned out to be.

The compromised phone felt like a brick in his pocket. As soon as the test was over, the first thing he was going to do was throw that thing overboard. It was the only piece of hard evidence that linked him to Angelina-Marie.

Even as he thought it, he knew it was a lie. He was fooling himself again. There were cameras everywhere in China. CCTV recordings, security footage, even private phones captured video that could be searched if the MSS wanted to do so. If they looked, they would find Han and Angelina-Marie together.

He hugged his arms around his chest, squeezed as hard as he could.

Then a new thought knifed into his overheated brain. What if Angelina-Marie came back? What if she wanted something else? Something even riskier...There would be no way he could say no. If she threatened to expose him, he would have to do whatever she wanted.

He thought about the first night he'd met her, in the karaoke bar, after she sang that song by Queen. In the clinical light of hindsight, he could see that everything—*everything*—had been a setup. Spilling his drink, striking up a conversation, her job as a software engineer recruiter, the "jobs" she gave him, the envelopes of cash.

Stupid, foolish, selfish man.

All around him, excited voices chattered about the excellent progress of the torpedo test. And the loudest of them was Gang Wei.

Chang tried to stand up straight and look interested.

The test director had wheeled in a large flatscreen TV and set it up in the empty space where the torpedo had been stored. There was a mission clock in the upper right corner, but the rest of the screen was dedicated to a graphic of the test range. The *Shinyan* showed as a red square in the lower left corner and the target ship as an X at the top of the screen. The space between them was littered with hundreds of white dots. Sonobuoys had been dropped from marine patrol aircraft all along the projected path of the torpedo so they could track the weapon.

The torpedo's progress showed as a solid red line cutting through the sea of white dots. The projected track ran to an open circle, which represented the transition point, the spot in the ocean where the torpedo would slow down and shift from the rocket booster to a normal propulsion system. From there, the Hu Jing torpedo would enter a search pattern just like any other torpedo.

The professional part of Chang's brain admired the torpedo's track. It was dead on target to intersect the projected transition point. The guidance system—*his* guidance system—was working exactly as planned.

Someone had brought in an office chair for Admiral Chin and positioned it in front of the flatscreen. The large man wedged his body between the arms of the chair.

At the admiral's side stood Chang's boss. Somehow, Gang's theatrics with the launch parameters upload had endeared him to the senior officer. In a feat of bureaucratic jiu-jitsu, Gang had managed to make himself more important than the test director. He crouched next to the seated admiral, providing running commentary on the entire test.

Since the mission clock showed that the torpedo had been fired sixty-one minutes ago, Gang's ability to capture and maintain the admiral's attention for that long was no small feat.

And Chang could tell the admiral was eating it up. The man had an actual smile on his fleshy lips and Chang even saw him laugh.

On the other hand, Gang did not look well. His long, patrician face was pale and sweaty, and he shifted his body as he spoke like a little kid who had to go potty.

Chang knew that with only two minutes left before the transition point, there was no way Gang was going to leave the admiral's side. He would tie his own intestines into a knot before he'd give up the opportunity to suck up to the man who ran weapons development for the entire Chinese Navy.

Gang got to his feet. He said in a voice loud enough for all the engineers to hear, "Any second now, the Hu Jing torpedo will shift to normal running mode and begin a search pattern to home in on the target."

As if he'd prompted it, a box appeared in the lower left corner of the screen. The decommissioned target hulk rode serenely at anchor. The image was sharp enough that Chang could see the rust stains down the flank of the old *Luda*-class destroyer and the fresh cuts on her deck where the salvage crews had removed equipment.

It was a beautiful afternoon. Sunlight gleamed on calm water, and the sky beyond the hulk was a cloudless, delicate blue.

The *Shinyan*'s commanding officer appeared in the doorway of the torpedo room. He made his way to the admiral's side and delivered a whispered report.

"Don't worry, Captain," Chang heard his boss say, "we don't need those escorts anymore." He pointed to the screen. "Please stay and watch the target get obliterated by the PLA Navy's newest weapon!"

The captain was not amused. He shot a baleful glare at Gang, then turned his attention back to the admiral. Chin waved his hand. "It's fine. We don't need them anymore."

Gang began to count down the seconds as the red dot of the torpedo's progress closed on the transition point.

"Thirty, twenty-nine, twenty-eight..."

Foolish, Chang thought. The transition point was not accurate to the second. Still, the weapon had performed flawlessly so far, so Gang was right to be excited.

"Transition!" Gang shouted when the counter reached sixty-three minutes. As if on command, the red dot stopped. Gang pumped his fist in the air. The engineers cheered, slapping each other on the back, high-fiving.

Chang felt a surge of pride at having been part of such a successful effort.

The red dot pulsed.

"What happens now?" Admiral Chin asked.

"The torpedo has shifted to a slower mode of propulsion that will allow it to search for the target," Gang explained.

"How much slower?"

"About 25 percent as fast as the rocket, Admiral. The speed of a normal torpedo."

Chin pursed his lips at the screen. "Shouldn't we see it moving, then?"

"Yes," Gang answered, "probably a lag in the signal. There are so many sonobuoys that we need to process..." His voice trailed off.

Chang watched the screen with growing horror as the mission clock logged the passing of another minute. The red dot had not moved. Even on the propeller, the torpedo would be traveling at over forty knots. That was fast. They should have seen movement by now.

Chang saw a spasm cross his boss's face, but it wasn't clear if it was because he realized the test had failed or he was undergoing intense intestinal distress.

A split second later, he had his answer. A brown stain appeared on the back of Gang's pressed khaki trousers. A ghastly, fetid smell filled the room.

"What is going on?" Chin struggled to stand, and one of his aides rushed forward to help him up.

Gang staggered backward and turned to leave the room, but the close-packed ranks of engineers blocked his path. Chin's beady eyes lit on Gang's backside. His sweaty face turned bright red.

"Where is the test director?" Chin bellowed as Gang fled the room.

"Here, sir." Mr. Li's thin face was ashen, the armpits of his polo shirt dark with sweat.

"What happened?" Chin was a quaking blob of sweaty outrage. His voice skipped an octave.

"It appears..." The director's voice was halting, as if not saying the words would change the horrible reality. "It appears the weapon failed—in the transition phase—we need to verify."

Admiral Chin's jaw flopped open. "The test is a failure?"

"Yes, sir—the indications are that is...so." He paused to swallow. "We need to verify..."

Chin bulled his way toward the torpedo room door. "No one leaves this room," he shouted. "I want the second torpedo ready to launch in less than one hour."

He grabbed one of his aides by the arm. "Find the engineer who shit himself and tell him he's fired."

"Aye-aye, sir."

The room was rank with disbelief and the smell of shit. Chang pressed his face against the bulkhead so no one could see him smile.

39

USS *Illinois*, 96 miles south of Pratas Island
1345 China Standard Time

The control room of the USS *Illinois* was as silent as a tomb, the atmosphere as tense as a loaded spring.

Thirty minutes ago, Janet had ordered the ship to general quarters, which had taken all of one minute, fifteen seconds—a new speed record for the ship, and an indication of how tuned in to the problem the crew was.

Part of setting the fighting condition for the ship meant securing ventilation. She often forgot how much the icy blast of air from the overhead vents contributed to the white background noise of the space. Now, the temperature in the quiet room was beginning to rise.

Janet tugged at the flash hood around her neck. The elastic fire-resistant hood was designed to be pulled over her head in the event of a fire, but now it was just clinging to her sweaty neck.

One of the fire control techs cleared his throat and was treated to a barrage of angry glares.

Janet cut a glance at the clock at the top of the nearest monitor. If the Chinese torpedo was launched at 1201 as Harrison had reported, then it should be here by now. Yet all they'd gotten was a brief burst of broadband noise in a long-range convergence zone, which could make it anywhere from twenty to a hundred miles away in water this deep.

She crossed to the sonar stack, where O'Malley sat hunched over the broadband monitor, eyes scanning the display, headphones clamped over his ears.

Janet touched him on the shoulder. "Senior chief?" she whispered. "Anything?"

O'Malley's eyes were red from the strain. He shook his head.

"Could we have missed it?" Janet asked in a still-low voice.

"No way, ma'am. That thing is about as subtle as a freight train. If it came within twenty miles of us, we'd hear it."

He left the real question in Janet's mind unanswered. What if it hadn't come within twenty miles of them? She had no idea how Harrison had programmed a new waypoint into a Chinese top-secret torpedo, but clearly something had gone wrong.

Her body was so tense she felt as if her muscles might snap like over-stretched rubber bands. She tried to draw in a deep breath, and it felt painful to expand her rib cage.

What now? she wondered. The time for the rendezvous with the Chinese weapon had come and gone, but how long should she wait?

Janet beckoned to the XO, who was posted next to the fire control team.

"Ma'am?" he asked in a low voice.

"Tom, do you recall the estimated range on this new weapon?" she asked.

"I'll look it up, Captain."

He was back in less than three minutes. "Maximum five hundred miles, ma'am. That's the best estimate."

Janet chewed her lip. The concept of a torpedo with that kind of range and speed still blew her mind.

"Okay, let's do some radcon math, Tom. Assume a top speed of two hundred nautical miles per hour, that's a max of two and a half hours of runtime on the rocket."

"That tracks," Savarino said.

"Add in thirty minutes of runtime for the propeller version of the weapon, and that gives us a total of three hours before that beast runs out of fuel."

Savarino looked at the clock on the nearest monitor. "It's been over two hours already, Captain."

"There's been no explosion, and it hasn't passed within sonar range of our position. So what conclusions can we draw from the data?"

Savarino made a face. "Either the weapon failed, or it's gone off in a direction where we can't intercept it."

"If the torpedo failed, there's no way anybody in DC can know that. On the other hand, if the weapon went rogue, what would the Chinese Navy be doing?"

Savarino's smile was wolfish. "A live torpedo gone rogue with a range of hundreds of miles? They'd be freaking out."

"Exactly, XO. Let's go topside and see what's cooking." Janet raised her voice. "Officer of the Deck."

"Yes, Captain." Lieutenant Taylor's instant response told her he'd been eavesdropping.

"Secure from general quarters. Prepare to take the ship to periscope depth."

Seconds later, the deck of the submarine angled upward.

Above her head, the familiar whoosh of air conditioning resumed. Janet pulled off her flash hood and stuffed it into her pocket. Then she found an air-conditioning vent and stood beneath the icy blast.

40

Special Activities Center, CIA Headquarters, Langley, Virginia
0248 Eastern Standard Time (1448 China Standard Time)

Harrison Kohl scrubbed his face with both hands. His entire body ached with fatigue and his overworked brain flitted from possibility to possibility —none of them good.

The massive Orca torpedo had been fired from the test platform at 1201 local time in the South China Sea. They knew that for a fact because the overwatch drone had recorded the plume of water shooting from the modified bow of the ship. Bob James had assured him that they would be able to detect the launch that way and it had gone down just the way the retired submarine captain had said it would.

Once it was fired, there was no way for US forces to track the weapon. The Chinese had dropped so many sonobuoys in the water between the launch platform and the target that it would have been foolish even to try to get a submarine into position along the launch path.

Less than an hour ago, James had declared, "Something's wrong."

Harrison, on his last nerve, resorted to sarcasm. "Bob, can you be a little more specific?"

James was unperturbed. "Even accounting for reasonable error in our calculations, by this time, we should have seen either the hulk explode or detected the decoy explosion to the north. Neither of these things has happened, ergo, something is wrong."

The problem was too many moving parts and not enough information on which to act. But the cost of inaction was piling up. An hour after the launch, eight Chinese warships detached from the security forces around the launch platform and headed south at flank speed.

While those eight combatants completely outclassed Ferrell's three littoral combat ships, even at top speed, it was hundreds of miles to Second Thomas Shoal. It would take half a day before the incoming PLA combatants posed a threat to the Philippine supply mission. The closest Chinese Navy combatants to Ferrell's ships were two guided missile destroyers moored in the lagoon at Mischief Reef, only about forty miles away from Second Thomas Shoal, but the overwatch video showed they had not moved from their location. It seemed that the Chinese were content to let their Coast Guard handle the incoming Philippine supply mission.

That, at least, was good news. The plan was for Ferrell's presence to draw Chinese attention, not start World War Three.

But it all depended on timing. Commander Ferrell's surface action group progress had been timed to arrive at Second Thomas Shoal in the middle of the afternoon.

One of the operators interrupted his train of thought. "Incoming priority traffic from the *Illinois*, sir."

"Send it over," Michael said. Harrison and James crowded around the screen, scanning the message.

Michael summarized, "Janet thinks the torpedo must have failed somehow. If it went rogue and drove off course, she thinks the Chinese picket ships would be freaking out. The pickets are calm."

Harrison tried to think. "Bob," he said to Commander James, "if you were running this test and the first torpedo failed, what would you do?"

James considered the question. "Normally, we'd stop the test and do a postmortem on the failure before we tried another launch." He hesitated. "But this is not normal."

He held up two fingers. "We know the Chinese are under tremendous political pressure to make this test successful. Billions of dollars and the fate of an entire new class of submarine rest on the outcome of this test."

He pushed down a second finger. "Second, we know they loaded two torpedoes. That's not unusual—these are beta units—but they never would have launched the first one if it didn't pass all the pre-launch checks."

"Which means what?" Harrison pressed, hearing his own frustration.

"Failure is not an option," James concluded. "They'll fire that second torpedo."

"When?" Harrison said.

James's face pinched into a frown. "Today, as soon as possible, most likely. They'll do it before someone higher in the chain of command pulls the plug on them."

Harrison made his decision. "Inform the *Illinois* that we concur with their assessment. Take station and prepare for a second launch. Advise the team leader on the *Arrogant* the same."

He listened as Michael issued the orders and dealt with the follow-up. There was one more piece of the puzzle.

The entire point of Ferrell's surface action group was to create a diversion, but now that the timing was screwed up, it could work against them. If the supply mission at Second Thomas Shoal caused too much of a commotion too soon, the Chinese might raise their defense posture across the region and cancel the weapons test.

On the other hand, the Chinese knew Ferrell's SAG was coming. The delay gave them more time to prepare, which put Ferrell and the Philippine supply mission in greater danger.

There was no getting around it. For this operation to succeed, he needed that diversion, and it had to happen at the right time.

"Michael," Harrison said.

"Sir?"

"Order Commander Ferrell to divert away from Second Thomas Shoal and slow down. Details to follow."

41

USS *Kansas City*, 29 miles east of Second Thomas Shoal
1515 China Standard Time

US Navy warship, you are approaching the territorial waters of the People's Republic of China. You are advised to alter course. Failure to do so may result...

Ferrell rolled his eyes at XO McKenzie. This was the third warning call they'd received from the Chinese Coast Guard vessels patrolling off Second Thomas Shoal.

Even though they were still almost an hour from reaching the claimed twelve-nautical-mile limit, the Chinese wasted no time stating their case. Ferrell imagined the sight of three US Navy warships joining the Philippine supply convoy had created an impression.

It suddenly dawned on Ferrell the Chinese were warning *him*, the US Navy, but hadn't said a word about the three Philippine Navy ships sailing a mile ahead of his surface action group.

I'm sure that's what the mysterious Mr. Kohl wanted, Ferrell reflected. He'd never felt more like a pawn than he did right now. It was not a pleasant sensation.

With three LCSs and the two Philippine Navy warships, they outnumbered the Chinese Coast Guard vessels five to four, but that was a false sense of security. The PLA had two destroyers at Mischief Reef, only forty miles northwest of Second Thomas Shoal, which was well within missile range. And that didn't even include the fighters stationed at three island airstrips arrayed across the Spratlys.

He'd also just received message traffic that eight Chinese Navy combatants were heading south at flank speed to augment the forces near Second Thomas Shoal. He wasn't that worried about the incoming warships. At their current speed, this operation would be over in the next few hours..

"OOD, transmit our standard response to the Chinese," he ordered.

The Officer of the Deck reached for the VHF radio, smiling grimly as he stated his case:

Chinese Coast Guard, this is a US Navy warship. Our units are operating in international waters in accordance with the established rules of the UN Convention on the Law of the Sea. We shall proceed at our own discretion. Out.

"Any sign of PLA aircraft?" Ferrell asked his TAO.

"Nothing from the PLA, sir," his tactical action officer responded. "The two P-8s launched out of Guam have an ETA of two hours, six minutes."

Ferrell studied the radar display, his mind churning with the possibilities—none of them appealing. This was shaping up to be a direct confrontation with the Chinese and he was the tip of spear.

The maritime patrol aircraft would arrive on station just as his ships were breaching the claimed territorial waters. What would the Chinese do once they realized where the US Navy P-8s were headed? They'd likely put fighters in the air to harass them, Ferrell guessed, making a tense situation even dicier.

He checked the latest update on his own air assets. The USS *Carl Vinson* carrier strike group was a little over six hundred miles south of him, but her threat posture was normal. She had only a single combat air patrol and an E-2D Hawkeye operating one hundred miles in advance of the strike group. Those guys were supposed to be his backup if things got ugly, and the clock was ticking.

Ferrell chewed his lip. The longer this went on, the more prepared the Chinese would be for his arrival. It was time to seize the initiative. He needed to shake things up.

His orders were to escort the Philippine supply mission to Second

Thomas Shoal. The normal cruising speed for the convoy was twelve knots, chosen as a balance between speed and fuel economy. But nothing in his orders prevented him from going faster.

If he pushed the convoy faster, they might catch the Chinese unawares. Maybe even give him a slight edge for what was to come.

"OOD," he called out.

"Captain."

"Inform the convoy and escorts that I want to increase speed to seventeen knots."

"Aye-aye, sir."

The call went out over the radio.

"Standing by, sir," the OOD reported.

"Execute."

"Executing increase speed to seventeen knots, aye, sir."

The call went out on the radio and Ferrell felt the engines respond. The *Kansas City* rose a little higher in the water and the wind rushing past the open doors on the bridge wings freshened.

"Let the Chinese coasties chew on that," Ferrell muttered. It was a small move, but at least he was doing something to help his tactical situation.

"Captain." The Radioman appeared at his elbow. "New priority traffic from Washington, sir."

Ferrell unlocked the tablet and scanned the message. The contents made him want to throw the tablet through the open doorway and into the deep blue of the South China Sea.

What the hell were they playing at? The muscles in his neck and shoulders tensed as he fought down the feeling of frustration. He knew the bridge crew was watching him, so he kept his face still.

"Officer of the Deck," he said finally, "slow the convoy down to four knots."

Ferrell went to the bridge wing and squinted at the horizon ahead. He gripped the railing until his forearms ached.

42

CNS *Shinyan*, 122 miles northeast of the Paracel Islands
1549 China Standard Time

Rumors ran through the ship like a virus, even reaching the engineering team sequestered in the torpedo room.

The Americans were escorting a Philippine Navy supply mission to Second Thomas Shoal—something they'd never done before.

Chang didn't know what to think. If you knew anything about the South China Sea, you knew about Second Thomas Shoal. Everywhere else in the South China Sea—the body of water was even named after China!—the neighboring countries had basically capitulated to the superior might of the PLA. There were protests and court cases at the United Nations, but it made no difference. It was a statement of fact: China *owned* the South China Sea.

Except at Second Thomas Shoal.

It was an embarrassment for the Philippines—that's the point that the Chinese political commentators always led with. Almost twenty-five years ago, the Philippine Navy grounded a rusting World War Two ship on the reef and maintained a ragtag contingent of military personnel, nothing more than pirates according to Chinese state TV, on board ever since.

The Chinese interest in Second Thomas had nothing to do with nationalistic goals, as the Western media claimed. It was strictly about security. The site of the grounded ship allowed the Philippine military a lookout over Mischief Reef, one of the most developed PLA military bases in the entire South China Sea. Given the strong relationship between the Philippines and the United States, that was unacceptable.

It was a losing game for the Philippines. There was no way they could match the resources of the People's Republic of China. They had already lasted longer than anyone in Beijing had thought possible, but the end was near. The supply missions were more sporadic and were turned away by the Chinese Coast Guard more often than not.

And the Americans? As usual, the Americans talked a good game. When their diplomats protested—Chang had seen them on TV—the Chinese news commentators didn't even bother translating what they said, they just made disparaging remarks about the United States' waning influence in the region.

But today, of all days, the Americans had chosen to get involved. Why now, when he was so close to his goal?

Chang felt like his entire body was just one bundle of nerves. His hands shook, his eyesight quivered, and his legs felt weak. After all he had endured to get to this place, he feared the news about Second Thomas Shoal would cause Admiral Chin to cancel the live-fire test of the second torpedo.

When the new rumor arrived that the Americans had backed down, Chang didn't believe it. He'd heard that the American ships outnumbered the Chinese Coast Guard ships. Everyone knew the American doctrine was overwhelming force. It was the same doctrine the Chinese forces used. Why would the Americans back down now when they had superior numbers?

But they had. Admiral Chin confirmed it when he showed up in the torpedo room. His dress uniform was wrinkled and he looked harried, but also visibly relieved as he reported that the Americans had turned away from Second Thomas Shoal. The Chinese Navy had won again.

"I want this torpedo launched by 1600," Chin told the test director. "And it had better work flawlessly."

"Yes, Admiral," Mr. Li replied. Then he found Chang. "You will load guidance system parameters. Gang Wei is not to set foot in this room."

Chang's body quivered like a bowstring. "Of course, sir."

The test director's eyes narrowed as he took in Chang's tired face and disheveled appearance. "Clean yourself up before the admiral sees you. I don't want another incident like the last one."

Chang raced back to his bunk, where he put on a clean shirt, washed his face, and combed his hair. He considered his reflection. He still looked awful, his eyes sunken and his skin pasty. He tried to pinch some color back into his cheeks.

When he got back to the torpedo room, the last weapon was on the rack in front of the gaping torpedo tube door. Chang unlocked his phone and called up Cassie's picture, then locked it again. All he needed to do was unlock the phone and touch her face to start the program.

The mechanical checklist of the torpedo began. The two technicians worked swiftly, under the watchful eye of the test director and the glare of the admiral. The techs presented their paperwork to Mr. Li, who scanned it and signed.

The ceremony of the first launch was gone, replaced by an oppressive, anxious silence. There were no video cameras this time.

"Connect the umbilical to the weapon," the test director announced. Chang stepped up to the desk where his laptop was open, placed his phone on the desk next to the computer. He realized immediately that he should have adjusted the desk for his height. A dozen eyes watched him as he fumbled with the knob to lower the work surface.

"What are you doing?" the test director hissed.

"What is taking so long, Director?" the admiral snapped.

Mr. Li's voice was near panic. "We don't have time for that, Chang. Do your job."

"Yes, sir," Chang whispered back. When he straightened up, he knocked his phone off the desk. It fell to the metal deck with a loud slapping sound. He picked it up and saw the screen was cracked. His heart hammering, Chang unlocked the phone and saw his daughter's face smiling at him.

"It's okay," he said. Then he touched the photo to start the hidden program.

Please work, please work, please work...

The test director looked like he was about to have a stroke. “I don’t care about your fucking phone, Chang. Do your job.”

Chang placed the phone face down on the desk next to the laptop just like he’d done in the dozens of practice sessions with Angelina-Marie. He called up the parameters and entered the data into the program. The screen cleared and a dialogue box popped up.

Ready to upload?

In one smooth motion, Chang ran his mouse up to the battery icon and clicked. Then, with a silent prayer, he tapped the Enter key.

Guidance system parameters loaded.

Chang stepped back from the laptop. “Parameters loaded, Director,” he said, his voice hoarse.

He’d done it. Chang half expected the admiral to yell *Stop!* and for police to rush into the room and arrest him.

Instead, the techs moved past him. They removed the umbilical and pushed the desk with his laptop out of the way. One of them handed Chang his phone. The picture of Cassie was still on the screen.

“Good looking young lady,” the tech said.

Chang blinked at the phone, then at the tech. He mumbled a reply.

Then he backed up to the bulkhead and used that vertical surface to keep his body upright as the massive torpedo disappeared into the tube and the door shut behind it.

43

Special Activities Center, CIA Headquarters, Langley, Virginia
0403 Eastern Standard Time (1603 China Standard Time)

The operator at the overwatch drone station sat bolt upright in his chair. "We've got a launch plume!" he shouted.

The room went electric. Harrison, who'd been dozing in an office chair at the back of the ops center, snapped awake.

"Put it on the big screen," Michael ordered, but the operator was already one step ahead of him.

Harrison studied the video image. A spear of white water shot out of the front of the *Shinyan*, then dissipated into a mass of bubbles. The big ship shuddered with the effects of the recoil.

"That's a launch, sir," Michael said quietly.

"Yeah." Harrison's mouth was suddenly dry. All this technology and they were reduced to watching for a flash of white water out of the bow of the ship. Based on that simple indication, he was about to put billions of dollars of hardware and American lives in danger. It felt surreal.

"Mark launch time," he said.

"1603 local," the operator replied promptly.

Harrison emptied his lungs.

"To all stations, Geronimo at 1603. Proceed with the plan."

He waited for the messages to go out.

"Put Commander Ferrell's surface action group on the screen," he ordered.

The image of the *Shinyan* vanished, replaced by an aerial view of surface ships dotting an ocean that gleamed like gold in the late afternoon sun. The ships looked like toys on the screen.

Ferrell's group formed a wedge, riding close behind the Philippine ships. The big Philippine supply ship was flanked by two vessels, one a small patrol craft, the other nearly the length of the US Navy combatants. Around them, in a loose ring, a cadre of four white Chinese Coast Guard vessels lurked.

As he watched, one of the Chinese ships sped up and angled toward the supply mission. It cut across the water at high speed, then veered off at the last minute. The slow-moving convoy traveled over the Chinese ship's wake a few seconds later.

"At least they're still five on four," Michael said, but without much conviction.

Harrison nodded slowly.

"Priority message to USS *Kansas City*. Increase speed, approach Second Thomas Shoal, complete supply mission." He paused.

Michael waited.

"Rules of engagement apply," Harrison added.

44

USS *Illinois*, 110 miles south of Pratas Island
1610 China Standard Time

"Raising the photonics mast for a look around," the Officer of the Deck called from his station. He toggled a switch on the panel and the optics broke free of the surface of the South China Sea.

Janet winced. It was a gorgeous afternoon, the water almost flat, the winds calm. Perfect conditions for an alert pilot or drone operator to spot the rooster tail caused by a periscope sticking out of the water.

The horizon was clear, but Janet's skin crawled with apprehension. At this depth, the ship was vulnerable, and they were deep in enemy territory.

"No close contacts. Lowering photonics mast."

"Scope exposure time eight seconds, OOD," the Pilot reported.

"Very well, Pilot. Set a timer for two minutes."

"Two minutes, aye, sir."

Taylor looked at Janet. "Captain, request permission to raise the SATCOM mast and query the satellite."

Janet nodded. "Permission granted, OOD."

Ninety seconds later, they had the intel update and their message traffic.

"Go deep, Mr. Taylor," Janet ordered.

As the ship got farther away from the surface, Janet's fears eased. On the surface, they were a target. Down here, she could fight on her terms.

The intel update arrived in control. Anxiously, Janet watched the central navigation plot update.

Their tactical picture had not changed that much. There were still four Chinese warships arrayed in a shallow semicircle to the northwest, and the closest was still fifteen thousand yards distant.

No Chinese submarines were known to be in the area, but Janet didn't believe that for a second.

"Where's the *Agamemnon*?" she asked.

"Here, ma'am," Navigator Avery answered. She slid the display field of view to the north. The last good location for the UK submarine was twenty thousand yards behind them. Janet checked the data tag to see the information was over two hours old. The HMS *Agamemnon* could be anywhere in their assigned water space by now.

"We have a Geronimo alert, Captain," the XO announced as he bellied up to the display. "Torpedo launch at 1603."

Avery worked the display controls, expanding the range of the display until she saw the target hulk on the lower center of the screen.

"Here's the projected track, Captain." She updated the screen.

Janet studied the new information. The dotted line ran northeast away from the hulk, then took a sharp dogleg to the right. The waypoint showed as a bright red dot on the screen.

She placed her index finger to the northwest of the waypoint. "I'm thinking here, XO," she said.

Savarino nodded. "We need to stay off the forward track in case that monster misses the turn, but..." He pointed to the Chinese warships. "That puts us within ten thousand yards of them."

"I'll take the devil I know over the devil I don't," Janet replied. "Navigator, give Mr. Taylor a course to put us six thousand yards to the northwest of the waypoint. Depth of three hundred feet, ship in hover mode."

"Aye-aye, ma'am," Avery replied.

"Mr. Taylor, load all four tubes with Mark 48 torpedoes. Make the tubes ready in all respects, with the exception of outer doors remain closed." He repeated the order back to her, his normally smiling face grave.

"Once that's complete, rig the ship for ultra quiet."

"Yes, ma'am."

She caught the OOD's eye and grinned at him. "Cheer up, Mr. Taylor. We're going hunting."

45

CNS *Changcheng* 346, 87 miles south of Pratas Island
1615 Chinese Standard Time

"Steady on depth five-zero meters, Captain," reported the watch officer.

"Very well," Kai responded. "Conduct a full sonar search."

"We are receiving underwater comms from the *Zunyi*, Captain."

Kai did not look away from the sonar display. "Acknowledged, watch officer. Make a record of the transmission. Continue with the sonar search."

"Do you want us to respond to the flagship, Captain?"

Kai ground his teeth in frustration. He turned to face the young lieutenant. "Continue with the sonar search, Mr. Wong. That is all."

"Yes, sir."

Kai should have known that would not be the end of it. He should have recalled that Lieutenant Wong was a great admirer of Commander Mao. Instead, he'd been focused on the sonar search.

The USS *Illinois* was out there. He could feel it. The American submarine was inside the perimeter of picket ships and he was going to find her.

He'd been searching for this submarine for long enough to have a healthy respect for her captain. He was up against a formidable opponent with a very capable platform at his disposal. Anything could happen.

It was more than just professional pride driving Kai now. If he could expose the American submarine, he would be vindicated. His chain of command would be forced to acknowledge that he was right. The Americans knew about their secret weapon.

Kai watched the narrowband sonar display, watching the snaking line of processed noise. Occasionally, a spike would appear, making Kai's heart race, but inevitably it would drop away just as quickly.

"Request permission to enter control," said a voice from the doorway.

"Enter, Commander Mao," the watch officer said loudly.

Kai turned from the display, surprised. He and Mao had been studiously avoiding each other since their last public clash.

"What are you doing here?" Kai demanded.

Mao did not waste time on pleasantries. "May we speak in private, Captain?"

"I'm busy. What do you want?"

Mao shrugged as if to say, *I warned you*. "I understand the flagship has been trying to contact us by underwater telephone. You have been ignoring them."

"Who told you—" Kai broke off, shot a furious look at Wong. The young lieutenant had turned away, but his back was rigid with tension.

"It doesn't matter how I know, Captain," Mao replied smoothly. "Is it true?"

"It's none of your concern, Political Officer," Kai shot back. "The operation of the ship is under my command. You may return to your duties."

"I think maintaining communication with the admiral is part of my duties." Mao's tone held some fire. He was not backing down this time.

Kai clenched his fists. He didn't have time for this. "We were at periscope depth only thirty minutes ago. We have the most current intel and we have our orders. If we respond to the flagship on the underwater telephone, we will be broadcasting our position."

"Broadcasting our position..." Mao scowled at him, then his face cleared. "You still think there's an enemy submarine out there."

Kai took a step forward. "I *know* there's an enemy submarine out there, Commander."

Mao leaned close. "You're acting like a crazy man, Kai," he said in a low voice. "Haven't you done enough damage to your career and your crew? We're hundreds of miles from the real action, and you still think the world revolves around you. You believe that some fanatical American submarine captain is lurking out there right now, waiting to do what? Listen to the sound of the target being destroyed?"

Kai was stunned into silence, then the rage bubbled up. He'd been right about the American sub all along. Mao knew it; they all knew it. But they would not acknowledge it because the facts didn't fit with their worldview that China was superior in all things.

Mao leaned in until Kai could taste the coffee on his breath. "You are sick, Kai Jun, and you're making everyone around you sick."

"Captain—" the sonar supervisor began, but Kai held up a hand to stop him.

"Get out of my control room," he said to Mao.

"You can't order me—"

Kai poked him in the chest with a stiff forefinger. "Get out. Now."

Mao held a hand over his chest as if the finger poke had actually hurt, his eyes wide with surprise. "You will regret this, Captain."

Mao spun on his heel and left the control room. The sonar supervisor's voice broke the silence. "Captain—"

"Wait!" Kai snapped. He felt his hands shaking with the surge of adrenaline from the confrontation. He balled his hands into fists, shoved them in his pockets. His breath came fast and hard as he tried to calm himself down.

Seconds passed. No one spoke, no one even moved.

"Lieutenant Wong," Kai said in a flat voice.

"Yes, sir." The young man posted to attention in front of his commanding officer, but he would not meet his captain's eye.

"Did you inform Commander Mao that I was not responding to the underwater comms?"

Wong's neck contracted as he tried to swallow. His voice sounded strangled. "Yes, sir."

"You are relieved of your duties, Mr. Wong, and your qualifications as watch officer are revoked. You may go."

For a second, Kai wondered if Wong was going to fight back, but instead, his shoulders sagged and he turned away.

"Attention in control," Kai announced as the door closed behind Wong. "The captain has the deck and the conn."

"Captain," the sonar supervisor said. "I have them. I have the tonal."

Kai stepped to the display. A strong peak showed in the center of the screen.

"Recommend a ranging maneuver, Captain."

"Helm," Kai said, "come to new course one-two-zero."

The signal on the towed array faded as soon as they turned. Precious minutes slipped by before they steadied on the new course and the towed array stabilized. The signal peak was still there. They had him.

"What's my range, Sonar?" he asked anxiously.

"It's at least twenty thousand yards, Captain. I think we have them in a sound channel."

The vagaries of sound in the ocean were playing in his favor for once. "How sure are you about that range?"

"If you can give me another leg of data, I should be able to confirm it, sir."

Kai turned again on a nearly reciprocal course. Behind him, he could just make out the warble of underwater comms from the flagship.

Not now, he thought.

More time, more data. "Range to target is estimated at twenty-one thousand yards, Captain," the sonar supervisor reported. "They're moving slowly, three knots or less."

Kai consulted the navigation display, his stomach churning with anticipation. He needed to get closer, but if he sped up, he would lose contact with the enemy submarine. On the other hand, if the sub moved slowly and held to a steady course, he could race ahead and surprise them.

It was a risk, a big risk, but bagging an American submarine inside the perimeter of the weapons test area was worth it.

"Diving Officer, make your depth one-five-zero meters. Helm, come right to new course one-eight-zero." The deck slanted downward steeply. When they passed one hundred meters, he gave his next order.

"Increase speed to all ahead full."

Kai leaned back against a stanchion and crossed his arms as the activity of the control room unfolded around him. He pictured the look on Mao's face when he showed the political officer a sonar image of an American submarine at close range.

46

CNS *Shinyan*, 122 miles northeast of the Paracel Islands
1720 China Standard Time

Following the launch of the first Hu Jing torpedo, the atmosphere was festive. On the second launch, the torpedo room had the air of a pandemic-era hospital waiting room. Everyone hoping for the best, but knowing that death lurked in the background, waiting to strike.

On the first launch, during the hour it took the high-speed torpedo to transit the 180 miles to the first waypoint, Gang Wei had acted like an emcee at a charity event. He narrated the action, kept the energy level in the room up, and made sure there was never a moment of doubt. Chang had little respect for Gang as a person, but the man had people skills.

On the second launch, with the admiral wedged into the same armchair and planted in front of the flatscreen monitor, time seemed to stand still. Chang had already chewed his fingernails bloody, but still he gnawed at his cuticles. And he was desperately hungry. He realized that in his high state of anxiety, he hadn't eaten anything since yesterday afternoon. It was as if the launch of the second torpedo allowed his body to feel again.

For the hundredth time, he extracted his mobile from his pocket and stared at the picture of Cassie. For better or for worse, he had done what he'd set out to do. Angelina-Marie had promised him that she would take care of his daughter, and he clung to that promise like a life preserver.

"Two minutes to the transition point," the test director announced into the silence.

From his position at the back of the room, Chang's head jerked up. He'd been so lost in his own thoughts that time had passed without him even realizing it.

Then a new burst of anxiety flooded into his system. What if the torpedo failed to transition again? His knowledge of the weapon design told him that the last failure was probably mechanical. These two weapons had been manufactured together. There was a possibility that a manufacturing error had been duplicated into the second torpedo.

Chang could see the test director in profile and could tell that Mr. Li's mind had settled on the same train of thought. His features were pinched and sallow, and a trickle of sweat ran down his temple.

"One minute to transition point," the test director said. His voice had a strangled quality.

Unlike the first launch, there was no countdown of the remaining seconds, just a solemn group stare at the mission clock. Chang held his breath, along with every other person in the room.

"Transition point now." The test director's voice cracked. Nobody laughed.

The red dot representing the torpedo slowed, the dot pulsing, then stopped. In the silence, Chang's racing pulse thundered in his ears.

The seconds stretched into impossibly long moments...

The red dot moved—or had he imagined it? He blinked and the display updated.

"Successful transition!" the test director announced.

The red trace of the torpedo's track began to curve into an S-pattern.

"The weapon is searching!" the test director's voice sang with relief.

Chang watched the search routine emerge on the plot. He had programmed these patterns a thousand times. Give him a marker and whiteboard, he could draw them blindfolded.

One...two...three...four peaks of a sine wave, then run straight and turn ninety degrees. Search in a new direction. One...two...three—

The torpedo found the target.

"Target acquired!" the test director squeaked.

Chang watched, mesmerized, as the torpedo turned toward the target. The weapon would emit three pings in rapid succession to verify target acquisition, then speed up for a final kill.

"It's range gating!"

When a torpedo locked on its target, it was designed to continuously ping the target to refine the distance to the detonation point, known as range gating. The distance between the red dot of the torpedo and the red X of the target narrowed.

In the corner of the screen, the old *Luda*-class destroyer floated serenely in the afternoon sun. The test director enlarged the image of the target to encompass the entire screen.

"Any second now," Li announced. A face-cracking smile stretched across his pale features.

The entire room leaned forward, hands clenched, eyes straining.

Chang felt his heartbeat slow down. Each pulse like a drum in his chest.

Boom...boom...boom...

On the screen, nothing happened. A white pennant on the bow of the target hulk fluttering in a light breeze offered the only clue that they were looking at a live video feed.

The test director gagged. His fingers scrabbled at the keyboard as he shifted the screen back to the torpedo track.

On the screen, the red track of the weapon had perfectly bisected the red X of the target...and continued to travel north.

"What's happening?" Admiral Chin's jaw gaped. He seized the test director's arm. "Tell me what is going on!"

"The weapon did not explode, sir."

"I can see that!" Chin stood. The chair clattered to the floor as he launched himself erect. All the engineers backed away from the test director.

"Everything worked perfectly...it just didn't...explode."

Chin's face looked like he might explode. "Where is it going?"

"I—I" The test director looked faint.

"How do we shut it down?" Chin demanded.

"We can't, sir. It will continue until it runs out of fuel."

"Oh no," someone said.

All eyes turned to the screen.

"What now?" Chin screamed.

"The rocket booster just reengaged."

47

USS *Illinois*, 112 miles south of Pratas Island
1720 China Standard Time

"New sonar contact!" called out Senior Chief O'Malley. The sonar supervisor's gruff voice sounded like a bullhorn in the hushed control room.

"Designate new contact Sierra eight-eight." He paused. "Classified as Chinese Orca torpedo."

The tension in the room snapped like a twig. A buzz ripped through the silence.

"Quiet," Janet snapped. She stood behind O'Malley's broad back. "You're sure, Senior?"

O'Malley's head bobbed and he turned in his seat to grin up at her. "Absolutely, ma'am. It sounds like a herd of buffalo in the water."

Janet slipped on the proffered headphones. It wasn't a bad description. The sound did have a rumbling quality not unlike the hoofbeats of dozens of heavy animals racing toward them. She just hoped they weren't about to get trampled to death.

She handed the headset back. "Time to waypoint?"

O'Malley was already working the problem. "Eleven minutes, Captain."

Janet's stomach clenched as the full realization of what she was about to do landed. She took a beat. "Officer of the Deck, set general quarters."

"Set general quarters, aye, ma'am," Savarino replied.

The general quarters alarm pulsed and the *Illinois* came alive with motion. Janet stayed still, calm, letting the action flow around her. On her ship, she was the standard.

"The ship is at general quarters, Captain. Hovering at two-five-zero feet, heading one-two-zero."

"Very well." Janet crossed to the central navigation display, where Jen Avery had already pulled up the intel plot and overlaid the sonar data for the incoming weapon.

"Target will reach the waypoint in nine minutes, ma'am."

"Send the data to fire control, Nav," she ordered.

"Already done, ma'am."

Janet smiled. This team was ready for action.

"Attention in control," she announced. "Our mission is to fake out the Chinese Navy. If things go according to plan, the incoming weapon will make a sharp right turn at the programmed waypoint. My intention is to fire two Mark 48 torpedoes, a primary and a backup, in advance so that they will arrive at the waypoint at the same time as the Chinese weapon. As soon as we detect the doppler shift indicating the weapon has turned, we will detonate the primary Mark 48 by wire. If the primary fails for any reason or the wire breaks, we will shift to the backup unit." She paused. "Then we will get the hell out of here."

Janet looked across the tense faces staring back at her. "Are there any questions?"

No one moved.

"Very well, then. Fire Control, weapons status."

"Tubes one through four are loaded with Mark 48 torpedoes, Captain. Wire continuity is good on all four units. All tubes flooded and pressure equalized, ready to open outer doors, ma'am."

"Very well, Weps." Janet turned back to the central plot where Avery waited. "Navigator, what's the countdown on launch?"

"Projected waypoint is six thousand yards, Captain, bearing one-three-six. Intercept requires torpedo travel time of just under four minutes, ma'am. We need to launch in"—she consulted the display— "three minutes. Countdown clock is running."

Janet went back to Senior Chief O'Malley. "Any change, Senior?"

He shook his head. "Steady as a rock, Captain. The Orca's right on track."

Janet resisted the urge to pace as she waited. She planted her hands on the edge of the navigation display in the center of the room. "Weapons Officer," she ordered, "open outer doors on tubes one and two."

"Open outer doors, aye, ma'am." A pause. "Torpedo tube doors one and two indicate open. Wire continuity checks on all units are still good."

At one minute remaining, Janet cleared her throat. By the numbers, she told herself. You've done this a thousand times.

"Firing point procedures, tube one."

"Plot ready," the Navigator reported.

"Ship ready," reported the XO.

"Weapon ready," announced the Weapons Officer. "Standing by to steer by wire on course one-three-six."

Janet swallowed. "Fire tube one."

A second later, her ears popped as a slug of seawater, driven by thousands of pounds of air pressure, ejected the torpedo from the tube into the ocean. *Wa-WHUMP*. The massive plunging sound was like a beacon in the ocean.

"Torpedo is running," Sonar called out.

"Wire continuity is good," sang out the Weapons Officer. "Steering torpedo to course one-three-six."

"Very well, Weapons Officer," Janet replied. "Let's do it again, people. Firing point procedures, tube two..."

48

CNS *Changcheng* 346, 104 miles south of Pratas Island
1736 China Standard Time

Captain Kai Jun checked the clock. It was time to see if his gamble to get ahead of the American submarine paid off.

"Helm, all ahead one-third. Diving Officer, make your depth seven-five meters."

He listened to the repeat back of the orders, felt the momentum of the ship slow in the water. The broadband display was still a sheet of white static. At twenty knots, the submarine sensors were useless. He was driving blind to a point in the ocean where he hoped his prey would be.

Given what had transpired an hour ago with Commander Mao, it was a risk he did not wish to dwell on. If he failed to find the American submarine, his career was as good as over. His own political officer would see to that.

He strode to the three-man sonar team. "Commence a full spectrum search as soon as your sensors are stable."

The order was completely unnecessary. Of course the sonar team would start searching for their target as soon as possible. The sonar supervisor turned in his chair to acknowledge the order. "Aye—"

He looked past Kai, his mouth open, the words dying on his lips.

Kai turned. Commander Mao had entered the control room without permission. Anger, fresh and hot, surged in Kai. He strode across the room to confront his political officer.

Three more men filed into the room. Enlisted men, wearing side arms. Part of the ship's security force.

"What is the meaning of this?" Kai shouted.

Mao's thin face was pale, but infuriatingly calm. "Captain Kai Jun, on behalf of the People's Republic of China and the Chinese Communist Party, I rel—"

"Captain!" the sonar operator shouted. "It's the Hu Jing!"

Kai spun around, lurching toward the sonar operators. A thick white stripe ran across the broadband display, indicating a very noisy contact was approaching them at a high rate of speed.

"On speaker," he ordered.

The Hu Jing? His brain tried to process the information his sensors were reporting. What was the Hu Jing torpedo doing this far north of the target?

The speaker energized, and a rumbling, grinding sound filled the room. He'd heard that sound twice before on the other weapons tests. It was the Hu Jing—and it was headed for them.

Mao grabbed his arm. "Captain Kai, you are relieved of your command—"

Kai spun around, pushing Mao in the chest. "Not now, Commander."

Mao made a hand signal. Two of the enlisted men stepped forward, flanking Kai.

"Get back!" he ordered.

The men hesitated, looking at Mao.

The political officer smiled grimly and stepped close to Kai. He opened his mouth to speak.

"Launch transients, bearing two-one-two!" the sonar supervisor's voice pitched into a scream. "*Torpedo in the water!*"

Kai heard a new sound on the speaker, loud and insistent, like the buzzing of an angry bee. He knew that sound. In every war gaming scenario in the simulator, that sound was played at least once:

The sound of a Mark 48 torpedo. The American submarine was firing on his ship!

Kai lashed out with his fist, catching Mao on the chin. The taller man went down and Kai raced toward the fire control console.

"Snapshot, tube one," Kai ordered. The fire control tech on duty reacted as he'd been trained to do. Hours of drills had burned the movements into his muscle memory. His hands flew over the control panel, but precious seconds drained away.

"Bearing two-one-two," Kai ordered. "Hurry!" The technician entered the data and flipped up the clear plastic cover from the blinking red button.

The button turned green. "Ready, Captain!" he shouted.

"Fire!" Kai smashed down the button. The ship rocked; his ears popped.

"Second torpedo in the water!" Sonar called out.

His ship was in mortal danger. Standard tactics called for Kai to put the torpedo behind him and try to outrun the weapon. He'd practiced the evasive maneuver a hundred times in simulators.

But Kai hesitated. His ear detected something that his brain had not processed yet. Under the rumble of the incoming rocket, the whine of the American Mark 48 torpedo was getting fainter. It was traveling *away* from the *Changcheng*.

He strode to the sonar broadband display. The thick white stripe of the incoming Hu Jing torpedo and the thinner trace of the one—now two—Mark 48 torpedoes were converging.

The Americans weren't aiming at him. They were aiming at the Hu Jing.

"Fire Control," he ordered, "standby to launch tube two."

49

USS *Illinois*, 114 miles south of Pratas Island
1738 China Standard Time

"Second torpedo running true," Senior O'Malley reported.

"Steering the second fish by wire to heading one-three-six," the Weapons Officer reported. "Wire continuity on both units is good."

Janet did not reply to either report. Her eyes were locked on the sonar display, trying to detect the slightest tremor in the thick white trace that represented the Chinese Orca weapon.

This is going to work, she told herself. That wire just needed to last one more minute and they were home free.

The sonar tech to her right sat bolt upright in his chair. "New contact bearing zero-three-zero!" He gasped, "Torpedo in the water!"

"I'm on it," O'Malley shouted. "Torpedo bearing zero-three-two, range six thousand yards and closing."

Janet's eyes snapped from the sonar display to the countdown clock. A modern torpedo would close that distance in a shade over three minutes.

"Captain—" the XO began, but she held up a hand.

"Sound the collision alarm, XO." The clock in her brain showed the seconds melting away, faster and faster.

"O'Malley," she barked. "Talk to me."

"Doppler shift!" The sonar chief shouted. "The Orca is turning!"

"The enemy torpedo is accelerating! It's range gating!"

"Weapons Officer," Janet ordered, "detonate both torpedoes now."

The blare of the collision alarm blocked out the Weapons Officer's response, but she saw him slam his hands down on both buttons. For a heart-stopping moment, Janet thought the wire had broken, then...

Ka-WHUMPF!

Two torpedoes detonated as one, creating a massive bubble in the ocean that expanded in an instant, then collapsed in on itself. The deck heaved as the force of the blast pushed the submarine back, then dragged it forward.

"All ahead flank!" Janet ordered. "Engine room, max power NOW!"

The deck bucked as the massive propeller churned the water behind them, driving them forward into the vortex created by the explosion. Janet's feet left the floor, her head connected with something hard, and she dropped to her hands and knees.

When she looked up again, the XO had a grip on the back of the Pilot's chair, yelling in the man's ear. He understood Janet's last-ditch plan: Drive the ship into the heart of the explosion and hope the enemy torpedo lost them in the chaos.

She made out O'Malley's round face, ghostly pale, his headphones dangling around his neck. Sonar was useless now. The ocean was a sea of chaotic noise.

Her ship was blind.

The submarine heeled to the right, throwing Janet into a metal stanchion. A stabbing pain radiated up her side.

The roll continued, the nose of the ship tilted upward.

The lights flickered. The deck beneath her hands went still. The thrum of the main engines driving the ship forward had stopped. She knew instantly what had happened. The blast had knocked the reactor offline. The *Illinois* was dead in the water.

"Reactor scram." The engineer's voice over the 1MC sounded preternaturally calm. "Commencing emergency startup."

Even an emergency startup took precious time and that was the one thing she did not have. There was an enemy submarine out there hunting them. Their first torpedo might have missed, but...

Savarino hauled her to her feet. "Recommend emergency blow, Captain."

Janet shook her head, the pain in her side leaving her unable to speak for a second.

"No," she gasped, "we hide here. Inside the explosion we're safe."

She didn't verbalize the rest of her thought, but Savarino understood. If they surfaced in the middle of the Chinese live-fire exercise, the entire operation would be exposed.

The skin on Savarino's face was tight, streaked with sweat. He had a cut over his right eye, and a line of blood ran down his cheek. He opened his mouth to respond, but Senior Chief O'Malley cut in:

"Active sonar, bearing zero-three-zero!"

50

CNS *Changcheng* 346, 101 miles south of Pratas Island
1740 China Standard Time

"Stand by to launch tube two," Kai repeated. He seized the fire control technician by the shoulder. "I gave you an order."

Strong fingers gripped his biceps on both arms, pulled him away from the fire control station. He fought back, but the two security guards were strong.

Mao stepped in front of him, saying in a formal voice, "Captain Kai Jun, on behalf of the People's Republic of China and the Chinese Communist Party, I hereby relieve you of command." He turned to the fire control tech. "Shut down the torpedo."

The young man looked from Mao to Kai. The third security guard stepped close, put a hand on his sidearm.

"Do it!" Mao ordered.

"I can't, sir. The wire broke."

Mao whirled on Kai. "You fool. Do you want to start a war? You don't know what—"

Ka-WHUMPF!

The deck tilted. Kai's feet left the floor and the hands holding his arms dropped away. He fell flat on his back, his head connecting with the deck. Stars cartwheeled across his vision.

A torpedo had exploded, but which one? He had to make sure the American submarine was dead. He had to be certain.

Kai rolled onto his hands and knees and used a stanchion to haul himself to his feet. He staggered to the helm. "Steer two-one-zero, all ahead one-third."

"Aye-aye, sir."

Kai lurched to the sonar team. One of the techs held his hands over his ears. He'd been wearing his headphones when the explosion hit and his hearing was damaged.

The sonar displays were saturated with noise from the detonation. It didn't matter; any pretense of stealth was long gone.

"Line up to go active," he ordered. "Full power."

The sonar supervisor's eyes showed his uncertainty, but he did as he was told. "Ready to transmit, sir."

"Go," Kai ordered.

The first burst of energy reflected off the millions of bubbles in the water, returning a screen of white noise.

"Again," Kai ordered.

Another screen of reflected energy.

"Recommend lower power, sir," the sonar supervisor said.

"Half power," Kai ordered. "Go again. Continuous pinging. Find that American submarine."

The second transmission was slightly better, but still full of trashy returns. A third ping, then a fourth, then...

There it was. A solid, unmoving blob amid a sea of half-formed ghost returns.

"We have a contact, Captain," the sonar operator reported. "Three thousand meters, bearing one-nine-zero. It's dead in the water, sir."

"I've got you!" Kai whispered. He raised his voice. "Firing point procedures, tube two, bearing one-nine-zero."

"Belay that order!" Mao shouted.

"Flood tube two and open outer doors," Kai ordered. The fire control tech hesitated. "I am your captain. Do it!"

Three security guards tackled Kai. His face smashed into the deck. They wrenched his hands behind his back and clipped handcuffs on his wrists.

"Fire tube two!" Kai shouted.

Mao put his hand on the fire control tech's shoulder. "Stand down."

The fire control tech crossed his arms, tucked his hands into his armpits.

"Fire tube two!" Kai shouted again.

One of the security guards pulled a red bandana from his back pocket and stuffed it into Kai's mouth. The material tasted of sweat and grease, making him want to gag.

"Cease active transmissions," Mao ordered. The sonar operator shut down the active array. Kai could see the enemy submarine outlined clearly on the screen. The sonar team turned in their seats to look at the political officer, their new captain.

Commander Mao froze for a second, realizing that he was now in charge. "Tell Mr. Wong to come to control on the double," he ordered the messenger. The man left and an awkward silence settled in the room, all eyes on Mao.

He shifted from foot to foot, his eyes darting around the control room. Finally, he said, "Prepare to take the ship to periscope depth."

Out of the corner of his eye, Kai noticed a change on the broadband sonar display, but all the sonar techs had turned to look at Mao. All their headphones were hung on the hooks next to their workstations.

A white trace raced across the screen. A close, fast-moving contact. Very close, and very fast.

Kai bellowed, straining against his captors, but the bandana stifled the noise.

"Sonar!" he tried to yell, but with no success.

The sonar supervisor looked down at him and Kai tried to indicate with his eyes the incoming danger. The man frowned in confusion, then spun around to face the display.

"New sonar contact!" He slapped the headphones on. "Torpedo in the water!"

A trained watch officer would have acted on instinct: increase speed to all ahead flank, make a sharp turn, deploy countermeasures to confuse the torpedo.

But Commander Mao was not a trained watch officer. And he hesitated.

His eyes found Kai as if to say: *What do I do?*

But Kai was bound and gagged on the deck of his own ship, helpless to save himself or his crew.

"It's range gating!" The sonar supervisor's voice cracked, but the report was unnecessary. Kai could hear the rapid-fire pinging of the incoming torpedo through the hull of his ship.

He closed his eyes.

51

USS *Illinois*, 116 miles south of Pratas Island
1745 China Standard Time

"Active sonar is consistent with a Type 039 Chinese submarine, Captain." Senior Chief O'Malley held the headphones away from his ears as he watched the sonic energy splash across his screen. "Range four thousand yards. They're operating at max power, ma'am."

"Can they find us, Senior?" Janet asked.

"At that power, all they're gonna get is a massive reflection," O'Malley assured her. "The ocean is a hot mess right now."

The *Illinois* was near ground zero of the underwater explosion. The disturbed waters were full of bubbles, dead fish, and other debris. Using full-power sonar transmission in this environment was equivalent to using high beams in thick fog. Less was more. Lower power might allow the Chinese ship to see more deeply into the fog where the *Illinois* was hiding. She wondered how long it would take the Chinese submarine captain to realize his error.

"Engine room reports reactor back online in sixty seconds," the Pilot reported.

Every second felt like an eternity. Janet ran the numbers in her head and the math did not look good.

At four thousand yards, a torpedo could be at their position in minutes. Even if she ran at flank speed, the torpedo had a serious speed advantage on her ship.

No matter how many times she ran the problem, the math did not work out in her favor.

"Open outer doors on tubes three and four," she ordered. If they launched a torpedo at her, she had no choice but to return the favor.

"Outer doors on three and four are open, Captain," said the Weapons Officer.

"They've lowered power!" O'Malley announced, a touch of panic in his voice. "They'll see us for sure..." His bearlike frame sat bolt upright in his seat. "Torpedo in the water!"

Janet's skin crawled. "Firing point procedures—"

"Wait!" O'Malley half stood up. "It's not a Chinese torpedo! It's a Spearfish! The *Agamemnon* is firing on the Chinese boat."

Janet's gaze snapped to the sonar display. The screen was awash with noisy clutter, but the distinctive stripe of a high-speed contact was plain to see.

"The torpedo is range gating!"

Janet gaped. "Is the Chinese ship firing back?"

"No, Captain. It's not doing anything. It's—" He snatched the headphones away from his ears.

Ka-WUMPF.

Another shock wave rocked the *Illinois* and the sound of the detonation rang through the steel hull. Janet hung onto the stanchion, the pain in her side screaming in protest.

O'Malley's round face was pale and sweaty. He put the headphones back on and screwed his eyes shut as he listened.

"Breaking up noises...hull popping...She's going down. No sign of an emergency blow...." He paused, his voice grew soft. "She's gone."

The silence in the control room felt thick as oil, as if the whole world had just slowed down.

"Reactor is back online, Captain," Savarino reported.

"I don't get it, ma'am," O'Malley said. "They never fired back. They never even increased speed. They had to hear it coming and they just...sat there."

And died, Janet finished in her head.

She tried to imagine what that death must have been like and stopped herself. That was not a helpful train of thought right now. What she needed to do now was to complete her mission: Get the hell out of Dodge. Undetected.

"XO." Her voice sounded like a croak.

"Captain." Savarino's voice didn't sound any better.

"Head due east for twenty miles, then turn north. Let's go home."

52

CNS *Shinyan*, 120 miles east of the Paracel Islands
1745 China Standard Time

The compromised mobile phone felt like a brick in Chang's hip pocket. As soon as they let him out of the torpedo room, he was going to go to the nearest ship's railing and drop it overboard.

But right now, no one involved in the testing was allowed to go anywhere. As soon as the Hu Jing torpedo failed to detonate at the target hulk and continued north, Admiral Chin ordered an immediate review of every step of the launch procedure.

The information on the flatscreen monitor was painfully incomplete. While the marine patrol aircraft had blanketed the ocean with sonobuoys along the track between the launch vessel and the target, they'd put very few listening devices in the water between the target hulk and the line of picket ships fifty miles to the north.

Consequently, the red line of the Hu Jing torpedo track ended about ten miles past the hulk. The red dot pulsed as the screen waited for an update that would never come.

Admiral Chin immediately ordered marine patrol aircraft to lay more sonobuoys in the waters north of the target, but they had all been vectored south to the unfolding crisis near Second Thomas Shoal. They answered to higher authorities now. Operational commanders, not scientists and engineers.

Chin's second-best option was to use the picket ships to try to track the errant torpedo. He ordered the admiral in charge to the north to gather as much sonar data as possible and report back.

Mr. Li, the test director, was all but useless. His hands shook, and his expression seemed to swing between extremes of mood. Still, he carried on, walking through every step of the pre-launch procedure in detail. When he got to the guidance system upload, he reviewed the parameters that had been sent through the umbilical to the torpedo.

He found nothing wrong with the uploaded data. Although Chang expected that result, he breathed a sigh of relief all the same. Angelina-Marie's plan had worked: The mobile phone overrode the data stream at the last minute and reprogrammed the weapon.

The test director's shoulders quivered with worry. In spite of himself, Chang felt sorry for the man.

"I can't understand," Li said in a low voice that reeked of desperate pain. "How could two torpedoes fail?" He looked at Chang. "What do you think happened?"

"I don't know," Chang replied, also keeping his voice low. "The guidance system worked perfectly. It transitioned to search mode, found the target, we even heard it range gate on the target...but the warhead didn't explode."

"Yes," the test director agreed. "The warhead." He started to close the laptop lid, then paused. "Whose computer is this?"

"Gang Wei's," Chang answered truthfully.

"Why did you use his computer and not your own?"

"He ordered me to use his laptop. I did what he said."

The test director's eyes widened. "He *ordered* you to use his laptop?"

"Well." Chang hesitated. "It wasn't a direct order, not really. I only saw him for a second and he was very sick, but he did insist that I use his laptop. It was already set up, so I figured, why not?"

Chang proceeded with caution. He and Gang had exchanged a few words through the closed door of the toilet, but his boss had been distracted to the point of frenzy. In that moment, he probably could have confessed everything and Gang probably wouldn't have remembered. Despite explosive diarrhea, Gang still only heard things that were about him.

"You don't think..." Chang let the question hang in the air.

When Mr. Li stood up, the test director seemed to have more stiffness in his spine. He picked up the laptop. "I need to keep this."

"Of course," Chang said, "anything I can do to help."

"Admiral Chin!"

The captain of the *Shinyan*, a PLA Navy commander, stood in the entrance to the makeshift torpedo room. He seemed reluctant to enter, as if the stench of failure might cling to his uniform.

"What is it?" Chin snapped. "I'm very busy."

The commander licked his lips. "Message from the flagship *Zunyi*. They report a massive underwater explosion north of the target hulk."

Chin's face sagged with relief. "Thank you for the update. I think we can assume that the torpedo detonated on its own."

"There's more, Admiral."

"Well?" Chin's imperious nature reasserted itself. "What is it?"

"The submarine attached to the picket line, the *Changcheng* 346, is missing."

Admiral Chin's fleshy cheeks turned the color of ash.

"We have orders from South Sea Fleet headquarters to return to port immediately." The captain departed the silent room.

Thirty minutes later, Chang emerged on the weather deck of the *Shinyan*. The late afternoon sun was warm on his back as he rested his elbows on the rail and looked over the side.

A creamy white wave curled away from the bow. A brisk wind cut across the deck, ruffling his hair. He sucked in a lungful of moist sea air, savoring the taste on his tongue.

The taste of freedom.

He felt hollow inside, as if the stress of the last twenty-four hours had drained all the energy from his body, turning him into a husk.

But he'd done it. He'd accomplished his mission. Not only had he escaped suspicion, but he'd also thrown doubt elsewhere.

When the test director asked about Gang's laptop, Chang seized the opportunity to seed the blame on his boss. Admiral Chin would not stop until he had someone to blame—someone not named Admiral Chin, that is.

If Angelina-Marie's claims were true, then even a deep forensic analysis of Gang's laptop would find no trace of the corrupted data file that had been passed to the torpedo.

Everything she'd told him to date was true. Anyway, he had no choice but to trust her. His fate was in her hands.

And the fate of his daughter. He pulled his mobile phone from his hip pocket and opened the photos. Cassie stared back at him, a big smile on her face. The picture was from her eighteenth birthday.

Before the divorce, before she went to Canada, before it all went wrong.

She didn't smile like that anymore. *I will get her back to that place of happiness and security,* he promised. *Whatever it takes.*

Then he let the mobile phone slip from his fingers.

53

USS *Kansas City*, 15 miles east of Second Thomas Shoal, South China Sea
1745 China Standard Time

Commander Mike Ferrell had a growing respect for the officer in charge of the Filipino supply mission. Captain Raul Bautista, commanding officer of the BRP *Antonio Luna*, seemed to be a veteran of numerous supply missions and an expert on Chinese harassment tactics.

Two hours ago, both he and Bautista had received orders to break off from a direct approach to Second Thomas Shoal and loiter in the area. The orders infuriated Ferrell, but when he conferred with the Philippine Navy officer on secure HF, the man seemed to take it in stride. His voice even had a hint of a smile.

"These resupply missions are as much political theater as they are about delivery of food and water, Commander Ferrell," he said. "Follow my lead."

The *Luna* herded the supply mission along a route parallel to their destination at a pokey speed of barely five knots. Ferrell had expected the Chinese to back off when they'd slowed down and changed course. He was surprised when the de-escalation actions had the opposite effect: It seemed to frustrate the Chinese ships. The situation felt more volatile now, as if the Chinese Coast Guard ship captains were spoiling for a fight.

For every hour that passed, their tactical situation deteriorated. Eight PLA Navy combatants were sailing south at top speed toward Second Thomas Shoal, offering reinforcement to the two PLA Navy destroyers still inside the harbor at Mischief Reef.

If this went on much longer, he could be facing ten ships. Not Coast Guard, but warships, armed with lethal missile batteries, against his measly defenses. Against that kind of firepower, he was a sitting duck. Surely his chain of command wouldn't let it come to that.

Besides, he thought, there was reason to believe that the Chinese wanted to keep this situation under control. If they wanted to challenge Ferrell directly, the two PLA Navy destroyers at Mischief Reef were less than forty miles away. So far, those ships remained at anchor in the harbor.

Ferrell's surface action group maintained a tight V-formation a thousand yards to the rear of the Philippine ships. The *Luna* ran on the starboard side of the supply vessel. Although the lumbering converted tender was much bigger than Bautista's command, it appeared slow and dilapidated next to the sleek Philippine Navy flagship.

The other escort, a *Jacinto*-class patrol boat about half the length of the *Kansas City*, took station on the port side of the supply vessel. It lacked the speed, firepower, and maneuverability of the flagship, but Ferrell welcomed all the help he could gather for the coming confrontation.

The Chinese Coast Guard formed a loose ring two thousand yards around the supply convoy. The Chinese ships seemed to be egging each other on, as if the captains were in a competition for who could execute the most daring run at the convoy.

For his part, Bautista played it cool, maintaining a non-threatening course and speed and letting the Chinese take last-minute avoidance maneuvers to prevent an accident. Periodically, his flagship issued a radio warning that they were a peaceful supply mission executing their right to freedom of navigation in international waters.

As the afternoon wore on, the Chinese radio responses degenerated from canned diplomatic language into angry taunts.

When the order came for the convoy to approach Second Thomas Shoal, Ferrell contacted Bautista again on secure HF radio.

"The Chinese are very angry," Bautista said after confirming that he had the same orders from his chain of command.

"I agree."

"We will use that against them," the Philippine Navy commander said, in a voice that portrayed confidence that Ferrell did not share. "I'm going to draw them off and instruct the supply vessel to make a high-speed run toward the shoal. When I make my move, I want you to take my station on the starboard side of the supply ship and bring your other ships in behind the convoy." He paused. "Is that acceptable, Captain?"

I'm an escort, Ferrell reminded himself. This is not my mission.

Out loud, he said, "I'll follow your lead, Captain."

For the next twenty minutes, Ferrell watched as Bautista slowly edged his warship ahead of the convoy, gradually increasing the distance between himself and the supply ship. The Chinese Coast Guard vessel assigned to guard the frigate matched his progress, slowly moving off station.

Then the *Luna* made its move, accelerating forward. The Chinese vessel immediately responded in kind, leaving a gap in the coverage. The two remaining members of the supply convoy made a sharp turn and accelerated due west toward Second Thomas Shoal.

Kansas City used her water jets to spin in the water, another move the Chinese failed to anticipate, and accelerated to take station off the starboard flank of the supply ship. With the superior speed and maneuverability of the LCS platform, Ferrell was on station in a matter of minutes, before the other Chinese vessels could react.

Ferrell was pleasantly surprised that the supply ship had some horsepower. By the time he arrived a thousand yards on her starboard beam, the rust-stained ship was traveling at over twenty knots.

Ferrell raised the binoculars. The lead Chinese Coast Guard ship, realizing he'd been duped by Bautista, tried to swing around to meet the supply vessel.

But the *Luna* was faster. Bautista crossed the stern of the Chinese ship and took station off its right side, matching speed. The Chinese captain tried to shoulder the Philippine Navy frigate aside, but the *Luna* deflected the attempt.

"We've got company, Captain," his tactical officer announced. Ferrell stood behind him to view the radar picture. The three remaining Chinese Coast Guard vessels were converging on the supply mission at top speed.

To the right of the *Kansas City*, the Chinese Coast Guard vessel tried to cut in front of the convoy.

"OOD," Ferrell shouted, "put us on an intercept. I want to shoulder him off course."

He spun the *Kansas City* and the ship shot forward at a full bell. The water jets gave his ship a maneuverability for which the Chinese had no answer. He approached the speeding Coast Guard vessel at an oblique angle, not touching the other ship, but forcing him to either change course or slow down.

Through the open door to the bridge wing, Ferrell could look down into the bridge of the Chinese ship. He spied the captain, binoculars around his neck, looking back at Ferrell. He saw the man's lips move, and the ship slowed.

Ferrell let out a relieved breath that they had blinked first and he waved at his counterpart. The Chinese captain gave him the finger.

"*Mobile*'s in trouble, sir!" his tactical officer called out.

Ferrell's move had opened a gap in their coverage of the supply vessel. A second Chinese Coast Guard ship was barreling into the breach at full speed.

The *Mobile* shot forward, attempting to shoulder the oncoming Chinese ship off course, but the Chinese ship captain kept his speed up. The ship hulls scraped against each other, but the Chinese captain had the upper hand. The *Mobile* fell back.

"OOD!" Ferrell shouted. "Reverse course now."

As fast as the *Kansas City* was, the Chinese captain had the edge and he moved to exercise his advantage.

"Captain!" the tactical officer warned.

Ferrell, who had moved to the bridge wing, took in the picture through his binoculars. Two Chinese ships were converging on the bow of the Philippine supply ship from opposite sides. The one to the left was in the lead, cutting across the track of the slower Philippine escort on a collision course with the supply ship.

"They're gonna ram her, sir," the tactical officer said.

The supply ship captain made the only move he had left: He cut his engines and put his rudder hard to the right. He'd timed it perfectly, Ferrell thought. On their current trajectory, both Chinese ships would pass in front of him.

Unfortunately for the captain of the supply ship, the Chinese vessel on his right flank did not maintain course and speed. At exactly the same time as the Philippine captain made his maneuver, the Chinese captain cut his own engines and put his rudder hard left.

The Chinese captain's plan, it was clear to Ferrell, had been to cross behind the speeding supply ship. Instead, he put his ship broadside to the much larger Philippine supply vessel.

Too late, the Chinese captain realized his dire situation. Ferrell saw the water boiling at the stern of the Coast Guard ship as the CO put on an emergency backing bell.

It only aggravated the problem. The Chinese ship slowed, but the propeller was fighting against five thousand tons of forward momentum.

The supply ship, traveling at more than fifteen knots, hit the much smaller Chinese Coast Guard vessel broadside. The impact occurred just forward of the bridge, the massive flank of the supply ship obliterating the forecastle of the sleek white Chinese vessel.

From his position a mile away, Ferrell watched the supply ship ride up out of the water, topping and rolling the Chinese ship hard to starboard. Even at that distance, the scream of rending metal reached his ears.

The Chinese vessel never recovered from the roll. The massive bulk of the supply ship hung suspended out of the water for a few seconds, then the hull of the Chinese vessel shuddered as the keel cracked. The Philippine supply ship fell back into the ocean.

The broken Chinese vessel tipped up at the bow and stern, then both halves of the broken ship sank beneath the waves.

54

USS *Kansas City*, 9 miles east of Second Thomas Shoal, South China Sea
1749 China Standard Time

Through the binoculars, Ferrell watched a slick of oil spreading rapidly on the ocean. The Chinese Coast Guard ship had disappeared.

At his side, McKenzie said, "Holy shit..."

Ferrell scanned the sea for survivors but saw none. He turned the field of view on the Philippine supply ship. The big vessel had a tear in her rust-stained hull, and she listed hard to starboard.

His mind raced. This was a total disaster—worst-case scenario. They needed to fall back now. He reached for the radio handset—

"Vampires! Vampires inbound! Bearing three-five-zero, range three-eight miles."

Ferrell reacted. "Helm, come right to three-five-zero, all ahead full." The ship spun, surged forward.

"Radar, give me a number of missiles and time on target," he shouted.

"I'm tracking two vampires, sir. Forty-three seconds to impact." The young sailor on the radar suddenly looked very young to Ferrell's eyes. Her face was bone-white, but her voice was steady. "They're targeting the supply ship, sir."

Ferrell tried to make sense of what he was seeing. They were firing from Mischief Reef, but they'd only used two missiles, aimed at the supply ship. The Chinese clearly thought that if they could kill the supply ship, they'd kill the mission.

Ferrell wanted to shout into the wind in frustration. Like it or not, they were in the shit now and he'd be damned if he was going to let the Chinese shoot a defenseless supply ship. The only way to stop that was to give them a juicier target.

Seconds mattered. The countdown clock ran in his brain. Timing was everything.

"Twenty-nine seconds," the radar operator reported.

"XO, launch chaff at fifteen seconds."

"Chaff at fifteen, aye, sir."

Ferrell snatched up the VHF handset. "All units, this is KC actual. Weapons hold unless you are fired upon. I repeat, weapons hold unless you are fired upon."

In the back of his mind, he still held out hope that he could walk this whole situation back. The PLA had launched only two missiles. That showed restraint. If he took out those missiles, and didn't fire back at the Chinese, then maybe, just maybe, he could get his forces out of here without starting World War Three.

He wondered if that restraint would hold once the PLA Navy brass realized they'd just lost an entire Coast Guard vessel with all hands on board.

"Launching chaff," McKenzie reported.

Ferrell heard the rapid *bang-bang* sound of the RBOC launcher. Chaff canisters released their load of metallic confetti into the air behind them.

"Hard to port, steady new course two-five-zero. All ahead flank."

The ship spun and lifted out of the water as her speed cranked up to forty knots.

The countermeasures rose behind them like a glittering mountain, offering the incoming missiles a massive target. He saw twin streaks of smoke enter a final kill sequence where the missile rose above the target and dove straight down. The maneuver was designed to bury the missile deep in the hull of the target ship before it exploded.

In this case, the target was a phantom and both missiles ended up in the ocean.

Ferrell pumped a fist.

"Helm, steer due south. Maintain flank speed."

Ferrell alternated between the radar screen and the binoculars. The three remaining Chinese Coast Guard ships had converged on the oil slick. They were putting boats in the water, so maybe there were survivors.

The Philippine ships were...

Ferrell stared at the radar display in disbelief, then raised the binoculars.

The supply ship, carrying a twenty-degree list starboard, was making about nine knots toward Second Thomas Shoal. She was flanked by the two Philippine combatants with *Mobile* and *Oakland* two thousand yards behind in trailing positions.

Ferrell snatched up the VHF radio handset. "All units, this is KC actual, we need to fall back, now!"

"*Kansas City*, this is *Luna* actual, negative. The supply ship is not going to make it back to port."

Ferrell tried to process what Bautista was telling him. The supply ship was not going to make it home, so...

"We're going to run her aground on the reef, Captain." Bautista put into words what Ferrell's brain refused to process. "We'll get her as close to the *Sierra Madre* as possible, then withdraw."

"Jesus, sir," McKenzie said, "that'll start an international incident."

Ferrell did the mental math. At their current speed, Bautista would need at least twenty minutes to put the supply ship into shallow water.

His job to escort the Philippine supply mission just got a whole lot more dangerous. If they were lucky, he figured they had fifteen minutes before the Chinese figured out Bautista's endgame. When that happened, they'd come at the Philippine contingent with everything they had.

"Captain!" the radar operator reported. "Fast movers inbound from Mischief Reef at five hundred knots."

Make that ten minutes until the Chinese figured it out.

Ferrell picked up the handset. "*Mobile* and *Oakland*, this is KC actual.

We're going to form a screen a thousand yards behind the supply convoy. I'm moving into position now."

He gripped the handrail as the ship turned and put on speed. *Oakland* and *Mobile* roared into position on either side of his ship.

"XO, give me firing solutions on those PLA destroyers."

"Aye-aye, sir."

The ships slowed, took up station in a thousand-yard perimeter behind the slower convoy. Thick black smoke poured out of the stacks of the laboring supply ship, but she was maintaining speed.

Two black shapes raced across the sky ahead of them. A second later, he heard the sonic boom of the PLA fighters over the roar of the wind. Even in a hierarchical command structure like the Chinese military, this tactical situation was not going to take a long time to solve.

Five minutes, he thought. Max.

"Captain!" McKenzie shouted. "We're being painted by fire control radars."

Okay, less than five minutes.

"Very well, XO." Ferrell's voice sounded flat in his own ears.

"I have a firing solution ready, sir," the XO announced.

"Assign two Naval Strike Missiles to each of the PLA destroyers, Mr. McKenzie."

The XO's face was an open book saying, *Is this really happening?* Then the moment was gone, and McKenzie was back in control.

"Two missiles each on the PLA destroyers, aye, sir." A beat. "Missiles are targeted, Captain."

Ferrell picked up the handset again, his every movement deliberate now. There was still a chance, he thought. Maybe.

"All units, this is KC actual, unless you see me fire, you are weapons hold. Acknowledge."

"*Mobile* actual, acknowledged." Her captain's voice was tight.

"*Oakland* actual, acknowledged." When Ferrell heard Hibbard's voice, a thousand memories flashed across his brain. He pushed them away.

Ferrell closed his eyes for a second. The next move was not theirs. If the Chinese wanted a fight, then he'd give them one, but he hoped to God it didn't come to that.

"Vampires! Vampires inbound! Bearing three-one-zero, range twenty thousand yards. Time to impact, two minutes."

Ferrell's eyes snapped open.

"XO, launch missiles."

"Launch missiles, aye, sir."

Smoke and fire consumed the forecastle of the *Kansas City* as four Naval Strike Missiles blasted out of their shells and shot into the sky.

"Time to impact one minute, thirty seconds."

The acrid smoke from the missile launch wafted into the bridge, stung his nostrils.

"Stand by to launch countermeasures and take evasive maneuvers."

Ferrell snatched up the handset.

"All units, this is KC actual. Weapons free. I repeat, you are weapons free."

55

USS *Kansas City*, 7 miles east of Second Thomas Shoal, Spratly Islands, South China Sea
1756 China Standard Time

Commander Mike Ferrell had trained for this moment his entire naval career. The orders that came out of his mouth were equal parts muscle memory and responses to the tactical situation. From his perch in the captain's chair overlooking his bridge crew, he was an extension of his command—and he was in the fight of his life.

"Two missiles locked on!" the XO shouted. "Time to impact twenty seconds."

"Hard right," Ferrell barked out. The compass repeater reeled as the nimble ship spun on a dime. "Launch chaff."

Out of the corner of his eye, he saw McKenzie's hand slam down and heard the distant *bang-bang-bang* of the countermeasures.

"Steady as she goes," Ferrell shouted. "All ahead flank."

The *Kansas City* stopped her sweeping turn and shot away, lifting out of the water, leaving the geyser of silver metal flakes in the sky behind her.

"First missile splashed. Second missile is still locked on!" the tactical officer reported. "SeaRAM is engaging."

Even as he processed the report, Ferrell could hear the sequential *whoosh* sounds as the rolling airframe missile launcher mounted on top of the ship executed a ripple fire.

Five hundred yards off their port bow, there was a tremendous explosion.

"Splash two."

Ferrell let go of the breath he was holding, but there was no time for celebration.

"Reverse course," he ordered.

When the ship spun around, Ferrell's heart jumped. The *Oakland* was on fire, her bridge a mess of twisted metal.

Hibs...but the thought evaporated as heavy-caliber rounds pounded into the superstructure of his ship.

The Chinese Coast Guard had given up looking for survivors and they were out for blood. While one of the Coast Guard cutters engaged the *Kansas City*, the other two converged on the Philippine convoy. *Mobile* moved to intercept one. Bautista and the *Luna* took on the second Chinese ship.

More rounds impacted the hull.

"XO, target that ship with the big gun and open fire." Ferrell drove the *Kansas City* straight at the Chinese vessel, offering the smallest possible target. The raked bow of the *Kansas City* allowed them to fire even as they bore down on the smaller ship. At nearly forty knots, the *Kansas City* chewed through the distance between them.

The Chinese ship turned to flee, but her captain misjudged the speed and maneuverability of the LCS platform. Again.

Ferrell felt the hull absorb multiple rounds of the heavy Chinese shells. One ripped into the superstructure above his head. When he looked up, he saw blue sky. The aluminum hull of the *Kansas City* wasn't made for this kind of abuse.

"Target her bridge!" he yelled. The order wasn't necessary. McKenzie knew his business.

The bridge of the Chinese Coast Guard vessel exploded. The ship swung into a lazy turn to port, losing headway rapidly.

"Cease fire!" Ferrell ordered.

He steered his ship back toward the fight just in time to see the *Luna* shoulder violently into another of the Chinese Coast Guard ships, knocking it off its collision course with the supply vessel. The railing of the Chinese ship crumbled under the impact. A streak of gray decorated her white-painted side.

Machine gun fire poured across the water between the two ships, the air hazy with burnt gunpowder. *Luna* drove the smaller vessel away from the supply ship, then executed an emergency backing bell, positioning herself on the Chinese ship's rear quarter.

The Chinese captain realized his mistake just as the *Luna* brought her 76mm naval gun to bear and opened fire at point-blank range. The *Luna*'s main gun worked with deadly efficiency. It put a few rounds into the bridge, then concentrated fire on the ship's stern to knock out the rudder and engines.

In less than a minute, the Chinese Coast Guard cutter was dead in the water. The *Luna* poured rounds into her waterline until the ship started to list. Then she sped past to rejoin the supply ship.

"Vampires inbound!" The tactical officer paused. "I count one-six bogeys. Bearing three-zero-two, range thirty miles. Time to impact three minutes."

Ferrell cursed to himself. The Chinese were in this for real now and he had four Naval Strike Missiles left.

"Target the launching ships with remaining NSMs, XO."

"Targeting, aye, sir." Seconds ticked away. "Firing solution locked in, Captain. Standing by."

"Fire," Ferrell ordered. The ripple fire of missiles was deafening. The blasts hid the bow of the *Kansas City* behind a wall of smoke and fire. Through the bridge doorway, he saw *Mobile* do the same. *Oakland* was nowhere in sight.

"Steer new course zero-two-zero," Ferrell shouted. His voice sounded muffled after the loudness of the launch. Smoke stung his eyes. "All ahead full." The ship turned, but not with her usual zip. Ferrell could feel the speed falling off.

"We're losing power," the OOD reported. "I've lost one of the gas turbines. Diesel two is also failing."

Ferrell had no idea how many rounds his ship had absorbed from the Chinese ship, but at least a few had found their mark.

He moved to the tactical screen. "We stay on this course and launch every countermeasure we have to draw the missiles away from the supply ship."

McKenzie nodded. "Countermeasures are reloaded, Captain."

"Thirty seconds to impact," the TAO reported.

"Launch countermeasures," Ferrell ordered. "One-second intervals."

Bang...bang...bang...bang...

Twelve seconds later, the Super RBOC launchers were empty. The air behind the ship filled with chaff and infrared countermeasures designed to fool the incoming enemy missiles. Ferrell spun the ship to allow the SeaRAM point defenses to engage.

"Splash one...two...three..." the tactical officer called out.

On top of the bridge, the close-in defense system launched interceptor missiles, then went silent.

The rolling airframe launcher was empty.

"We're Winchester on SeaRAM, Captain," the XO confirmed. Then his voice spiked. "Missile lock! Incoming missile!"

Ferrell ordered a new course that would take them into the chaff cloud, but the ship was slow to respond. He seized the 1MC handset. "All hands, brace for impact."

He dropped the microphone, gripped the arms of the captain's chair with both hands.

Ferrell heard the missile make its pop-up climb, then the sound died, and he knew it had peaked and turned. A dark shape flashed down in front of the bridge windows. Ferrell slammed his eyes shut, bracing for the explosion that was going to blow him to Kingdom Come...

Nothing.

The ship slowed even more. They'd been hit, but not killed.

"Damage report!" he called out.

"Flooding in forward compartments!" came the report.

Ferrell launched out of his chair to the bridge windows and looked down at the hole in the forecastle deck of his ship. His heart skipped a beat.

The missile had passed through the aluminum hull and into the ocean below them. If the *Kansas City* had been made out of steel, they'd all be dead.

"OOD," he shouted. "What's our status?"

"Two engines out and a third is in trouble, sir," the OOD replied. "I can give you ten knots, maybe twelve."

When they cleared the dispersing cloud of chaff, the first thing Ferrell noticed was that *Oakland* was gone.

If they stayed here, they were dead. He needed to collect his survivors and clear the area, but first he needed some serious air support.

He grabbed the SATCOM handset, keyed the transmit button. "Almighty, this is *Kansas City* actual. Request immediate air support and relay of distress call to all nearby US units. We have one unit sunk, two damaged. We are Winchester."

Saying it out loud gave Ferrell a cold feeling. They were out of missiles, offensive and defensive, and the countermeasures locker was empty. Worse, his two biggest assets—speed and maneuverability—were questionable at best.

If the approaching Chinese launched another missile salvo, his ship was a sitting duck.

56

SS *Arrogant*, Dalupiri Island, Babuyan Island Chain, northern Philippines
2045 China Standard Time

"All stop," ordered Bill James. "Hold this position, Captain."

Claude Buettner nudged the engines into reverse until all their headway had dropped off, then slipped the throttle into neutral. "All stop. Holding position."

The shadowy figure of the SEAL commander nodded in the dim green glow of the instrument panel. All lights on the ship were extinguished, including navigation lights, and the ship's automatic identification system beacon had been turned off hours ago.

Claude had insisted that he be allowed to run the radar and the fathometer. This area of the Philippine Sea was littered with reefs and atolls, not to mention fishing boats and other small watercraft. With the *Arrogant* running dark, he needed to make sure he kept his command safe.

Despite the tension in the air, Claude yawned. It had been a long day, full of twists and turns that he barely understood. Bill's teams had been out on the water since midmorning tending to a series of hydrophones that they'd arranged across a twenty-mile arc.

There had been a flurry of message activity around noon, followed by a tense two hours, then another burst of back-and-forth messaging. Bill even broke out his satellite phone at one point and had a hurried conversation with someone.

They were trying to find a torpedo, Claude had figured out that much from Bill's hints about the Notice to Mariners, but the idea still didn't compute. How was a torpedo supposed to travel hundreds of miles off course?

Then, as the afternoon sun touched the horizon, Bill's radio exploded with updates. With Claude looking on, Bill consulted the chart of the area, drawing thick lines with a pencil, then issuing search orders.

The *Arrogant* reversed course to pick up a four-man team to their north. By the time Claude turned south again, the sun had set and Bill asked him to run dark.

The sliver of moon in the night sky shed little light on the quiet sea. Bill offered him a pair of night vision binoculars. "You want to take a look?" He pointed dead ahead into the darkness.

Claude raised the glasses and focused. A half mile off, his diving launch and an inflatable dinghy rode lightly on the gentle waves. There was only one man in the launch, which meant there were seven in the water.

"The EOD teams are done with their part," Bill said in a low voice as if reluctant to break the tranquility of the scene. "We're rigging the inflatables. It's tough going. That thing grounded itself pretty hard."

Claude could make out a dim glow in the water beneath the diving launch.

"How visible do you think that light is?" he asked.

"Good eye." Bill chuckled. "This was supposed to be a daytime operation, but best-laid plans and all that. How do you feel about using your ship as cover?"

Claude studied the SEAL commander. "You're sure the warhead is disarmed?"

Bill shrugged. "My guys get it right"—he flashed a smile— "most of the time."

Claude laughed at the joke, but he'd seen what a torpedo warhead could do. He did not want to be anywhere close by when one went off.

"I'll guide you into position, Captain," Bill said as he slipped out the door of the bridge. He reappeared a moment later on the bow. He raised a walkie-talkie to his lips.

"All ahead slow, Captain. Nice and easy."

Claude nudged the throttle and the *Arrogant* crept forward. He kept one eye on the fathometer as the ship neared a shoal. Divers surfaced on either side of the ship, disembodied heads floating in black water.

"Easy...easy...nice," Bill said. "Give us a slight backing bell to hold us right here."

Claude followed the directions.

"Perfect," Bill said. "You can drop anchor."

Claude cut his engines. In the quiet, he could hear the anchor in the bow splash into the water.

Bill appeared in the open bridge doorway. He flipped the light switch, flooding the bridge with bright light. Claude blinked in the sudden glare.

"Turn on every light you've got on this boat, Claude," Bill ordered. "Let's get some glare on the water. Just in case there's anyone watching from above."

By the time Claude got to the main deck, Helen had all the deck lights on as well as all the lights in the stern that shone down into the ocean. In the crystal-clear waters, Claude watched a moray eel poke his head out of a coral formation and quickly withdraw.

"Ready to see what all the fuss is about?" Bill asked.

Claude followed him down to the well deck. The catamaran hulls of the *Arrogant* created a covered well about thirty feet long and twenty wide. The designers of the ship had intended the space to house a small submersible for covert operations, but Claude usually slung nets across the space and used it for storage, as they'd done with much of the SEAL team's gear.

Tonight, the nets were gone and the pool of water framed by the ship's twin hulls was illuminated from below.

Claude gasped at the sight. The torpedo had the dimensions of a city sewer pipe—at least a meter across, Claude guessed, and the tail extended well past the end of the well deck. The torpedo was painted bright red and the wings of a dragon swept out of the coral as if the weapon was trying to take flight.

Bill's men worked on either side of the weapon, using drills, shovels, and gloved hands to move coral and sand out of the way.

"They're rigging an inflatable sling underneath it," Bill explained. "It hit the reef pretty hard, so it's dug in there deep. Not an easy job, but we'll get 'er done."

Claude couldn't take his eyes off the huge weapon. "I think you've got a bigger problem, Wild Bill."

The SEAL commander frowned. "Oh, yeah, what's that?"

Claude gestured to the stern of the torpedo. "Once you get it floated, how are you planning to hide it? It's not going to fit in here."

Bill's face creased into a tired smile. "Oh, ye of little faith, Captain Claude. This night is just getting started."

57

USS *Kansas City*, 45 miles northeast of Second Thomas Shoal, South China Sea
2138 China Standard Time

Commander Mike Ferrell sat in the pilot's chair on the darkened bridge of the USS *Kansas City*. His first command. *His* ship.

His hand trailed idly over the controls, the dials and levers that controlled the speed and direction of this magnificent piece of engineering. All the computer screens that the OOD normally used to navigate and fight the ship were dark, save one.

The display told him the basics of his command. All engines were offline. Her bow was pointed due north and she was sitting low in the water.

He could sense that. The *Kansas City* normally felt light beneath his feet, almost flighty, ready to spin and race away at a moment's notice. Now, even in these calm seas, it felt as if every wave might roll her on her side.

Her center of buoyancy was off. So far off that she was unstable. Unseaworthy.

His ship was dying.

It was hard to believe that a mere twenty-four hours ago, this bridge had been alive with people and equipment. He'd been the commander of a surface action group running drills in the open ocean, playing out scenes of war.

Then he'd lived those scenes. His ship and crew had acquitted themselves well, but the cost...

From his seated position, he could tilt his head back and see the stars through the jagged hole in the top of the bridge.

The ache in his chest felt like a stone. Out of a crew of forty-five souls, there were six dead and a dozen injured. The *Oakland* had fared even worse. A direct hit from a PLA missile had killed everyone on the bridge, including the captain, his best friend, John Hibbard.

Ferrell found it hard to even fathom a world without Hibs. He would deal with that reality tomorrow. Right now, he had urgent business of his own.

In one of the blank computer screens, he saw the reflection of Carlston McKenzie fill the doorway of the bridge.

The XO cleared his throat. "It's time, sir."

Ferrell sighed as he hauled himself to his feet. His muscles felt like he'd been worked over with a baseball bat. His insides were still staticky with nervous energy, leaving him feeling slightly nauseous.

McKenzie wore a sling on his right arm and had a white bandage over his eye.

"After you, Carlston." Ferrell followed his XO off the bridge for the last time.

"The crew is off, sir," McKenzie reported. "All watertight doors are latched open. The ship's been stripped of any sensitive material." He handed his captain a folded bundle. "This is for you, sir."

Ferrell ran his hand over the folded American flag, still wet with sea spray, then placed it inside the small duffel that held a few personal items from his stateroom.

"Thank you, Carlston," he managed.

They'd maneuvered the dying vessel to the deepest water they could find in this notoriously shallow area. Only about 250 feet, but it would have to do.

With the *Kansas City* at all stop, they'd supervised the transfer of the crew to the *Mobile*. Then, while the XO double-checked the abandon ship procedure, Ferrell had gone to the bridge to say goodbye.

In the hangar deck, the side hatch was open. Normally, the waterline was twenty feet below the lip of the hatch, but now water sloshed onto the deck. Ferrell waited until McKenzie had crossed to the waiting launch, then he moved forward. The *Kansas City* was riding so low in the water that he had to step up onto the gunwale of the rescue ship.

He nodded to the pilot, a chief petty officer wearing a *Mobile* ball cap. The launch turned and accelerated away from his ship.

Five minutes later, he climbed the ladder to enter the hangar deck of the USS *Mobile*. A bosun rang the ship's bell twice. "*Kansas City*, arriving," he announced.

How many times had he been rung aboard as the commanding officer of the USS *Kansas City*? A hundred? A thousand? Every time he came aboard or walked off any US Navy ship, that familiar sound had greeted him or wished him well on his departure.

It was a sound that usually filled him with pride, but this time it felt like a punch in the chest.

You can feel sorry for yourself later, he thought. You've got a job to do.

He forced his legs to march across the hangar deck, part of which had been set aside as a makeshift morgue. Through gaps in the tarps set up to screen the area, he saw black body bags lined up along the deck.

Ferrell looked away. Later, he told himself.

Mobile had taken her share of battle damage. A repair team was tack-welding a sheet of aluminum over a hole in the bulkhead.

He didn't need an escort, the *Mobile* was a carbon copy of his own ship, but one was provided anyway. When they arrived on the bridge, Captain Elizabeth French was waiting for him.

"Welcome aboard, Captain," she said.

Ferrell shook her hand automatically. "Thank you, Beth, for giving all of us orphans a home." He attempted a smile.

In contrast to the *Kansas City*, the bridge of the *Mobile* was alive with activity. Ferrell longed for that feeling again.

French handed him a pair of headphones, and they stepped onto the bridge wing, where she dismissed the lookout.

Overhead, a flight of F-35s from the air wing of the USS *Carl Vinson* screamed past them in the night sky. Their air escort would remain until they reached port. Two thousand yards away, Ferrell could make out the lights of the BRP *Antonio Luna*.

The Philippine patrol craft *Juan Magluyan* had taken a direct hit from a PLA anti-ship missile but somehow managed to remain afloat and stable. Against all odds, the supply ship successfully grounded itself on Second Thomas Shoal, a mere five hundred meters from the *Sierra Madre*. Ferrell imagined the Chinese were shitting a brick about that new wrinkle in their plan to dominate the South China Sea. The *Sierra Madre* was badly rusted out, slowly disintegrating on the reef. In comparison, the supply ship was almost brand-new. She would last decades as another outpost at Second Thomas Shoal.

It was almost enough to make him smile. Until he thought about what that operation had cost in blood and treasure. There had to be more to it than just sticking it to the Chinese at Second Thomas Shoal. This little freedom of navigation jaunt had come dangerously close to starting World War Three.

He thought about the mysterious Harrison Kohl—if that was even his real name. The CIA had used Ferrell and his entire surface action group for something.

Whatever it was, Ferrell just hoped it was worth it.

"I'm sorry about John," Beth said. "Captain Hibbard was a good man."

Ferrell didn't want to go there—not yet, anyway. Right now, he needed to stick to the matter at hand. When he ran out of things to occupy his mind, he might be strong enough to open that well of grief.

Or not.

"Let's get this over with, shall we?"

"Aye-aye, Captain," French replied. She raised her voice. "Stand by to fire the main gun. Your target is the *Kansas City*. Aim for the water line."

"Ready to fire, Captain," came the reply.

"All yours, sir." Beth put on her headphones.

Ferrell settled the headphones over his ears, welcoming how the insulation blocked out his senses.

He breathed in. All he could hear was the sound of his own respiration.

Peaceful. Isolated. Maybe he'd just stay here a while longer...

But duty called—as it always did—and he looked forward to the hulking 57mm gun on the bow that was aimed at his beloved *Kansas City*.

He closed his eyes, filled his lungs with air, and yelled:

"Fire!"

58

SS *Arrogant*, Babuyan Island Chain, northern Philippines
2320 China Standard Time

Claude Buettner was back in the captain's chair on the bridge of the *Arrogant*. The bridge was dark again, which was how he liked it. In the opposite chair, Bill James snoozed, his chin on his chest, arms folded, feet propped on the open windowsill.

After hours of digging by the team of divers in the water beneath the *Arrogant*, Bill James had given his seal of approval on the work. He ordered his men out of the water and the catamaran positioned away from the site of the downed torpedo—which was fine with Claude.

"What now?" Claude asked. He was curious to see what Bill and his team had in store.

"Now, we wait," Bill replied. While his men ate and rested from a very long day on and in the water, the SEAL commander retired to Claude's bridge and took a nap.

An hour ago, a thick layer of marine fog moved into the area. Using Bill's high-end night vision binocs, Claude could just barely make out the inflatable dinghy riding at anchor over the stolen weapon.

Bill started awake and dropped his feet to the floor. He extracted a satellite phone from his hip pocket and tapped the screen. He looked up with a quick smile, fully awake.

"Showtime, Captain."

Bill took the binoculars back and focused them into the fog to their north. As he did so, Claude became aware of a low hum in the distance. Bill unclipped the handset from the VHF radio and pressed the transmit button.

"Liberty, Liberty, this is Circus. How do you copy?"

"Circus, this is Liberty. I will be at your position in two mikes."

"Copy all, Liberty. Circus, out."

Claude checked his surface search radar. A huge shape was closing on their position at a very high rate of speed, far faster than a ship. It had to be an airplane, but it was flying dangerously close to the water.

Bill had turned his binocs to the dinghy over the torpedo. "All right, guys, let's pop the cork."

Four men went over the side of the inflatable while the remaining man moved the craft out of the way.

Bill shot a look at Claude. "If this doesn't work, we've got a long night ahead of us."

Over his shoulder, Claude saw a boil of water, and eight orange inflatable balloons popped out of the water. Between them, a long, sleek shape barely broke the surface of the sea.

The low hum grew in amplitude until it became a roar. Something out of sight hit the water and the tenor of the roar deepened. A series of slow waves rolled into the *Arrogant*, gently rocking the catamaran.

"There's our ride," Bill said. A long wing loomed out of the darkness above them, four turboprop engines shredding the fog.

Claude gaped. The wing was at least as long as his entire ship. A pontoon hanging down from the wingtip swept past the *Arrogant* and the enormous aircraft made a wide turn in the water.

"What the hell is that thing?" Claude asked.

Bill James spoke over his shoulder as he made his way to the main deck.

"It's the Liberty Lifter," he said. "Experimental cargo aircraft. Uses wing-in-ground effect to move heavy cargo long distances across water." His teeth flashed in a smile. "It's a DARPA prototype. The project was canceled, but the CIA borrowed it for this mission."

The rear of the aircraft faced the *Arrogant* now and a ramp lowered into the water. Claude could see that the cargo bay of the Liberty Lifter was a huge amphibious well deck.

The four divers carefully maneuvered the stolen Chinese torpedo into the open cargo hold. Two of them disappeared below the water. The orange inflatable balloons deflated in pairs, and the massive weapon settled in place. A team on board the aircraft swarmed forward to secure their precious cargo.

"Quickly, now, gentlemen," Bill called out.

Claude saw that the SEAL teams and their gear had been loaded into the inflatable dinghies. Two of them were already speeding toward the open cargo hold. The third was being held against the stern by one of Bill's men.

Wild Bill James held out his hand. "It's been a pleasure, Captain Claude, but this is where we part company."

"This is it?" Claude said, as he shook the man's hand.

"'Fraid so, Captain." He kissed Helen on the cheek. "Look me up next time you're in Pearl. We'll do dinner and hit the dance floor."

Helen kissed him back. "You're on, Wild Bill."

Bill stepped lightly down to the stern and hopped into the dinghy. The craft cut across the water and disappeared into the Liberty Lifter's cargo hold.

The ramp immediately started to close. The Liberty Lifter rose in the water as the pilot adjusted the trim and emptied the amphibious bay. Eight turboprops roared in the night, and the massive airship began to move away.

Claude listened to the engines change tenor as the enormous aircraft turned and gathered speed.

Then it was gone.

Quiet reigned over the misty ocean. Gentle waves lapped against the hull.

Claude looked around. The main deck was spotlessly clean, all the furniture replaced exactly where it had been when the SEAL teams had arrived on board. It was as if they'd never been there.

"Where to now, Claude?" Helen asked.

He sighed. "Our orders are to clear datum and get lost in the islands. By sunrise, I want to be far away from this spot. If the Chinese come calling, I don't want to be anywhere in the vicinity."

"Long night ahead," Helen said. "I'll put on the coffee and meet you on the bridge."

Claude climbed through the abnormally quiet and orderly ship to the bridge. Was it possible that he missed that pack of jackasses?

A black box lay on his captain's chair. Claude opened it to find the night vision binoculars. These were state-of-the-art field glasses, easily worth a few thousand dollars. He hefted the glasses in his hand and found a handwritten note underneath:

To Captain Claude and the crew of the Arrogant –

My sincere thanks for your hospitality. Fair winds and following seas for your next adventure.

Your friend –
Wild Bill

Claude placed the binoculars on the dashboard, then slid into his captain's chair. The engines of the *Arrogant* thrummed to life beneath his sandals.

He pushed the throttles forward and steered due south.

59

Vancouver, British Columbia, Canada

"Happy twenty-first birthday, *baobei*." Chang Han held up his wineglass. "I'm so proud of you."

"*Baba*, stop," Cassie said. "You're embarrassing me." But she touched her glass to his anyway.

Chang sipped his drink. The Five Sails Restaurant was a five-star experience. On the recommendation of the sommelier, Chang had selected the Willamette Valley pinot noir even though it was more expensive, and it had turned out to be an excellent choice.

Mere months ago, even though he had the money, an expensive bottle of wine like this one would have seemed like an extravagance. Today, it felt right.

"You've changed, Baba," Cassie said quietly. "I like it."

Her words sparked a glow of pride in Chang's belly. He took another sip to hide his embarrassment.

"You've changed, too, Cassie." He hesitated, then plunged ahead. "For the better."

A shadow of irritation flickered across his daughter's face, then she smiled. "Thank you. I feel better—about myself, I mean. For the first time in a long time, I feel *good* about myself."

Chang sighed inwardly. It had all been worth it. He'd sensed a change in his daughter from the first moment he hugged her at the airport. There was a fresh glow about her that he'd not seen in years, certainly since the divorce. She had a new internship, a new apartment, and a new boyfriend—all in the last month.

In each instance, his daughter described a situation that had somehow just worked out in her favor. If there was any hint of suspicion on her part of a larger force behind her sudden run of good luck, she hadn't mentioned it yet.

Chang's own fortunes were on the rise as well. Gang Wei had been fired from his position as head of the Guidance Division. Chang was awarded the job on an acting basis until his higher-level security clearance was approved.

Unfortunately, the work on the Hu Jing torpedo had been shelved in favor of a new autonomous underwater drone for the defense of Chinese harbors. Chang's division was leading the development of the guidance system for the project.

While they ate dinner, darkness settled over the Inner Vancouver Harbor. The floor-to-ceiling window next to their table turned into a dark mirror reflecting the room behind them.

Cassie excused herself and Chang settled back in his chair to savor the last of his wine. His eyes scanned the reflection, then snagged on a familiar face. The wine turned sour in his mouth.

From two tables away, Angelina-Marie Markov rose to her feet and glided to his table. She slid into Cassie's seat.

"How are you, Han?" Her eyes pinned him to his chair.

Chang sat up slowly. "I'm...well." The pleasant buzz from the wine evaporated.

She arched an eyebrow. "Congratulations on your new promotion. You earned it."

Chang's mouth was dry, his head swam. What could she possibly want with him now?

"Your daughter is beautiful. I understand she's doing much better."

Chang nodded, swallowed.

"I'm so happy for you, Han." She winked at him. "We take care of our friends. Remember I told you that when we met for the first time?"

"Yes," Chang managed.

"Speaking of friends." Angelina-Marie palmed a business card and dropped it next to his plate. "Call that number and they'll give you access to your new bank account. $250,000 in a numbered account, untraceable." She smiled. "Thank you for your service, Han."

Angelina-Marie glanced at her watch. "I must be going, but I'm so glad we ran into each other." She stood in one graceful movement. "I may be in China on a recruiting visit in a few months. May I look you up?"

There it was, Chang thought. The give and the ask. His heartbeat ticked up.

I could say no and see what happens. He spied Cassie making her way across the restaurant toward him. Or I could say yes and ensure her future.

Chang steeled himself and stood, forced a smile. They were just two business acquaintances who happened to run into each other in a fine restaurant. He held out his hand.

"I look forward to it."

Her touch was cool and brief, then Angelina-Marie sidled away just as Cassie arrived back at the table. His daughter's eyes were wide.

"Who was that woman, Baba? She's *beautiful.*"

Chang sat back down. "I interviewed for a job with her company once," he said. "It didn't work out."

Cassie took her seat and leaned across the table toward him.

"May I have dessert?"

He recognized that innocent smile, the same one that Angelina-Marie had loaded on his phone. The same phone he'd thrown into the South China Sea.

He pretended to consider her question, then slapped a hand playfully on the white tablecloth.

"Only if we get another bottle of wine."

Chang waved the sommelier over to their table.

60

Joint Base Pearl Harbor-Hickam, Hawaii

Janet Everett placed her leather folio inside the cardboard box on her neatly made bunk and stepped back to survey her empty stateroom.

It looked just the way she'd found it three years ago. In the space of an hour, she'd taken the place she called home for the most rewarding years of her professional career and turned it into just another impersonal berthing space.

By this time tomorrow afternoon, it wouldn't be her stateroom anymore. It would belong to the next captain of the *Illinois*.

He'd make the space his own for as long as he had the honor of commanding the ship, then he'd turn it over to the next guy.

The idea that she could be replaced that easily depressed her. It made her wonder if what she did mattered. The Navy was a massive enterprise, and she was a tiny, insignificant cog. The machine would carry on whether Commander Janet Everett existed or not.

She'd changed duty stations before, leaving people that she'd come to care about. But this time was different. Whatever challenges lay ahead, they would never match her time in command of this magnificent ship and her crew.

"Get over yourself already," she whispered. "You're pathetic."

She turned to more practical matters. The white dress uniform hanging in her closet had been pressed and cleaned, the medals carefully arranged, and the white shoes polished. She'd even liberated her Navy ceremonial sword from the back of the closet in her condo and spent an hour making sure it was pristine for the upcoming ceremony tomorrow.

This was how she'd spent the last six weeks since they'd returned from the South China Sea. Making much-needed repairs. Cleaning. Organizing. Marking time.

At noon tomorrow, the wait would be over. Her final duty as captain of the USS *Illinois* was to present her crew to their new commanding officer and walk across the brow for the last time.

Janet crossed to her mirror and stared at her reflection.

"Whatever happens tomorrow," she ordered herself, "you will not cry."

She'd been practicing. In her mind, she imagined hearing the call, "*Illinois*, departing" as she walked across the brow for the last time and let the emotions flow over her. Her breath caught, her eyes watered, but she held it together.

"Not bad," she said to her reflection. "You just might pull this off."

The phone on the wall buzzed.

"Captain," she answered.

"Captain, XO, we have a...situation topside, ma'am."

"What kind of a situation, XO?"

Savarino seemed to be at a loss for words. "The kind where I need you up here, like right now, ma'am."

As she hung up the phone, Janet wondered if this was some sort of practical joke on her last day as captain. She'd expect that from Lieutenant Taylor, but the XO? For weeks, Savarino had been pulling his hair out preparing for the change of command ceremony. She hardly expected he'd be in a joking mood, but then again, Taylor could be convincing.

A tiered platform had been erected over the curve of the submarine hull, complete with an awning and a podium, and covered with white canvas and tri-color bunting. The utilitarian steel brow connecting the submarine to the pier had likewise been decorated.

What Janet noticed first was that the traffic on the pier seemed abnormally light. At this time of the afternoon, there would be hundreds of sailors leaving for home or coming on duty as well as forklifts and the occasional supply truck.

But the pier was empty except for two black GMC Suburbans idling next to the brow.

A tall, rangy man wearing wraparound sunglasses and a blue blazer stood next to the XO by the topside watch station. Petty Officer Wilson, the topside watch, looked frozen in place, the look in his eyes a combination of awe and fear.

“Captain,” the XO began, “this is Special Agent Forester.”

Janet’s hand was lost in the man’s huge mitt. “FBI?” she asked.

“Secret Service, ma’am. You have a visitor.”

“I have a visitor...” Janet’s voice trailed off as she saw President Eleanor Cashman emerge from the back of the lead SUV. Don Riley followed.

Behind her, Janet heard Forester say in a low voice, “Granite’s on the move.”

Cashman mounted the steps to the brow and turned to acknowledge the American flag flying on the stern of the *Illinois*. Then she began to walk toward Janet.

“What do I say?” Petty Officer Wilson asked in a frantic whisper.

“United States, arriving,” the Secret Service agent supplied.

Ding-ding, ding-ding. United States, arriving. Ding-ding, ding-ding.

Janet heard the ceremonial announcement and watched the President draw closer, as if it were happening to someone else. Suddenly, Cashman was standing in front of Janet, holding out her hand, saying, “Captain Everett, Eleanor Cashman, it’s a pleasure to meet you finally.”

Janet grasped the outstretched hand and looked down. The President was wearing Brooks running shoes.

“Donald advised that I wear sensible shoes, so I left my high heels in the car,” Cashman noted wryly, looking over her shoulder at Don.

Janet laughed and the spell was broken. “Good advice, Madam President.”

Cashman’s eyes swept over her. This was a woman who didn’t miss much. “I understand tomorrow is a big day for you, Captain.”

"I'm only the captain for a few more hours, ma'am." Janet had to talk around an unexpected lump in her throat.

"Perfect timing, then." The President took her arm. "Perhaps I could get a tour while you're still in charge, Janet."

The next forty-five minutes were surreal for Janet. She led the President through the forward section of the ship. Torpedo room, mess decks, control room, even crew's berthing areas. The President wanted to see everything.

Cashman was a good student, listening carefully to crew members explain their jobs, then asking questions. Two Secret Service agents ranged ahead of them and two followed with Don Riley and the XO bringing up the rear.

At one point in the tour, the President said, "My word, Captain, your ship is so clean! I could eat off the deck."

Janet could practically hear the XO swell with pride. In anticipation of the change in command, Savarino had been on a savage cleaning frenzy and the ship had never looked better.

The tour ended in the wardroom. There must have been a signal that Janet missed because she found herself alone with Don and Cashman. Everyone else, including the security detail, had disappeared.

"Would you like some coffee, Madam President?" Don prompted.

"That would be lovely, Donald."

Janet rang for the mess attendants. The door to the galley was opened by a Secret Service agent who stepped aside to let a young man with a silver tray enter.

"Thank you," Cashman said as the culinary specialist placed a cup and saucer in front of her. Janet noted that the Supply Officer had gotten out the ship's china for the visit. "What's your name, young man?"

"Baxter, Madam President. Ralph Baxter." His voice warbled with anxiety. "From Scranton, Pennsylvania."

"I know Scranton very well, Ralph. How long have you been part of the crew?"

Janet watched the exchange, noting how easily the President connected with one of her youngest crew members. It was a quiet kind of leadership. The kind that made her crew not only feel seen, but made them proud of their jobs.

When Baxter departed, the President turned her gaze back on Janet. She had the unsettling feeling again that she was being X-rayed on an emotional level.

"It must be hard for you, Captain. Giving up command, I mean."

Janet fought the lump in her throat again. "Is it that obvious, ma'am?"

Cashman smiled tightly, nodding. "I hope when it's my time to leave the stage, I'll be able to demonstrate the same grace you've shown me today. You made the tour about your crew and your ship, not about yourself. I admire that in a leader."

Janet's cheeks grew warm. "Thank you, ma'am."

"After reading your report, I decided that I had to meet you in person. You performed a great service for your country, Janet. You accomplished something that I think few officers could have pulled off."

"So, it was worth it, then?" Janet asked. "You recovered the torpedo?" Like most highly compartmented covert actions, the people involved in the operation never knew the outcome.

The President's face tightened for an instant. "I fear those are two separate questions, Captain. I'll take the second one first.

"Yes, Don's operation was successful. The weapon was recovered, and the Chinese have discontinued their development program for the Hu Jing torpedo. I must admit, I get a certain perverse satisfaction from hearing that we are reverse engineering a Chinese weapon for once, instead of the other way around."

Janet laughed politely.

"But was it worth it?" Cashman's expression grew somber. "I'm here in Hawaii to visit the families of the sailors killed in the Second Thomas Shoal incident. When I meet the widows and the children of the men and women killed in action, I see a different answer to that question."

"The Second Thomas..." Janet's voice trailed off as she made the connection. The freedom of navigation operation was a diversion to cover her actions as she helped the CIA steal the Chinese torpedo. Off the top of her head, she didn't even recall how many were killed and injured in the skirmish.

"I'm sorry, Madam President."

Cashman sighed and Janet felt the depth of emotion. "So am I. Those men and women will weigh on my conscience until the day I die. What grieves me more than anything is that I can't tell them what really happened and why it made a difference for their country."

Cashman smiled, slow and sad. "But right now I can honor you and your crew's accomplishment, Janet."

She placed a leather-covered box on the table and opened it. Inside was a round medallion with a raised star, dark gold in color, with words around the perimeter:

Central Intelligence Agency. At the bottom of the medal, between two points of the five-sided star were two words:

For Valor.

"Ma'am, this is—"

"An Intelligence Star, awarded for services rendered with distinction under conditions of grave risk." She turned to Don. "Did I get that right, Donald?"

"Yes, ma'am."

"But—" Janet began.

Cashman waved her hand. "I know, you're not with the CIA, but you were a CIA officer in the past, and for this mission, you operated under the auspices of a CIA covert action, correct?"

"Yes, but—"

Cashman put her hand on Janet's arm. "Can you let me have this win, Janet? I'm the President, and I decided you should have this award. Deal with it."

"Thank you," Janet said finally.

"You earned it, Captain, and so did your crew. At the change of command tomorrow, the CNO will announce that the *Illinois* is being awarded a Presidential Unit Citation for your last deployment."

"Thank you, again." Janet felt herself start to choke up. "I—I don't know what to say."

Cashman found her hand and squeezed. "I didn't come here just to give you an award, Captain. I came here to meet you. I wanted to know what kind of person possessed the courage and the skill to put her ship in harm's way. I wanted to see you with your crew, see how they acted with you."

A final squeeze. "I got what I came for. Congratulations, Captain. Your country owes you a great debt."

Cashman sighed, got to her feet. "I know someone will be knocking on that door any second now telling me I need to be somewhere else."

Don reached across the table and picked up the box with the medal. "For obvious reasons, this award and the citation will be redacted in your service jacket. A classified version will be available for the promotion board to review in a secure environment."

Janet made a face. "You know how much my chain of command hates that, right?"

Don grinned, shrugged. "We all have our crosses to bear, Captain Everett."

The group headed topside, sandwiched between the President's security detail. The gentle empathy that Cashman had shown in the wardroom was gone, replaced by a professional veneer.

At the quarterdeck, they said their formal goodbyes. The President of the United States, wearing running shoes, walked across the brow, turned to pay her respects to the flag, and disappeared inside the black SUV.

Janet lingered on deck, enjoying the cool evening breeze, while the XO directed a small work party on some last-minute details for the upcoming ceremony. As the sun slipped under the horizon, her shadow on the water grew longer.

The evening call to colors began to play over the loudspeaker on the pier. Janet mounted the brow, faced the American flag flying at the stern of her ship, and raised her hand in salute.

Alpha Strike
Third Option #2

A new geopolitical alliance is spreading like wildfire—and it's threatening to ignite a global crisis.

After years of confronting state-level threats from China and Russia, the United States and its allies now face something far more unpredictable: a powerful, shadowy syndicate forged between Mexican cartels and extremists in Africa's Sahel region.

Their goal is simple—maximize chaos, reap profits, and tear at the seams of the liberal democratic order.

Harrison Kohl, Director of the CIA's Special Activities Center, is handed a single directive from President Eleanor Cashman: dismantle the network at any cost.

But Kohl quickly discovers this enemy doesn't play by familiar rules. Armed with cutting-edge weapons, cloaked by advanced operational security, and backed by billions in illicit funding, the syndicate is more than a threat—it's a revolution in organized violence.

When conventional operations fail, Kohl is forced to make a desperate move: activate disavowed assets and launch an off-the-books campaign that could either destroy the syndicate or drag the United States into scandal—and defeat.

ACKNOWLEDGMENTS

In many ways, we owe this book to a well-timed research trip to San Diego in October 2024.

David hadn't set foot on an active-duty warship since he'd left the Navy in 1994 and JR since before his retirement in 2011, so the field trip was a sort of homecoming for both of us. Although the primary goal of the trip was to update ourselves on how the US Navy had changed, we were struck by the fact that if you look past the latest technology, things haven't changed much.

The Navy is—and always has been—about the people. We'd forgotten how many bodies there are on a Navy ship and how *young* they are. An aircraft carrier, like the USS *Carl Vinson*, has a crew of 5000 sailors with an average age of just twenty-four years old. Every sailor we met took pride in explaining their role and how it contributes to the overall operation of a US Navy warship.

We saw that same pride when Lieutenant Commander Mike Ferrell, Executive Officer of the USS *Kansas City*, gave us a tour of his ship. The littoral combat ships have a bad reputation in Navy Procurement, but the ships are amazing. When we stood on the bridge of the *Kansas City*, we knew we had found the missing piece to our next novel.

We asked Ferrell if he wanted to be in a book. When he said yes, we asked him if he wanted to die a hero.

He said no. We honored his wishes and gave him a promotion to O-5.

Carlston McKenzie, a former student of JR's, is now a Lieutenant Junior Grade serving on the USS *John P. Murtha*, a *San Antonio*-class amphibious transport dock. Although his ship was in the shipyard when we visited, he managed to wrangle us a tour. In our fictional world, Carlston got a promotion to O-4 and a billet as XO of the *Kansas City*.

(Also, the well deck of the *Murtha* inspired the same feature on the Liberty Lifter at the end of the book.)

Lastly, we were hosted in San Diego by Bill and Bob James. Longtime readers will recall that "Wild Bill" James made his first appearance in a Bruns-Olson novel in *Proxy War,* but this time he was joined by his brother, Bob.

Speaking of longtime readers, several of Janet's crew on the USS *Illinois* are familiar names to us. Although we've never met any of them in real life, we are forever grateful for their continued readership and their reviews. Thank you, David Taylor, Jenny Avery, and Thomas Savarino.

We have a long-standing rule that a character named after a real person never dies in our story unless we have their permission. Thank you, John Hibbard, for your long service in the US Navy and your brief service in our novel.

Shannon Petersen, another Bruns-Olson friend, was spared a gruesome death because we couldn't bring ourselves to take out such a gentle human being, even fictionally.

As always, we need to thank our publisher for their support. Our sincere appreciation to Andrew, Amber, Lisa, and especially Cate, for all your work to bring this project to life.

Lastly, we want to thank our families. The year 2025 marked our tenth year of co-writing and none of that would have been possible without the love and support of those closest to us.

Sincerely,

David & JR
12 August 2025

ABOUT THE AUTHORS

David Bruns

David Bruns earned a Bachelor of Science in Honors English from the United States Naval Academy. (That's not a typo. He's probably the only English major you'll ever meet who took multiple semesters of calculus, physics, chemistry, electrical engineering, naval architecture, and weapons systems just so he could read some Shakespeare. It was totally worth it.) Following six years as a US Navy submarine officer, David spent twenty years in the high-tech private sector. A graduate of the prestigious Clarion West Writers Workshop, he is the author of over twenty novels and dozens of short stories. Today, he co-writes contemporary national security thrillers with retired naval intelligence officer, J.R. Olson.

J.R. Olson

J.R. Olson graduated from Annapolis in May of 1990 with a BS in History. He served as a naval intelligence officer, retiring in March of 2011 at the rank of commander. His assignments during his 21-year career included duty aboard aircraft carriers and large deck amphibious ships, participation in numerous operations around the world, to include Iraq, Somalia, Bosnia, and Afghanistan, and service in the U.S. Navy in strategic-level Human Intelligence (HUMINT) collection operations as a CIA-trained case officer. J.R. earned an MA in National Security and Strategic Studies at the U.S. Naval War College in 2004, and in August of 2018 he completed a Master of Public Affairs degree at the Humphrey School at the University of Minnesota. Today, J.R. often serves as a visiting lecturer, teaching national security courses in Carleton College's Department of Political Science.

You can find David Bruns and J.R. Olson at
severnriverbooks.com